The Dinosaur Knights

TOR BOOKS BY VICTOR MILÁN

The Dinosaur Lords

The Dinosaur Knights

The Dinosaur Knights

VICTOR MILÁN

TOR

A TOM DOHERTY ASSOCIATES BOOK

NEW YORK

This is a work of fiction. All of the characters, organizations, and events portrayed in this novel are either products of the author's imagination or are used fictitiously.

THE DINOSAUR KNIGHTS

Interior illustrations by Richard Anderson

Maps by Rhys Davies

Designed by Greg Collins

A Tor Book
Published by Tom Doherty Associates, LLC
175 Fifth Avenue
New York, NY 10010

www.tor-forge.com

The Library of Congress Cataloging-in-Publication Data is available upon request.

ISBN 978-0-7653-3297-4 (hardcover)
ISBN 978-1-4299-6612-2 (e-book)

Our books may be purchased in bulk for promotional, educational, or business use. Please contact your local bookseller or the Macmillan Corporate and Premium Sales Department at 1-800-221-7945, extension 5442, or by e-mail at MacmillanSpecialMarkets@macmillan.com.

First Edition: July 2016

Printed in the United States of America

0 9 8 7 6 5 4 3 2 1

To the memory of Emma Lou Who Milán, beloved dog,
companion, and protector of us all, who died two days after the
launch party. You'll always be missed, old friend.
This book is your memorial in more ways than one.

ACKNOWLEDGMENTS

The number of people who have helped make this book possible has only grown. I can do no more than hit the high points.

Thanks to my friends in the Albuquerque Science Fiction Society and at Archon in St. Louis for your love and support.

Thank you, again, to my fellow writers of Critical Mass, past and present, who helped me do this thing: Daniel Abraham, Yvonne Coats, Terry England, Ty Franck, Sally Gwylan, Ed Khmara, John Jos. Miller, Matt Reiten, Melinda Snodgrass, Jan Stirling, Steve Stirling, Lauren Teffeau, Emily Mah Tippetts, Ian Tregillis, Sarena Ulibarri, Sage Walker, and Walter Jon Williams.

Thank you to my agent, Kay McCauley; my editor, Claire Eddy, and her indefatigable assistant, Bess Cozby; and to Richard Anderson, for what Walter Jon Williams called "the greatest cover in the history of the Universe." And to Irene Gallo for signing off on it.

Thanks to all the folks at the Jean Cocteau Cinema and GRRM's minions for your help: Raya Golden, Melania Frazier, David Sidebottom, Laurel Zelazny, and Lenore Gallegos. And a special thank-you to Patricia Rogers and Sage for riding to the rescue.

A big thank-you to Ron Miles, Webmaster Supreme, for resuscitating my website from the dead—in style! And to Theresa Hulongbayan and Gwen Whiting for creating and wrangling my Facebook fan page!

A heartfelt thank-you to George R. R. Martin, for so many things.

Thank you to my Dinosaur Army for keeping the faith.

And thanks to Wanda Day for all she's done for me. Did you know—after my disclaimer that she was not the inspiration for the name of Rob Korrigan's axe and everything—she actually dressed up as the damn thing for the Bubonicon Masquerade in 2015? Yeah, she did that.

And as always—thanks to you for reading.

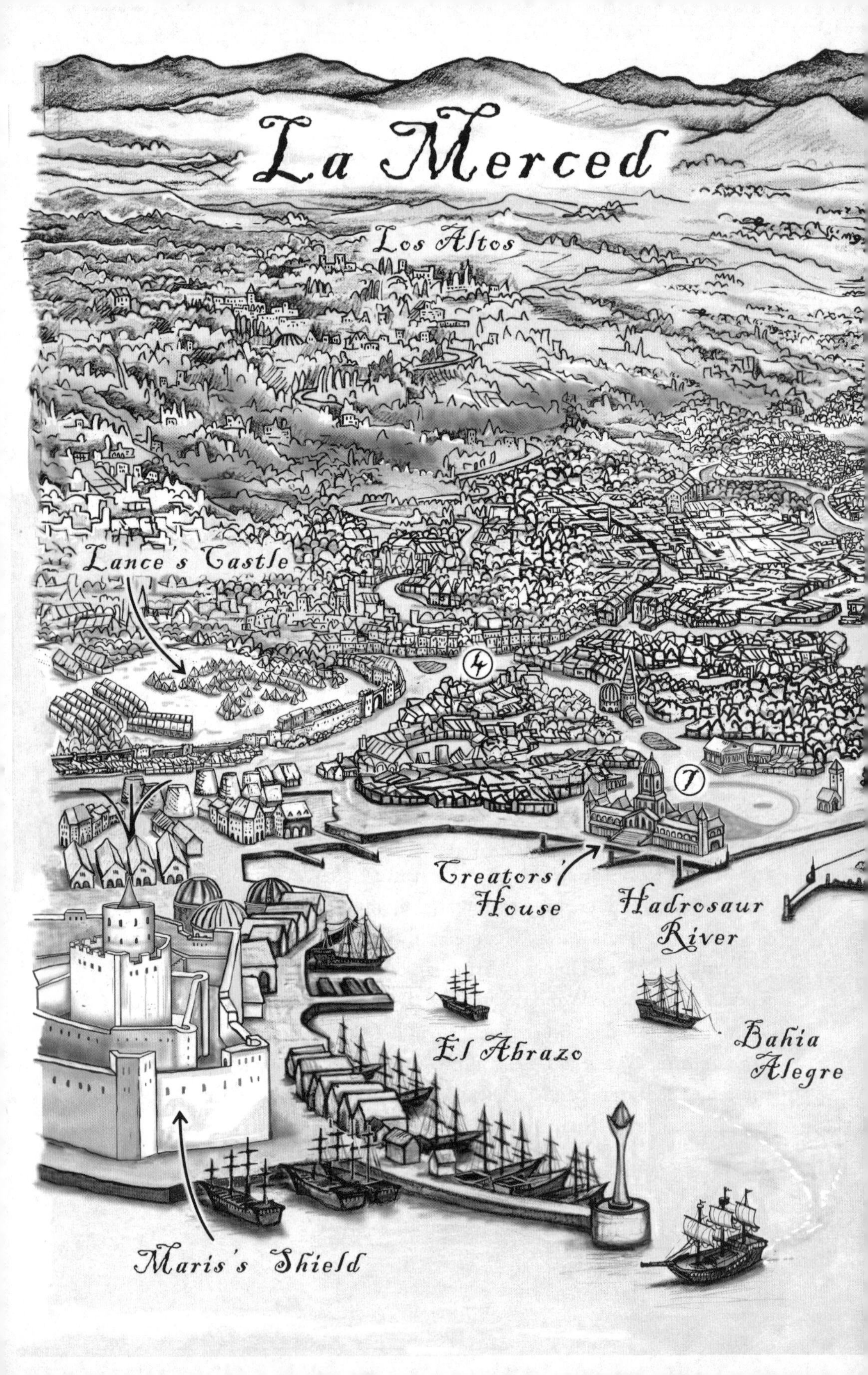
La Merced
Los Altos
Lance's Castle
Creators' House
Hadrosaur River
El Abrazo
Bahia Alegre
Maris's Shield
4
7

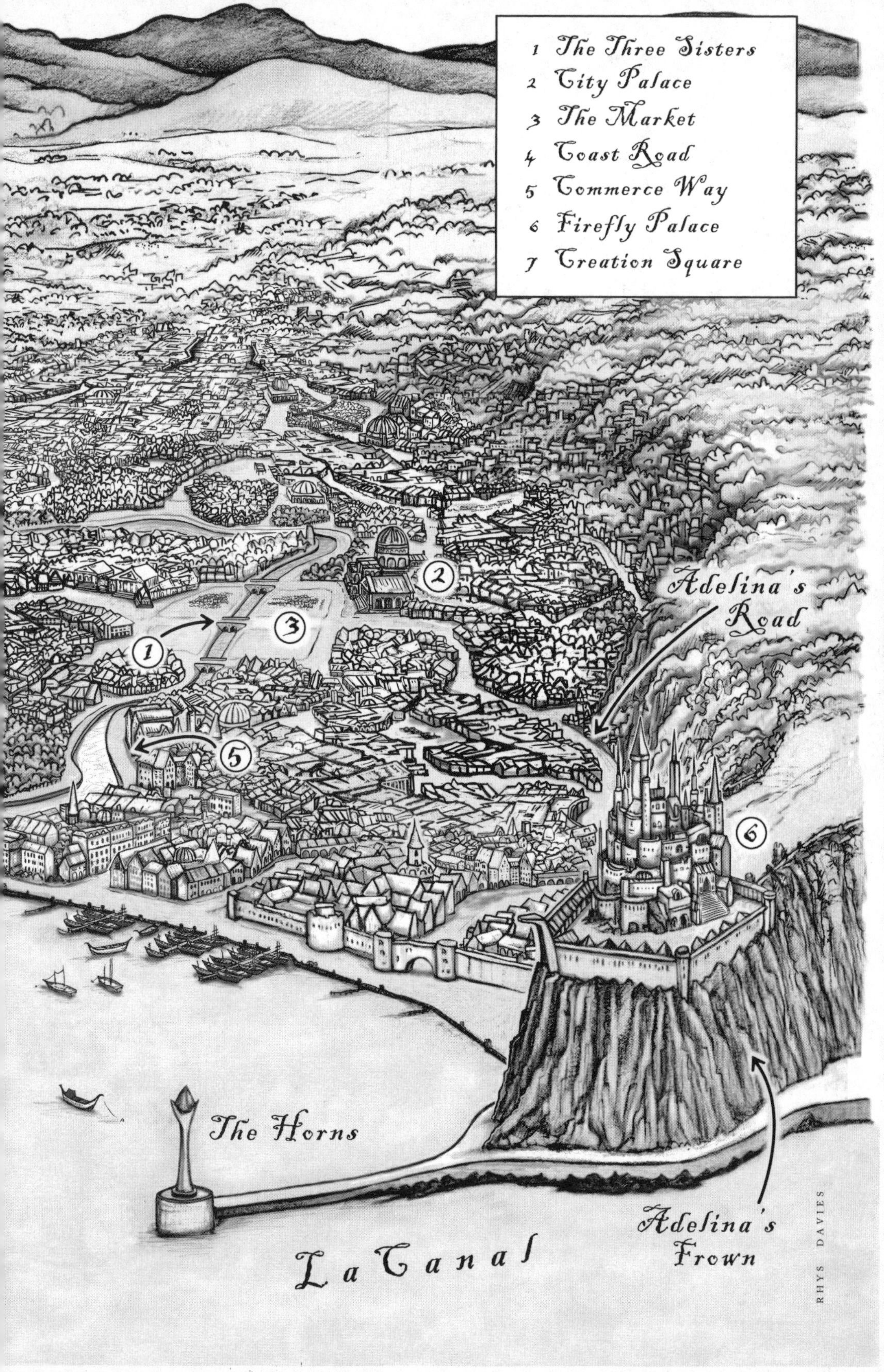

1 The Three Sisters
2 City Palace
3 The Market
4 Coast Road
5 Commerce Way
6 Firefly Palace
7 Creation Square

Adelina's Road

The Horns

Adelina's Frown

La Canal

RHYS DAVIES

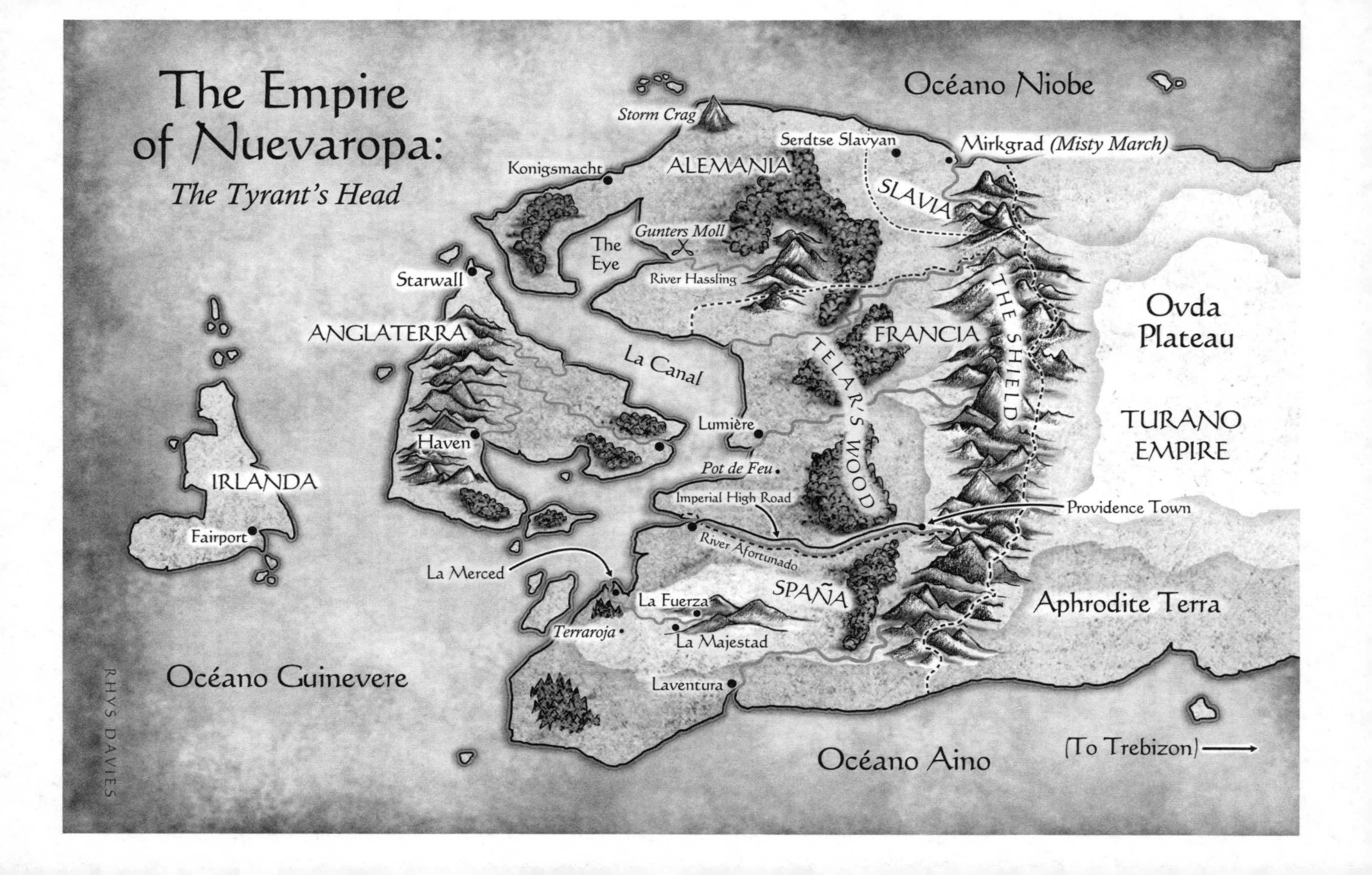
The Empire
of Nuevaropa:
The Tyrant's Head
Océano Niobe
Storm Crag
Serdtse Slavyan
Mirkgrad (Misty March)
Konigsmacht
ALEMANIA
SLAVIA
Gunters Moll
The
Eye
River Hassling
Starwall
ANGLATERRA
La Canal
FRANCIA
TELAR'S WOOD
THE SHIELD
Ovda
Plateau
TURANO
EMPIRE
Lumière
Haven
Pot de Feu
Imperial High Road
IRLANDA
Fairport
Providence Town
River Afortunado
La Merced
SPAÑA
La Fuerza
Aphrodite Terra
Terraroja
La Majestad
Océano Guinevere
Laventura
Océano Aino
(To Trebizon)
RHYS DAVIES

The wise young person will keep this always in mind:

In Nuevaropa, living is easy. But so is dying.

—**A PRIMER TO PARADISE FOR THE IMPROVEMENT OF YOUNG MINDS**

Part One

Colloquy in a Sewer

Prologue

Los Ángeles Grises, **Grey Angels,** *Los Siete,* **the Seven. . . .** —The Creators' supernatural servitors: Michael, Gabriel, Raphael, Uriel, Remiel, Zerachiel, and Raguel, who are charged with maintaining sacred Equilibrium on Paradise. They possess remarkable powers and mystic weapons, and when they walk out in the world, they often take on a terrifying appearance. They are not humane, and regard all things as straw dogs.

—A PRIMER TO PARADISE FOR THE IMPROVEMENT OF YOUNG MINDS

Firefly Palace—*The sewers far beneath.*

URIEL: Before you go, my friend—a moment.

RAGUEL: You're not going to try to change my mind again, are you?

URIEL: No. I'll abide by the compact—until my turn arrives. I only wonder how you plan to return to Providence?

RAGUEL: Release this body back to dust and reanimate the one there. It's waiting for me in a safe place, nice and dormant and ringed about with the strongest protections. It probably won't even have decayed appreciably, in such a brief interval by Outerworld standards.

URIEL: But aren't you the least bit nervous there might someday be a duplication error—and, you will forgive my saying this, cause you to undergo the True Death?

RAGUEL: The prospect does not unduly worry me.

URIEL: Don't think it can't happen just because it hasn't happened yet.

RAGUEL: It hasn't happened to any of us. Not that way.

URIEL: The prospect chills me to the core. What about her? Might Aphrodite intervene to cause such a thing?

RAGUEL: She wouldn't dare. That would bring her the same fate.

URIEL: She dares much, though. She walks the narrowest of lines, with her meddling on behalf of the dirt people.

RAGUEL: But she's bound no less than we, by the same terrible threat that compels us all. Anyway, given the way she always prates about it, she does take seriously her role of preserving Paradise and all its creatures. Including us.

URIEL: And therein lies the problem.

RAGUEL: The one thing that concerns me is my Providence avatar getting destroyed.

URIEL: What a shame that would be.

RAGUEL: I'm sure you'd weep bitter tears that our faction lost, and had to yield to yours. You're not getting too eager, are you?

URIEL: Not enough to cheat. It's your turn, you and your fellow frothing Purifiers.

RAGUEL: And I shall yield to you and your fellow Fundamentalists. If I should fail. I just won't.

Part Two

Rebirth

Chapter 1

Chillador, Squaller, Great Strider—*Gallimimus bullatus*. Fast, bipedal, herbivorous dinosaurs with toothless beak. 6 meters long, 1.9 meters tall at the hips, 440 kilograms. Imported to Nuevaropa as a mount. Bred for varied plumage; distinguished by a flamboyant feather neck-ruff, usually light in color. Frequently ridden in battle by light-riders, as well as occasionally by knights and nobles too poor to afford war-hadrosaurs. Extremely truculent, with lethal beaks and kicking hind-claws.

—THE BOOK OF TRUE NAMES

Somewhere in central Francia:

Unseen, the hunter crouched in dense brush, watching with scarlet eyes.

Her belly rumbled so loudly with hunger that she feared it might give her position away. Her every instinct raged at her to strike, to rush down, snap the tailless two-legs in half, kick over their wooden shell-on-wheels, sink her teeth behind the frill of one of the hornfaces tied to it and rake its belly open with her powerful hind-talons.

But she would not. Could not.

Her mother, her lost mother for whom the longing was a constant ache, had taught her well. She must not kill two-legs, no matter how hungry she was or how tasty they were. Not unless ordered to by her mother, who wasn't here to do so. Or unless they attacked her.

The Allosaurus was cunning, intelligent for her kind and in her fashion. That did not equip her to persuade herself that her mother would, if present, give her leave to eat two-legs because she was hungry. Her thoughts were simple as a blade and direct as an arrow's flight.

Besides, she had learned the hard way that if the two-legs spotted her, they were liable to turn out armed with spears and bows and torches, in numbers too great even for her to think of killing them all. They were persistent and resourceful, worse even than horrors. Like those vicious little raptors, they could endanger even a full-grown matadora if enough of them attacked.

So, breathing shallowly, the monster stayed crouched, and let the small trade-caravan wind its way out of the copse of saplings through which the narrow track ran without attacking it.

When they were gone she rose from the brush and stepped out on the road. As she looked longingly after the carts, she saw a small figure standing atop one of the wooded gentle hills that dominated the terrain: a two-legs with a strangely pointed head.

Her mother could put on different heads at will, she knew. Her mother was a great sorceress. Though she knew it was not her mother, the hunter had come to recognize this two-legs and its peculiar head. And as always happened when she saw it, a hint of her mother's long-lost scent reached her nostrils. Joyous certainty filled her, that somehow she was coming closer to her mother, day by day.

A shift in the wind brought her a whiff of fresh nosehorn. Wild ones, from the tang of ferns and berries, not the tame beasts hitched to wagons and fed on gathered fodder and grain. A small herd grazed somewhere nearby.

She was a good girl. She had not eaten the two-legs. And she wouldn't go hungry much longer.

She allowed herself a soft, happy cry: *shiraa.*

She turned. Despite her tonne and a half of weight and eleven meters' length, she flowed back into the brush like a fish among water-weeds, making little more noise.

"I can't take it anymore."

Letting the reins fall in the middle of a sun-dappled forest roadway, La Princesa Imperial Melodía Estrella Delgao Llobregat clutched her hair with her fists and screwed up her face in misery.

That hair was dungeon-depth black now. Pilar had slipped into a town and bought dye to hide Melodía's distinctive dark-wine hair. Her own hair, a black so deep as to seem blue in certain lights, she left as it was; she was insignificant, the only reason for anyone to identify her being that she was the fugitive princess's companion. And anyway her coloring wasn't exactly rare here in the south of the Empire of Nuevaropa. Her eyes, startling emerald green, were a problem. But not even her gitana wiles offered any means of disguising them.

Pushing their mounts as hard as they dared, the young women had quickly crossed the border from Spaña into Francia. Avoiding the major Imperial High Road they then made for County Providence as rapidly as they could. There they hoped followers of Melodía's lover Jaume's doctrines might shelter them. It was a thin strand, but the only one in reach.

Once her first flush of mad elation following her escape had faded, Melodía traveled in a state of floating numbness. The physical pain of the rape by Falk had gone away even before that. She didn't think, she didn't feel. She mechanically did what Pilar told her. It was as if her senses, her body, even her mind had been swaddled in down.

But now, without warning, the numbness had vanished. Sudden weight crushed her like an anvil falling. It drove the breath from her, the strength. And tears.

"I miss Montse," she said in a voice like a fistful of pottery shards. "I miss Daddy. I miss my friends. I miss sleeping in a bed. I just can't stand this."

Pilar stopped her white ambler and turned back.

"Princess," she said gently. "We need to move. We don't want to be caught here in the open."

Both were dressed as hidalgas, in loose silken blouses and linen, with boots, belts, and broad-brimmed wayfarers' hats. Master plotter Abigail Thélème had suggested that looking like young women of consequence was the least risky of bad options for their flight from the false accusations of treason that had led to Melodía's imprisonment, violation, and desperate flight into exile.

To start with they were well mounted, suspicious for the lower orders. If they seemed affluent they admittedly risked being robbed or grabbed for ransom. But their apparent breeding would still likely win them a measure of respect for their persons, for reasons of habit as well as potential reward versus risk.

But as commoner women traveling alone they'd run terrible risks of rape, enslavement, or murder—and not just by the bandits who swarmed the Imperio's byways.

They carried a few weapons Pilar's coconspirators had provided: smallswords for each, a shortbow and arrow quiver for Melodía. Pilar was at least a vigorous, determined young woman, while Melodía had been well trained to use weapons. But as far as Melodía was concerned right now they might have been wet blades of grass: dank, limp, useless.

"It's just so hard," she sobbed. "What's the point, anyone? We don't have a chance. Not really. Everyone's against me. They're just going to chase us down like rats. Or bandits will swoop down on us and gobble us like a flying *dragón*. I'm tired and dirty, and my legs and butt ache all the time."

"Come along, Princess," Pilar said, grasping for the reins that slung slack over Melodía's pommel. "At least let's move off the highway. Please?"

Melodía batted her hand away. "I can't take it anymore! Don't you understand? Aren't you even listening?"

Pilar pressed her lips and drew a deep breath. "Very well. Then listen to me, and listen well. You need to grow up now, Melodía. You're not a Highness anymore. You're not a princess. You're a fugitive criminal, a renegade with a price on her head. You're also a young woman on the road, with the Fae alone knowing what is following you, amidst a countryside crawling with bandits. We're in deadly, constant danger."

Melodía stopped sniffling, dropped her hands, sat up and blinked. Her serving-girl's voice, always pleasant and deferential before, now cracked like a whip.

"I know you're intelligent. Lots more than you're showing now. You've got all the strength of will you could ever need too. I know you better than anybody—even your sister; I've known you longer than she. But you need to grow some sense, and in an Old Hell of a hurry, and bend that intelligence and that will to something bloody useful. Because both of our wits and wills together won't be too much to keep us alive to reach Providence.

"So if you want to live—if you want to clear your name, reunite with your sister and your father, reconcile with Count Jaume who loves you, and get vengeance on that filthy belly-crawler Falk, you need to straighten up and you need to do it now."

At last some sensation broke through the squishy and previously impermeable layers of Melodía's self-pity. Lightning outrage flashed through her brain, down her throat to the pit of her belly.

"How dare you? How dare you speak to me that way?"

"Because I still serve you," Pilar said. "And because I'm your friend."

Meravellosa had briefly tried reaching back to reassure her mistress with a lick on the cheek. Finding no success at that, she dropped her head to crop the lush green grass that grew beside the crushed tufa, the long-frozen volcanic foam that metaled the roadbed. Now she pricked her ears and whickered low in her throat. Pilar's mount and their cranky bay pack-marchador began to snort and sidestep.

"Shit!" Pilar said. Around a bend in the forest road behind them a horse whinnied greetings to others of its kind. "Quick, now, into the brush—"

But the riders were on them before Pilar could do any more than make another grab for Meravellosa's reins.

There were seven of them: six men-at-arms on coursers, led by a splendid young knight on an extravagantly ruffed blue and yellow Great Strider. They wore dinosaur-leather jacks over light tunics, and high boots lined with felt to keep from chafing bare legs. All carried long spears and yellow shields with red nosehorn heads on them. The knight wore a morion with a poofy yellow plume nodding above the crest. His horsemen made do with peaked steel caps and less splendidly tooled boots.

Melodía and Pilar had been overtaken by your basic baronial bandit-hunting patrol.

Melodía's heart felt like a small bird trying frantically to escape through her throat. *We're caught!* she thought. Her despair of a moment ago now seemed mere childish tantrum. *Now I've got something to cry about.*

"Ladies," the young knight said courteously. His goatee and moustache and the hair that hung to his shoulders from beneath his helmet were a yellow only slightly less gaudy than that on his shield. He was handsome and slim, and his facial hair couldn't conceal the fact he was little if any older than Melodía.

Dropping the butt of his spear into a holder by his saddle he swept off his helmet and bowed low. "Mor Tristan of L'Eau Noire, at your service. I ride for Baron Francis of La Licorne Rouge. Whom have I the honor of addressing?"

The riders were all around them. Pilar had pulled her ambler up alongside Meravellosa. Fortunately the two beasts were at peace with one another, and didn't flatten their ears and try to bite or kick.

Pilar shook back her heavy hair and sat up straighter in the saddle. "I am Lucila, la Baronesa de la Castilla Verde, off to visit my cousin Montador Cédric, who serves Comte Modeste of Tempête de Feu." Which happened to be the next county but one along the way to Providence.

"And who might this beauty be?" asked Mor Tristan, eyeing Melodía appreciatively.

"My maidservant Marta," Pilar said. She spoke Francés flawlessly but with a strong Spañola accent—such as any self-respecting Spañola noblewoman might affect, even if she could speak without the accent. All the Towers of Nuevaropa, *Mayor y Menor*, were equal before Imperial law. But the Spañoles were, as the saying went, more equal than the others, and appearances must be preserved.

"She's been weeping," Tristan said.

Even in her surprise and terror and renewed outrage—*a servant, am I?*—Melodía felt fresh discomfort. This young knight was uncommonly observant for his kind. Which could be uncommonly inconvenient. Or fatal.

"The impudent wench spoke back to me," Pilar said. "Do you believe? I let her feel the edge of my tongue. And she responds like this. The weakling! But that's the lowborn for you. They have no steel in their spines."

Tristan tipped his head to one side. "It's been beaten out of them, over time," he said.

"Say," said one of his men, bending close to Melodía. "Don't these two look like the fugitives we were told to look for?"

Melodía's outrage was suddenly sidetracked by a sensation as if her heart, that fluttering flier in her throat, had turned to lead and dropped straight to the pit of her stomach.

"Perhaps so, Donal." Tristan rooted in a saddlebag and produced a handbill printed on springer-skin parchment for durability. "The Princess Melodía of Torre Delgao, no less—the Emperor's daughter. Apparently she's been very naughty. And her own serving wench."

He looked at both of them. "But it's hard to tell anything from these damned secondhand scribblings. And anyway, the renegade princess has red hair. It says so clearly here. Whereas neither the Baronesa nor her slattern shows so much as a glimmer of red."

"Slattern?" Melodía yelped. "Why, you dirty—"

Pilar backhanded her across the face.

It was a smart blow, driven by a strength surprising in one who hadn't had the extensive physical training afforded to women of the upper class. Although perhaps it shouldn't have surprised Melodía, given a servant's life spent washing and lifting and carrying. But more than arm-strength it was the sudden pain in cheek and nose, and sheer shock that it even happened, that knocked Melodía off her saddle and into the crunchy light gravel between her horse and Tristan's dinosaur.

The strider gobbled alarm and hopped back like a startled bird. Tristan fought to control it as the horses shied away. Melodía had landed on her butt, which though padded well with muscle was already sore, and gotten a jolt to her spine, adding both insult and injury.

"What the Hell do you think you're playing at?" she shouted at her serving-girl.

Or started to. When she opened her mouth Pilar brought her riding crop down in a whistling-vicious slash. It took Melodía across the crown of her head. It hurt like fuck, despite the cushioning of hat and hair. She flung up both hands protectively.

"How dare you talk back to me?" Pilar yelled. Even in a seethe of pain and indignation it rang uncomfortably familiar in Melodía's ears. "I'll teach you to be impertinent."

And leaning from the saddle she proceeded to thrash Melodía most thoroughly on her upflung arms, and then her back and shoulders, until the Princess collapsed, sobbing helplessly, in the pumice.

"There," Pilar said in satisfaction.

Looking up through a waterfall of tears Melodía saw her servant straighten in her saddle and let her crop—which she had never used on her actual mount—dangle by a strap.

"She'll remember that lesson a while, don't you think, Mor Tristan?" she said, smoothing her hair and white blouse.

Tristan bowed low again. "I shall certainly remember it, Mademoiselle," he declared, and Melodía could hear unmistakable irony in his voice. "It would be our honor to escort you to the border of our county."

"Stop sniveling," Pilar said imperiously. It actually took Melodía a moment to realize she was talking to her. By sheer process of elimination, mostly, at that: she was the only one sniveling after all. "Pick yourself up and get back on your horse. Or I'll give you something to *really* whine about—and at the next farm I'll sell that mare, who's much too fine for the likes of you, and buy you a bony nag far more in keeping with your station."

Melodía's arms and back blazed with unaccustomed pain. Her pride hurt scarcely less. But that pitiless voice sounded as if meant what it said. Feeling older even than la Madrota, the unbelievably ancient Queen Tyrannosaurus of Tower Delgao, she picked herself up, pushed away Meravellosa who was trying to nuzzle her comfortingly, and hauled herself onto the saddle with approximately the same grace as she would have loaded on an equivalent weight of meal in a sack.

The unlikely cavalcade set out again. The "Baronesa" rode knee to knee with the handsome young knight, gossiping with cheerful malice about what Melodía realized were thinly veiled personalities from the Corte Imperial. Having never seen young Tristan's face at court, Melodía knew he'd have no way of recognizing they weren't really hangers-on of some bent-centimo magnate of La Meseta.

Young Mor Tristan restricted his contributions to agreeing gallantly with whatever had fallen most recently out of Pilar's mouth during her infrequent pauses. As Melodía's pains and passions settled back from the boil she found her perceptions unnaturally keen: the rustle of the broad splayed leaves above them, the smell of the forest and the sweating beasts, the usual chittering debate overhead between toothy birds and furred fliers, the feathery touch of a breeze on her face. Which now felt as if a red-hot iron mask had been clamped over it.

The men riding behind her also spoke, pitching their voices low. "Did you see the rack on that Baroness? Shitfire or not, I'd love to bury my cheeks between them."

"I'd pay to see you try, Corneille. Me, I'd rather try to screw a red-feathered horror. Safer in the long run."

"How about the wench, then?" persisted Corneille, who was manifestly hornier than was good for him. "She's almost as hot."

Almost? Melodía thought. She carefully kept her shoulders slumped and eyes downcast. But she did wish for soldier ants to bite Corneille most enthusiastically on the genitals at the next stop.

"You'd be almost as great a fool to lay a finger on her," said the other man. "Me, I'm afraid to touch anything that belongs to that she-spider. Even her shadow."

Chapter 2

***Los Compañeros de Nuestra Señora del Spejo,* The Companions of Our Lady of the Mirror**—An Order Military made up of dinosaur knights sworn to serve the Creator Bella, which was founded by its Captain-General, Comte Jaume dels Flors, to serve beauty and justice and aid the oppressed. Their churchly charter restricts them to no more than twenty-four serving members, picked from the most heroic, virtuous, artistically accomplished, and beautiful young men of Nuevaropa and beyond, not all of noble birth. They are encouraged to form lasting romantic pairs among themselves to further cement their bonds. Nuevaropa's most renowned warriors, led by its foremost living philosopher and poet.

—A PRIMER TO PARADISE FOR THE IMPROVEMENT OF YOUNG MINDS

"—and in the heat of the Battle of Blueflowers"—the round man's tenor voice bubbled with outrage—"they held back and did nothing—nothing!—while our beloved brother Sieur Percil was cruelly slain, and the heroic lords Yannic and Longeau suffered the wounds whose marks you see before you!"

Though Rob sat under guard at the back of the villa's banquet hall, he could clearly see Yannic, seated up front near the Council dais. The nobleman's narrow head was wrapped in bandages that left only eyes, mouth, and nostrils uncovered. Rob reckoned whatever lay beneath could hardly help being an improvement on what Yannic had started with.

He did find it an interesting commentary on the current balance of power in Providence, or at least the town, that the only town lord privileged to sit at the high table was Longeau, himself a Council member.

"As for our country brethren, Baron Ismaël of Fond-Étang was captured and carried back to Crève Coeur to be held for ransom. Baron Travise, sorely wounded, barely escaped the fray. His squire and servants carried him back to the Glades to recuperate."

The speaker himself was unwounded in his well-filled robes of green and gold. "Melchor, you fat, treacherous bastard," Rob muttered to Karyl, who sat beside him on the bench built out from the hall's rear wall. "I thought he was the most reasonable of the lot. And here he was working to undermine us all the time."

Karyl returned the slightest of shrugs. "No doubt you're right."

Rob glared at him. "Isn't that something of a cavalier attitude when we're on trial for our lives?"

"The play's only begun," Karyl said. "Providentials like their drama. This production will be long drawn out. Let's wait to see the climax, shall we?"

"As long as it fails to involve a black hood, an axe, and Rob Korrigan's young neck."

Karyl laid his head back against the wall and closed his eyes. Rob scowled even more furiously. Which did him as much good as you'd expect any face made, to appearances, at a sleeping man.

Karyl wore his usual mendicant-monk outfit, and cradled his blackwood walking-stick against one shoulder like a child its stuffed toy. The instant the town guards had stepped up to arrest them on the rainy Western Road, Karyl had spontaneously developed a grievous limp. Whether they thought he'd been hurt in the rout at Blueflowers, or an old campaign injury was acting up, the guardsmen hadn't interfered when Karyl asked an archer to bring his stick from the farm. Nor had anyone bothered to inspect it.

"What of our Brother Cuget, who set aside his dislike for violence to put himself in the path of those who despoil our Garden?" Sister Violette's voice rang like a malicious bell.

Melchor's head-shake made his sideburned jowls jiggle portentously. "Dead, Sister Violette. Dead and abandoned on the battlefield by those cowards there."

He thrust a theatrical arm like a spear at Karyl and Rob. Heads turned. Faces flushed with fury or furrowed with interest or hung slack with incomprehension.

Rob stood up and took a bow.

Violette nodded her head of long, silver hair, done up in a complicated bun at the back of her fine head. Her eyes, which matched her name, flashed with passion and triumph.

"Allow me to sum up the indictments against you," she declaimed to Rob and Karyl. "The terrible raids by Count Guillaume of Crève Coeur's knights forced us, in violation of our principles, to hire you to defend us. Yet when the time came to face a Brokenheart invasion in the field, you hung back. And so because of your cowardice—to call it plainly what it was—disaster befell our nobles, and our people."

"That's a lie!" a voice shouted from the crowd.

It was the old farmer Pierre. Mud still caked his face and streaked his raptor-scarred leg. A rag whose bloodstains barely stood out against the filth encircled his head. A knot of his fellow peasants stood around him at the hall's left front.

Violette's face became a mask of almost insane rage. But only Rob, it seemed, was looking at her.

"The captain tried to stop a foolish attack," Pierre said. "He ordered us to stand fast. We—I disobeyed. To my bitter cost. My eldest son lies in that field. Raptors rip his limbs, and fliers are pecking the eyes from the head I used to tousle when he was small. It was the lords who did it, and Karyl and his lieutenant who tried to stop it."

If Melchor could have incinerated the old man with his eyes, he would have. But he left it to Violette to reply.

"Who's most to be believed? A man of gentle birth, or some rude farmer who brings his dirt with him into our hall?"

"Does our Garden value birth over worth?" asked Bogardus. "Haven't you always been among our most insistent, Sister Violette, that each shoot be allowed to grow as high as it can, without regard to antecedents?"

Her face pinched like a sea-scorpion's claws. "Melchor's a man of education."

"Undoubtedly. Does that make him infallible?"

"You saw what happened," Pierre called to the town craftsmen who had fought in the battle. Cleaner and more neatly dressed for visits to their own homes before coming here, they mostly stood clumped at the other side of the room. "You were there. Tell them."

They looked to Reyn the carpenter. After a moment, he grimaced and nodded.

"It's true. Captain Karyl told us to set up a strong defense and wait. The lords rode out in front and ordered us to charge."

He shrugged big shoulders. "We obeyed. Betrayed by habit, I guess. We all lost friends and kin too, thanks to the lords. Or no thanks to them!"

"You'll pay for this!" Yannic hissed through his head-swaddling. "I'll have your ears for this!"

"I'm no serf of yours, Yannic. City air is free air. And what about the Garden and egalité?"

That set off a clamor like a harrier-pack screeching at the Moon Visible. Longeau's tenor rang above the racket.

"All this to the side, no one disputes the foreign mercenaries held back, instead of joining us at the forefront of battle. What's that, if not cowardice? Do you call that beauty, Eldest Brother?"

Rob looked to Karyl. His companion had his head tipped back against the mural that was his dead protégé's only monument. His eyes were shut, his bearded lips slightly parted, as if he soundly slept.

"You know the truth!" Rob raged at him. Out loud: he could have screamed it without being heard anybody farther away. "You've got to tell them! Why won't you defend yourself, man?"

As if that were his cue Bogardus raised his hands outward from his sides, unfurling his robe's wide sleeves like wings. Once again he worked his magic and stilled the crowd.

"Perhaps we should let our captains tell their story," he said. "Brother Karyl, if you please?"

Karyl opened his eyes and stood up briskly. He didn't act like a man who'd been dozing an eyeblink before. Rob doubted he had, in fact. But he also knew Karyl could wake from the deepest sleep in an instant. When the nightmares let him sleep deeply.

"The facts are as you've heard them, Eldest Brother. If our actions don't speak loudly enough on our behalf, what can words do? We'd proclaim ourselves in the right whether we were or not."

And he sat. Rob stared at him in horror.

"You've killed us, man," he said, in Anglés thick with Traveler accent.

"It's only the second act," Karyl answered him in Francés. "Wait for the finale."

"That's what I'm afraid of," he said. "Specifically, mine."

Yet Karyl had it right: the show was far from over. If these mad Providentials loved one thing more than art, it was arguing. Preferably at the top of their lungs, faces red and spittle flying like Ovdan horse-nomad arrows. Which they duly fell to now, with a will.

Clearly Bogardus believed Karyl—perhaps because he hired the outsiders in the first place, and badly wanted to. At least he seemed to listen as attentively when the lowborn spoke as the high, which was more than most of the Council did. Or for that matter most Gardeners. Rob couldn't help thinking of the softness of their hands, and how notably toil hadn't stained their simple yet costly garb. Only the raw acolytes did anything useful—even tend the namesake gardens.

"Why won't Bogardus speak up for us?" Rob muttered. He wasn't sure what was actually being said: plucking out words like *treachery* and *dismemberment* from the general tumult had made him shut his ears. Instead he tried to track the collective passion. Which seemed to go up and down like a seesaw. "He carries the whole damn town in the palms of his hands."

"He wants this settled once and for all," Karyl said. "If he imposes a solution, it'll be like face-paint over a festering boil. Maggots would breed beneath."

And sometimes Himself shows quite the streak of poetry, Rob thought. He sighed. For once he decided to keep his tongue on a short rein. He'd already mentioned headsmen and nooses as often as good taste allowed, in any event.

An urchin slipped in the doorway to Rob's left, past the guardsman, who frowned officiously but made no move to stop him. Or her. Rob could never tell. But he instantly recognized the shock of ragged black hair, snub-nosed face, the shapeless grey sack of frock.

Like a ferret, Petit Pigeon never took a direct route across the open unless there was no choice. Sidling up to Rob, the child-spy whispered in his ear. As Rob listened his eyebrows slowly rose toward the shock of bronze-tawny hair he knew was standing up all awry from running anguished fingers through it.

"Good work," he said when Little Pigeon finished. He dug in his pouch and gave the child a copper centime. Little Pigeon grinned, showing startling-white teeth, and slipped quickly back out between the town guards at the door.

Not five breaths later Emeric strode in. His face showed grim and rough-hewn humor. The sentries made as if to stop him. A narrowing of forest-green eyes snapped them back into their places like spring-mounted toys.

The woods-runner took his turn whispering in Rob's not so shell-like ear. Fighting back a laugh that threatened to boil over like water from an unwatched pot, Rob thanked him. Emeric went out, flicking the guardsmen with a glance like spit.

Rob leaned his head near Karyl's. "I've just had two pieces of information drop into my lap," he said. "Together they make the most remarkable whole."

Circumstance overriding his own rhapsodic nature, Rob gave Karyl a succinct account. Then he leaned back, no longer fighting a beard-splitting grin, inviting his friend to admire his news.

Karyl cocked a skeptical brow. "Convenient, that one comes on the heels of the other."

"Not really," Rob said, shifting his butt on the hard bench with impatient energy. "The events they report happened close together. And for all Little Pigeon's guile and Emeric's gift for intimidation it took them a while to get past the guards."

"Well. They've done a splendid job." And unbelievably Karyl made to settle back into his nap.

"What the Old Hell's wrong with you?" Rob hissed. "This proves our case!"

"Not necessarily," Karyl said. "It doesn't exculpate us, only spreads the guilt around. At best, it might deflect attention from us briefly."

"But the debate's going against us! A little less attention might be just what we need. For instance, to make a quick nocturnal dash for the frontier. . . ."

Karyl opened one eye. "Worried?"

"Shouldn't you be?" Rob asked.

Karyl smiled slightly. Then he laid his head back against the cool painted wall and to all appearance dozed peacefully off.

I hope you've got some bloody plan in that dented, nightmare-haunted skull of yours, Rob thought savagely, *and aren't just sinking back into the cold-comfort muck of fatalism.*

But Rob's psychic powers failed him. Which was small surprise, since despite his heritage he had none. Which was just as well, or he'd likely be held in thrall by some bloody banking-house, Creators' Law against slavery be hanged.

Which on reflection didn't look so bad a place to be, just now. Bogardus clearly favored the men he'd hired. So did the commoners, peasants and townsfolk alike, who had fought at the blueflower field. But sentiment among the townsfolk who had crowded in to watch, and more to the point, among the surviving Council members, ran strongly against them.

Despite the tension, and sleeping from the time they'd been locked into villa rooms in lieu of cells—not very restfully, for some reason—until summoned for trial, Rob dozed off.

As he discovered when a voice blaring like a trumpet too close to his left ear jarred him awake.

"Can I be heard?"

In the darkness the horse whickered and tossed its head as Jaume cinched the saddle on top of the pad. He ignored the beast. It might have a name; he didn't know or much care. To him it was a mode of transport—a living being to be treated with kindness, of course, because that was the Lady's way, as well as his natural inclination. But it meant nothing special to him, not the way a good dinosaur did. Certainly not like his beloved Corythosaurus Camellia. In that he was the opposite of his estranged lover, who cared little for dinosaurs but doted on horses, especially her mare Meravellosa.

Melodía. The name tolled like a funeral bell in his mind, and left a taste of ashes on his tongue.

The orange glow that danced suddenly upon the polished leather of the saddle told him the horse wasn't in fact reacting to this unaccustomed nocturnal activity, but to the approach of living beings.

He turned. His first reaction was to frown. The torch was held up by the trembling hand of none other than his arming-squire, Bartomeu. It illuminated the glum faces of five Companions.

"Wouldn't it be easier if you had light to work with, Lord?" asked Florian with deceptive lightness.

"I learned to saddle a horse in the dark when I was a boy," Jaume said, "campaigning against the miquelets in the mountains of Dels Flors."

The Companion horse-paddock was next to the stouter enclosure where their war-dinosaurs lowed and grumbled to each other, in a little valley near the town of Red Crag. The Companions had sited their cantonment so that the winds mostly kept the stench of the rest of the army away.

Tree-frogs sang in the copse from which the party of Companions had emerged.

"I'm sorry, Lord!" Bartomeu blurted. "I—"

"Don't blame the boy," rumbled huge Ayaks. "We intimidated him."

"It's all right, Bartomeu," Jaume said. "You didn't do anything wrong. My actions stuck you between two stones, I'm afraid."

"Where were you going, Lord?" asked Manfredo.

Jaume smiled. *I won't lie*, he told himself. *These are my friends—my Companions.*

Besides, it wouldn't do any good.

"Following Melodía, of course," he said.

"Pay," Florian said to the Taliano. "I told you he'd try to go after her. You just don't understand passion."

A wave of pain washed over Manfredo's square-chinned face. "Don't talk about things you know nothing about," he rasped.

Florian raised a brow. Then his mouth set, as if he realized what he'd said to a man who had so recently given his own longtime lover the final mercy.

"Your pardon," he said, lowering your head. "I spoke without thinking. The captain's right to have his doubts about me, I suppose."

Manfredo frowned, but said gruffly, "Pardon granted."

"You can't leave us!" said Wouter, with more emphasis than was usual for him. "We're just about to march against Conde Ojonegro."

Word of Melodía's bizarre arrest, imprisonment, and escape had been the second body blow Jaume in as many days. The first came when, instead of the expected command to march the Army of Correction back to La Merced to be dissolved, orders came bearing Felipe's seal to turn the army's attention to the fief near the border with Francia, whose lord had been defying the throne in a complicated matter involving ownership of several choice fiefs.

Jaume shook his head. "You don't need me for that. It's not as if I did such a marvelous job in the campaign against Terraroja."

"Don't sell yourself short," said Machtigern.

"You can't leave your appointed post in command of the army," Manfredo said severely. "That would be a dereliction."

Jaume smiled thinly. "I thought I was the Constable," he said, "commander of all Imperial Armies. I could put you in charge of the army, if I chose."

But Manfredo shook his curly red locks. "You're also Marshal. The Emperor put you in command of the Army of Correction. You must remain at your post. You can send out Companions, or whomever you choose, to search for the Princess. But at that, only so that she might be returned to La Merced for trial."

"Jaume's not going to drag his lover back to captivity in chains," Florian said. "Nor send anyone else to do it. He shouldn't either. This whole thing stinks of a setup. You know her better than anybody, Jaumet. You've known her since she was a child. Would she plot against her father, for any reason whatever?"

"Never," Jaume said.

He scanned the faces of his beloved comrades. "This comes as no surprise to you, I belatedly see."

"Rumors of the upheavals in La Merced reached camp two days ago," Ayaks admitted. "We kept them from you as best we could."

"Thank you, I suppose. But now I do know. And—I must go to her."

"What will you do for her?" Machtigern asked. "What could you do?"

"Help her. Shelter her. Bring her here, I suppose."

"You can't do that," Manfredo said gravely. "She's a fugitive from justice."

"I know what lies behind all this," said Machtigern. "Falk."

The normally taciturn knight all but spat the name of his fellow Alemán.

"Who killed Duval in duel and took his place in command of the Imperial Guard? Who killed the Emperor's own kinfolk while trying to arrest them, had his infernal white pet of a tyrant bite the head of Prime Minister Mondragón on the plaza before the Pope's own Palace? Who arrested your own beloved Melodía on charges of plotting against her own father, which everyone in the Empire knows for a trumped-up travesty? Why not lead us Companions straight back to La Merced and deal with that damned rebel goblin, Captain?"

Ayaks laid a hand on Machtigern's wide shoulder. "You have said something there, my friend. Nor should we neglect this mysterious confessor of His Majesty's, this Fray Jerónimo. I'd bet he's the one behind all this insanity!"

"Not a good idea, brothers," said Florian. "Jaume leaving his post plus marching the army on La Merced? That would equal plain treason against the Fangèd Throne, if not in his uncle's loving eyes, then in those of too many powerful figures for even Felipe to disregard. And his Holiness Pío's only looking for an opportunity to yank our Charter."

Jaume stared at him. "You? Mad Florian, advising caution?"

Florian shrugged. "I can't let myself become too predictable. But the idea of taking the Order back to La Merced races past rash. It's just foolish. Still, I agree you've got to do something, Captain."

"If you abandon the army, what will become of it?" Manfredo asked. "It will ravage the countryside worse than ever. And probably wind up destroyed, which, while small loss in terms of the villains who'd actually do the dying, would deal a terrible blow to Imperial arms and prestige."

Jaume knew the former law student had a point. But unaccustomed anger bubbled up inside him. "And if I abandon Melodía? What kind of man would that make me?"

"One who follows the law he's sworn to uphold," Manfredo said. "What can you do to help Melodía, if you won't take her back to stand trial? Go into exile with her? That'll be your only recourse, if you violate the Empire's Law."

"Have you forsaken Beauty then, Manfredo?" Jaume said in cold fury. "Have you lost faith with the Lady we all serve, and gone back to worship Torrey and the rigidity of His Law?"

Even in the spitting torchlight Jaume could see the color fall out of Manfredo's face. The Taliano turned and walked into the night.

Jaume deflated. He realized his wrong at once. He longed to call after his friend—his Companion. To apologize for letting his temper seize control of his tongue.

But the hellbrew of passion that had driven him since he read his uncle's oddly bloodless letter had deserted him abruptly. Now he felt little but cold clamminess inside, and bewilderment at the dizzy wheeling of events in the normally placid court. Duval and Mondragón were Felipe's friends, he thought, and as loyal as I am. And who could believe Melodía, of all people, of wishing her own father harm?

But one man in particular, he knew, must have believed those things. *—I cannot shape that thought now.*

He sagged. Then, feeling a strong grip on his shoulder, turned.

"Whatever you decide," Florian said, "we're behind you. Us Knights-Brother, and most likely the Ordinaries as well. Even that dry stick Manfredo. You are our Captain-General, and our friend."

Jaume squeezed his eyes shut. He felt tears weight down his lower lids.

"I suppose I can only do what I have all along," he said, opening his eyes and forcing a smile. "My duty to my uncle and the throne."

"And Melodía?" Machtigern asked.

"I can only hope for the best for my true love. She's smart, stronger and more resourceful than she knows."

But inside he asked himself: *Have I made the worst of choices? And could it be,* once again*?*

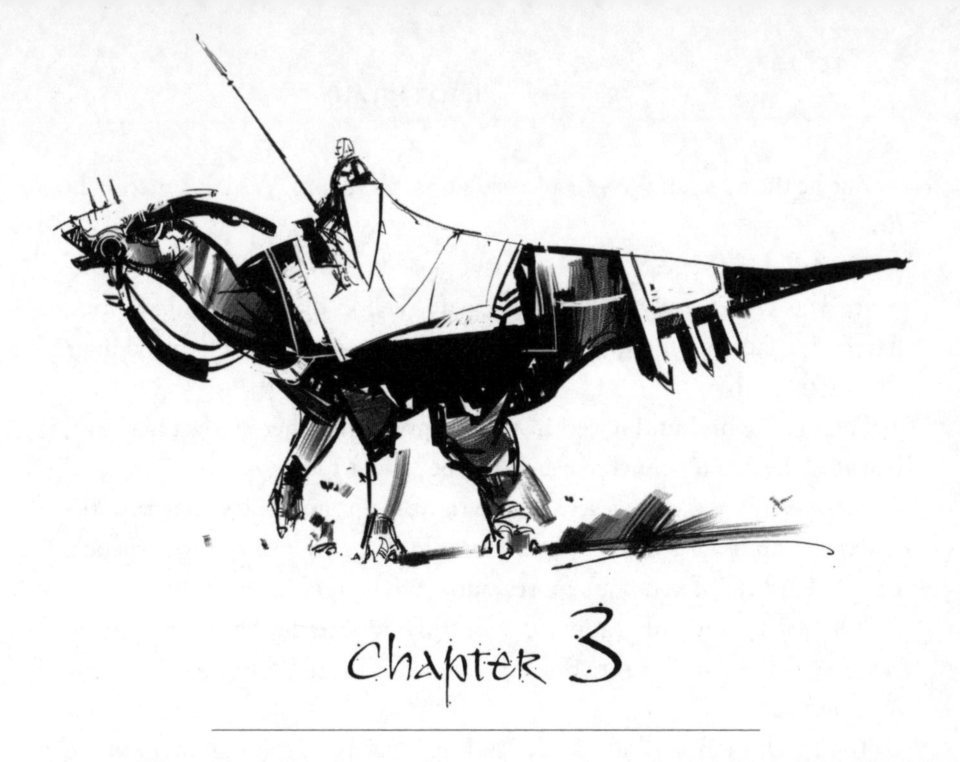

Chapter 3

Trono Colmillado, **Fangèd Throne**—Throne of the Emperor of Nuevaropa in La Majestad, supposedly fashioned from the skull of an unprecedently huge and terrible monster, an imperial tyrant (*Tyrannosaurus imperator*), heroically killed by Manuel Delgao, progenitor of the Imperial line. Since no confirmed reports of the existence of such a monster have ever been discovered (although it is duly listed in *The Book of True Names*), the Fangèd Throne is widely presumed to be a sculpted fake, if a glorious one, and the Creators to have an arch sense of humor.

—THE BOOK OF TRUE NAMES

"People are scared by the news of a Grey Angel Emergence in Providence, your Majesty," Duke Falk von Hornberg, new head of the Imperial bodyguard, the Scarlet Tyrants, told his master as he walked beside him across the Palace yard in the dim dawn light spilling over the western walls. "Many voices are calling for immediate war, in the La Merced streets as well as at court."

"Well," said Felipe, Emperor of Nuevaropa, as he hopped one-legged, trying to pull his right boot off without stopping, "we can't rush into this. I'm getting pressure from the family not to do anything too rash, you know. They truly believe we've held on to power since the Empire's inception by not exercising any of it. Shortsighted, but there you have it."

But he didn't sound too displeased at Falk's report. Which suited Falk fine.

"There," His Majesty said in satisfaction. He tossed the boot to a servant, who was already carrying its mate. Felipe did not mind walking barefoot, a fact of which Falk approved. "Any word how Melodía's doing? Or where she is?"

He skinned his hunting-jerkin of thin springer-leather off over his head, baring a chest and paunch covered in fine ginger fur.

Falk set his jaw. "Majesty, there are underground ways that run between the dinosaur stables and the Great Hall for your morning audience. I really must insist you not expose yourself to danger in this way."

"Oh, pshaw. I'm only Emperor. Not truly important. Although we may yet change that, am I right? But I'm damned if I'll skulk like a thief in my own home."

The Firefly Palace, Palacio de las Luciérnagas in the regional tongue and main language of the Empire itself, wasn't strictly speaking his home. It was actually owned by Prince Heriberto, the local ruler. But he rented it out to Felipe, who in turn preferred it to the official Imperial residence in the capital, La Majestad.

Felipe stripped off his linen trunks and the loincloth beneath at one go. Falk averted his eyes. These southerners had a scandalous lack of body modesty.

"Now, tell me, what have you heard of my daughter?"

"Nothing, I fear," Falk said. "She and her wench are doing an excellent job of hiding from dutiful nobles and their vassals despite our sending alerts throughout the Empire to keep a watch for the fugitives."

"Good," Felipe said.

As a devotee of the Creator Torrey, or Turm in his native speech, as well as a firm believer in the principle of *order*, Falk should have spoken right up about how the Empire's own law was not to be taken lightly—least of all by the Emperor himself.

He did not. For one thing, Felipe *was* the Emperor, and belief in order meant belief in the hierarchy: that those above ruled those below by right. Nor was Falk so single-minded in his devotion to his principles as to be unaware that contradicting one's boss isn't always the soundest career move.

But mostly it was because he was thinking, *Good indeed. Better if she isn't captured at all.*

"She *did* escape imprisonment for treason, your Majesty," he settled on saying. "With the help of her serving-maid, also a fugitive from the law."

Felipe was just tying up a fresh loincloth. "And I quite agree with you that, drastic as it was, arresting her was the best way to get her out of the bull's-eye lantern glare—and away from the turmoil of Palace intrigue you've so ably been putting to rest, my dear boy."

So pleased you feel that way, Majesty, Falk thought. Inasmuch as "putting to rest the turmoil" had so far consisted of personally using his albino Tyrannosaurus war-mount Snowflake to publicly decapitate the Emperor's longtime friend and Prime Minister, Mondragón, and killing several of Felipe's own relatives. Granted, they were scurrilous rogues, and no one would miss them. Nor be the wiser that Falk's rise had entailed actively if briefly conspiring with them. And all that also left aside that Falk had acceded to his current post of chief Imperial bodyguard by the expedient of challenging its former older, also long in Imperial service, to a duel and then killing him.

Amazingly, all is actually going to plan, he thought. *Or most of it.*

Mother, are you proud of me? She wouldn't be, he knew.

One of Felipe's trailing servitor-gaggle tossed an elaborate ceremonial yoke of yellow ridiculous reaper feathers over his shoulders.

"There!" Felipe said, plucking the harness more satisfactorily into place as another servant fastened it with a brooch inset with a thumb-sized ruby. "Now I'm suitably Imperial to meet those beastly Trebs this morning. No doubt they'll be whining at me to give them an answer in the matter of marrying Melodía off to their Crown Prince Mikael. Which she's dead set against, not that I blame her."

He turned his face to grin boyishly at Falk, frustrating the efforts of a servant to place a semiformal crown of gold set with rubies on his head right-way-to.

"Say, they can hardly blame me if my daughter's not to hand, can they? I couldn't hand her over to their fat, unwashed heir, even were I going to. Which the Creators give me strength and wisdom not to, since it's when you have formal alliance with the Basileus that those confounded intriguers find it most convenient to put the knife in. Plus she's not having any of it, of course."

He shook his head. A second attempt at applying the circlet ended with it tipped at a dangerous if rakish angle forward and over one bulbous pale-green eye. The exceedingly stylized tyrant skull looked like some creature perching on His Majesty's close-cropped head like a cat and winking at Falk.

"Strong-willed girl, that," Felipe said. "Say, just between you and me and the wall—"

And the servants, Falk thought. *Who hear everything. And repeat it to* my *servant.*

"—be a good lad and quietly send out a stand-down on the alert, will you?

Falk managed to keep his answering smile tight-lipped, instead of splitting his beard with a foolish grin.

"As you wish," he said.

Since I can't hope to order the bitch killed without losing my own head, he was thinking.

Having Falk's head off was the kindest thing that His Imperial Majesty was likely to do to him if he found out what his new security chief had done to his adored daughter while she was in his custody, and the Creators' ban on torture be damned.

He must tread carefully—more so now than ever, precisely because of his powerful position. Most particularly he had to guard against a tendency to take Felipe for a rambling, ineffectual fool. Which error had led the Electors to choose to place his broad buttocks on the Fangèd Throne, under the misapprehension he'd be safe and do nothing to upset the Empire. Or the death grip his family, Torre Delgao, had held on the Empire's rule since its inception.

In fact the Emperor was highly intelligent—and highly ambitious to exercise the power latent in the throne in the face of centuries of calculated inaction. His activism had sparked a rebellion among the nobles of Alemania, among them Falk himself. And his nature, impulsive yet easily led—and not eager to reconsider an action, once taken—had also set Falk on the path to his present status, once he'd presented himself at court to repent theatrically of his error and throw himself on Felipe's mercy. Felipe did love his grand gestures.

He also loved his daughters, even though he tended to forget they existed when distracted by matters of state or his love for hunting, say. Falk's excess, drunk with triumph as well as wine—and the sly words of his manservant—could yet cost him and his mother everything they'd worked for over the years.

Still, Falk was well-pleased with the situation. Albeit not smug. *And that hada Bergdahl will prevent smugness from ever gaining a foothold in me.*

Rob jumped. Karyl sat up crisply.

A man stood in the doorway. He had a heroic paunch, with chest and shoulders to match or more. Coarse dark-blond hair was swept back from sun-reddened features of the sort called leonine, after the bestiaries of fabulous animals of First Home that were a favorite of every child. His green-trimmed brown tunic, tan hose, and brown suede boots were plain but clearly of expensive make. A belt supported a scabbarded broadsword. From the wear visible on the hilt it was no prop.

The town guards at the door stood deferentially away. Clearly, Rob noted, here stood a man of Consequence. Although his sheer presence would command attention regardless of his standing.

"Merchant Évrard," Violette said. "I thought I sensed an unsavory smell."

"Insult us as you wish," Évrard said with a smile. "So long as you continue to pay us in the Count's good silver, we'll continue to feed you. Now, if it pleases the Council, allow me to rephrase: will you hear, not me, but my son, who fell sorely wounded protecting us all?"

For a moment Melchor, Longeau, and Violette looked ready to refuse. A feral growl rose from the crowd. Gaétan was popular to begin with. Whatever they felt about Karyl, the mob was eager to seize upon his unquestioned heroism despite the Blueflowers debacle. Perhaps the more so because of it.

Not leaving time for the hostile Councilors to object, youthful members of the merchant's extended family carried in a litter. On it lay Gaétan, still deathly pallid except for a fever-flush on his cheeks. As his kinsfolk bore him to the front of the hall, the onlookers packed into the central hustled aside, not scrupling to knock one another onto those seated on the benches.

Who muttered curses but made no effort to thrust them back toward the pallet and its being carried forward. So deeply ingrained was the terror of disease, even though everyone knew the kind that sometimes followed injury wasn't infectious. Ignoring them, the bearers set the litter on the open maroon tile floor at the foot of the dais.

"I want to give my testimony, if I may," Gaétan croaked. He struggled to sit.

"Please, brave boy, don't trouble yourself," Bogardus said.

"No. I won't lie like a lump. I need to speak. You need to listen."

Like an eel through rocks his sister Jeannette made her way through the crowd to kneel at his side. With the help of his litter-bearers she helped him sit, half upright and propped in her lap. The thin sheet that covered him fell away from the bandages wound about his chest.

Violette said nothing. But her lips compressed to the vanishing point and her eyes turned briefly to slits. *Brave girl*, thought Rob, to risk the wrath of that one.

He knew the powerful Council member could make his sometime-lover's life in the Garden into Old Hell on Paradise. But he feared worse, somehow. Violette and her supporters had taken on an edge, recently. Something he couldn't put a name to.

He couldn't see Violette lowering herself to wielding a dagger herself. But she and her cohort Longeau had been willing, eager even, to adopt a rabidly aggressive strategy even as they continued to mouth words of pacifism. He didn't find that reassuring.

Haltingly, Gaétan spoke. "We'd marched a kilometer or two west from Pierre Dorée, that village abandoned last year after the bastard Guillaume sacked and burned it. Master Rob's scouts reported they'd found Salvateur's forces not far past a rise just ahead. Captain Karyl ordered us to take up positions blocking the road, in and in front of the woods we were just passing through, where the goblins couldn't all come at us at once.

"Then suddenly the town lords were out in front of us, asserting their ancient right of command, so-called. Longeau gave a rousing speech about how we had to attack at once. And most of our people went charging forward, obedient as dogs."

Gaétan paused. His face twisted briefly. Rob could only guess at the pain from his wound stabbing through his chest.

"I wanted to go with them," Gaétan said. "I really did. But Karyl ordered us to hold back. I obeyed."

The audience recoiled, with a joint hissing inhalation. "Stop helping us," Rob muttered under his breath. "Any more such favorable testimony and the mob'll forget all about hanging or beheading and jump straight to pulling us apart with nosehorns."

"And Karyl was right," Gaétan said. "We felt the awful terremoto that broke our brothers before they got within bowshot of the enemy. Watched them stream back over the rise toward us in panic flight. Watched them ridden down by a couple dozen of Salvateur's cavalry and a handful of dinosaur knights. With nothing in the world we could do.

"You all know Lucas, the genius lad who painted this place? He was Karyl's special student at swordsmanship. He learned fast and well. I saw him empty a courser's saddle of a Crève Coeur knight. Then another one killed him."

Seeing an opening, Sister Violette slid in words like a silver knife. "So Karyl lured our greatest painter away on this mad errand of his, got him killed—and didn't even avenge him?"

Rob saw Karyl flinch as though struck. His face tightened, went pale and stark. A scar Rob hadn't noticed before glowed like a white thread down the right side of his forehead.

Grief throbbed in the silver-haired Councilor's voice as well as anger. And they're both genuine, he thought in surprise, or she's as great an actress as ever Lucas was an artist with a brush.

He wasn't sure he liked knowing what that told him. Easier by far to think of Sister Violette as nothing more than a cynical foe, a viper coiled in the ground cover, awaiting the opportunity to strike.

Gaétan shook his head, grimaced again. "No. Karyl didn't avenge Lucas. I did, for all that's worth. Shot the Brokenheart bastard who speared him right out of the saddle.

"No, all Karyl did then was save us all."

Yannic was glaring through his bandages as if deranged. His lips opened as if to speak. Melchor grabbed his arm to silence him. The fat man's grip must have been unexpectedly strong; Rob could see his fellow lord wince through his bandage-mask.

"Karyl shot the leading morion through both cheeks with his horn-bow," Gaétan said. "She threw her rider and turned right about, knocking over two other duckbills who were following too close behind. The dino-saur knights were all clumped together, you see.

"That stopped them cold. As for the Crève Coeur chivalry, few wore full plate—why put themselves to the heat and bother, to trample a handful of peasant scum like us? Instead most wore chain and open helmets. So as they closed with us, even our shortbows were able to hurt them. Karyl and I emptied some saddles with our Ovdan bows. The crossbows may have gotten some too."

He shook his head wearily. "Then I got stuck. I—I can't tell any more. But if Karyl hadn't kept us archers back, none of us would be here now. That . . . I know—"

His blue eyes rolled up in his head and he slumped against his sister. Rob felt like applauding. If that was genuine—and it certainly appeared so, especially the way Jeannette cried out and began to weep—Gaétan's body, at least, had a Fae's own sense of timing.

Into the silence that gathered like spirits of the dead around the young woman's sobs, Bogardus said, "Who can tell us what happened next? You, you—"

He gestured at Reyn and Pierre. "Come close, my friends, if you please. What happened after gallant Gaétan fell?"

Despite his earlier defiance, Reyn shot Yannic a fearful glance. But he complied. Pierre strode forward as forthrightly as his limp would allow. *There walks a man who feels he's little left to lose*, thought Rob.

"Some of us who'd run rallied behind the archers, took up a stand in the woods," Pierre said. "We were afraid, still. But we—I—I saw the rich boy Gaétan fall, and the lord Karyl stand. They could've run away as soon as they saw us come over that cursed hill with Old Hell on our heels. Instead they risked their own lives to give us a chance to keep ours."

"Do you seriously expect us to believe that a few paltry archers and some frightened peasants crouching in the underbrush not only stood off Crève Coeur knights, but routed them?" asked Violette in a bone-dry tone.

"It's true," said Reyn. He sounded glum. Clearly he didn't like the choice he was making. But then if he hadn't found it more palatable than the alternatives—silence, or a lie—he wouldn't have chosen it, thought Rob.

And there's your cue, lad. He stood up and walked toward the dais.

Halberds clashed in front of him. Rob extended a finger beneath the X they made and pushed upward.

"Out of my way, pencil dicks," he told the town guardsmen. They raised their weapons and stood aside. "Smart lads."

"This man's on trial!" exclaimed Longeau. "How can he be permitted to speak?"

"In justice, how can he not, my friend?" Bogardus asked. "What have you to tell us, Master Korrigan?"

Nothing bloody Karyl shouldn't be saying in his own bloody defense, Rob thought. He successfully fought off the urge to glance over his shoulder at his codefendant. In for a penny, in for a pound.

As he reached the clear space between dais and dining tables Rob took a step to his left. *No point blockin' the Council's view of the lovely Jeannette and her fallen-hero brother now, is there?*

"Eldest Brother," he said, "please understand: it's not as if we chased the Brokenheart knights away. We just made them think better of pressing the issue at that particular moment. They pulled back up the rise to wait for their foot to catch them up."

"I don't understand," said Councilor Telesphore. His whey-bland face looked genuinely puzzled. Rob quailed: if not an ally of his and Karyl's, Telesphore was one of the least overtly hostile on the Council, and no friend to Violette. "Knights are renowned for courage. Rashness even. How could they be so easily . . . discouraged?"

"Ah, and it's true: not for nothing are they called bucketheads, your Worship. But they'd ridden over that hill expecting easy meat. Instead we gave them a faceful of steel, the like of which they found not to their taste."

"Are you saying they were afraid of you?" Violette asked.

"Not that. But like wasps we stung them. Knights don't much fear death, Sister. But they fear ignominy. Scarce a one of them could make much of a noble cause out of hunting for scratchers to steal and women to rape. They weren't set in their minds for battle, you see, but for mischief. The same does not make for a death long sung in ballads."

"So now you're a mind reader?" Violette sneered.

"No. But I'm a dinosaur master by trade. I know how a nobleman's mind works. If such a thing can be said to exist."

"It happened the way he says," Reyn said. "They didn't run. But they did stop chasing us, and they did draw back to the height."

Pierre uttered a caw of laughter so loud and wild it made even Rob jump. "Why are we even arguing about this?" he demanded. "We're here, aren't we? What Karyl did worked. Or we wouldn't be!"

Bogardus nodded. "Thank you both. Clearly, we all see with different eyes. You've certainly opened mine.

"I thank you all for your testimony. With the best faith in Paradise, we all can see each one of you has spoken the truth as best you know, out of partial knowledge. Now I'm satisfied we've heard the whole."

The hall went silent. Jeannette had given off crying and looked up at the Council with her pretty young face beseeching. Bogardus smiled at her.

"On behalf of the Garden I thank your brother for everything he's done," he said. "You as well, Younger Sister. Please, take him where he can rest and heal."

Nodding gratefully, she eased her brother's head back down to the pillow and stood. The sweat in his hair had stained her nut-brown smock. The bearers picked him up gently. She followed them out of the hall.

When they were gone Bogardus rose. "I've come to my decision. Clearly, everyone acted as they thought best, out of nothing but concern for our people, our province, and our Garden. And clearly Karyl acted rightly. He saved what could be saved, so that we may yet hope to defend ourselves against Count Guillaume's depredations."

He held out his hands. "Voyvod Karyl, approach, please."

Exuding quiet dignity, Karyl walked forward. He didn't bother leaning on his staff.

"Lord Karyl, Master Korrigan," Bogardus said. "Evidence compels me to find you innocent of all charges. Your liberty is restored. You shall continue in charge of our army, if you will."

Lady Violette turned a hot purple glare on Longeau. Standing close by, Rob was half surprised the Councilor's robe didn't catch light. Longeau nodded, as if reluctantly, and slowly got to his feet.

"Brothers and sisters and children of the Garden," he said. "People of

Providence. The time has come to face the truth, unpleasant as it is to behold. Our good Eldest Brother has taken too much upon himself. It's time he stand aside, and let the Council's will rule Providence."

They reached the border of the next county as shadows lengthened away from what would soon be the setting sun. They had left the woods behind, and rode through broad fields green with ripening grain.

"That way lies Castle Feather itself, señorita," Tristan said, pointing north of their track, which ran generally northwest. "Countess Eulalie would doubtless be honored to host you for the night. Or as long as you wished to stay."

"I thank you, Mor Tristan," Pilar said. "It's so rare to meet a knight of your intellect. I can't remember when I last had a more diverting conversation."

"I assure you, ma'amselle, the pleasure was mine."

And sweeping a final bow, he turned his blue and yellow dinosaur and sent it trotting back along the road, with his six riders following. Even the mounts seemed glad to be shut of the women.

Pilar sagged in her saddle. "Whew," she said. "Let's find shelter, shall we, Princess? I don't think I've got another performance like that one left in me."

"Me neither," said Melodía meekly.

Chapter 4

Los Creadores, **The Creators, Los Ocho, The Eight**—The gods who made our Paradise and all things that live upon it out of Old Hell: Chián, Father Sky or the King; Maia, the Mother Land or Queen; Adán, the Oldest Son; Telar, the Oldest Daughter; Spada, the Middle Son; Bella, the Middle Daughter; Torrey, the Youngest Son; and Maris, the Youngest Daughter. Each has a usual appearance and attributes, yet can manifest opposite gender—and opposite attributes. Each has a unique trigram of three solid or broken lines drawn one above the other. The Creators are served by seven Grey Angels of nearly divine power and often terrifying aspect.

—A PRIMER TO PARADISE FOR THE IMPROVEMENT OF YOUNG MINDS

"Who said you rule Providence?" a voice shouted from somewhere in the crowd. But everyone ignored the outburst.

Bogardus turned a hooded look toward Longeau. His shoulders slumped ever so slightly.

"We have treated our Eldest most unkindly." The words seemed to pour from Longeau's mouth and spread out over the hall like honeyed oil. "We've asked him to carry the burden of our physical welfare as well as spiritual. Can any mortal bear so much weight? I know I couldn't.

"Not, of course, that I presume to compare myself to our Brother

Bogardus, the brightest and most beautiful bloom in our Garden. Yet even the most splendid flower can wilt when subjected to too many stresses. Is it not true?"

The crowd began to murmur. To Rob, standing dubiously between them and the Council, they sounded at least receptive.

"What's the devil up to now?" he muttered to Karyl.

"What you'd expect," the other said imperturbably.

"Some of us who fought Baron Salvateur's marauders may have been overhasty in our assessments. Yet, the unfortunate facts remain. Our army failed. The raiders carry fire and sword into the very heart of our province. Shouldn't the army's commanders—foreign hirelings, after all, not Providencers born—be held to account for that failure? No matter how successful they proved at containing its disastrous effects?"

"That's truth," a man shouted from the audience. It may even have been spontaneous.

Longeau smiled sad indulgence. "No one here holds greater esteem for our Eldest Brother's wisdom, insight, and goodness than I. Yet clearly, we must ease his burden. Take up our share. Therefore I propose that certain core Council members—Brother Absolon, Sister Violette, and, asking forgiveness for the presumption, my own humble self—form an advisory committee, to make everyday policy and trouble Bogardus only when necessary. Gardeners, brothers and sisters of the Council, what say you?"

He looked around the high table. Absolon looked surprised, Violette smug. The others seemed merely confused. Startled babble ran through the hall.

Karyl nudged Rob. "Your cue."

"Me?"

"You're the showman. Show them."

Rob cleared his throat. "Titan shit," he said loudly.

That shut them up. Longeau actually goggled at him. "Excuse me?"

"I said, and I quote, 'titan shit.' You were fools to send the army against Count Guillaume's dinosaur knights and gendarmes in the first place, when we were too few and far from ready. Only through Karyl's actions did you ever have an army to begin with. Only through his actions do you have anything that can be called an army now."

He was in fine voice. His words echoed from the vine-painted rafters.

The crowd heard. They listened. Up on the dais Violette was almost spitting and Longeau had gone first red, then white.

"Surely this is intolerable!" he shouted.

Rob smirked at him. *You lose points for yelling, lad*, he thought. *Yell louder.*

"That this outland—mercenary—be allowed to speak in our sacred Garden Council, and to spread such calumnies—"

"I thought our Garden embraced everything that grew," a woman cried from the rear of the room. Rob was astonished to recognize Jeannette's voice. He swung around to see her stalking back in through the door out which her brother had just been carried, glowering like a whole storm front.

"Everyone has the right to speak here, foreign or not," she said. "I for one want to hear them. And if you want to throw the word 'calumny' around, what about you trying to give the lie to the testimony my beloved brother rose from what could be his deathbed to deliver to this assembly?"

"Oh, brava, child, brava," Rob muttered into his beard. He damned well doubted Gaétan was going to die unless somebody smothered him with a pillow. He'd seen enough battlefield injuries to know that if Gaétan's were going to kill him, they'd have done so by now. Jeannette surely knew that as well as he: their father's healers, the best the family's extensive fortune could secure (which was to say, the best) would have told her that much. But both his poet's soul and his self-interest, key influences in Rob Korrigan's life, applauded her performance.

He bowed to her. "Thank you, Sister Jeannette," he said. "And now I have something further to contribute to the debate. Send in Little Pigeon and friends."

All the comings and goings had completely discombobulated the town guards manning the door. One made a halfhearted clutch as Rob's child spymaster and two other ragged urchins darted in. They easily evaded him, and he succeeded only in dropping his halberd with a comic clatter.

The identifiable boy and girl who came in with the androgynous child acted reluctant. Little Pigeon, who had no more fear than a ferret, seemed to tow them after by sheer personality. She or he stopped right in front of Bogardus with chest thrust out like its namesake.

"These children of Providence town must surely be known to some of you," Rob said with a grand gesture. "As I sat at the back of the room, these children came to me with a most curious story. Will you tell it again, Little Pigeon?"

"Yes," the child said, quite calmly.

"Bogardus, this is absurd!" Longeau said. But his face had gone ashen, and his lips showed a bit of quiver.

"They're children, brother," Bogardus said gently. "Let them speak."

"Earlier this morning," Little Pigeon said, "I was in the square by the Maris fountain. I spotted a tall man talking to another in an alley. Both wore cloaks. The shorter, wider man had short hair, brown or blond. Rain had soaked it so I couldn't. Chloé—"

Little Pigeon indicated the girl, a freckled redhead. "—saw he wore armor. Olivier saw his cloak was blue and green."

That raised a sharp noise from the crowd: the Crève Coeur colors.

"And the other?" Rob said.

"He wore a hood. But we saw his face."

"Can you identify him?"

"I'd know that long nose anywhere. It's him, the one who looks like he's sucking on a green persimmon!"

As one all three children pointed to Longeau.

"Bogardus, this is intolerable," Violette all but shrieked. "How can you allow this farce—"

"Farce, Sister?" Rob said loudly. "Or tragedy?"

He turned again to the rear of the hall and roared, "Bring in the captive."

A man marched in, barrel-bodied beneath a sodden green and blue tabard with a mail hauberk clinking beneath. Rain had darkened and spiked his cap of hair. Broad and coarsely handsome, his face was given a devilish cast by a long sword-cut that ran from left eyebrow to bristle-covered right jaw. Full lips wore an insouciant half smile and murk-green eyes were calm, despite the fact that his hands were bound behind him.

And, more impressively, despite the point of a spear pricking the back of his thick neck.

Whereas the appearance of a captive Crève Coeur knight startled the crowd, the spectacle of his captor made them reel on their benches. The woods-runner Stéphanie carried the spear. She had her short brown hair bound up in a brown kerchief band. A feather panache in drab woodlands greens and browns was pinned at her left. A long narrow braid, feather-tipped, swung by each shoulder. A thin green braid that signified allegiance to Telar encircled her waist. She wore a leather bracer around her left forearm, a dagger strapped to her right, and low boots. And that was all.

Ceremonial nudity was a recognized way of accentuating the gravity of an occasion. It had more impact here in Providence, where people normally went clothed, than in the hotter, wetter lowlands.

Not that she didn't make sufficient impression on her own. Rob hadn't fully appreciated before what a remarkable figure she made, long-limbed, with the lithe muscles and assured lethality of a matador. The brutal knife scarring on her face, and incidental gouges and slices on her tawny hide, now only reinforced the splendid barbarism of her appearance. Her breasts were large if somewhat flat, with wide brown nipples. Rob couldn't help noting with interest her pubic hair was an almost dainty patch, soft and brown, not the exuberant bush he'd expect from such a wild woman.

For some reason the men in the audience seemed more appreciative than the women, but no eye looked anywhere but at Stéphanie as she marched the captive to the Council table.

Bogardus seemed to have trouble restraining a grin. "Your name, Montador?" he asked the knight.

"Laurent of Bois-de-Chanson, knight in service to my lord Baron Salvateur, and to his liege Guillaume, Count of Crève Coeur."

"And to what do we owe the presence of such a distinguished guest, Mor Laurent?"

The man snorted as if at a joke. "The woods-rats and their mounted farmer friends caught me as I rode away from town this morning."

At the phrase *woods-rats* Stéphanie went pale and drew back her arm as if to drive her hunting-spear through the knight's neck. Rob quickly laid a restraining hand on her arm. It felt like wrapped wire under velvet.

"And did you meet someone in an alley near the square?" Bogardus asked.

"Yes." He jutted his square chin at Longeau. "That one."

"Don't listen to this nonsense," Longeau said. "This—this is a feeble attempt to defame a man whose only crime is zealously serving the Garden of Beauty and Truth and the people of Providence!"

Mor Laurent barked laughter. "Is that what you call it here? Back home across the Lisette we call it treason."

Violette shot to her feet as if she had a spring up her butt. "You lie!"

The broad face darkened. "Release me, and I'll challenge you or any champion you care to name for that slander."

"Will you want to fight me if I ask why we should believe you, an enemy, Mor Laurent?" Bogardus asked.

Laurent glared at him a moment. Then he shrugged. "Believe what you want; all your opinions matter to me as much as those of as many fatties. If you want to kill me, get to it. I'm easily bored."

A large portion of the crowd enthusiastically seconded the suggestion. But Bogardus said, "If you satisfy us you're telling the truth, we'll set you free. The only conditions are that you ride straightaway across the border, and never bear arms against Providence again."

He looked at Karyl. Rob did likewise. Karyl nodded crisply. Stéphanie glared at Rob.

"They'll be plenty more for you to skewer, my dear," Rob muttered to her. "We need this one unpunctured, please."

He knew that if Mor Laurent had been among her rapists and tormentors she'd have killed him already no matter what anybody told her. The woods-runners had no more stomach for obedience than Rob did himself.

Laurent shrugged again. "Very well. It's cheaper than a ransom, and the pickings have been thin of late. I agree to your terms, on my honor as a belted knight. The man's treason served us well enough, but I've no more bloody use for a traitor to your side as to my own, as Torrey's my witness. He said he'd smooth our road to take over the town if we spared him. And the whole bloody Council, why I don't know."

"And had you spoken to him before?"

"Oh, yes. He said he'd help us see off this rag-tag rabble army of yours, and discredit your mercenary captains. Or better make an end to them. Said he thought them a greater threat than we were. A damned fool thing to say. But a traitor will say anything to justify his treachery."

"You bastard!" Longeau hissed. "How can you tell such lies? What did the foreigners pay you?"

"A spear at my neck, as any fool can see, handroach. Brave man, to spit on the honor of a trussed-up captive. But I'll serve you back the same."

He looked around, bold as Bogardus. "Who saw this soft-fleshed sack of wind in the fighting? Anyone? Then how'd he get the wound? It can't have been shaving: a kitten could lick his whiskers off for him."

Rob stepped up on the dais, snatched Longeau's arm from its sling with a big square hand, and ripped off the bandage. Longeau struggled but couldn't free himself. Rob held his arm up for all to see.

The skin of his arm was white and intact.

"A miraculous healing!" Rob declared. "That, or bouncer's blood sprinkled on bandages to cover a fraud."

The crowd jumped to its feet, shouting fury. Longeau cringed. Rob let him go.

"Release the captive, please, Brother Rob," Bogardus said beneath the tumult.

Rob turned to Stéphanie. "Lend me your dagger."

Her green-hazel eyes blazed like stirred bonfires. "Please," he said, acutely aware of how close he was to feeling his own guts wrapped around that spear. "We'll give you all the vengeance you can stomach, Karyl and I. Promise."

Lips twisting in a snarl, she whipped her dagger from its arm sheath and threw it clattering to the tiles. Then she turned and stalked out. Rob watched the play of her muscle-rounded buttocks beneath the smooth brown skin until they vanished out the door.

Shaking himself, he bent to pick up her knife. He raised a brow at Karyl as he straightened. Rob stepped up behind the knight's back and cut the ropes. Despite temptation—*self-denial is good for the soul, lad*—he made himself work carefully so as not to cut the captive.

"Go now," he said, as Laurent shook his hands free, "and sin no more."

For a moment the knight stood frowning thoughtfully and rubbing his red wrists. Then he looked Karyl in the eye.

"You've won them for now," he said. "But they'll turn on you for sure."

"I know," Karyl said calmly.

Mor Laurent blinked at him. Then he laughed. With his laughter echoing from the painted rafters, he walked down the aisle toward the door and out.

The crowd watched him go. While they were distracted Longeau lunged with startling speed. He yanked Sister Violette up from her chair behind the table and against his chest. A short broad dagger appeared from somewhere, dimpling the white skin beneath her jaw.

They found a little ancient cinder cone with its crater fallen-in in the middle. Some hole must have still led underground because there was no more than a boggy patch at the bottom of the depression. Its walls rose comfortably higher even than the horses' heads.

Which were kept low to the ground anyway. The cone was well overgrown, sides brushy, top crowned with saplings. The interior was upholstered with green grass and fragrant, soft-leaved scrub.

Happily a stream ran not fifty meters from the cone. Pilar stood watch while Melodía stripped, bathed, and washed her clothes. Then Melodía guarded while her servant did the same. Naked and refreshed, the two long women led their mounts, the wet laundry draped over their backs, up the short slope and back down to their chosen campsite.

Pilar got fresh silk loincloths from their luggage. As Melodía put hers on, Pilar carefully arranged their garments on a thorn-free bush to dry. Then as the rough circle of sky above them shaded from indigo to near-black, and stars began to peek with increasing boldness through tears in the clouds, she laid a small fire.

"There," Pilar said, standing up. "The crater'll hide the fire from passersby. And on the off-chance anyone sees the smoke they're likely to think the cone's waking up again, and run away as fast as their legs can carry them."

Melodía had draped her saddle-pad over a conveniently sized lava rock near the fire and sat gratefully on it. She laughed. "You think of everything, don't you?"

Pilar reacted as if Melodía had showered her with curses. The easy, brisk, competent assurance with which Pilar had managed everything suddenly fled. Her face sagged, aging what seemed like fifty years in the orange underlighting. Her shoulders sagged. She drew the dagger from her belt. Kneeling before Melodía, she held the knife toward her mistress hilt-first.

"What on Paradise are you doing?" Melodía demanded in genuine consternation.

"I dishonored you, mistress," Pilar said. "I abused you and struck you. I'm willing to pay the price for my unforgivable acts."

"Oh, don't be an idiot, Pilar. Stand up and put that silly knife away."

Pilar looked up at her. Despite her look of despair, for the first time in what seemed like years Melodía had realized just how beautiful her servant was.

It probably has been years, Melodía thought. She sighed. Taking the other woman by her outstretched arms she gently but decisively pulled her to her feet.

"Listen," she said. "I know I was acting like an idiot back there. I was being weak and self-indulgent. I'd say childish, but that makes me think of my baby sister, Montse, and that hardly seems just. Beneath those dreadlocks and those round cheeks she seems about as soft as a mace-tail's backside. I can't see her breaking down like that."

Just to help her feel worse a wave of homesickness washed over her and made the last few words stumble on their way to the door.

"Don't sell yourself too short, Highness. You've been through a terrible ordeal."

"Nothing justifies my breaking down like that. Certainly not in the middle of the damned road, where, just as you warned me, we were promptly snapped up by the next patrol along."

"But—what about—"

"Don't even say it! You don't need to remind me. I'll feel that little lesson in my arms and back for days. And my poor head! I'm surprised you didn't split my scalp with that first lick."

She shook her head. "Not even Doña Carlota's dared lay a hand on me since I was twelve. Not that she needed to do, once it penetrated her thick skull that telling me I'd disappointed my daddy hurt worse than any strap."

Pilar still wouldn't meet her eyes. To Melodía's astonishment she saw tear-tracks shimmering on her cheeks.

"I'm so sorry, Princess."

"You saved our lives, Pilar. You saved me. Your quick thinking back there was all that prevented disaster. You do a scary-good job of portraying a snotty noblewoman."

Pilar sniffed but showed a slight, shy smile. "I've spent a lot of time observing, your Highness."

"I hope I heard a comma, there, Pilar. I'd hate to think I inspired a single iota of that hateful Baroness Greencastle."

As she spoke her cheeks burned. Helpfully her mind was replaying instances where she had treated people in a fashion little if any kinder. And most of those "people" happened to be Pilar.

Melodía licked lips that felt cracked like dried mud. "You had no choice about—what you did back there. Nothing could put down their suspicions I might be the fugitive princess faster than giving me a thrashing like that. Thanks for sparing my face, anyway."

Pilar's smile was a little stronger. "A whip-weal on your cheek would raise questions we didn't want to answer at our next encounter," she said. "Anyway, I'd hate to spoil your loveliness. I've put enough effort into maintaining it, after all."

Melodía laughed. "So you have."

Suddenly the women were hugging each other and weeping. After a lengthy cry they broke apart.

"Here," Pilar said, lifting a lock of tear-sodden hair away from Melodía's face and smoothing it back away. "Let's get you looking a proper princess again. I'm afraid that cheap dye will leave streaks on your cheek. The way things are going, the stain would probably still be stubbornly in place weeks after your hair's gone back to its normal shade."

Melodía laughed. "Just one question, Pilar, querida."

"¿Sí, Alteza?"

"Did you have to be so damned enthusiastic?"

Chapter 5

Marchador, Ambler, Palfrey—A horse trained to a gait called "ambling": a smooth yet rapid and tireless-seeming walk. The favored traveling mount of those who can afford them, for their price can rival a war-trained courser's.

—A PRIMER TO PARADISE FOR THE IMPROVEMENT OF YOUNG MINDS

"Back away," Longeau shouted, dragging Violette around the table. The other Council members fled, leaving Bogardus alone on the dais, his handsome oblong face a blank. "Stand back or I'll paint the room red with her blood!"

She went along in an uncharacteristically passive way. Rob had often seen that reaction among folk the first time they had sudden personal violence directed against them. Of course, most people Rob knew had that experience at an age much less than Violette's, no matter what that actually might be.

Longeau might have hauled his hostage out the nearby door that led to the kitchen. But instead he pulled Violette toward the center of the dais, causing the front rank of onlookers to scramble frantically over each other to get away from him. Clearly he wanted, not escape, but an audience. Seasoned performer that he was, Rob had frequently found himself compelled to choose between those exact same things.

Bloody amateur, was his assessment of Longeau's pick.

Rob and Karyl stood their ground. Rob wondered at Karyl's reaction. *After all, she's the most persistent thorn in his ass*, he thought. *In both of ours*. Himself, Rob would only regret to see her cut out for the fact it was done by the handroach traitor.

"Please, Bogardus," Longeau moaned, looking up at the other man. To Rob's amazement tears streamed down his face. "You know why I had to do this."

To the hall at large he said, "You can't know, you mustn't know—pray the Creators, you never know . . . oh, terrible beauty. The secret rituals of power. And the cost; ah, the cost; I feel it in my belly even now. You know, Eldest Brother."

"Enough, my friend," Bogardus said softly into the terrible silence. "Give me the knife and we'll end this."

"End this?" He uttered a wild laugh. "That was what I hoped. Our only hope. I thought I'd save us from ourselves. I couldn't see any other way. The power, the terrible majesty . . . that inhuman beauty, too great to quit or to endure. Lady Violette, you know. Don't you? Don't you? Everything I've done I did for you. For us. For our souls. Souls. For everybody's soul!

"I didn't do it for the silver, but for *deliverance*. For all of us, I swear by the Creators! Crève Coeur's ravagers are kinder than what is to come."

"Shut up, you fool," hissed Violette.

Longeau sighed. His shoulders slumped. He pressed a fervent kiss on his hostage's lips, which went visibly slack from shock.

"At least I can save you from yourself," he murmured. The knife blade withdrew ever so slightly from Sister Violette's pale neck as he cocked his arm to thrust.

At his eye's edge Rob saw a flash. In quick succession he heard a swoosh, a sort of wet crunch, and a thud.

Then blood was spraying in an amazing fan from the stump of Longeau's knife-arm, just below the elbow. It drenched Violette instantly in red. Screaming, onlookers whom curiosity had sucked back up toward the dais jumped away, upsetting a table into jingling silver and shattering crockery to escape the blood-fountain.

Near him stood Karyl, holding his staff-sword's wooden hilt in both hands. The rest of the staff, which served as concealing scabbard, lay on the tiles a couple of meters away. Howling in terror Violette tore herself free of Longeau's suddenly slack grip. Placidly Karyl flicked his meter-long single-edged blade to clear it of blood, and wiped both sides with quick strokes against Longeau's smock.

Rob reeled as Sister Violette ran straight into his arms, of all places. Lean as she was she proved surprisingly substantial, and wirier than she looked. Unable to think of anything better to do he patted her tentatively on the back.

He jerked his hand away. It was sticky-red with Longeau's blood.

With eyes like boiled onions Longeau stared at his gushing stump, and at the rest of his arm, which jerked like a landed fish on the maroon floor tiles. Pallid fingers still clutched the knife.

"Strike me dead," he said, almost wonderingly.

"I have," Karyl said, turning away and bending over to retrieve the scabbard. "You've perhaps two minutes left with that artery severed."

Longeau gaped at him. His eyes rolled up and he slumped to the floor. The crowd watched, shocked to silence.

"Shouldn't we help him?" Absolon asked after a moment.

Slowly Bogardus came around the table and stepped down from the dais to stand looking down at his friend. The pulses of blood from his wound grew visibly weaker with each repetition.

"Why?" Bogardus asked sadly. "To preserve him for the noose? This is a kinder death, as well as a far more aesthetic one. He'd choose it himself if he could."

"What about those things he was saying, then?" Rob said. "All that about terrible beauty, and what was to come being worse than a marauding army?"

Violette pulled free. "A madman's ravings," she said. "His desire to justify his actions drove him insane. To think I trusted him!"

She ran to Bogardus and threw herself against him. He embraced her with one arm, disregarding the blood that soaked her hair and gown.

"Who but a madman would trust Crève Coeur enough to bargain with them?" he said. "A sad case, my friends."

He reached up, took a spray of fresh forest flowers from a vase on the Council table, and tossed them on the body.

Rob frowned. *That doesn't sound right,* he thought. *But then, nothing here does.* He felt questions pressing outward on his skin, but for the moment even he couldn't quite fit words to them.

At a sign from Bogardus husky townsmen came and picked up Longeau's now-lifeless body. Cradling Violette against his chest, Bogardus watched them carry him out the door to the kitchen.

"Ah, my friend," he said sadly. "That it had to come to this."

He gave a final hug to the shaken Councilwoman and helped her sit on the edge of the dais. Then he turned to the address the hall at large.

"Now, my brothers and sisters, hasn't the time come to apologize to these gentlemen, and confirm them in the roles we have given them? Which, we've now seen, they've carried out with exceptional skill and courage."

But the Councilors, standing off by the left end of the dais, tossed nervous looks around among themselves, like hot embers.

"Things are complicated, Bogardus," said Iliane, who had shown no active hostility to the outlanders—if no overfriendship either. "We've seen and heard some horrible things tonight. Things I never imagined I'd witness have disturbed our hall's serene beauty. You can't ask us just to wave our hands and pretend nothing's happened."

"No, Sister," Bogardus said, smiling sadly. "What I ask is the opposite: take note of the frightening things we've experienced, and act accordingly."

But the surviving Councilors wouldn't meet his eye.

Rob sidled close to Karyl. "It's a brave show we've put on, any must admit," he murmured. "But now we might think of edging toward the door and exiting stage left."

"Salvateur!"

The woman's voice rang off the rafters. Everybody jumped and turned to stare at the rear of the hall.

Stéphanie stood there, still naked and spear in hand. Her magnificent body and scarred face streamed rain. Her eyes were wild and fierce as a hunting horror's.

"Salvateur!" she shouted. "His riders are fast approaching down the west road! While you loll around here on your fat butts listening to fools and liars, your enemy comes to burn your towers around your swollen heads!"

Melodía raised her face to the morning sun shining through the perpetual daytime overcast. She inhaled deeply.

"It smells as if something died," she said,

They rode up a river valley, wide, flat, and shallow, in the county of Métairie Brulée near the border of Providence. The river itself, currently more a stream, wound through marshes and stands of thin, pale-green weeds. The valley's most remarkable feature was the limestone islands, each about five meters tall, which dotted it. These had flat tablelike tops and white sides scooped and smoothed into shiny concave waves by water.

And, perhaps, the wind that quested ceaselessly down from the mountains. The Shields were close enough now to be visible most of the time as a blue wall. Despite altitude and the breeze off the perpetually snow-clad peaks the morning was hot, the overcast seeming no thicker than a vast linen sheet. Unusual numbers of birds and big fliers circled overhead; Melodía kept a wary eye on these, although none seemed large enough to be true dragons, hence dangerous to full-grown humans.

Aside from wrinkling their noses the young women paid the smell no further thought. Death was commonplace, after all.

"Tell me one thing, Pilar," Melodía said.

"Anything, Melodía."

Melodía insisted that Pilar refrain from calling her Highness, and was trying to break her from using honorifics of any kind. They were both outcasts, now. Outlaws together. And friends—a fact Melodía found herself clinging to with a certain desperation, the more so for having recently recovered it after losing it so long ago.

"Where'd you learn to speak Francés so well?"

That skill had served them well on that chance encounter with the bandit-hunters in Licorne Rouge, and several times since, when Pilar had used the same ruse to talk their way past other wayfarers. She had also used them to buy some feathered twist-darts.

Melodía had put the bow to good use shooting small game for the pot, and it could help defend their camp. But Melodía couldn't shoot at all well from horseback—horse archery was an incredibly abstruse skill, and Melodía gathered you practically had to be raised to it to be much use, like the wild steppe-nomads of Ovda. She was fairly proficient throwing darts from the saddle, though, enough to discourage bandits or other minor predators.

She now rode with a quiver of half a dozen darts by her right knee. Like the smallsword they wouldn't raise eyebrows among those the women encountered. It was common for servants to go armed to protect their masters against the bandits that infested the roads.

Melodía and Pilar hadn't run into any actual bandits yet. For which Melodía thanked her luck. After her traumatic experiences in La Merced she was even less inclined than before to believe in the Creators.

"Where'd I learn Francés? Why, the same places you did, naturally. Didn't I sit in on all your lessons from girlhood on? And your conversations with the Lady Abigail Thélème? I got to practice, sometimes, with lesser folk I met in the course of my Palace duties. Which gave me a firmer grip on the tongue, if not exactly its courtlier aspects."

Melodía laughed. Quickly she sobered. *How did I come to take her so much for granted, this childhood friend of mine? For ten years at least I've been no more aware of her than of my own shadow.* The thought made her feel sticky and cloddish.

Pilar's face rumpled. "Ay, that smell—" she said.

The stink seemed to have suddenly redoubled. Overt before, now it battered Melodía's head and shoulders like an inflated bladder at some riotous Mercedes street carnival.

"Mother Maia, what died?" she exclaimed. "A titan?"

They came around a rock-island like a white mushroom, swinging wide to clear a big clump of debris, limbs and brush and the like, which the last flood had left stacked against its upstream side, and saw what caused the smell.

"Good call," Pilar said. "That's certainly a titan. And it's most definitely dead."

It lay like a ridgeline athwart their path and the stream itself. Sunlight glinted on the temporary pond it had made by damming the flow. It had been a big one, a true matriarch, a good thirty meters long. What kind it had been was unclear: its body was blackened and grotesquely swollen. All Melodía could tell was that it was some fur-legged monster, such as a spine-back or thunderbeast, though not a treetopper. She could see no sign of the rest of what had probably been a goodly herd of enormous dinosaurs. The sandy, weedy soil, frequently washed by rain and river-rises, wouldn't hold tracks for any length of time.

"We have a problem," Pilar said, reining in her ambler.

Melodía stopped Meravellosa beside her. The mare kept an ear cocked back toward the gelding-marchador, which followed Pilar's mount on a lead, lest it try to sneak a nip at her fanny.

"So we do," Melodía said.

Vast as it was the titan would take no more than a minute or two to ride around. In life the plant-eater had been too huge for any predator to bring down, except perhaps tyrants operating in a pack. Dead, by accident or starvation or festering wound, it provided a bounteous feast that drew every predator of every size from kilometers around.

Hordes of meat-eating dinosaurs crowded around like trenchermen at table. Multiple generations of horrors jostled each other and perched on the high-arching ribs to snap in fury at scavenging fliers impertinent enough to try to land and rip off a beakful. Blues snarled and shrieked and flourished arm-feathers at reds that got too close to their territory, while greens nipped in to take advantage of their distraction, for all the planet like street gangs in La Merced's nastier slums.

Behind the horrors orbited packs of smaller harriers and little vexers, dashing in under their big cousins' terrible claws to snatch a bite and whip away again.

Even they stayed well clear of two matador packs that worked the hulk. Out of practical necessity the big horn-browed hunters had staked out either end: long neck and tail, and the body immediately adjacent. One clan was blue-green and yellow, the other a more unsettling blackish-red shading to tawny gold on their bellies. Both groups displayed the distinctive sharp striping, dark over light.

They stayed far enough apart to ignore one another with honor, reserving their bellowing wrath for younger kinfolk who got too grabby, or the occasional incautious flier or raptor. As Melodía and Pilar watched with horrified fascination a matador bull brought its big head up to clash its jaws on a corpse-tearer with a short powerful beak and nasty flesh-tone-and-purple crest that winged too near. The monster's agility apparently surprised the flier even more than it did the women.

Growling like a volcano about to blow the matador shook the black-furred flier until its long wings flopped limp as water weeds. Then it tossed the corpse away into the grass and resumed tearing at the titan.

Ignoring the giants, countless lines of even less enumerable black ants wound out of the mountain of decay. Mammalian scavengers, emboldened by hunger and mostly the fact they were too small to bother with in the face of this giant feast, rummaged in the narrow nooks and crannies of the vast cathedral of decomposition.

"Whew," Melodía said. She hadn't even known she was holding that breath. "This is a pretty dilemma, isn't it?"

"It'll take us hours to backtrack to anyplace where we can get the horses up the cliffs," Pilar said. Sheer four-to-seven-meter limestone walls half a kilometer apart defined the valley. "And the longer we spend around that thing the more likely we are to run into latecomers to the banquet. It's a miracle we didn't get snapped up as we rode here all unsuspecting."

She made a quick, clearly ritual gesture, which Melodía, a thoroughgoing agnostic even though she had been schooled in Church ritual, failed to recognize. It clearly wasn't one of the eight simple sigils of three lines, whole or broken, stacked upon each other that signified each Creator. Nor was it the more complex ideograph from the Holy Tongue, which textbooks said and traders confirmed was the everyday language of far Chiánguo. It gave Melodía a curious feeling in the pit of her stomach.

"There's a whole barony's worth of meat-eaters all crowded together here," Melodía said. "A county's perhaps. More than a human hunter might see in a long lifetime. But they're the real problem."

"No."

Like the small furred predators who provided humanity's companions and helpers, dogs and cats and ferrets—like humans themselves—meat-eating dinosaurs sometimes chased prey for sport. Raptors, in particular the big, clever horrors, were notorious for their cruel games. It was one reason they were called horrors.

But no carnivore would abandon the boundless bounty of a dead titan while meat remained. From twelve-meter matadors to hopping raptors no longer than Melodía's arm, all were fixated on the fragrant corpse. When finally gorged—it took a lot to satiate a meat-eating dinosaur—they waddled off to find shelter and slept for a day or two to digest. Then, if flesh still clung to the bones, they'd feed again. Until the last scrap was consumed they would either eat or wait to eat more, distracted only by suspicion that their neighbors would try to cheat them of their stinking mouthfuls. Which of course they would.

"The feasters aren't the ones we have to worry about," Melodía said. "It's the ones who aren't strong enough to force their way to the trough."

She saw some of them now, a couple of hundred meters off to the left: a trio of bachelor male matadors, gleaming black and red in the sunlight, stamping in frustration in weeds that came to their knees and occasionally snapping at one another.

"They do look mightily pissed off," Pilar said. "And they're just the ones we can see."

"You aren't going to like this," Melodía said, "but let's ride in as close to the dead monster as we can get our mounts to go. The diners will barely notice us."

"You're right," Pilar agreed. Her complexion was less dark an olive than normal. "Let's go. But we'll still have to run the gauntlet of the unhappy excluded. We'll look to them like consolation prizes."

For some insane reason Melodía laughed. "Then we'll have to trust to our wits and our horses!"

"Let's pray our wits are sharp. A matador can outrun a horse on a short field. Or an ambler."

Melodía grinned at her. "Good thing we're well mounted, then, isn't it? Yah! ¡Vámonos, queridas mias! *Let's ride!*"

The sturdy mare shot forward as if launched from a ballista. Pilar's white marchadora followed a beat later, the gitana bent low over her neck, her long black hair streaming behind. Whatever she thought of the wisdom of Melodía's chosen course she wasn't going to let the Princess ride into danger's literal dripping jaws alone.

And the plan was insanely dangerous in fact. But Melodía was young, and vigorous, and found that she thrilled to the hunt even when she was the prey. Her heart sang with more than exhilaration's song: *What did I do to earn such devotion from Pilar?*

Wishing she dared whoop with exhilaration, Melodía swept behind the feasting monsters' tails, Pilar beside her, so close their horses' hooves raised glittering fans of spray from the impromptu pool, which had gathered around the hulk. Winged beasts perched higher up the mountain of softening, oozing flesh than land-borne predators could climb beat wings and screamed as if in outrage. Melodía wondered if they might actually be clever enough to try to divert some of their rivals into pursuing the strange horse-human hybrids, clearing the way for them to eat in peace.

If so, it didn't work. A couple of blue horrors flicked quick yellow gazes at the women as their mounts and pack-marchador splashed past. But they didn't so much as twitch their feathery tails.

Glancing at Pilar, Melodía saw her companion rode with mouth wide open. *She doesn't dare breathe through her nose either*, Melodía thought. The stench was almost visible here—and not just the shimmering cloud of flies, the buzzing of whose myriad rainbow wings almost drowned out the sounds of tearing and crunching.

They passed the corpse's far end. Whether tail or neck they couldn't tell; whatever tipped it lay hidden among grass and boggy pools. Melodía couldn't hold back a skirling cry of triumph.

Pilar gave her a wild-eyed look. Then her laughter joined Melodía's.

Ten meters their beasts' hooves drummed on more-or-less solid white soil. Twenty meters on they rode, then fifty.

"We made it!" Melodía sang out.

And naturally that was when the matador lunged from hiding in the shade of a concave-sided stone island, roaring like an avalanche.

Chapter 6

Matador, Slayer—*Allosaurus fragilis*. Large, bipedal, carnivorous dinosaur. Grows to 10 meters long, 1.8 meters at shoulder, 2.3 tonnes. Nuevaropa's largest and most-feared native predator. Famed for its often-incredible stealth.

—THE BOOK OF TRUE NAMES

Baron Salvateur was a big man in black armor on a big black horse. Or at least they looked black in the pissing-down rain. His shield was blazoned with a winged golden figure armed with a sword on black. Or anyway dark.

Perhaps mindful of the arrows his men had met at Blueflowers, which had prevented them from turning their victory into a total massacre of the Providence militia, he wore full plate and an armet. The visor was up, revealing a face that at this distance was an olive blur with a black smear of moustache. Rob thought he saw stubble darkening the jaw.

He stood with Karyl and Bogardus behind a barricade of a couple of wagons, one loaded with wine casks, one with stones, which had been pushed together end to end to block the Chausée de l'Ouest. Bogardus had tricked himself out in steel cap and leather jack from the arsenal, whose ancient caretaker had handed out spears, halberds, and crossbows to the numerous citizens now manning the barricades. Karyl, like Rob, wore the clothes he'd come to the trial in that morning.

A hundred meters west riders, mounted on coursers and dinosaurs, appeared from the brush at the edge of the woods. Among them came armored foot, shields, and archers. The distance was too great for Rob to read their expressions. Their attitudes suggested trepidation and frustration.

The Providentials hooted. The riders looked at their commander. He looked at the bristling defenses, the steep roofs and narrow streets. Clearly he had expected to fall upon a city virtually undefended, by way of either demoralization or simple surprise.

He proved his reputation for astuteness by showing that he recognized what he was really looking at: a trap. If his marauders continued, they would find themselves outnumbered, surrounded, in terrain that took away their every advantage and gave them to their enemies.

Without further word or signal the baron turned his stallion and high-stepped the beast back into the woods.

Most of his men, riders and infantry, turned to follow, some sullenly, some—the brighter—with attitudes of relief. One horse-mounted knight, a young buck with long braids and his helmet still attached to his saddle behind him, wheeled his white courser. As the beast sidestepped and whickered he stood up in his stirrups, pulled up the skirt of his mail coat and pulled down his breeches to bare his ass.

A bow thrummed from the barricade. Even without the rain to stretch and weaken the string it was a heroic shot for a shortbow. Yet an arrow sprouted instantly from the knight's pale left buttock.

He howled. His horse bolted into the brush. Emeric stood on the board of a wagon brandishing his bow.

"Missed, a handspan right!" he shouted after the knight, whose own comrades Rob could hear laughing at him most unchivalrously as his horse crashed through the undergrowth. "Come back, Mor Knight! My sister will plant her spear right between those pink cheeks of yours!"

The defenders cheered uproariously. They hadn't really believed they could stand off a powerful raiding party, especially after the debacle at Blueflowers. And now they had.

They tried to put Emeric on their shoulders. Instead he waved them off shouting, "It's Karyl who saved us! Praise him!"

Somebody began to chant the name: Karyl. Karyl. Rob turned to his companion in a combination of delight and astonishment. *Truly, the Fae must smile on you, my friend*, he thought.

Bogardus strode toward Karyl, his practiced presence commanding every eye. Two meters from the smaller man he stopped, doffed his steel cap, and knelt.

"Captain Karyl," he said, his face streaming rain—and tears as well, or at least his voice suggested them. "I pledge to follow your commands in war. Will you lead us?"

"Lead us!" the crowd yelled. "Lead us."

Rob had thrown his fist in the air and was shouting the chant as well. It may have been that he started it.

Karyl's brow knit. Uncharacteristically he paused before saying, loudly and clearly, "I shall."

Bogardus grabbed his left hand—his sword hand—and kissed it. As he bent his head Rob saw a stark look come over Karyl's face. And though Rob had never known a touch of the mind-reading gift, it came clear as a shout to him that his friend was remembering the captive knight's parting words.

Like a vast pink Paradise flytrap lined with yellow daggers, the monster's mouth spread open scarcely ten meters to Melodía's right. The way her heart practically exploded in her chest, it might have been the same in centimeters. She felt the hot gush of its bellow.

They had outridden the dead titan's stink, carried away downstream on the wind. The reek of decaying meat-bits caught between those serrated slashing-teeth struck Melodía like a fist.

"Shit!" she yelped. Meravellosa who, like all her short and somewhat chunky kind, was no racehorse, had been running at what Melodía had always known as her best speed. Now muscles bunched and exploded between the rider's trim muscled thighs. The mare accelerated.

Melodía dared a fast glance back. Their pursuer was skinny, and not just from hunger: little more than a snake with two huge pumping hind-limbs. Teal on the back, shading to greenish-yellow on chest and belly, he would in time darken and acquire the stripes that are characteristic of his kind. But his eyes were already that terrible matador blood-color.

Clearly the Allosaurus was an adolescent male, aggressive and obnoxious enough to be driven from his own family by the prime, not yet strong and seasoned enough to win entrance to another pack. Misjudging his quarry's speed, he had charged at ninety degrees to their course rather than leading them like a marksman shooting fliers on the wing. That lack of skill was doubtless part of the reason he hadn't found a new pack.

Trying to correct its aim, the dinosaur skidded sideways into a shallow outlier of the main watercourse. Slipping in the mud, it fell onto its side in a colossal splash, with hind-feet and smaller forelimbs clawing comically at the air.

Youth-agile, it jumped back onto its feet in an eyeblink and hurled itself forward again. It roared as if Melodía's witnessing its humiliation had made this personal.

Stomach filled with fluttering like a hundred frenzied moths, Melodía turned her head forward again to sweep the valley ahead in a desperate search for cover. The young matador had hips scarcely wider than Meravellosa's. Melodía knew there could be few hiding places he couldn't follow them into. Or root them out of by sheer strength and fury.

Then her eyes brushed something promising. They widened. *If we can reach it. . . .* , she thought.

Pilar's marchadora had pulled out in front of Meravellosa. Now Melodía found herself overtaking rapidly. By the elevation of the ambler's head and the action of her hindquarters Melodía saw to her horror that Pilar was reining her in.

"What're you doing?" she screamed.

"We can't outrun the monster," Pilar shouted back. "I'll let it take me—"

"You'll do nothing of the sort. Ride, you crazy gypsy!"

Perversely, Pilar opened her mouth to argue. Melodía snatched up the riding crop that dangled unused from her saddle. Pilar's mount was still too far ahead. But the pack-ambler followed Pilar on a lead, rolling eyes and squealing protests at slowing down with a huge meat-eating dinosaur breathing on his tail.

Veering in close, Melodía slashed the bay marchador viciously across the cruppers. It shrieked—not, it seemed to Melodía, without a note of triumph—and raced forward and bit Pilar's mount on the rump. The white ambler squealed, seized the bit in her teeth, and bolted.

Breathing like a bellows, sweat flying from her flanks and froth from her mouth, Meravellosa actually managed to overtake and briefly pace the leggier marchadora. It was all Melodía needed to head her a hair to the right.

She glanced back again. The monster had lost a good forty meters with his slapstick slip-and-fall. But he was making back the difference at a terrifying rate. *If he holds that pace another fifty meters he'll have me*, Melodía thought. And as mad as he looks he'll run till his heart bursts.

Looking ahead she saw Pilar's green eyes, huge as a startled tomcat's, staring back at her from a face that looked as if it were coated in fine wood-ash.

"Princess, he's almost got—"

"Eyes forward!" Melodía screeched. "*Now, now, now!*"

The saucer-wide eyes blinked. Then Pilar obeyed, turning the right way in her saddle.

And ducked low over the ambler's outstretched neck just in time to avoid smashing her brains out.

A true forest giant, thirty meters long, it had been uprooted and denuded of branches by some prior flood and fetched up against a sinuously carven jut of rock. Stripped of bark, its trunk, as wide as Melodía was tall, angled upward to a ball of mighty root-stubs a good six meters across.

Pilar, her mount, and the pack-ambler passed safely beneath bare wood bleached grey-white like a bone. Melodía ducked and followed at full gallop. Less lucky than her companion she gasped as a short, sharp stump of branch raked down her back. Hot and bright, the pain momentarily left no room in her chest for mere air.

Gritting her teeth, she looked around. Huge jaws gaped not three meters from the tip of Meravellosa's glossy white tail. Red eyes glared into Melodía's. The adolescent matador vented a shrill scream of rage and triumph, its entire being focused on the prey it was about to seize.

Then it slammed face-first into the trunk.

The impact actually cracked the driftwood giant. The matador's hindquarters kept moving. Tail and pedaling legs foremost, it slid twenty meters on its back, under the dead tree and beyond. Then it lay in the weeds feebly waving its limbs in the air.

"You meant that to happen?" Pilar called back in amazement.

Melodía grinned. "I sure did. If that bad boy's not dead, he won't be aware of anything but the ache in his head for a week. Now let's ride like the wind, before we meet any of his cousins!"

Chapter 7

Tricornio, **Three-horn, Trike**—*Triceratops horridus*. Largest of the widespread hornface (Ceratopsian) family of herbivorous, four-legged dinosaurs with horns, bony neck-frills, and toothed beaks; 10 tonnes, 10 meters long, 3 meters at shoulder. Non-native to Nuevaropa. Feared for the lethality of their long brow-horns as well as their belligerent eagerness to use them.

—**THE BOOK OF TRUE NAMES**

When Melodía and Pilar rode into Providence's seat up La Rue Impériale, they found broad, well-kept cobbled streets between narrow buildings roofed in colorful, gleaming tiles, and the main square abuzz with talk of a herd of fabulous horned monsters supposedly glimpsed in the woods to the west just moments before. Road-worn but energized by the prospect of journey's end—both hope and fear sizzling in Melodía's veins like fat in a skillet—they paid little attention to the wild-sounding rumors.

They quickly got directions to the Garden of Beauty and Truth's villa east of town. Flower-smells and strains of lutes and flutes floated over the wall that surrounded the grounds.

"I thought they were pacifists," Pilar murmured as they drew up before stone water troughs in the shade of a fig tree outside the front wall.

A pair of guards in morions and enameled leather breastplates, intricately figured with thistle insignias, stood flanking the red-painted gate. They held serious-looking halberds. The effect was spoiled somewhat by the man's bare spindle legs.

Melodía swung down off Meravellosa. Her body was stiff. She was an expert horsewoman, but days of hard riding had taken toll.

"Well, Jaume's no pacifist," she said quietly, hitching Meravellosa in the shade. The mare dunked her muzzle eagerly in the water and began to slurp it up.

Even indomitable Pilar showed signs of road-weariness. She was a beat slow dismounting. Melodía was already detaching the pack-ambler's lead from her saddle by the time Pilar swung a long leg over the saddle and dropped to the ground.

The two women hitched their animals to weathered granite posts and approached the gate.

"Who might you be?" asked the male sentry, who had a moustache waxed into ridiculous spikes. His manner showed slightly nervous curiosity more than wariness, much less stern authority.

"I'm Melodía Delgao."

"Melo—the P-princess? The Emperor's daughter? Really?"

The female sentry's dark eyes narrowed in her broad, brown face. She looked to Melodía like a fellow Spañola. Which was not unexpected on a major trade route through a province that bordered Spaña as well as Ovda.

"Maybe," she said, "maybe not. Don't be so credulous, Philemon."

"It's all right, Raúla," a mellifluous masculine baritone said through the opening gateway. "These are guests. They are expected."

A tall man appeared in the entryway to a small courtyard beyond the wall, with a much-shorter woman by his side.

"You are Eldest Brother Bogardus?" she asked. She had read about him, of course—he was a controversial figure in the Empire these days, to say nothing of a professed acolyte of the philosophies of her own estranged lover, Jaume. He was, as advertised, a handsome man of mature years, in his eighties, per report, with clear grey eyes and square-cut iron-grey hair hanging just past the corners of a square jaw. He looked more like the erstwhile warrior he was said to be than the former priest of Maia he acknowledged being. Despite the name his own saturnine coloring suggested Spañol roots to her.

Most of all it was the sheer presence that beat from him like heat from a forge. Who else could he be, than the master of the Garden of Beauty and Truth, and by extension, allegedly of the entire County? She shut her mind to thoughts of her own Jaume. Too much depended on the outcome of this interview to blunder into the maelstrom of grief and loss and rage—mostly self-directed—those thoughts would lead her to.

"I am," he said, smiling.

Melodía did wonder just how he knew of their coming. But only briefly. It seemed only right that so masterful a man would know everything that happened in his domain. Even if Providence was still technically ruled by Count Étienne, she had no doubt who was in charge.

"La Princesa Imperial?" his companion asked. She was striking in her own right, once Melodía could break her eyes from the magnet of Bogardus's face: slim and pale in a simple gown of the same silver white as her hair, which she wore drawn severely back from a face of sculpted, high-cheekboned beauty. Her eyes were a strange purple, and fixed on her intently.

"No princess here," Melodía answered. "An exile, rather. A weary traveler and her companion, seeking sanctuary. And your teachings, if you'll share them with us."

She shook her head. "I must warn you, if you shelter us, you risk retribution from the Empire."

The head-toss of disdain with which the purple-eyed woman responded dispelled any doubts Melodía might have harbored that she was a true grande. She knew the hauteur trained into blue bloods virtually from birth. And more to the point, could recognize when it was faked.

"We're not afraid of the Empire here," the woman said.

"This is Sister Violette," Bogardus said to Melodía, "a member or our Council of Master Gardeners. And your companion?"

He finally transferred the beacon of his smile to Pilar, who stood half a step behind Melodía's left shoulder.

Melodía glanced back at her maid, who wore the studiedly neutral servant's expression she knew so well. She looked back with a smile of her own.

"Pilar," she said. "My good friend."

Bogardus nodded, then took both newcomers firmly by the shoulders.

"Sister Melodía, Sister Pilar," he said, "welcome home."

"I'm over the moon," said Rob, who was over the moon.

Hands on hips, he stood in the road above the farm, watching the dinosaurs approach like houses walking. Their vast frilled heads swung in time to their steps.

Three-horns, he was thinking, and he had to think loudly to drown out the pulse that hammered in his ears. *Fighting three-horns from Ovda itself. Six of them, Mother Maia,* six*!*

They were beautiful. And then again, they weren't. It was nothing for Rob to be split in two contradictory parts. He was lucky when it wasn't more.

There was no question the Triceratops looked bad. Their tan sides, streaked with darker brown from spines down, were sunken from their journey through the high Shield passes. At least two showed signs of lameness. Such things were to be expected from rapid forced travel up and down steep paths with little forage or water. They could also be signs of something worse. Only careful inspection, and possibly time, would reveal which.

One bull sported a broken brow horn. Rob saw it was the horny sheath, not the bone core, that was broken, meaning it would eventually grow back. In the meantime it would be remedied by one of the sharpened iron caps the monsters were customarily equipped with for battle anyway.

So, roughly worn though they were by travel, the six Triceratops were the most beautiful things Rob had ever seen. So far as he was concerned, they were the true lords of battle: the real dinosaur lords. *And in mere moments I'll have my hands on one for the first time in my life*, he thought. *It's enough to make a dinosaur master ten years in the grave hop up and dance a jig.*

He glanced at Karyl, who stood beside him with arms folded across his chest, holding his staff in his left hand. The midmorning breeze stirred the topknot that hung across the unbound hair at the back of his head. Rob expected him to make some disparaging remark about Rob's ill-concealed enthusiasm.

Instead Karyl's face hung grey and slack behind his beard, and moisture actually glittered in his dark eyes.

The sight hit Rob like a belly punch. *Ho, what thing is this?* he wondered. *I thought he'd look the way I feel, like a child seeing his Creation Day presents spread out beneath the tree.*

Karyl lowered his face—and Rob cursed himself for being a witling. *Can't you see your own hand in front of your nose?* he thought. *He's mourning the men and women and monsters he lost at the Hassling.*

A normal man would have missed the power and prestige that had been stolen from him that day, in the middle of the blood-reddened river—in no small part, through the actions of Rob himself, though Karyl blamed Imperial treachery delivered by the hand of the Emp's pet hero, Count Jaume dels Flors. But Rob had long since given over thinking of Karyl Vladevich Bogomirskiy as *normal.*

And when Karyl looked up at the nearing beasts again, the beginnings of a smile showed on a face more recognizably his own.

A rider straddled each three-horn's neck behind its big bone frill. Ovdan, by their dark skin and black hair and eyes, small men and women wearing long jackets against what to them was lowland chill. Pacing the herd beside the elevated road came the lesser figure of Zhubin the spike-frilled hornface, with Gaétan aboard. The young man's broad face showed a broad smile despite the sling that immobilized his left arm, to keep him from tearing his recently healed chest wound through overexertion.

Gaétan nudged his mount into a stiff trot to draw ahead of its colossal cousins. Rob winced. Zhubin had a similar gait to Little Nell's, and her trot always felt like getting kicked repeatedly in the tailbone by a very large man wearing very heavy boots. *It can't feel good in his chest, that,* he thought.

Gaétan's smile faltered. But not from pain, it seemed.

"Do you like them?" he asked tentatively.

Karyl looked at Rob and cocked a brow. "They'll want a keen inspection first," Rob said gruffly. Then he grinned.

"But seeing them close up makes me believe in love at first sight, almost."

A skinny teenaged girl in an unbleached linen smock ran up carrying a hemp bag. Rob took it with thanks. He didn't know her name. Since the successful repulse of Baron Salvateur's probe, recruits had poured into Séverin farm, from the town, the province, and even beyond.

Anyway, she's not one of mine, he thought.

He was having enough trouble keeping track of his new scouts. As for the woods-runners, except for a notable few he was hopeless at them; they came and went as if blown on the breeze. He honestly didn't think they cared whether he knew their names or not. They helped out of respect for Stéphanie and Emeric—and hatred for Count Guilli and his Rangers.

The trike-riders halted their mounts by clucking, and clattering what looked to Rob like shillelaghs on their frills. The Ovdans were free about banging the beasts with the things. It wasn't cruelty, he knew. It took a lot to get the attention of something that big, with that thick of a hide.

And now he truly appreciated for the very first time just how *big* Triceratops were. Titans were vaster, of course. But you couldn't train those for war. Or at least no one Rob knew of did, although legend had them being used in battle in any number of exotic locations, from Zipangu to Tejas.

A dinosaur knight's duckbill was easily as long as the three-horns, which ran around nine to ten meters in length and sometimes longer. But where the largest sackbut or morion ridden to war seldom weighed more than three tonnes, the lead trike, a female who was obviously the herd prime, must go upward of ten metric tonnes if she weighed a gram.

Rob walked right up to her snout, bold as you please. And considerably bolder than he felt. But that was how you treated a hornface of any ilk. His direct approach made her point her massive head straight at Rob in case he was crazy-suicidal enough to attack.

What you did *not* want was to go creeping up on one of the monsters from sides or rear, where the frill blocked its vision. If you did it would simply take you for a Horror looking to leap on its back, and stomp you into a carpet accordingly.

Instead of goring or trampling Rob the Triceratops lowered her huge head inquisitively. The tip of her nasal horn came level with the tip of Rob's own nose. He reminded himself that the horn wasn't much use in a fight, since if it rammed something too hard it could break the monster's snout. But it was as long as the span of his outstretched fingers, and big around at the base as two fists, and came to a nasty if not exactly needlelike point.

And "too hard" was a relative term. It meant, if she tried digging the horn into the flank of a rival hornface, or the gut of a marauding meat-eater. That horn would still serve quite nicely to split open a thin-skinned lightweight like a raptor, or a man. Yellow, it was, shading to brown so dark as almost to be black at the end.

And those great horns jutting a meter and a half from either bony brow—those were meant to kill the largest Tyrannosaur. They were weapons as formidable in their way as any tyrant's teeth.

The trike's nostrils were big, protruding to either side of her beaked snout. Moving deliberately but confidently Rob shifted to blow into the left one. She jerked her head slightly, then blew back. Plant-eating dinosaurs were just like horses that way: they breathed in each other's noses to get acquainted.

Having reassured the big female that here was a tailless two-leg who knew how to talk Triceratops, Rob went to the trebuchet in his arsenal. He dug in the bag the nameless recruit had fetched him and brought out a handful of dried figs. He let her smell them, then held them to her mouth.

And, as it opened, Rob hoped that she'd react to that the same as his own Little Nell would—docile and minute by comparison as she was. That great yellow beak could take his hand off effortlessly; the shearing teeth behind would mince it, bones and all. But instead, a fat yellowish-pink tongue emerged and swept the figs from his open palm with surprising gentleness.

The trike munched them right down, rumbling with satisfaction. Rob reached up to scratch the wrinkly flesh beneath her yellow eye, taking care not to seem to threaten the eye itself.

She bobbed her head appreciatively. It was as long as Rob was tall. Yellow-tan like the body, the horned face bore a striking pattern of darker brown that highlighted its frill and the bony structure of its face.

"So we're friends, now, girl," he muttered. "Gently now."

She blew through her nostrils again as if in acknowledgment.

"Well handled," Karyl said.

Rob grinned immoderately but tried to pass it off: "Beasts are simpler than men."

"Not necessarily," Karyl said. "We're just more likely to take their acquiescence for granted."

Rob wasn't about to take a ten-tonne monster for granted. Hoping he'd done enough to win her trust he moved back beyond the frill. The mahout looked quizzically down at him, then shifted his leg, clad in sturdy brown cotton-twill trousers, to let Rob scratch his mount's relatively thin-scaled neck.

She rumbled and nodded happily. Her rider called out something in his beastly tongue. Gaétan laughed and answered.

"He says he's surprised," Gaétan translated. "Most lowlanders are afraid of a three-horn."

Rob laughed—softly, so as not to startle the beast.

"Are they all daft up on the Plateau, then, that they don't fear such a monster as this? Me, I fear well anything that can crush me by no more than a moment's inattention."

He drew in a deep and satisfied breath. "Well, this one seems sound enough at any rate. Let's have a look at the rest of ye, then."

Chapter 8

Torre, **Tower**—One of the ruling families of the five Kingdoms which make up the Empire of Nuevaropa, plus the symbolic Torre Menor or Lesser Tower, which represents the recognized Nuevaropan minorities in the Diet, and Torre Delgao, the family from which the Emperor or Empress is always Elected.

—A PRIMER TO PARADISE FOR THE IMPROVEMENT OF YOUNG MINDS

The first thing Melodía noticed about the farm was the stink. Or rather, the lack of it. The afternoon breeze blew the smells of the horse and dinosaur enclosures away. But Karyl kept a clean camp or she'd have been able to smell the stench regardless.

She knew enough, from her own reading and Jaume's tutelage, to approve of that much.

She touched Bogardus on the arm. Despite his seemingly sedentary life as a sect leader it felt firm with muscle. *Maybe he actually does garden*, she thought.

"Which one's Karyl?" she asked.

"The snake most dangerous," said Sister Violette, who walked on Bogardus's other side from Melodía. "Because he looks the most innocuous."

Melodía wasn't sure what she felt about the Councilwoman, largely because she was none too sure how Violette felt about her. She acted friendly. But Melodía thought to see a certain wariness in her. She acted almost proprietary toward the Eldest Brother. And while jealousy was considered a risible vice, especially here in the south of the Tyrant's Head, it still ensnared some. Melodía had no way of telling whether Violette simply felt affection for Bogardus, or might see her as a threat to their relationship.

"Our Colonel's not in view," Bogardus said, with just a trace of extra emphasis on the first two words. "But don't fear, Sister. He won't be far away."

Séverin farm seethed with purposeful activity. It gave Melodía a homesick twinge: it reminded her of nothing so much as everyday life on the expansive grounds of the Firefly Palace. Despite a breeze blowing down from the passes, carrying an edge that chilled Melodía's skin slightly through her long trousers and sleeves, most men and women wore nothing but loincloths, though most women bound their breasts for comfort and convenience as they worked or drilled.

At the center of it all stood, or wallowed six enormous hornfaces in a stream that ran slaunchwise across the property. They were the wonders that had brought the group from the Garden villa to see. Melodía knew what to expect. Yet the actual sight of the creatures made Melodía stop and stare, her relative lack of affinity for dinosaurs notwithstanding.

"Impressive, aren't they?" asked Bogardus with a warm, deep chuckle. She could only nod. "That's Rob Korrigan, our dinosaur master, there."

A man wearing a sort of cloth skirt stood shin-deep in water next to one of the Triceratops. He, not the dinosaur, seemed to be the focus of attention of eight or nine others gathered around.

He was a man of medium height or a little over, she judged. His bare torso resembled a wine cask, if those sported curly red-brown fur on their upper halves, which in Melodía's experience they did not. His arms seemed unnaturally long, as if he might be able to scratch the kneecaps of his bandy legs without bending over. But his face, though his chin almost rested on his collarbone without much by way of interference from a neck, was surprisingly handsome: strong jaw outlined in a neat beard, well-defined profile marred only by a somewhat flattened nose. His hair was an unruly shock the same bronze as his beard and body hair.

Neither he nor his rapt circle paid the least attention to the new arrivals.

Instead he cocked back his axe—which had a meter-long hardwood haft and a spike to back its bearded head—and whacked its flat against the outside of the three-horn's near rear hock. She snorted and bobbed her immense frilled head but didn't seem unduly bothered.

It occurred to Melodía to wonder what it would take to get the attention of such a gigantic beast. And whether it might really be such a good idea to do so. Seen up close, those horns that jutted from her brow, each a good meter and a half long, were flatly terrifying.

A clump, mud on the outside, grey-white dust on the inside, fell away from the wrinkled brown leg. Rob grinned and squatted, hands on thighs.

"Look here, now," he called. He pointed with a blunt forefingers. "Just as I thought: here's a growth of flaying-fungus. Nothing serious now, but let it go and it'll eat her hide like an army of soldier ants."

"Eat hide like that, off a beast that big?" asked a woman with brick-colored hair cropped short over fisted features.

Rob laughed. "Well you might wonder how something which seems so trivial can defeat armor that sheds arrow and spears like water. And the answer is: time and persistence. Just as ants and other tiny scavengers can strip what the big meat-eaters leave of a titan carcass in a matter of days."

He stood. "Mix up lye, a large spoon to four liters of water, and use that to scour the spot well with a stiff-bristle brush. Then rinse and rinse until you're sure you'll wear through the hide yourself, and rinse again."

"Shall we bind it after, like a wound?" asked a stocky male peasant, one of the older recruits, whose nose and front teeth had clearly been broken by a blow at some point in his career.

"No, indeed. The good sweet air of Providence will work cure enough."

Melodía felt herself frowning at his failure to notice her, Pilar, or their austere escorts. *I should hope I'm more interesting than fungus.* She felt the anger inside her—which though she kept buried deep, most of the time, never let her forget it was there—start to roil like black tentacles in her gut.

Then she caught herself. She'd had plenty of experience with masters in the course of her education and life at court. It was the nature of the breed to obsess on the object of their mastery. Jaume claimed that was how they got to be masters, which made sense to her, when she thought about it.

As if sensing her displeasure Bogardus cleared his throat. "Master Rob," he called, "we've a new arrival to our Garden whom I'd like you to meet."

The burly man looked around. His beard came to a small point, Melodía saw. His eyes were large and green-hazel.

"Is this the fabled Princess Melodía we've heard so much about, then?" he said.

"This is our new sister and her servant," said Violette.

"Friend," Melodía corrected. She felt Pilar briefly grasp and squeeze her hand. *I hate myself for treating my childhood friend as a mere* appurtenance *all these years*, she thought. *I won't let it go.*

"Well, you'll forgive me my informal dress, Highness. Or you'll not. Either way, welcome to our camp. And who's this ravishing creature here?"

Melodía had to glance around to follow his gaze—straight to Pilar. Who seemed to be blushing. Something Melodía had never seen her lifelong companion do before, in memory.

"This is my *friend*, Pilar. And as for informality, Master Rob, you didn't have much advance notice of our visit. And anyway, I'm happy to be a plain Gardener now, since I'm not even sure I'm legally a princess anymore."

Rob approached, unself-conscious, water dripping from his hairy calves. "Ah, yes. We've heard about your arrest in La Merced, and your daring escape. There's quite the price on your head, I understand, so."

She must have looked alarmed at that. He laughed.

"We'll all be Imperial outlaws here soon enough, mark my words," he said. "You need have no fear of being turned in for the reward, I'm thinking."

He came right up, and past her, to take Pilar's hand in his and press it to his bearded lips.

"Enchanted to meet you, señorita," he said. Then to Melodía: "You too, of course."

She smiled thinly. Inside she was trying to still the reflexive surge of panic the man's casual talk of outlawry had roused in her, to momentarily blanket the always seethe of rage.

Bogardus assured me they could tie the Empire up in courts for years, if

Daddy tries to make them give me back, she made herself recall. *My father may not uphold all the traditions that have helped our Torre remain sole holders of the Imperial throne for centuries, but he won't want to make the family look worse than it does already by throwing an armed snit about me.*

Surely, Bogardus knows more about the Empire's law and noble sensibilities than this rough creature?

She had thought about mentioning the report of a Grey Angel Emergence in Providence that so fortuitously reached La Merced as Falk succeeded Duval as her father's chief bodyguard. That could provoke a hysterical response not just at court but in the streets of La Merced—and lead to the Empire taking action against the Garden for reasons having nothing to do with her.

She had thought better of it. *We're guests here*, she reminded herself again, *by sufferance of Bogardus and the Council. It just seems rude to bring that matter up.*

And the Garden itself, the community and the literal garden it nurtured at the villa, were so calm and beautiful as to render the notion of some mythical monster's presence . . . as absurd as it was.

"Where's Karyl?" Bogardus asked. His deep, smooth voice was like oil poured on the fears Rob's insouciance had raised.

With visible reluctance Rob let go of Pilar's hand. The gitana had gotten over her bout of shyness—or dropped the façade, Melodía guessed—and was smiling openly at the dinosaur master now. He was, candidly, a bit coarse for Melodía's tastes. But she had to admit there was charm to his hada grin and the mischief-light dancing in his eyes.

"Himself will be on the other side of these great beasts," Rob said, "admiring them in the guise of inspecting them. Where else would he be?"

Bogardus smiled at Melodía. "Shall we?"

Ignoring Bogardus's proffered hand Melodía splashed through the stream—upstream of the large dinosaurs, of course. Though she and Pilar had bathed and donned fresh clothing after being welcomed to the villa, she wore the same boots, still scuffed and stained from worse than mountain-shed water and a little bottom mud. She noticed with amusement that the ever-capable Pilar wasn't at all backward about accepting the assistance of Rob's crooked elbow.

On the far bank a slight man in a nondescript dark skirt not too different from Rob's stood talking with three other people. Her eyes slid right past him, before stopping with a bit of a shock and snapping back to him. *The snake most dangerous. . . .* she recalled.

This *is the devil in human form whom my father ordered Jaume to throw away his own honor, and that of the Empire, in order to bring down?* She could hardly believe it. *Why, he's shorter than I am!*

On second glance there was no mistaking him, from Jaume's account, reports from the Princes' War, and yes, the songs that celebrated both his long and epic rise and meteoric fall. The long, dark, grey-threaded hair, worn in a sort of horsetail from the crown that hung over unbound hair at the back of his head. His bearded face, so gaunt it reminded Melodía of a Life-to-Come sectary who took their eccentric self-denial doctrines too much to heart. His ribs, a washboard to fit the most extreme ascetic.

But the ropy muscles that twined his limbs and torso definitely did *not* belong to any cloistered monk. Nor did his air of total physical assurance—his movements graceful yet slightly abrupt, like a lizard moving on a cool day.

Without so much as a glance at the newcomers he continued talking to his companions. One was a sturdy, good-looking young blond man with an arm in a sling. The other two were even smaller than Karyl himself. Judging by the olive skins, the long blue-black hair both man and woman wore in braids, and the quilted jackets they wore, they must be Parsos or Turcos from the Grand Turanian Empire of High Ovda. Probably they had come with the three-horns; the huge hornfaces didn't live in Nuevaropa, but abounded on the grassy semiarid plateau east beyond the Shield range. Which roughly exhausted Melodía's stock of knowledge about the beasts, other than that they were truly fearful to meet in battle. Which the merest glimpse of them was enough to show.

"Voyvod Karyl," she said, walking toward him, "I'm Melodía."

He turned a rumpled brow to her. "Who?"

She stopped. Her stomach went tense and cold. She drew a deep breath. *Down*, she told her anger. *I am a guest here. And this man serves my hosts.*

"Melodía Delgao," Bogardus said, joining her.

"Emperor Felipe's daughter," said Violette.

Karyl grunted. "Apologies, your Highness," he said.

"Oh, that's not necessary. For one thing, I'm an outlaw. I may not even be a princess anymore, technically."

"Of course you are," he said blandly. "Felipe can't attainder you without giving up his own lands and titles—including the Fangèd Throne. Welcome to Providence."

She frowned. This wasn't going at all the way she anticipated.

She had intended—well, she wasn't entirely sure. Something involving apology for what her lover had done to him—at her father's behest, and dutifully, but a terrible injustice. She wanted to assure him Jaume himself knew what the wrong had been, and felt contrition.

And here he was dismissing her like a foolish child. The way her father had rebuffed her efforts to take some active role at Corte Imperial.

"Count Jaume—" she began. Saying the name cost her pain, and caused the anger to flame up inside her. At herself and her beloved.

But Karyl himself stiffened at the name. "I mean," she said, "we're betrothed—practically—and, well—"

I'm making a fucking fool of myself, she realized. *I'm trying to apologize, here! Why won't this man* listen?

But Karyl's face had closed like an iron gate. "We prepare for war here, Princess," he said curtly. "You will excuse me."

He turned his back on her.

She was left standing rigid, eyes stinging, hands wrapped into fists so tight the backs of them ached. *I abased myself to make things right with him and he, he spurned me! He treats me as less than filth. The way Falk did—*

The rage made her want to vomit.

Then Bogardus touched her lightly on the arm. "Come on, Melodía," he said gently. "You and Pilar must be exhausted by your travels. Let's get you back to the villa."

She made herself swallow her bile, and her fury, and force a smile at him.

"Yes, of course, Eldest Brother. We need to rest."

Chapter 9

***Hada*, the Fae**—Also *demonio*, demon. An individual is called a **Faerie**. A race of wicked supernatural creatures, who defy the Creators' will, and seek to tempt humanity into ruin. Fighting together, humankind, the Grey Angels, and the Creators Themselves defeated their attempt to conquer all Paradise during the dreadful Demon War. Notorious for their pranks, which can be cruel, and their fondness for driving bargains with mortal men and women. Which they keep, but seldom as expected.

—A PRIMER TO PARADISE FOR THE IMPROVEMENT OF YOUNG MINDS

Not long past sunset Rob walked the Imperial High Road toward Providence town. It was a beautiful evening. Overhead the clouds had already broken apart to reveal a sky shading from indigo toward black the farther it got from the eastern horizon, where the clouds were lit with fading glows in peach and lilac. The stars shone forth in glory. Late-summer insects trilled competition to the frogs in the ditch and along the riverbank nearby. The air was soft as a maiden's kiss, and smelled of evening blossoms and distant suppers.

Rob Korrigan swaggered along in his bandy-legged way, his bootsoles crunching the tufa pebbles of the roadway, humming a song to himself. It was a ballad he was composing, a satire on the conduct of the town lords in the Battle of Blueflowers Fields. He did not expect to perform it at the Garden villa anytime soon.

He carried his axe across his shoulders. Its head was uncased. Though the land hereabouts wasn't as mad-fecund as that lower down, there were few areas outside Nuevaropa's higher mountains that were hard to get a living from. And Providence prospered at least as much through trade as farming.

But banditry had never, it seemed, been a great problem in Providence—at least, not until its highborn neighbors began to supply it in abundance. The major trade caravans, like those run by the house of Gaétan's father, Évrard, offered fat prey, true enough—and safeguarded with packs of well-compensated bravos. Indeed the merchant clans grew bravos of their own, as Gaétan himself attested.

So the targets rich enough to draw attention from large, well-organized gangs tended to be too formidable to be worth the game. And the lesser traders, tinkers, and farmers simply weren't worth the taking, when living was so relatively easy.

That had changed, though, with the refugees swarming to Providence town, especially in the wake of Salvateur's fire-and-sword sweep. But not that much. Providencers were openhanded folk, if prone to argue the merits of poets and painters ferociously at the drop of a critical remark.

The woods-runners now gave vast respect to Karyl, and scarcely less to Rob, whose mounted scouts had helped them chase the hated Rangers back into Crève Coeur. They proved willing to let go of their traditional distaste and distrust for the Seated Folk enough to help the dispossessed. At least those who showed goodwill. Those who didn't vanished; and Rob for one, wasted scarce thought on them, and less pity.

So Rob expected no trouble of this fine evening. But he hadn't survived the life Fate had led him through by taking his own safety for granted. So often did he run the craziest risks that, when chance allowed, he took extra care.

When the shadowy figure emerged from the weeds at the causeway's side he raised the axe-haft from his shoulder.

"Master Korrigan," a female voice said. "You have an unmistakable silhouette."

"Pilar?" he said, frowning into the gloom. "Why are you lurking in the weeds, then, lass?"

He saw her smile gleam white in starlight literally before the rest of her began to resolve as if materializing from the gloom. "For the same reason you carry your axe with naked head."

He laughed. "Sensible girl."

"What brings you out on the highway by night?" she asked. Her accent was strongly spiced with Spañola—and something else whose familiarity spooked him.

No, he told himself, *leave off. That cannot be. It's starting at phantoms you are, me lad.*

"I'm, ahh—on my way to the Gardeners' villa," he said. "They set a better table than our mess, I fear. Even if there's, um, no meat to be had."

"Is that so?" Her tone and the glitter of starlight in green eyes challenged him. "Well, I was coming to see you, Master Korrigan."

"Rob," he said. "Just Rob. Er—you were?"

"Come now," she said with a laugh. "I'm not drawn to bashful men. Nor does bashfulness seem to come naturally to the likes of you, Just Rob."

"Don't call me that either, for I'm not just at all," he said.

But it was mere flippantry, reflexive as catching an apple tossed at his face. He wondered himself at his bashfulness. It wasn't his style, for a fact.

"Since you wanted supper," she said, smiling, "would you like to come back to the villa with me?"

"It seems I was headed that way anyway. So, certainly."

They fell into step side by side. Eris, the Moon Visible, rose in the west, her silvery face lopsided from having just passed half-full. She flung their shadows against some trees beside the road, through whose pallid trunks Rob glimpsed fields beyond.

He suspected Pilar was adjusting her stride to match his. She had to be; her legs were as long as his were short. She was, he had no trouble admitting to himself, a devilish well-set-up young woman, with a face to make the Lady Bella herself smile in approval, that blue-black hair, big jade-green eyes, and big round breasts to set them off proper.

Under normal circumstances he'd charm her with words that might have been penned in honey with a silver nib. Then, a tickle of the titties, bend her over, whip her skirt up above her waist, grab a handful of bum, and Bob's your uncle.

It wasn't that he didn't want to do that. He did, more fervently than he could remember since he was a lad and bursting at the seams with horniness. And that despite that he'd hardly been going without in Providence. And especially not since they'd seen off Salvateur and his thugs in the pelting rain.

But . . . there was something more. Something that tightened his throat as much as lust tightened his scrotum, and tickled his belly much as his imagination would have her tickling the underside of his cock.

"Why so quiet?" she asked.

"It's your sauciness, as Torrey's my witness," he said. "Confound you, woman. You're unexpected."

She laughed. It was a full and throaty laugh. He could but approve.

"Oh, I'm glad you won't curse me," she said. "Cursing by the Korrigan has power."

"Now, why would you say a thing like that?"

It was all he could do not to slap himself immediately on the forehead. *It's my own witling self I should curse, for letting that roll out my mouth!* he thought fiercely. *Ah, and why didn't Ma Korrigan do a better job of beating it into me, not to ask questions I didn't want answered?*

She was looking at him, those green eyes disconcertingly keen, as if they were focused past the skin and muscle and bone of his face onto the thoughts behind—those traitor, seething thoughts.

"Do you really think you can play coy with me?" she asked.

"Hmm. No," he said. "Evidently not."

Then he stopped literally in his tracks. She hadn't spoken Francés, or Spañol, or even Anglysh. She had spoken the secret tongue, the forbidden tongue, known by many names, even to its own speakers, but known to his own folk as *rromani ćhib.*

"I should curse you, for trapping me so, lass," he said. In Anglysh.

She laughed. "Why bother?" she asked in the same gitano tongue she'd just used. "Would any gadji know the language well enough to say that?"

"No." He looked furtively side to side.

"You think we might be overheard, out on the road after dark like this? And would you care if someone skulking in the weeds learned the secret you seem to cherish, that you are rom?"

Actually, it might be entirely in character for Petit Pigeon to lurk along the road and spy on her boss. His boss. Would be, he corrected. She thought he was on good terms with his androgynous chief spy in the town. But ah, that's the thing with spies, he thought. You cannot trust the goblins.

"Besides," she said, "why worry if someone did find out? Do you fear these Providencers will think you a great rogue, because you're gitano?"

"They know I'm a great rogue already," he said. "But it can be dangerous for others to know that other thing, nevertheless. As well you know, lass. I'll bet you didn't advertise your lineage in the fine castle at La Merced!"

She shrugged. "Melodía knows. So does her father, of course. Anyway, what does that matter? We're all outlaws together, here in the foothills of the Shields. And who here is likely to know your surname means 'touched by the Fae'?"

He scowled. "You've scarcely met me," he said, the aggrieved tones only half-feigned, "and here you've winkled out all my deepest darkest secrets!"

"Not all of them, I'm sure," she said.

"Now how do I keep them secret, then?"

She laughed. "I grew up as maidservant to a scion of Torre Delgao. I know how to keep secrets. So what of your Colonel, then—Karyl? Does he know your secrets?"

After Karyl's and Rob's acquittals at trial Bogardus had ramrodded a promotion for the army's commander through the Council. Violette was right pissed, which tickled Rob no end. He seemed more excited about the new rank than Karyl, though.

Now it was Rob's turn to laugh. "Child, I've told him a hundred tales of my past. None of them true. And all."

She nodded as if that made perfect sense. Clear it is she really is a gitana, then, he thought. Is it possible she's one of my countrywoman as well?

Regretfully he let go the notion. Romani from his Ayrish homeland tended to have similar coloration to his own. By her looks her clan had lived in Spaña for generations, maybe centuries.

"And if my very life depended on the teeniest, tiniest little speck escaping those dragon eyes of his," he said, suddenly sober as if he'd never known the taste of ale, "I'd count it lost."

"You think he knows what your name means, even?"

"Not that. Though if any man has been touched by the Fae, it's him."

She nodded. They walked a while in silence.

When he began to fear he'd overplayed his hand and shut a door between them she shot him a glance, sly and sidelong.

"It may be," she said, "that I feel unusually loquacious tonight."

"Your education's not suffered for growing up the Princess's maid, and that's a fact."

"We'll be eating soon—I'm ravenous, aren't you? But afterward, perhaps we can go to the garden and you can find some other way to occupy my mouth than spilling all your precious secrets?"

And she took his hand and practically towed him toward the villa.

Chapter 10

Compito—Compsognathus longipes. A small, fuzzy-feathered, meat-eating dinosaur; 1 kilogram, 1 meter long. Native to Alemania, but common throughout the Empire, and indeed on many continents of Paradise, apparently introduced by traders and travelers, as pets or simply stowaways. Sly and shy, it feeds on tiny animals such as lizards, frogs, and mice.

—THE BOOK OF TRUE NAMES

"I'm happy here," Melodía said.

She walked with Pilar beneath ash trees, beside a stream which meandered between fields of ripening beans and grapevines on stakes south of the Garden villa to the River Bonté that ran through Providence town. It was a placid late-summer morning. The birds and fliers were still in the early heat. The drowsy buzz of insects mostly drowned the rustle of leaves in the light breeze. The sun shone hot through a thin covering of clouds when they passed from shade to light.

"Oh, yes," Pilar said. "I've found certain satisfactions here as well."

Her smile—and now that she let herself notice, or bothered to, Melodía had discovered her friend had a lovely smile—had an oddly dreamlike quality to it.

"I'm so glad to hear that, Pilar."

Actually Melodía felt that some of the Gardeners still tended to treat Pilar as a servant. *Not through malice*, she thought. But perhaps through habit. Then again, the younger newer acolytes did tend to wind up with most of the scut work of keeping the Garden vibrant and growing. Even if Melodía herself seldom found herself performing arduous or unpleasant tasks unless she herself sought them out.

"Bogardus is more than I'd even hoped," Melodía went on, "strong and patient and wise. A good teacher. And while I'm not sure I agree with his extrapolations from—from my cousin's philosophies, he does make a persistent case for them."

She was undergoing a protracted spell of reluctance to say Jaume's name. It stirred up so many contradictory feelings. Not least was how she longed for intimacy—but shied away from it as well, in the wake of what had been done to her, a handful of weeks before.

"Sister Violette—I don't really know what to make of her."

"She treats you well," Pilar said. "She seems to like you. And I think, defer to you more than the other acolytes."

"True. But I'm not sure *how*. I don't think I'm ready for everything she seems to offer me. Nor am I altogether sure yet whether she also somehow regards me as an interloper. A rival for Bogardus's affections, which is absurd, of course. Or—something else. Which I can't quite pin down with my finger."

Pilar made encouraging noises. Melodía, still smarting at the way she had somehow in her mind transformed her best friend and playmate into a mere servant during her transition from girlhood, realized she had a great deal of practice doing that, and was made uncomfortable in a whole different way. But with rueful amusement—*at least I can still do that!*—she recognized her friends at court had often done it to. As she had to them.

She missed her friends terribly: cool Abi, scion of Sansamour; her current best friend Princess Fanny of Anglaterra; her bumptious cousins Lupe and Llurdis from the courts of Spaña and Catalunya. Even weepy Josefina, daughter of their host in La Merced, Prince Heriberto. They were nominally ladies-in-waiting, ostensibly hostages for their ruling mothers' and fathers' good behavior—by tradition more than practical purpose, for most of the Empire's history—and her closest friends. Even more she missed her baby sister, Montserrat, solemn and playful and oddly practical, brown-skinned with a mop of dark-golden dreadlocks. Though half Melodía's age she and Pilar had been the ones who roused the others, as well as the Firefly Palace servant-staff—in honesty, more out of love for Montse than her less approachable elder sister—in an unlikely plot to free Melodía from her unjust and absurd imprisonment.

Melodía missed her father, the Emperor Felipe, too. But she couldn't bring herself to think of him too much either. He must have signed off on her arrest on charges of treason apparently trumped up by his new chief bodyguard, Falk. Although he could not have had any inkling of what the Northern nobleman had done to his daughter and heir when she was in his custody.

Could he? She shivered in the warmth. *No. Of course not. He loves you. When he remembers you, of course.*

Hold on to that thought.

The last came to her in the manner of a drowning woman clutching a plank in a tempest.

She shook her head. The Garden's teachings—and Jaume's—were right that Beauty held healing powers, at least. Although, confirmed agnostic as she was, she doubted that the Creator Bella, the Middle Daughter, functionally goddess of Beauty in Paradise's official eight-person pantheon, existed to help make it so, as fervently as Jaume and Bogardus believed she did.

Instead she admired a tangle of wildflower vines in a clear space between the pale-trunked ashes, some purple with yellow hearts, some an orange-red not too dissimilar to that of Jaume's own heraldic colors. Intertwined amidst a deeper green than the leaves of the trees, their disparate colors somehow failed to clash, but found curious harmony. Gazing at them soothed the conflicts in Melodía's heart and mind.

She stopped to soak the serenity in. Pilar paused beside her. Her silence now had the quality of the comfortable silences between friends, not the half-respectful, half-fearful types of a servant not spoken to by her grande mistress. Or so Melodía hoped and believed.

"Isn't that adorable?" she asked softly, as a tiny tailless flier, not longer than her hand, landed next to the flower-tangle. It showed its full new pelage, bright and even gaudy in scarlet and yellow limned in black, for the rapidly approaching autumn.

"It is," Pilar said, as the flier commenced to hop about and peck among the lower-lying ferns.

Melodía thought to notice the slight catch in her voice that indicated she'd only just stopped herself from using the honorific *Alteza*—Highness. She opened her mouth to twit her for it.

From amidst the flowers a tawny head shot out. Tiny-toothed jaws snapped shut on the glorious flier with a crunch of lightweight bones being crushed. The flier squeaked.

Melodía yelped and jumped back in something like terror. Fixing her with a curious topaz eye, the predator raised its head, which was only roughly the same size as its doomed prey, and with a couple of gulps swallowed the faintly struggling pterosaur. With a final toss of its crest of yellow feathers, the head disappeared back into the vines.

"See!" Melodía shrieked. "That's how he is!"

"How who is?" Pilar said. "It was only a *compito*. Common as mice, and only doing what compitos do."

"Don't you see? He's like that! A thorn in the rose. An adder in the beauty!"

"A what? I think compitos are kind of cute. They're predators, sure. But so are kittens. Or Montse's adorable little ferret friend, Mistral."

"But don't you see? It hides among the beauty to kill the beautiful! Like him!"

"Like who?"

"Karyl!" Melodía shook her head in exasperation. It was so clear to her now. All clear. Why was Pilar being so obtuse?

"Who? What?"

"He lurks in the Garden, biding his time before he crushes the beauty from it! He's what's *wrong* here."

"But I thought it was the raids by Count Guillaume of Crève Coeur that were what was wrong here in Providence," Pilar said. "Weren't they what Karyl and his friend Rob were hired to stop?"

"That's the pretext! They always have a pretext, the men of war. They always have an excuse. And the poison of his militarism is seeping out. It's why Violette and some of her followers are starting to turn from the soft path of the Garden!"

"Wait—"

"It's his fault! He's a violator. Just like Falk!"

Even in her state of angry agitation, she saw her friend's face, normally even darker than her own, go ashy-pale.

"I don't think Captain Karyl is anything like Falk . . . Melodía. He may have his faults. But not even his many enemies ever hinted that he's a rapist."

"Men of war. Karyl and Falk. They're both men of war! Not like—not like Jaume. War isn't his first choice. Don't you see?"

Pilar took her hand and squeezed it. "I'm with you, Melodía. No matter what."

She sensed her friend was humoring her. But the fever was already ebbing.

"Someone has to do . . . something."

Pilar nodded and smiled.

Melodía took her friend's hand in both of hers and squeezed it tight. She lowered her face, and felt tears drop on the back of her right hand: one. Two.

She sighed deeply, raised her head, and let go of Pilar's hand.

"Let's get back to the villa," she said. "I'm hungry. And after lunch Bogardus is speaking in the Garden about the nature of divinity."

Pilar smiled in a less tentative way than she had been. "I didn't think you believed in divinity."

"I don't necessarily believe what he says. But he says it so beautifully! Let's go."

Next morning Melodía and Pilar were awakened with the dawn, when autumn chill blew sharp down the wind from the passes, and the villa halls bubbled with the word everyone had feared.

Rob Korrigan's scouts reported that Count Guillaume himself had crossed the Lisette River, at the head of his whole army of vassals and allies, hungry as horrors for rape, plunder, and power.

Melodía wept for what would become of the Garden and the people she had come to love.

But she could not banish the horrifying conviction that the real enemy was among them already.

Chapter 11

Cruzada de los Ángeles Grises, Grey Angel Crusade—The most feared form of divine punishment levied by the Grey Angels, in which one or more Angels raises a horde of human minions to wage wars of extermination against populations who sin too grievously against the Creators' Law. Grey Angel Crusaders are said to be indifferent to privation, fear, and pain. While Grey Angel Crusades are occasionally reported from elsewhere on Paradise, Nuevaropa has been spared their horrors since the High Holy War.

—A PRIMER TO PARADISE FOR THE IMPROVEMENT OF YOUNG MINDS

"Try some of these, your Grace," said Bergdahl, holding out a waxed-paper bag with sides stained dark by grease.

Duke Falk von Hornberg hoisted a skeptical brow. "What is it? Not fried squid suckers again?"

Whitewashed walls and the stones of the street three stories below concentrated midday heat on the little balcony. It was still cooler than the young Alemán was accustomed to in his Equatorial homeland at the Tyrant's Head's north end. He wore a splendid royal-blue feather cloak thrown to shade his shoulders, a loincloth of matching silk, and buskins with leather thongs wound up his calves. A black hornface-leather belt supported scabbarded arming-sword, dagger, and a purse lined with mail to foil thieves.

"No, no," said his tall and lank-haired servant, working his long jaws around a mouthful of whatever the bag contained. He had on a greasy loincloth, sandals, and a shoulder-yoke of feathers as drab and bedraggled as the rest of him. His wide, conical straw hat leaned against the wall beside his master's much finer headgear of silk stretched on a framework of pterosaur wing-finger bones. "It's fried bouncer-skin. Tejano delicacy."

He gestured vaguely with his bag. "I got it from a booth on the edge of the plaza."

Noisy Mercedes thronged the vast square two blocks away. A semicircle of Papal guards in silver-inlaid blue morions and cuirasses held them clear of the wall of Creators' House, the public temple that jutted from the east wall of the enormous Channel-side fortress which was the Papal stronghold. At the stroke of noon his Holiness, Pope Pío, was scheduled to speak from the ceremonial balcony. Like this one it was railed with spikes of verdigris-covered bronze—a testimony to the tenacity and athleticism of La Merced's burglars.

The inhabitants of La Merced weren't famed for their piety, unless one meant their lack of it. But they were renowned for their love of spectacle. And criers and handbills had assured them for the last two weeks solid that today Pío would deliver his most important sermon ever.

Of course no one Falk had talked to, in the Palace or this strange, undisciplined southern city, could recall his Holiness doing or saying anything memorable at all, ever. But rumors had got their hopes up today. Rumors that had largely emanated from Bergdahl, his local network of spies and hirelings, and a distressing number of silver pesetas from Falk's war-chest. To such effect that Falk had been compelled to shell out a whole good gold trono to rent a balcony the size of a modest bed to watch the proceedings.

"Well—all right," Falk said.

He dug tentatively into the bag, not best pleased by the prospect of eating food that Bergdahl had been picking over with his perpetually grubby fingers.

But the crisp, curled, squarish morsels certainly smelled enticing. Falk picked up a couple in his big thick fingers, popped them into his mouth, and chewed.

And chewed. At first the skins crunched most satisfactorily, like fresh celery. But they just kept chewing.

Then the flavor hit him, and his stomach declared open opposition.

"Well, your Grace? How do you like them?"

Falk turned a watering and displeased gaze on him.

"The Tejanos eat them with hot-pepper powder sprinkled on them, I hear," Bergdahl said defensively. "These plain ones were all I could find."

"On the whole," Falk said, still chewing, "they appear to have the flavor and consistency of a nosehorn-driver's loincloth, boiled and fried in stale Protoceratops lard."

He spat the skins, which as far as he could tell remained intact, over the green metal railings.

"Your Grace would know best, I'm sure," said Bergdahl with a smirk.

Falk sighed theatrically.

"I don't know why I put up with your impertinence, Bergdahl," he said.

"I do," Bergdahl said smugly. "Send to your Dowager Mum and ask, if you're hazy on the concept."

Falk scowled. *You might as well cut my balls off and brandish them in the palm of your hand*, he thought. He didn't say so. It would only make it—well, more so.

"If I'm supposed to be advancing the principle of the strong ruler," he said, "why won't Mother give me more leeway to actually act on my own?"

"Don't whine," Bergdahl said, stuffing a whole fistful of the nauseating chips in his mouth and chewing. Little fragments sprayed from his mouth like brick-dust from a wall hit by a trebuchet stone. "It's unseemly in one so large."

Why do I let him talk to me like that? Falk thought, retreating into sullen silence from a fight he knew he'd never win. *I'm a man of consequence here: a man of Power. I command the Imperial bodyguard. All the young courtiers and favor-seekers flock to me. And I've the ear of the Emperor himself. I'm his favorite, I might even say, what with his pretty-boy nephew off subduing some wretched hedge-knight or another.*

So why do I have to let myself be treated with contempt by a lowborn lout with shit under his fingernails?

He knew why. Far too well to need to articulate it to himself again.

The crowd bellowed sudden anticipation, like a tyrant menagerie at feeding time. Gaudy flocks of feeding fliers took flight, with booming wings and brisk complaint. Falk felt gratitude for the occasion for his eyes to look outward again.

The Pope had stepped onto his projecting balcony. Shrugging off the hands of a bevy of red-gowned cardinals he tottered forward on his own. He was over two hundred and looked it: like a white silk bag of sticks, topped with a miter-crowned nosehorn's egg.

That was ancient, even by Paradise standards. Although people could live indefinitely barring misadventure, the world had a knack of providing such misadventures. Pío's accomplishment in getting so old was made more remarkable by the fact that, as Pope of the rich and powerful Nuevaropan branch of the universal Church of the Creators, he arguably disposed of more actual *power* than the Emperor himself.

The Pope reached the rail. The crowd cheered. Falk wondered whether it was genuine approval or mere hope he'd topple over.

"They're in a particularly receptive mood," Bergdahl said, stuffing the last of the bouncer-hide chips in his face, wadding the bag and tossing it over the rail. Unseen below them one of the Scarlet Tyrants who secured the building—mostly Riquezos with necks wider than their heads—cursed as it bounced off his horsehair-plumed helmet. "An hour ago a dwarf-titan ran amok, kicked free of its wine-cart, and trampled half a dozen bystanders."

"Aren't the Merced rabble notoriously softhearted?" Falk said. "They certainly acted sullen when Snowflake and I had the head off that tiresome old rogue of a Mondragón."

"Oh, they're compassionate enough, as rabble go, your Grace. But they love a good show. And this was an accident." As if that explained things. Or made sense.

Pío raised quavering hands and began to orate. Miraculously the crowd fell quiet. Not that Falk could hear his words, across two blocks of flat roofs and a good two hundred meters of mob.

He didn't need to. He knew perfectly well what the Pope was saying: he preached fire and steel against the Garden of Beauty and Truth. He was doing nothing less than demanding his hearers take up arms and march to destroy the heretics in Providence before their evil ways brought a Grey Angel Crusade down on the Imperio.

Falk and his servant had worked hard the last few weeks to stack the wood and pile on the tinder. Bergdahl was a wonder at getting things done, Falk had to admit. He continued to perform his Palace-servant duties while expanding his network of spies and informants—and utilizing them to stoke terror over the Grey Angel Emergence reported in Providence in every level of society.

But getting people excited wasn't the same as getting them to *act*. Much as they loved sensation, Mercedes's feet were firmly planted on the ground of everyday business. They had their fun and got back to work.

"He'll never pull it off," Falk muttered, gripping the railing between ornate green spikes. "He can barely stand up without help, he has a voice like a moribund frog, and all the personality of his morning bowl of gruel."

"Ahh, but you overlook one thing, your Grace," Bergdahl said. To Falk's astonishment he produced a small dead fish from his pouch and casually bit off the head. "He believes in his cause with a passion that consumes him utterly."

He munched. Scales spilled over his grey underlip.

"Some say such total surrender to passion can lend a man greater than normal powers," the servant went on.

"I'd think you'd say it would make him a fool."

"Perhaps. But what's more useful than fools?"

Bergdahl tipped his head to look sidelong at his nominal master. Falk knew that look, and hated it.

"After all, His Majesty's proving most useful indeed."

"Hold your shit-encrusted tongue!" Falk hissed in Alemán.

"Why? You fear spies? My lord, to whom do you think they'd report, if not to you?"

"We both know better," Falk said, knowing for once he had the right of it. "I've tipped over too many kiosks on the way to where I am. There are plenty at court who think I've come too far, too fast for a foreign upstart. And former rebel, at that."

He shook his head. "I honor Power above all things. It's what separates us from beasts, who have only muscles and teeth. But sometimes it's like water: the harder I try to grasp it, the faster it squirts through my fingers."

"Perhaps my lord could learn the patience to cup his hands."

"You know what I mean! Anyway, Felipe understands power. He intends to really *rule*. Perhaps it's the iron in his good Alemán blood."

Instead of coming back sarcastically Bergdahl stiffened. He leaned forward, like a raptor tipping forward and raising its counterbalancing tail to spring to the chase.

"What?" Falk demanded.

"Something."

"That's no answer. Tell me plainly—"

Bergdahl raised a peremptory hand. "Hush."

The Pope's voice had risen to surprising volume and clarity. The crowd actually quit shuffling its collective feet and stilled. For the first time the old man's words reached to the balcony.

"—divine retribution hanging over us!" he was crying. "We must prove ourselves worthy of the Creators' mercy! Our only reprieve from the Grey Angels' soul-reapers is to leave them no work to do! Our only hope, to cut down the foul shoots of heresy ourselves, trample them into the dust, and burn the remains! Providence must be—"

He clutched his sunken chest and reeled back from the rail. Cardinals rushed forward to his aid.

He lunged away from them to lean far out toward the crowd.

"—destroyed!" he screamed.

His body jerked. His head snapped up. Then he pitched forward over the railing to plummet ten meters to the yellow limestone flagstones below.

For a moment the crowd stayed still as stone. Then with a single many-voice roar it surged forward, pressing the halberdiers back upon the body of their fallen master.

"Outstanding," Bergdahl breathed.

Falk's stomach lurched. A moan escaped his lips.

"What's the matter, Lord?" demanded Bergdahl, who'd already turned to enter the apartment behind. "You look as if you'd seen the Old Duke's shade."

"Oh, Chián, King of All Thrones, protect us," Falk all but sobbed. "We're well and truly fucked."

Bergdahl arched a brow. "You really think so?"

"What else can I think? The loudest voice in favor of our enterprise just cut off with a croak and fell on its head. Those weak sisters in the College of Cardinals despise Pío's militancy. They'll stumble all over themselves in their haste to elect someone who'll disavow our Providence Crusade and everything to do with it. Don't you see, you fool? It's over. We've lost!"

Bergdahl put his head back and cawed with laughter, like a harvester-of-eyes flier perched above a battlefield of dead stares.

"Your Grace, you know so much, yet understand so little! Do you truly not see? We haven't lost. We've won it all!

"All I need do now is to scatter a handful of silver into the right pockets, a few words in the proper ears, and by sundown all of La Merced will know it's just witnessed a miracle. And know for a fact the Creators Themselves endorsed the Pope's last wish."

He shook his head in something akin to admiration.

"To think the ineffectual old Fae-spawn did most of our work himself. By somehow contriving to martyr *himself*!"

Chapter 12

Año Paraíso, **AP, Paradise Year**—A year contains 192 days each of twenty-four hours (reputedly longer than those of Old Home). The year is divided into eight months named for the Creators' domains: Cielo (Heaven), Viento (Wind), Agua (Water), Montaña (Mountain), Mundo (World), Trueno (Thunder), Fuego (Fire), and Lago (Lake). Each month consists of three weeks of eight days, each named for a Creator: Día del Rey (Kingsday), Día de Lanza (Lanceday), Día de Torre (Towersday), Día de Adán (Adamsday), Día de Telar (Telarsday), Día de Bella (Bellesday), Día de Maia (Mayasday), and Día de Maris (Marisday).

—A PRIMER TO PARADISE FOR THE IMPROVEMENT OF YOUNG MINDS

"So come fill up your glasses
"With brandy and wine.
"Whatever it costs, I will pay.
"So be easy and free,
"When you're drinking with me,
"I'm a man you don't meet every day."

Applause bounced off the vine-painted rafters of the Garden Hall as Rob struck the last chord on his lute.

It was an ancient ballad. Older, some said, than Paraíso itself. It seemed to stir something atavistic within Rob and his hearers alike, at a depth nothing born of this world could touch.

Or maybe that was just the ale he'd drunk to lubricate his vocal cords.

Smiling and nodding he rose from the foot of the dais where the Council table stood, and walked—not any too steadily—back to the chair awaiting him at a table in the front row. Karyl nodded gravely to him as he dropped down into it.

Rob wasn't sure whether he believed Karyl lacked any appreciation for music or not, despite the way he claimed he had tried to suppress the arts when he was voyvod of the Misty March. But one thing was sure: the man admired a thing well done.

Rob felt a warm glow of more than applause and a bellyful of alcohol. The army marched with the dawn. Which meant he was marching, yet again, and quite irrationally, straight toward danger.

But he wouldn't be carrying around the dreadful weight of responsibility. At least, not for the quartermaster's job.

A young man took Rob's place and began to declaim bad poetry badly. He seemed to have trouble keeping black bangs out of his eyes.

Two days earlier Gaétan's cousin Élodie had joined the army to take Rob's place in charge of logistics. Évrard was miffed with Karyl and his son, since Élodie had been his bookkeeper-in-chief up until the point she marched into his office and demanded a leave of absence to join the fight against Crève Coeur in her own special way.

Gaétan said he hadn't even asked her. He claimed she was outraged when she found out a minstrel was in charge of the militia's supplies.

I'd take that amiss, Rob thought with amiable muzziness, *save for the fact it outraged me most of all.* Anyway, being scout-boss as well dinosaur master took as much as he had, if in a far more congenial way.

The poet had grown strident. He appeared to be delivering himself of a polemic against those who spurned the "purity" of the Garden's vision. Whomever they might be.

It struck Rob as a peculiarly harsh message for a movement devoted to appreciating Beauty. But he'd heard complaints recently that Gardeners were beginning to take undue interest in the everyday doings of citizens of Providence town. And Gaétan said the Council was trying to raise tariffs on certain goods, seemingly not so much to raise revenue as to discourage their importation.

Which struck Rob as poor sense, given the ease of smuggling over the Shield Mountains, formidable as they might be. And which in turn seemed right typical of the Council of Master Gardeners. Excepting Bogardus, of course.

He looked around the hall. It was even more packed than usual for the after-dinner entertainments. Most of the few actual Gardeners who had volunteered for the defense force had come to be seen off by their brothers and sisters.

He didn't see Pilar. Despite Melodía's insistence she was no longer a servant, the Garden mostly kept her acting as one. To Rob, she insisted she was happy to do so. He wasn't so sure. But he couldn't tell if she were lying or not.

He could usually tell if someone was lying. That presupposed they were less skillful than he. Which he had learned to take all but for granted.

But not this lass. Whether Pilar had learned the skill growing up a servant, eventually at the Imperial Court, or whether it was true what their enemies—which was most folk in Nuevaropa—said, that gitanos had a natural gift for dissimulation, or some combination, he didn't know. But if she lied about how she felt about the Gardeners treating her as a servant again, he couldn't tell. She did make clear Melodía insisted on being treated herself as just another acolyte, although if the Delgao chit thought they'd actually do that, she was even more naïve than Rob judged her.

Thoughts of his emerald-eyed witch-girl jabbed Rob most uncomfortably, like a sharp stone to the fundament when he sat to take a rest from tramping some forest trail. He hated to leave the relative comfort of the farm, with its reliable shelter—and reliable lack of dangers, dinosaur and human. Traveling with the army meant less privation than traveling as raw as he and Karyl had done on the journey here, but it was still an uncomfortable business. And danger at some point of the voyage was a certainty, not supposition.

But what he'd miss, more than a feather bed and the free-flowing wines and ales of Providence town, was Pilar. Not just the loving either. She was more than a mere bedmate. He loved her flashing wit and ready laugh—and her understanding nature, which seemed not to tolerate but embrace his foibles, for all that she could see them as clearly as anyone he'd met.

And maybe all that means I should be glad to be setting out with the clouds' return, he told himself.

But he had learned to make the most of merriment when it came within reach. So he took a jolt of the hefty, chewy ale, and forced his attention back to his surroundings.

His and Karyl's tablemates were a handful of young Garden men who had recently enlisted. He hadn't got their names yet. Doubtless Karyl had. Few details of his command escaped his dark dragon eye.

"It's called 'opera,' you see," said the overly handsome youth called Rolbert. "Comes from Talia, they say. It's all the rage in Lumière. I heard about if from a Walloon come up the Imperial street looking to trade emeralds from Ruybrasil for spices from Turanistan."

"So they sing, and tell stories," said Dugas, who had eyes like currants crowded rather too close for comfort on either side of a long, skinny nose. "What's special about that?"

"Ballads tell stories," offered a redheaded man whose name Rob didn't know.

"Well, but they act it out as they sing, you see," Rolbert explained. "Kind of. They all play parts, or rather sing them. So it's like a play, but sung."

"It's not new, this opera," muttered Rob. "It's only just coming back in vogue, is all. It's been around for years and years. And blighted every one of 'em."

The fiery young poet finished declaiming, to fevered clapping from Sister Violette and her cronies and pro forma applause from the rest of the hall. He didn't get even that much from Rob and Karyl's table. *Not that my lord Karyl would applaud the man who pissed on his pant-leg if it was afire*, thought Rob in fond exasperation.

Bogardus—and Melodía, who sat beside him—clapped hard but without evident conviction.

"And what have we here?" Rob said aside to Karyl. "I do believe our little fugitive Princess may have flown from one daddy to find another."

His companion didn't deign to glance his way.

The clapping died away. The whole hall seemed to inhale in horrid apprehension that the polemical poet might feel called on to do an encore.

The collective exhalation stirred torch-flames like a breeze when instead he dropped his eyes shyly and blundered back to his table.

Bogardus rose. He spread his wide-sleeved arms like white wings in what Rob had come to recognize as his characteristic gesture. *It works for the lad*, he thought. *Why would he change it?*

"As most of you know, my friends," Bogardus said in his roundest tones, "we're honored to have among us a charming visitor, whom I hope will consent to join our community in whole heart. I am pleased and honored to present to you Melodía Delgao Llobregat, late of La Merced."

She rose, blushing prettily and thanking the diners for their applause.

"Sister Melodía has graciously agreed to sing a song for us," Bogardus said. "She's asked that Rob Korrigan accompany her on his lute. Master Rob, would you be so kind, to her and to us?"

Rob stood up. To cover a sudden attack of nerves he plucked at his beard with both hands, once each, as if trying to pull point to two.

Then he bowed low. "I'd be a greater churl than even I am, to refuse such a gracious lady."

He saw Melodía's pretty face tense up a bit at that. *She loves playing up to the Garden's egalitarianism*, he thought, amused. *And why not? It's her own lover taught them to believe in it.*

Although perhaps the dashing Count Jaume has himself a rival, now.

As he reclaimed his lute from the rack by the wall and returned to the dais, he noted Violette gazing keenly at the fugitive Princess. Her sharpish pallid features were drawn into a smile, half as if she'd invented Melodía, half of raptor intensity.

And what's this, then? he wondered, settling his rump comfortably on the edge of the stage.

From Pilar he knew Violette liked playing with Gardener girls as well as boys, which he did not begrudge her. He liked the lasses too. And Melodía was a tasty morsel, no question, although too full of herself for his taste. He also knew from Pilar that Melodía had resisted frequent sexual overtures from some of her ladies-in-waiting. But they were mere girls, and made pests of themselves. Whereas in Sister Violette Rob recognized an accomplished player of the game.

But ah, he thought, *what game does she seek to play with our rogue Princess Imperial? A game of pleasure, or a game of thrones?*

"What's your pleasure, my lady?" he asked Melodía as she joined him on the terra-cotta tiles in front of the head table. She wore a frock of purple linen, embroidered around the bodice with pink roses on green vines. A modest enough garment in cost and cut, to be sure. But it did little to hide her altogether grown-up charms from Rob's accomplished eye.

"Melodía, please." She smiled. "There's no lord or lady here. It's one of the reasons I love it."

"Suit yourself. What song would you like me to play?"

"'Amor con Fortuna.'"

He nodded. It was a favorite of his, and said to be more ancient still than the tune he'd played earlier.

"Be warned, lass," he said, "I play it lively. Some there are as play it like a dirge. Which I suppose suits such crabbed souls as deem either love or fortune a thing to lament. Of which there are none here, I trust?"

She laughed. A little wildly, he reckoned, and a little brassily; there was a tint to her cheeks and a glint to her eye.

"That suits me as well, Master Rob," she said, prettily enough.

I used to think love a subject well-suited for dirges, myself, once upon a day, he thought. *But now—*

He shook the thought away like a three-horn dislodging a drill-fly from its eyelid. He was only ready to stray so far down that path.

He played the song as promised, fast and merry. To his mild and pleasant surprise Melodía sang not just with a clear lovely voice, but technically quite well.

When they were done he complimented her singing. "It's not to be remarked on, I suppose," he added, "given you're half Catalan. Of which folk I hear it said, if you pinch them, they cry out in pitch."

Again Melodía laughed. Her face was even more flushed than before.

"I can't really credit my mother's heritage for more than the inclination," she said. "Whatever skill I have, is a gift from my cousin Jaume, my teacher."

"Teacher of us all," added Bogardus.

Rob blushed hot to the roots of his beard. *Walked into that with eyes open, didn't you?* he jeered at himself. He dreaded going back to sit beside Karyl, who still hated the Imperial Champion for destroying his White River Legion.

But, dismissed, he had to. He replaced the instrument and resumed his seat, studiously not looking at his companion. Who of course said nothing.

But Melodía had stayed where she stood. She swept the hall with an imperious glance.

"Master Rob has given us beautiful music," she said. The diners clapped. "I wish that was all he gave us.

"By itself, his playing would be a worthy gift indeed for Providence and its Garden. Our Garden, if I may be so bold. But he, and his companion, bring us something far less beautiful: the curse of war."

Violette and her claque at the Council table applauded briskly. The hall reacted with less enthusiasm. Some applauded. At least as many murmured rebelliously.

Rob's reaction wasn't mixed at all. He sat up sharply. The Princess's preamble washed away his embarrassment at indirectly bringing up Karyl's nemesis Jaume like a bucket of cold stream-water to the face. Ale-induced fuzzy-headedness went with it.

"I thought it was Count Guilli who brought us the curse of war," one of their companions said.

Rob ignored him. Seriously pissed and seriously fuming, he now doubly feared to look at Karyl. Then, forcing himself, he met a dark, sardonic eye.

"It would appear our juvenescent Princess has set you up," Karyl said.

"Like a duck-pin," Rob admitted sourly.

"Can't be much dishonor in that," Dugas said, evidently trying to be helpful. "She was nursed on court intrigue, after all."

"If she's so bloody good at intrigue," Rob muttered, "what's she doing here?"

"I have treasured the few short weeks I have spent among you," Melodía was saying. "I hope to pass many more here, and contribute what I can of Beauty.

"And of Truth. And one truth troubles me, though I hesitate to bring it up—"

"Please," Bogardus said, after only a beat or two. "You're our sister now. Please speak freely."

Rob thought he had gone a little grey around the jowls, though he spoke as graciously as ever. He wondered why.

"In just in the short time I've passed in the Garden," Melodía said, "I have noticed a . . . a hardening. Of hearts and minds. I wish I could say otherwise."

Even Violette frowned at that one. Rob smiled bitterly. *Ah, youth*, he thought, frisky as a filly—and heedless as a fifty-tonne titan ambling through a village. If the silver-haired Sister thought she could control Melodía, she had a better think coming.

"You have hired hard men to protect you," she said. "I understand that. You face a cruel enemy.

"But can you really defeat cruelty with cruelty? I've studied war—in books, and at the feet of a man who's mastered it along with many gentler arts. And that's what war is: cruelty.

"The Garden preaches nonviolence. Jaume doesn't; you know that. Bogardus, who brought my good cousin's teachings here, has never hid the fact. As he himself says, Jaume has planted the seeds, he has cultivated them, and the flowers have grown in their own ways. Beautiful ways."

She paused a moment, her lovely face troubled. Whether it was show or not, Rob had to nod. The girl performed masterfully at more than singing.

"But—perhaps the edges of the flower wilt. Poisoned soil can't long nurture Beauty, can it? And by bringing the practice of war into our Garden, do we not risk poisoning our own soil?"

Violette's violet eyes positively lit. She made to clap like a mad thing. Yet Bogardus, who played a crowd like Rob his lute, raised his right hand. It was a slight gesture—but it froze Violette.

"What can we do, Melodía?" he asked. "The threat is real. If it wasn't, we—I—would never have risked breaching our doctrine to bring these men here to teach, and practice, war."

"But where's the greatest danger? War is seductive, my friends."

She waved a hand at the rafters and the muraled walls. Rob cringed. He saw it coming, like a trebuchet-flung boulder tumbling lazily toward the bridge of his nose.

"Didn't you lose the incredibly gifted artist who brought these flowers and forests to life all around us, because he followed Karyl to war?"

The grumbling that had answered her question about the greatest danger turned into a sort of moan of shared pain. These Gardeners had no way of knowing Lucas's death had wounded Karyl more deeply than any of them.

Still—"Credit where it's due," Rob said, "the lass has a positive gift for denunciation, and no mistake. Hearing her I'd be after condemning myself, if I hadn't long since forgiven myself worse."

He glanced at Karyl. His face looked more like that of a marble statue than normal. The scar down his forehead was bright white on ivory. Rob used humor like a shield. But it wouldn't protect them both.

Doesn't do me that well, truth to tell, he thought sourly, and tossed back the last of the ale in his stoneware mug. It had gone stale. It figured.

"What would you have us do," a man's voice shouted from the hall, "lie back and let Guilli have his way with us?"

Melodía froze, and her dark eyes went wide in her cinnamon face.

"Be still!" snapped Councilor Absolon at the unidentified questioner.

That brought Melodía smartly 'round. "Wait," she said. "I'm a guest here. Please correct me if I misunderstand: doesn't everyone have an equal voice here? I thought that, in the Garden, there was no such thing as high and low?"

"It's a Council matter," the lank-haired Absolon blustered. "We're the Master Gardeners. We're in charge of keeping the Garden clear of weeds."

"Is asking a fair question a weed, then?" Melodía challenged.

"Faith, she has sincerity," Rob said quietly aside. "Once a body can fake that, now, the rest is gravy."

Absolon blinked and looked for support to Violette. She kept staring at Melodía.

"Melodía has the floor," Bogardus murmured. "Courtesy is a beautiful thing."

"To answer your question," Melodía told the man who'd challenged her, "I don't know. I don't pretend to have the answer. I only know—meeting violence with violence can't be the only answer!"

Her eyes misted, and in a clouded voice she said, "If, in the end, Beauty and Truth can't enough to survive on their own, what does it say about the world? What does it say about us?"

She lowered her face and slumped her shoulders, clearly finished. Violette leapt to her feet, shouting "Brava!" and clapping furiously.

An eyeblink later her surviving Council allies jumped up. They put Rob in mind of a toy he'd seen offered for sale by a Traveler band his own wayward group had encountered in his childhood. You turned a crank and small painted wood dolls, the size of clothespins—which they probably were—bobbed up and down through holes in a board.

Simple as it was, the toy entranced young Rob. Of course his mother had met his pleas to buy it with a cuff to the side of the head. Not that they had the coin to spare. And when that night he tried, naturally, to steal it, he learned an even sorer lesson on the risks of trying to rob a fellow Rom.

More deliberately than Violette had, Bogardus got up clapping his big square hands. The hall applauded too, but more tentatively.

Rob's initial admiration for the girl's performance was evolving into outrage. The warmth that spread from his gullet through his gut after a hearty draft from his refilled mug kindled the embers.

He turned to Karyl. "How can you just sit there passively listening? Could you not be bothered to defend yourself?"

Karyl cocked a brow. "I don't bother defending against words."

"Don't you see? Truly? It's not what's *real* that moves people. It's not even what they think. It's what they believe. Else how would minstrels make our living? The right words can twist even the plainest action in people's minds, so that what they remember is something other than what happened. Didn't you learn that in your father's court?"

"I did," Karyl said. "I also learned I cannot win such wars of words. And I try never to fight when I can't win."

Rob drained his mug again. He shook his head and blew like one of his magnificent new three-horns.

"But you cannot deny the heart, man," he said. "Didn't you learn that, when you were voyvod, Karyl, me lad? If you try to do so, it becomes your worst enemy. Especially when it's your own."

But he was talking to an empty chair at an empty table. Karyl had risen, picked up his staff, and walked unhurriedly from the hall. Around them the crowd was breaking up. Whatever the Gardeners thought of

Melodía's impassioned speech, it had well and truly doused the festive mood.

The story of my life, Rob thought. Rising uncertainly to his feet he stumbled off to steal what comfort he could from a final few hours in Pilar's sweet arms.

Chapter 13

Artillería, **Artillery**—Missile weapons too heavy to be carried by an individual person. Types commonly used in Nuevaropa include the stinger or ballista, a large, cart-mounted crossbow for shooting spears, which may be easily and quickly moved about the battlefield by teams of horses; the catapult, a generally heavier engine using a large bow or twisted rope to power a lever-arm, which casts stones or fireballs; and the trebuchet, a huge machine with a long, hinged wooden beam, in which the dropping of a metal box filled with massive weights propels a throwing-arm to hurl large missiles up to 300 meters. Devastatingly powerful, the trebuchet cannot be moved, and is used almost exclusively in sieges. It requires teams of large draft-dinosaurs such as nosehorn to cock it between shots.

—A PRIMER TO PARADISE FOR THE IMPROVEMENT OF YOUNG MINDS

With a moan of wooden axle in bronze bushings, the three tonne counter-weight fell toward the yellow soil. The trebuchet's stout framework, held together by rope windings and the bronze brackets Maestro Rubbio had produced from the vaults beneath the Firefly Palace above La Merced, groaned and bucked and clattered amidst a cloud of dust. The longer arm hit the top of its arc, whipping a hundred-kilogram chunk of granite in a high arc against the grey-clouded afternoon sky.

The shot having gone off properly, the seven Companions gathered on the hilltop turned their attention back toward their commander, who had paused in reading from a parchment in his hand to eye the trebuchet warily when the command to launch was given. The Nodosaur engineers were fully as proficient as the élite browned-iron infantry. But the trebuchet was a trickish beast. Sometimes, inevitably, things went wrong. Which was why, two days before, a hundredweight boulder had flown, not toward the castle walls, but almost straight up.

And landed square on the unprotected head of their fellow Companion, Mor Étienne. In a way that was a blessing from the Lady: had the rock struck his armor-clad body the excellent plate might have protected him from immediate death, allowing him to linger in agony for days before finally passing—or requiring of one of his brothers the terrible duty of speeding him on his way with the misericordia, as Manfredo had done for his lover Fernão after the Battle of Terraroja. Thus had the Companions lost one of their longest-serving brethren.

"So that's it, then," Manfredo said. He had his square, handsome face turned to the stiff morning breeze and his blond hair blowing out behind. "His Holiness is dead."

Drovers tapped the haunches of a brace of nosehorns with long willow switches. The dinosaurs obediently plodded forward, drawing the trebuchet's long arm back down by means of a pulley staked to the ground to cock the machine for its next shot.

"Long live his Holiness," said Florian sardonically.

Timaeos uttered something between a wail and a moan and collapsed onto a nearby granite outcrop. Cradling his face in his hands he began to sob disconsolately and mumbling in his native Greco.

His heart full of conflict, Jaume watched the stone strike. It gouged a puff of ochre dust from a crater that looked as if it had been crudely peened into the sandstone curtain wall by a giant hammer. Above it, the flag of Ojonegro fluttered from the rampart. It was a visual pun. The county was named for the nearby Black Springs, where the town stood. But "ojo negro" also meant "black eye"; the Count's insignia was a staring black eye on a field of gold. Whether a clever sleight on the artist's part, or simply of Jaume's admittedly energetic fancy, when the wind whipped it just right the banner seemed to wink derisively at the besiegers from the ramparts. As it did now.

"What's he on about, then?" Wil Oakheart of Oakheart asked with a nod to Timaeos. They all wore their white-enameled breast-and-backs with the Lady's Mirror in orange on the fronts. The Imperial artillery had smashed every ballista the defenders shot at them from the rampart. But none of them was virgin enough to assume that the canny Conde might not be holding one back to impale one of his key tormentors if opportunity offered. "Pío hated the Eastern Church. And he particularly hated the fact we took in some of its adherents as knights-companion."

"All faiths are one in the Creators' eyes," said Manfredo.

"Ah, but in the eyes of the late and not universally lamented Pío," Florian said, "perhaps, not so much."

The crunch of stone hitting stone reached the men's ears.

"Pío was a holy man," sobbed Timaeos, in Francés even more broken than usual. "He was our Holy Father."

The Companions' other giant, the Ruso knight Ayaks, had come to loom at Timaeos's side. The two were best friends, and occasionally lovers, although both preferred slighter men. With a bare hand like a fatty hamhock he patted the paldron that protected the red-bearded Greco's mountainous shoulder.

"You big baby," he said, not without affection.

El Condado de Ojonegro lay on the border between Spaña and Francia, squarely athwart the Imperial High Road—which led to the troublesome County Providence, object of the recent war-hysteria in La Merced. Its ruler, a small and skinny man with more than a touch of the ferret to him despite being named Robusto, was less odious than the Count of Terraroja had been. But legally speaking the Fangèd Throne had a much stronger bone to pick with him: he was charging tariffs, steep ones at that, of travelers and traders along the High Road. That was a clear and serious violation of Imperial Law.

Black Springs had prospered moderately, whether through its liege's road piracy or, possibly, in spite of it. Lying in the transition zone between the arid Meseta and the immense forest, Telar's Wood, that spanned most of the Tyrant's Head, Ojonegro boasted mines, fields of flax, hemp, and cereal grains, and rolling lands covered thickly in enough grass and ground cover to support decent-sized herds of fatties and domesticated nosehorns.

Count Robusto possessed neither the army nor the allies the wicked

Leopoldo had. Unfortunately, he did possess an almost equally sturdy and well-supplied stronghold. Faced with the overwhelming onslaught of the Army of Correction he had retired behind the thick walls to thumb his nose at his besiegers. Literally. Daily.

The place was simply too strong to take by storm without breaching the walls. The Nodosaur pioneers reported that, though the castle was built of relatively soft local sandstone, it stood on bedrock of granite. The pioneer captain, a man as formidably competent as he was literal-minded, had informed Jaume that his experts, working the clock around, could mine the walls sufficiently to cause a breakthrough in almost exactly twenty-five weeks. Since Jaume doubted he had eight days over a year to reduce the fortress, he'd set the trebuchets to work, and the army to lay siege,

Unfortunately, it wasn't just political practicalities that dictated Jaume didn't have eight months and more to conquer Ojonegro. The army was already straining the resources of the surrounding countryside. Not to mention that the Ordinaries and the Knights proper found themselves forced to spend much of their energy controlling the depredations of the rest of the army. As Jaume had predicted to Tavares, the knights' and house-troops' taste for plunder, rape, and sheer vandalism was inclining the peasants to torch their fields and food stores, poison their wells, and simply run away with their livestock, without even waiting to be subjected to forced sales of supplies.

What the wily Count Blackeye was counting on was that hunger and thirst would simply drive the besiegers off before their engines could knock a hole in his walls.

Before reading more of his uncle's letter, Jaume paused to dab away moisture that blurred Felipe's overly minute and finicky penmanship. Pío had been among the bitterest enemies of Jaume and his Companions—certainly the most influential. Only Felipe's unswerving patronage prevented the Pope from dissolving the Order.

But he was a good man, in his way, thought Jaume. *And harsh though his views could be, in person he was kind.*

He read more aloud. He paraphrased. His Imperial uncle had a tendency to overelaborate.

"His Eminence Victor del Vallegrande has been elected Pope, and assumed the name Leo."

Unlike the news of Pío's demise, revelation of his successor produced an entirely unmixed reaction from his listening Brothers. Manfredo actually smiled—an act that had grown even rarer with Fernão's death.

"He is highly orthodox," he said.

"I'm astonished," said Florian. "Even more than at finding I agree with Manfredo. Vallegrande's a young man. Barely eighty. Usually the factions of the Colegio won't agree to seat a pontiff who's not scratching feebly at Death's door, so that none of them enjoys supremacy for too long."

Even Jacques's prematurely aged face was alight with satisfaction. "The Cardinals were clearly eager to repudiate the old man's warlike policies," he said. "So they set aside their differences to rush in the candidate furthest from old Raúl del Pico Alumbrado." Which had been Pío's birth name.

"If we're living right," Oakheart said, "he may even talk sense to Felipe, and get him to negotiate an end to this fiasco."

The others nodded. Machtigern turned to look at Castle Blackeye as a rock hurled from another of the battery of three trebuchets bounced off the walls.

"The Count would have surrendered by now," he growled, "if those rabid horrors we're saddled with hadn't worked treachery in Terraroja."

Jaume sighed. Ojonegro was just grabby, not a sadist or murderer. Unlike the army's first target he hadn't forfeited his head. Technically his were capital crimes as well, but in practice they were always settled by public contrition and payment of a hefty fine to the Fangèd Throne. Indeed, if it wasn't for Felipe's mad new spirit of adventurism, Don Robusto would probably have capitulated had Jaume done no more than show up at his gate with a Companion or two.

But now Ojonegro knew what happened to those who trusted the Ejército Corregidor. Everyone knew. And old Pío had indeed encouraged his crony the Emperor to make war on his own subjects.

And then Jaume read further, and felt as if he'd taken a ballista bolt to the belly.

He stopped, moistened his lips, read the lines over again.

"Captain?" Florian asked. "Are you feeling well?"

"No," he said. It came out as a croak.

"Ahh—no, as in you don't feel well?"

"That," Jaume agreed. "And also—his Holiness Pío was preaching a great Crusade against Providence for heterodoxy, to the masses at Creation Plaza. He dropped dead at the very climax."

"But there's no evidence they deny the Creators!" Pedro the Greater exclaimed, shocked from his usual elegant reserve. "How can they be condemned as heterodox?"

"Arguably they're less so than Pío himself was," Florian said. The late pontiff's—*sympathy*, Jaume preferred to think it—for the hyperascetic, hence heresy-skirting, Life-to-Come sect had been an internal Church controversy that bordered upon scandal.

"The Imperial Court's possessed by terror," Jaume said. "They fear the errors of the Garden of Beauty and Truth are so grave and extreme as to risk incurring a Grey Angel Crusade against the Imperio."

That brought a momentary silence: the Companions knew little enough about the Garden, but they all knew the Garden at least claimed to base its aesthetics-based philosophy on Jaume's own.

"Our new Pope Leo will put paid to that nonsense, quick enough," Machtigern said.

The parchment crumpled in Jaume's hand. "Leo has endorsed his predecessor's last sermon," he said through a throat that felt as if it had inhaled flame. "Felipe has acceded. We are ordered to gather up the Ejército Corregidor and march to join the Imperial Army by the quickest routes and fastest marches."

"But how is that possible?" exclaimed Bernat, shocked out of his usual amiable stolidity. "Victor—Leo's orthodox in his views. He's not one of these crabbed Life-to-Come cranks, with their hatred of pleasure and cleanliness, and their love of militarism for its own sake. How could he of all men go along with this Crusade insanity?"

Florian smiled a mad smile and shook his head, so wildly his golden locks fluttered like banners in a shifting wind.

"Don't you see?" the Francés knight said. "Our freshly minted Pontiff had no choice. He couldn't renege on the cunning old Velociraptor's final sermon, when it culminated in his own most public death.

"Gentlemen, we are screwed."

"I'm troubled," Melodía said.

She was walking with Bogardus alongside the same stream where, a few days earlier, she'd been surprised and horrified when the compsognathus had suddenly devoured the tiny, colorful flier.

It was another of what she'd learned to regard as a typical Providence autumn afternoon: warm, smelling of flowers and the trees that dappled the ferny green and lavender ground cover with shadow. The nearness of the mighty Shield mountains lent just the slightest touch of cool to the breeze that rustled the leaves overhead. Small fliers chirped and cawed from the branches.

"What about, Sister?" The Eldest conversed with her in Spañol, as he frequently did when they were alone. He seemed to be doing it as a courtesy to her native tongue, although his accent convinced her she'd been right in her initial surmise it was his as well.

A spotted frog uttered a croak of annoyance. Even after spending a couple of weeks amidst the Garden of Beauty and Truth, Melodía smiled to hear Bogardus call her that. It felt good to be appreciated for herself, not for her titles, or as a conduit to influence.

But her smile faded on the outside as it did within. "I thought the Garden stood for freedom as well as equality," she said.

"So we do."

"But the Council's begun trying to extend its rule to the city," she said, "instead of just running the Garden."

Bogardus frowned. She shied away slightly, emotionally, then recognized the look as pensive, not angry.

"Some of our members have begun exerting their influence, yes," he said. The ground cover crunched softly beneath their sandaled feet, releasing their sharp, ferny fragrance. "But doesn't there have to be authority of some kind?"

Melodía agreed that this was so.

"And which would you rather feel: the Gardener's gentle, guiding hand? Or the fist of command?"

"The first," she admitted.

She wore standard Garden garb: a modest muslin frock, off-white, with flowers embroidered on the bodice by Sister Jeannette. Pilar had braided her hair that morning, and wound it around her head. Despite the fact she didn't want her friend playing "maidservant" to her anymore, she hadn't resisted too hard. Pilar seemed to enjoy doing it.

Bogardus had on his usual long, grey academic gown trimmed in purple. He looked like a priest. Though he never spoke of his past, she had heard that's what he had been: of Maia, some said. Others claimed he had been a votary of Torrey the Law-Giver, and still others that he was a nonsectarian who served all Eight impartially. Although he based his teachings on those of Jaume, the Empire's most famous devotee of the Lady Bella, he seldom referred to individual Creators. Indeed he seldom referred to the Creators at all, invoking mostly Beauty and Truth as his guiding principles.

"But it's just—since I've arrived, things have changed," she said. "The air is changed. When I go into town people on the streets are no longer so easy in their manner or free in their expression."

"Isn't that the burden of war?"

"That may be," she said. "I do think all the preparing for war has poisoned minds and souls. More so now that it has truly come upon us. But that's not all I'm seeing."

"I certainly don't mean to doubt you, my child," he said. "But isn't it possible you're just seeing things through eyes more accustomed to the ways of the Corte Imperial?"

"But what I see is people acting more restrained than courtiers do. I've heard some say they fear that if they say or do or even sing the wrong thing, they'll have the town guard on their necks."

Bogardus sighed. "I see," he said. "I hadn't realized things had gone so far."

"But you're the Master Gardener!"

"All on the whole Council are Master Gardeners."

"But everybody calls you Father behind your back. You're the unquestioned leader."

He laughed. *It had a bitter ring*, she thought.

"Perhaps my leadership's more symbolic than actual," he said. "Still, I understand the argument: that those who possess special insight and wisdom have an obligation to lead others on the proper path. Even by force if need be."

"Sister Violette's explained that to me," Melodía said. "I still don't agree."

Far from being jealous of Bogardus's interest in the younger woman, not to mention Melodía's evident infatuation with Bogardus, Violette had adopted Melodía as a special sort of pet. She had also hinted strongly, though no more, that she wouldn't mind having Melodía join the two of them in bed.

She had declined, by pretending not to take the hints. Bogardus had become a strong and warming presence in her life. Violette's age suggested she had the experience to ease Melodía's first experience of sex with another woman—unlike Melodía's friends Llurdis and Lupe back at court. Their own love-play was alarming and sometimes outright violent, enough to make it easy for Melodía to rebuff their occasional importuning.

But Melodía felt no sexual desire that she could recognize at all. She hoped that Falk hadn't robbed her of that too when he raped her. But she was simply uninterested in such intimacy.

"You're wise beyond your years, querida," Bogardus said. "Perhaps you'll soon be ready for a higher mystery."

Her pulse picked up. "Do you really think so?"

"I do. But you must be sure within yourself. For there is such a thing as beauty so intense as to be terrible."

She dismissed the notion from consideration as soon as she heard it. It didn't seem possible. Instead her heart danced with the joyous anticipation of learning secrets.

How can I prove myself worthy of such an honor? she wondered.

"But still," she said, recalling her own vehement words from her walk with Pilar. "This growing reliance on force troubles me. I can't help but wonder if this Karyl's not poisoning the very soil the Garden grows in."

Bogardus sighed. The army had marched out from Séverin farm that dawn, leaving a small detachment behind on guard, mostly those mildly injured in the inevitable accidents that troubled even the best-run enterprise of such a size. Especially where dinosaurs or even Melodía's beloved horses were involved.

"I feared the possibility when I invited him here. But what else could I do? If I could have thought of any alternative—had anyone ever suggested one that worked—I'd never have compromised our principle of peace. But Count Guillaume has proven notably resistant to recourse to Beauty, or even Truth. And little as I like to fall back on the facile, Jaume himself defends those values with the sword he's named the Lady's Mirror."

"Yes," she said. "But Jaume himself would be the first to admit he doesn't have all the answers. He fights himself only when he can find no other way."

Thinking of her lover—especially speaking his name aloud—set her emotions to boiling inside her. She felt anger, at him and at herself; and likewise resentment. A sense of loss and a fear of inflicting unhealable wounds. Yet thinking of their times together—his smile, the rich music of his voice, his touch—something else welled within her as well. Something that overrode the seething, and smoothed it away.

"I know," she said abruptly.

Bogardus cocked a brow at her.

"You know many things," he said. "Which in particular?"

"What to do. I see it now."

"What do you mean?"

Her mind raced so fast that diverting her attention to speaking threatened to trip her up. Her heart raced faster at the beautiful clarity.

"I see a way," she said, speaking hurriedly so as to be done with distraction. "It's just a chance, yes; I admit that. But how can I live with myself if I don't do what I can to stop the slaughter?"

"That's a beautiful sentiment indeed," Bogardus said. "But how?"

She smiled at him with only a little of the malice of youth triumphing over age. "As to that," she said, "you'll have to wait and see."

Chapter 14

***Sacabuche*, Sackbut**—*Parasaurolophus walkeri.* One of the most popular war-hadrosaurs. Bipedal herbivore: 9.5 meters, 2.5 meters tall at shoulder, 3 tonnes. Named because its long, tubular head-crest produces a range of sounds like the sackbut, a trumpetlike musical instrument with a movable slide.

—THE BOOK OF TRUE NAMES

Dust or mud. The eternal choices faced by armies on the march. Like most who marched, Rob would generally take dust. Which was today's menu. Not that *choice* ever really came into it.

With no more reluctance than any other, the Army of Providence trudged to war.

In particular, Rob was eating the dust of the men-at-arms' horses, and behind them the war-dinosaurs. The road they traveled showed signs of neglect, the crushed-tufa metaling wearing through in places to show bare dirt already grooved by rain-erosion. Whether that was because pressure from Crève Coeur raiders made maintenance difficult, or because the Garden seemed increasingly uninterested in such mundane concerns, Rob didn't know. To either side wide fields lay bare and brown. The autumn harvest was being taken in. The winter crops were not yet planted, or at least not visibly sprouting.

Not even Karyl could have prevented the bucketheads and their retainers from claiming right of precedence on the march—even the second sons and daughters who made up most of the heavy cavalry. They were volunteers, after all, like the common soldiers.

But as it happened the arrangement satisfied Karyl. The knights leading the long column rode their travel horses, lighter, steadier, and more durable than their mettlesome war mounts, courser or dinosaur. Even though they were but lightly armored in chain or leather or just their shirts, armed with sidearms like swords and axes with a few spears thrown in, they were still the best-trained warriors in Providence. They should give a good account of themselves in the unlikely event of sudden attack.

Unlikely because Rob, thanks to the eyes and ears of his scouts and woods-runners, knew more about Count Guillaume's movements than Guilli himself did.

He rode his plodding, nodding spike-frill Little Nell along the road beside the six massive Triceratops. The monsters had filled out under his careful (and plentiful) feeding. Their tough, thick hides shone with health.

Baggage-bundles were piled high on the three-horns' backs. The durable personal belongings of the dinosaurs' attendants and fighting-crews, mostly—things that would suffer little from being cut loose and dumped in the ditch if danger threatened. Their negligible weight would add nothing to the monsters' fatigue.

The rest, particularly the disassembled fighting-castles, rode behind in carts pulled by nosehorns, the three-horns' smaller but still formidable cousins. Who in turn were larger than the Einiosaurus Nell. The massive trikes could pull the carts themselves without noticing the added work, but Karyl, who knew the beasts better than any Nuevaropan alive, didn't want the bother of unhitching them from wagon-harness to deploy for battle. While Triceratops, the largest practically domesticated dinosaurs Rob knew of, were unmatched for clearing obstacles from their road, it wasn't as if there were any shortage of powerful draft-dinosaurs available.

Small knots of chattering children perched atop two of the baggage mounds. Once they'd satisfied themselves the small, noisy creatures posed no threats, the trikes ignored them. A big flier rode in splendid isolation aboard the bull Broke-Horn's cargo. It was rather a splendid beast itself, tailless, a meter high, with a crest as tall again. Its belly fur and crest were white, its wings slate grey. To Rob, who knew little and cared less about flappy or swimmy things that fell into the range of "too big to eat" and "too small to eat him," it had a curiously nautical cast for a creature found so far inland.

At an easy canter, Karyl came riding back toward Rob along the weed-choked ditch. After making sure Karyl's mount wasn't making a beeline to attack her, Little Nell resolutely refused to look at the grey mare. And waspish as she was, Asal showed no inclination to get frisky with the three-horns. It may simply have been their sheer intimidating size, although Rob reckoned their warning snorts and shakes of their frilled head—the least of which must have weighed fully as much as the mare herself did—would freeze the heart of a bronze statue of a horse. Even one as mettlesome as Asal.

"You seem remarkably well set up for a man who passed the kind of night you did," Karyl called to Rob as Asal turned about to fall in alongside a manifestly uncomfortable Nell.

Rob laughed. "A liter of cold water swilled down, and another couple poured over the head, work wizardry to restore a lad," he said. "And, truth to tell, it's just as happy I am to put the town behind us. The Garden and its stinking intrigues, the more."

Except Pilar, of course. *But maybe it's no bad thing to separate yourself from the lass as well, fine as she is,* Rob told himself. *Precisely because she's so fine. It's perspective you're needing now, Robby, me lad.*

"Why now, more than before?" Karyl asked.

Rob looked at him. He knew the man was never the one for mere rhetorical questions. "The Council's showing a most unhealthy inclination to poke their noses into other folks' affairs. And no nose sharper than that silver-haired witch Sister Violette's." He shook his head. "What's trying to forbid people wearing purple feathers in their hats got to do with Beauty or Truth, or forcing them to petition the Council every time they want to build a new wall?"

"I'm told the Master Gardeners feel called upon to extend the benefit of their superior aesthetic vision to the population as a whole," Karyl said dryly, "improving their poor lives thereby."

Rob snorted. "Next they'll be banning the singing of bawdy songs in the ale-houses! Or the ale-houses themselves, which Mother Maia forfend. They're working the strong arm, and that's the fact."

"The little Princess wasn't wrong," Karyl said. "Not altogether. When they saw Salvateur stood off, it gave the Council a taste of the power *soldiery* confers. Apparently they like it."

"But it's Violette and her pious pacifist choir who're gaining the upper hand!"

"It's pacifists who are most prone to grow entranced by force," Karyl said, "once they taste the forbidden draft. Not that Violette and her claque love us. But don't confuse their contempt for the implement with their lust for what they perceive that implement can do for them. Our greatest challenge now isn't Guilli. It's beating him before our own employers pull us down."

Strange, Rob thought. *That captive rogue of a Crève Coeur knight said much the same thing.*

"What about Bogardus?" he asked. "Has the power gone to his head too, then?"

"Not yet, I think. Though he was our first champion, and in some ways remains our only one of consequence. He's seen battle from the bloody, sweaty inside, that one; a priest isn't all he was, before coming here. He knows what's real. More than the rest of the Council, anyway."

He shrugged. "But he'll go along with them in the end. No choice: otherwise they'll take him down. Or make him a mere figurehead. Which would be worse for a man like him."

Rob's face fisted in a scowl. Resentment against Violette and her claque had flooded his stocky body, as well as remembered annoyance at Karyl for not speaking up more briskly in his—and Rob's—defense. Despite the fact he was no slouch in a fight, he knew the other could squash him like a blood-bloated mosquito, with approximately the same exertion. Notwithstanding that—or was it because?—Rob suddenly couldn't resist baiting him.

"You're as infatuated with Bogardus as ever that Imperial chit is," Rob said. "You put too damned much faith in him."

Karyl rode a few breaths in silence. It was a time of cold belly-turning fear for Rob: that he had gone too far. It was a usual consequence of letting his imp of the perverse—never long dormant—take control of his mouth.

But instead of drawing the conventional, cross-hilted arming-sword he wore to battle and cutting short Rob's young life, Karyl answered quietly, "I know."

Rob literally swayed in the saddle.

"You know?"

"Of course. I'm . . . a seeker, I suppose. It may be all I'm really living for."

"Seeking what?"

"Some kind of certainty. What the Witness told me, the things I've experienced, have brought all that I knew, or thought I knew, about my world and myself crashing into ruin. I don't even know why I'm alive."

He held up his left hand. His sword hand, now tanned and strong and in no visible way different from the other. Even now, with it slowly dawning on Rob that he was likely to be allowed to keep his head a while yet, said head couldn't help swelling with a hearty case of *I told you so*.

A domesticated horror belonging to a pack set on Karyl by Duke Falk's mother, the Dowager Duchess of Hornberg, to make sure he was dead after the Battle of Hassling had bitten Karyl's sword hand clean off. When the self-proclaimed witch Aphrodite had hired him and Rob on Bogardus's behalf to come to Providence and raise an army to fight, she had performed a magic she claimed would grow it back. Skeptic to the core, Karyl openly doubted the existence both of witches and of magic.

Rob had taken a different view. And when the lost member in fact sprouted anew, good as ever, on the long journey hither, Karyl had seemed as much soured by it as overjoyed.

"Even skepticism's played me false," he said, as if sniffing Rob's thoughts. "I don't what to believe anymore. I need the hope that I might find answers, somewhere. Bogardus is wise; he practically glows with certainty. Maybe he has what I need."

"Why not ask him?"

Karyl shook his head. "My need shames me. Its intensity, its urgency."

"I don't mean to make light of your feelings, my friend, but after all you've faced and all you've survived, surely you'll not let shame get the better of you?"

Karyl's face was a naked plea. "But what if he tells me he doesn't *know*?"

Rob sighed. Putting hands on thighs he hoisted himself off his seat on a fallen log.

The evening conference had been quick. It was early yet. Despite the fact sunlight still shone nearly level between slim sapling boles a small fire danced yellow, chuckling to itself. The tang of its smoke was already noticeably mingled with the smells of meat roasting and legumes boiling for two thousand or so evening meals.

The sun was still a red ball beyond the clouds above the eastern horizon when Karyl ordered a halt for the day, amidst country that had begun to roll noticeably more than the earlier pure farmland. It struck Rob as early. Clearly Karyl was in no hurry.

It's Himself's decision to make, and I've no interest in the why and wherefores, he thought. *All I am is glad it isn't mine.* Even though he'd been relieved of the crushing burden of being quartermaster, he found himself with more responsibility than he wanted or ever had wanted, thank you kindly.

It was strange, he thought. A dinosaur master had plenty of responsibility, and that was the trade he'd chosen, and was happy to be practicing it again. It seldom felt like a burden when he was doing it. And being master of the scouts and spies, now—that was more like what the grandes called a *hobby*. The achievement of a mischievous childhood dream—more play than anything else, really. Yet add them up and you got—

Responsibility. *Ugh. I can't seem to get the awful thing off my back.*

Most of Karyl's captains had quickly departed the little clearing in a sapling-stand atop a low hill. One of the last to leave laid a hand on the commander's shoulder and said something that made him shrug.

Baron Côme was a man of Rob's height or a little more, a muscular sixty-five-year-old with a shock of tan hair, and a face like an old shoe that was rescued from plainness by bright blue eyes and a smile roguish enough for an Irlandés. He and a few dozen retainers had joined the army within days of Karyl and Rob's acquittal. The blue-jowled Baron Salvateur had taken out his fury at being repulsed from Providence town by driving Côme from his domain, *Le Vallée de la Sérénité.*

Rob would've resented the Baron's late arrival, if not for the fact that his fief on the Lisette had stood a bulwark against the invaders since the incursions began, long before Rob and Karyl got here. And that Côme's beloved wife, Zoé, had fallen fighting the Brokenhearts the year before. He was that near-oxymoron, a genuinely clever buckethead, as opposed to simply sly or cunning. He was popular among both lowborn and high. Rob liked him himself, for a wonder.

More than he liked the taller, red-haired man who hung back with Côme. Eamonn Copper was Ayrish, and it may have been his share of native charm the Francés, Côme, had hogged for himself. A noted mercenary captain on his own hook, he had joined the army with a contingent of eighty mailed spear and shield men, the most of them former housetroops, like as not deserters.

Copper had trouble keeping employment. The anger many of his and Rob's countrymen shared crackled along the surface of his skin like static electricity. Men said he was overly fond of drink.

Although he made no claims of noble birth, or knighthood—he was as chary of details of his own history as Rob Korrigan was with truth about his own—he was known to be skilled on a war-hadrosaur. Having satisfied both Karyl and Rob of his ability to use her, he had been given Brigid, as Rob had dubbed the somewhat flighty orange sackbut female they'd taken from the knight at Whispering Woods, the same having no further use for her.

The two moved on. All but yapping at their heels like a pug dog, and equally ignored, went a rotund, bearded figure. Rob spat after him as they went away out of sight through the brush and down, not caring if he saw or not.

"Why do you put up that treacherous, fat fuck Melchor?" he asked Karyl. The other surviving town lord, Yannic, still sulked in his manor, claiming incapacity from the wounds he'd had at Blueflowers. Rob reckoned he was malingering, and good riddance.

"Better to have him where we can keep an eye on him."

"Which presupposes a man can stand the sight of him."

Karyl shrugged. "I told him that if he showed any sign of getting out of line, I'd kill him."

Rob laughed. Not because he thought Karyl was joking. But precisely because he wasn't.

"So, what chance do you give us, Master Rob?" Karyl asked.

Rob clucked thoughtfully, low in his throat, rubbed his beard and nodded.

"We've scarce a thousand effectives," he said. "Count Guillaume has at least half again as many, with twice the heavy-horse and three times our own dinosaur knights. He outnumbers us in every way, for a fact, except in missile troops, and in light-horse, which he's got none to speak of. And while our common pikes are nothing to raise more than a horse-laugh from a Nodosaur centurion, they are trained at least halfway, with even some leather armor and iron hats from the Town Armory among them. So I fancy their chances against his larger mob of unhappy peasants with sharp sticks.

"Crève Coeur's got no more field artillery to speak of than we do, which isn't any. He does have some siege engines, but correct me if I'm mistaken, if we find ourselves on the receiving end of *those,* we're doing something grievous wrong. And of course no one in all the land has anything like our six living fortresses. We're better equipped than any scratch force has a right to be. But the Brokenhearts are better trained and experienced, along with there simply being more of the brutes. So, all taken with all—they'll win. Unless, of course, we cheat like a bastard."

He grinned, all wild and sudden. "And you're just the man for that, Karyl Bogomirskiy!" he exclaimed.

Karyl flashed a rare smile. "I am."

"So what about you?" Rob said, as the flash passion passed and left him chilled. "Do you think we've any chance, then?"

"You may recall I expressed my distaste for fighting battles I know I can't win."

Rob nodded. "Aye. And I note you didn't kick, this time, about taking the field, but rather told the Council straightaway you were ready to march. So—what is it gives us this chance, against a foe who seems to be holding every trigram card in the deck?"

Karyl smiled. "Why, you, Master Korrigan," he said. "You and your mad young men and women."

Rob's jaw fell open. Before he could think of anything sensible to let out of it—

"Master Rob," a hesitant voice called.

Poised at the clearing's verge, like a yearling springer ready to bolt, stood a young woman dressed in the leather jack and high boots typical of Rob's scouts. Her blond hair hung in pigtails, framing a pretty, blue-eyed face. She wore a longsword slung across her back. The hilt was plain black wood and looked to have been polished by use.

"Valérie," Rob said. "Come ahead, lass. We'll not bite your head off. Have you something to report, then?"

Shyly she stepped forward, nodding. She dealt easily enough with Rob. But as far as he knew she had never met Karyl. And a lot of the newer recruits, having imbibed not only survivors' tales that exaggerated the heartbreaking debacle of the Blueflowers into brilliant victory, but songs of Karyl's epic past as well—no few penned, and frequently sung, by none other than Rob Korrigan—regarded him with near-worship.

She was a city girl, youngest child of a trading family. Évrard's house was easily the biggest and richest, but Providence town was far too prosperous to support only the one. The important details were, she knew how to ride well, and was willing (or mad) enough to serve as one of Rob's scouts.

It was a perilous undertaking, and no mistake. Over a score had already gone down, dead or injured. Only a handful had been captured. But the Brokenhearts treated them as they did captive woods-runners. It may have had the effect of making fewer willing to enlist—Rob honestly had no way to know—but it certainly inspired the remaining scouts to savage vindictiveness that matched their *coureur de bois* allies'.

"So, what have you to tell us?" Rob asked.

She flicked a nervous glance at Karyl. He nodded.

"We spotted a party north and west of here, riding through the woods," she said. "Eight people, mounted on amblers. There was Councilor Absolon and several other Gardeners. Uh, all from the better families. And . . . the Princess, sir, and her black-haired friend that came with her from Spaña."

"And they're going—?" Karyl prodded.

Rob felt absurdly gratified that she glanced to him before replying, as if to confirm it was all right. And then the awful impact of the girl's inevitable next words struck him.

"West, Captain, sir. Toward Count Guillaume's lines."

Chapter 15

***Cabeza de Tirán*, Tyrant's Head**—Home to our Empire of Nuevaropa, the Tyrant's Head forms the western end of the continent of Aphrodite Terra. Taken with the large island of Anglaterra across La Canal (the Channel), it supposedly resembles the head of a *Tyrannosaurus rex*. The mighty Shield Mountain range, *El Scudo*, separates it from the Ovdan Plateau. Its climate is mostly tropical, though it doesn't have distinct rainy seasons. Humid coastal swamps and forests rise to a fertile central plateau, including Spaña's arid *La Meseta*. The Tyrant's Head is spanned from north to south by a forest of mixed conifer and deciduous trees called Telar's Wood.

—A PRIMER TO PARADISE FOR THE IMPROVEMENT OF YOUNG MINDS

"My lord Count Guillaume," said Melodía, her knees feeling the morning warmth the soft grass of the clearing through the fabric of her plain white gown. "We've come from Providence town to beg you for peace."

Before her sat the Count of Crève Coeur on a folding gilt chair, with his elbow propped on one arm and his chin in his palm. He was a big man, not all of his size muscle, dressed in a silken gown, one side blue, the other green. The Broken Heart emblem was sewn in gold on the right breast: the blue side. His big, red face frowned beneath his shock of prematurely white hair. His expression showed perplexity rather than displeasure. Melodía hoped.

"Do you actually have the power to negotiate?" he asked. A knock-down awning of gold-trimmed green silk shaded him from morning sun already fierce through a high, thin screen of cloud. A half-dozen retainers clustered around him.

"I am Master Gardener Absolon," said the tall, lank man who knelt on Melodía's right. "I speak for the Council."

"And these others?" Guillaume asked. He had a voice surprisingly high-pitched for a man of his size.

"Good Gardeners," Melodía said. Three young women and two men, some of the most passionate believers in Melodía's cause, had ridden hard with her from Providence town the day before. They camped the night in the forest, and set out at first light to kneel at the feet of the Count of Crève Coeur.

"And my friend Pilar." Melodía was keenly conscience of her companion hovering at the edge of her vision, half-surrounded by spearmen with blue and green tabards over their mail hauberks. The gitana looked most uneasy.

You worry too much, dear friend, Melodía thought. *I've seen the way. You'll see.*

Behind the supplicants stretched fields left fallow by farmers who fled the invading army as they would any natural disaster. Paradise had moved quickly to reclaim them with green grass and flowers in white and blue. Before them stood old hardwood trees with trunks stout as boulders. Around them Melodía heard the ruckus and rumble of a large army. Men shouted, sang, or cursed. Hornfaces grunted. Huge feet stamped. Weapons clacked on weapons and ladles in pots. War-duckbills droned and piped at one another as they fed on mounds of grain and vegetation fresh-cut by bustling grooms.

"It's a trick, Lord," said the tall, bulky-bodied man who stood at Guillaume's right. Black brows glowered over a fleshy nose and heavy blue-shadowed cheeks. *This must be the infamous Baron Salvateur*, Melodía thought.

Guillaume waved a beefy hand at him. "Do they look threatening to you, Didier?"

"It's not these poor nosehorn-calves who worry me," the Baron said, "but the mind that may have sent them."

"If you keep on like this," Guillaume said, "next thing I know you'll be checking beneath your cot before going to bed each night, to see if this bugbear Karyl is hiding there."

Melodía's cheeks flushed hot. "Captain Karyl hasn't got anything to do with our mission, my lord. If he did, he'd hardly approve."

"So. You offer surrender," Guillaume said.

"I offer peace. Once we agree in principle we can discuss terms."

"What do you offer me," he said, "that would lead me to agree to give you peace, if not full submission? The Garden is the most troublesome neighbor, you know. They keep trying to infect my realm with their twin plagues of anarchy and egalitarianism. A Grey Angel has been seen Emerging in your county. Do you think those facts are unrelated?"

She frowned. "I heard a rumor to that effect in La Merced." *But why would I have taken it seriously?* she did not say. But only so as not to anger the man she was trying to reason with.

"Which no one in Providence has heard," Absolon said. His voice faltered a trifle. "I—the Count must be misinformed."

"Your lack of order may have affected your intelligence-gathering," Guillaume said.

"We offer you love, Count Guillaume," Melodía said hastily.

For a moment they seemed to inhabit a bubble of silence that stilled even the invading army's clamor.

"'Love,'" said Guillaume, as if the word was some unfamiliar, funny-tasting food.

"Love," she said, striking again while the iron was—she hoped—hot. Also she hoped to proceed quickly to the sit-down phase of negotiations; the bumpy hardness of the ground was beginning to tell on her knees. "The *Books of the Law* bid us love one another. If we act in a spirit of love, obedient to the Creators, what grounds can that give the Grey Angels to act?"

As if they existed, she thought. But she wasn't here to argue theology—much less insult the Count's. No matter how deeply mired he was in superstition.

Guillaume frowned. He sat up straight and scratched his clean-shaven chin as if genuinely intrigued.

"You're serious," he said.

"I am, Lord."

"Wellll . . . what can love win me that force of arms can't?"

Feel free to chime in any time now, Melodía thought furiously at her companions. They seemed unwilling to preempt a princess. *We may need to work on this egalitarian thing.*

"Perhaps nothing," she admitted. "But at how much less cost to you than war?"

"And are you, or the people you claim to represent, willing to let my troops plunder and rape, with maybe a bit of torture thrown in?"

She recoiled. It felt as if she had been kicked in the stomach. "This isn't something to joke about!"

"Who's joking?" He held out a hand, took a swig of wine from a pewter flagon a lackey thrust into it. "The boys and girls have had a hard campaign; they need to take the edge off. And that seems a lot to ask people to undergo voluntarily. Which may have something to do with why it customarily isn't."

Melodía's thoughts whirled like a wind-hada behind eyes that suddenly blinked at hot tears. "But—how can you take this so lightly? I offer peace. I offer *love*."

"Haven't you been listening to me, girl? I can impose peace, on my own terms. What do I want with love?"

He drained the mug and wiped his mouth with the back of his hand before tossing the flagon over his shoulder without looking. His servant fielded it deftly.

"In any event," the Count said, "I can always find more peasant levies and mercenaries to make good my losses. Granted, peasants are more easily come by. But then again, dead mercenaries are notoriously lax about insisting on their pay."

His retinue laughed uproariously at that. Except for Salvateur. He was staring at Melodía with what seemed to be increasingly narrow focus. With her heart sinking faster than it was already, she remembered his reputation for astuteness.

"If you'll pardon me, Lord."

"Oh, what's that? Speak up, Baron; you've no need to wait upon ceremony with me."

"Aren't you Melodía Delgao Llobregat, Imperial Princess and scion of the Archduchy of Los Almendros?" Salvateur asked. "And isn't that other woman your maidservant?"

Defiantly she tossed back the lock of hair that had escaped her Francés braid and begun to tickle her forehead.

"What's that got to do with anything? I still kneel before the Count in all humility, and beg him to make peace."

"'What's that got to *do* with anything?'"

The Count looked around at his retainers. After a moment they decided he was making a joke and laughed. Even Salvateur, who didn't seem much used to the courtier's role if Melodía was any judge (and she was), joined in.

"'What's that got to do with anything?'" the Count repeated. "Oh, come on, girl. Your Imperial Highness: stand up."

She glanced back to nod at her companions. All rose as one. Melodía's knees worked more stiffly than she liked, but she was glad to be off them.

"What it has to do with anything," Guillaume said, "is that you're now my honored guest, while I negotiate with your Imperial father about payment for your safe return. As for the rest of you lot—"

He looked to his shield-bearers. "—take them away. Let the troops amuse themselves with them. It'll whet their appetites for the pleasures to come when we've whipped down these leveling Providence scum. Then bring out my hunting-pack. My horrors need the exercise; we could use the sport."

"You don't dare—" Melodía shouted.

Hands grabbed her arms. Hard fingers dug deep. She smelled man-sweat and sun-heated dinosaur leather.

"My dear, silly little Princess," Count Guillaume said mildly, "of course I dare. After all, you're a renegade and fugitive from Imperial justice, aren't you? Be grateful to me for sparing you and your serving-wench. I could send back both your heads to La Merced, you know. And your father would have to thank me for the gift!"

And he guffawed as if that was the grandest joke of all.

In the afternoon stifle of the tent, Melodía lay on her side and suffered.

Her arms ached from her wrists being tied behind her back. The physical was the least of her hurts.

Twice recently she had known what she felt like utter despair. First, in her cell after Falk raped her. Then on the road, when the exhilaration of her escape had faded and the terrible reaction set in.

Yet this was every bit as bad. It might be worse.

The tent smelled of horsehair, warm silk, her own sweat, and limestone-stringent dust. Outside the camp vibrated with the usual sounds of an army in the field. She strained her hearing, half trying to hear cries if her friends were being tormented, half dreading to hear them.

She didn't. The fact did not comfort her.

I brought them here, she thought. *I got them into this.*

Though she had blamed herself a thousand different ways for her arrest on trumped-up charges, she knew, intellectually, it wasn't her fault.

But she had gone passive. She had trusted her father. Imperial justice. Her own innocence.

It had gotten her literally fucked in the ass.

Now innocence of another kind had dropped people who trusted her into deadly danger. Possibly herself as well. That remained to be seen, although she trusted Guillaume's assurances he meant her no harm. She was too valuable to him intact.

To think I thought love *could sway a creature like that.* Her naïveté of minutes before now turned her stomach.

But even as she imploded into despair, pressing outward against that was the urgent desire to *do something*. She had to help her friends. She hadn't collapsed so far as not to realize that meant she had to do something for herself first.

But how? She had been left with wrists and ankles tied in silk scarves—no doubt to further impress upon her that she was the Count's captive and must accept his will.

She couldn't think. Far easier to slump, to dwindle to a point in darkness and let the outside world do as it would.

But she couldn't. Quite. *They counted on you. You're their only hope.*

She recalled a conversation with Jaume. Long ago, long before romance was any more than a child's idle dream. Her father was still an Archduke, then, and Jaume a brash young hero/poet, widely celebrated, but struggling to build his newly chartered Order and to attract the best of Nuevaropan chivalry, the smartest, most talented, bravest, most moral, and most beautiful knights to become his Companions.

She mentioned—she forgot now why—that her dueña, Doña Carlota, had told her anger was bad and should be banished. Jaume smiled and said it wasn't possible. Nor even desirable.

How, she wondered, could anger can be good?

Is fire bad? he asked her. It can cause horrific pain and injury. It can destroy beauty faster than almost anything else. Yet how could we live without it? It also gives us beauty, and helps sustain the life to enjoy it.

Fire, she admitted, could be both good and bad.

Precisely! he exclaimed, with that happy enthusiasm she loved so well. Fire has two opposite values. It can be used for good or bad, like a knife. Like any tool. So with some emotions.

Some? she wondered.

Some, he said. Envy, worry, despair—these can't help us, only hurt. Think of them as Poison. Other emotions can be good or bad. Love is one. Hate another, albeit dangerous. And anger. Anger is the most, in ways, like fire.

Among other ways in this: the fire of anger can burn away such poisons as despair.

So now Melodía started getting mad.

And then a knife-blade poked through the silken wall of the tent a handspan from her eyes.

Chapter 16

Horror, Chaser—*Deinonychus antirrhopus.* Nuevaropa's largest pack-hunting raptor: 3 meters, 70 kilograms. Plumage distinguishes different breeds: scarlet, blue, green, and similar horrors. Smart and wicked, as favored as domestic beasts for hunting and war as wild ones are feared. Some say a *deinonychus* pack is deadlier than a full-grown *Allosaurus.*

—THE BOOK OF TRUE NAMES

Melodía's righteous anger, mostly at herself, evaporated in a mouse-terror squeak. *Soldiers! They've decided to disregard Guillaume's orders, sneak in and—use me. . . .*

A dark-olive face thrust in through the cut. Green eyes looked at her in concern.

"Highness?"

"Pilar," she breathed.

Pilar's face withdrew. A shaft of white lanced into the tent. Although the sun had passed the zenith and the cloud-filtered light was indirect, it dazzled Melodía's eyes, accustomed to the gloom. She screwed her eyes shut on big pulsing purple balls of afterimage.

She heard the sizzle of silk being cut. Then Pilar was kneeling beside her, sawing through the scarf that tied her wrists.

"Where on Paradise did you hide that knife?" was all she could think to say.

"Somewhere they didn't find it," Pilar said. "That's a good lesson for you, Princesa dear: a woman always needs a final friend."

"How'd you get clear of your guards?"

"Pointed out to them that it would hardly do for an Imperial Princess, even a hostage one, not to be properly attended by a serving-maid. That, and promised them blow jobs."

"Ew," Melodía said. "Did you deliver?"

"We need to move rapidly now, Alteza, and leave particulars for later, yes?"

She helped Melodía out the hole in the back of the tent. A stand of green bamboo screened it. Melodía blinked, swayed as the blood prickled back into her limbs.

Pilar reached to steady her. She shook her head.

"I'm fine."

Pilar knew that was a lie, of course. But she didn't call Melodía on it. Instead she took her hand and led her into dark-green brush, away from the clearing where the tent stood among a number of others.

When they had gone a few meters Melodía stopped. "Take me to the others," she said.

Pilar shook her head impatiently. "I can't."

"I've got to help them!"

"I'm sorry, Melodía. They—"

"I command you to help me rescue them."

Green eyes flashed. "Am I your servant, or your friend?"

Melodía's lips pressed to a line. She nodded. "You're right. You are my friend. Now, please take me to the others!"

"But I can't," Pilar repeated. "It's too late."

She pointed east. Through gaps in the lance-leaved vegetation Melodía saw a field of ripened wheat, abandoned to rot by farmers who had fled the Crève Coeur advance. It was already being choked by weeds which had sprung to half its height. A pallid figure ran through the wheat with gangling high-kneed strides and flapping elbows. Behind it the dying stalks wavered as if from a wind. Among them Melodía caught cobalt flickers, as of blooming wildflowers.

It took her a moment before she realized the fleeing man was Councilor Absolon. Blood that shone bright red in the sunlight streaked his naked body. It occurred to Melodía that the breeze seemed awfully localized. Could it be a wind-hada, as they called a miniature whirlwind back home?

Then something blue and lean blurred from the vegetation to land on Absolon's shoulders. *That's no wind.* Realization chilled Melodía. *Those aren't flowers. They're* feathers.

Three meters long, the horror as likely weighed as much as the gaunt, gawky Councilor himself did. Its impact sent the running man pitching forward onto his face. Even before he vanished from view, the outsized killing-claws on its hind feet were gouging into his back as it clung to his face with winglike arms.

Absolon left a trail of blood spray in the air behind him when he fell, and screams like a girl-child's. They were shockingly high and ululating, pleading without words for mercy from a creature that thirsted for cruelty as it did for the hot blood of prey.

Pilar's grip on Melodía's arm had no more give than black iron.

"You—can't—help—him," she hissed.

More plumed monsters sprang on the shrieking man. They had blue and white crests, white bellies, black masks at their eyes. A yellow snout whipped skyward, flapping a long red strip of something it held in its teeth like a rag. A rag that shed red drops. . . .

And you did this to him, an accusing voice said in Melodía's skull.

Out into the field loped a party on horseback. Guilli rode in the lead on a white hunter mare. Four or five of his noble favorites followed, dressed as he was for the hunt in jaunty caps, tunics, loincloths, and sword-belts. Melodía heard the hateful music of their laughter even over Absolon's screams.

With dagger-twisting-in-the-entrails certainty, Melodía knew how foolish she had been. But she wasn't stupid. Neither was she slow.

He's gone, but— "The others—"

"The only ones better off than he are dead already," Pilar said. "Let's go."

"I can't just abandon them."

"You're still heiress to Los Almendros," Pilar said. "You're a Delgao. You have a duty. You have a destiny."

"But how can I live with their blood on my hands?"

"Learn," Pilar said. "You can always die later. It's easy. Now, stop being a fool. Come on."

She led the unresisting Princess south along the field's verge, keeping them screened by brush and trees. Melodía's every fiber longed to simply dart straight away from the camp of her enemies. But she fought the panicky urge. That would mean fleeing into more open, derelict cropland. Into the sight of the terrible yellow eyes of the horrors.

She and Pilar didn't run, but they did move fast. The undergrowth crackled around them. As Melodía got control over thoughts and fears chasing each other in a mad vortex she began to wince at every rustle of branch or crackle of fallen twigs underfoot. Then she realized the noise they made hardly mattered, between the steady rumble of the army camp, and the terrible cries, and even more terrible laughter, of the hunt.

They jumped a narrow stream running through the woods. Beyond the undergrowth it flowed into a straight ditch with a windbreak of plane trees with white boles planted alongside it. High weeds marked the ditch's course as clearly as they obscured actual sight of it.

"Why are we so close to the camp's edge?" Melodía asked. "Instead of right in the middle of it?"

"Prevailing winds blow from the east," Pilar said. "The Count pitched his tents on this side of camp to avoid his army's smell."

Evidently he had no fear the Providence would fall on him suddenly. *And why should he?* Melodía thought bitterly. *They're crazy if they think they can face him at all. Was I really so wrong—*

From somewhere to the right, not far, rose a chilling sound: the deep baying of a hound. Other dog-voices quickly joined.

Yes. The word slammed into her skull like a mace. *Yes, I was so wrong.*

"The dogs are on us," Pilar said. "We have to run for it now."

"Maybe Guillaume just wants us brought back."

"I doubt it. Does it matter now?"

Melodía was a seasoned enough hunter to know the answer. Horrors of whatever color were sight hunters. Killing had their blood-lust up: they'd chase and bring down prey now for sheer love of the hunt. And they were trained to follow the baying of hounds—

"Across the open fields?" she said. "We don't have a chance!"

"Until those things have our guts in their teeth," Pilar said, "there's always a chance."

Even in her extremity that reasoning sounded questionable to Melodía. Her reflex panic did her a favor then. It overrode her mind's inclination to think-through and debate, and made her body run.

She bounded after Pilar into the field. This one had clearly been harvested. Dry stalks nodded among the weeds, and broke at their passing. The tilling of the rows and relatively soft soil made running hard. Melodía quickly found herself panting.

From the sound, the dogs had broken through the trees behind them. They were halfway across the field now. Another copse rose less than two hundred meters ahead of them. If they made it they might at least make a stand.

A trumpet's skirl smashed that hope. Melodía stumbled over a furrow. As Pilar grabbed her arm and helped her recover she looked back over her shoulder.

Count Guillaume himself was just riding through the weeds on this side of the ditch. He lowered a hunting-horn from his red face. His laughing courtiers flanked him.

From the tall weeds came wiry brown men and women in peaked green caps and tunics: Rangers, Crève Coeur's scouts—and huntsfolk.

And with them came blue horrors, ten or more, their jaws red and snapping.

Melodía ran so hard it felt as if her heart would explode. Pilar raced at her side. The traitor dirt crumbled beneath them, slowing their steps.

The pursuing dromaeosaurs seemed to skip lightly across the tops of the rows. Laughing, the hunters followed.

Ahead of Melodía the trees and brush grew larger, tantalizing. It felt as if safety waited there. Though Melodía knew better, she still drove herself as fast as her long flashing legs could carry her. Reaching the woods would at least be a final triumph to carry with her to her next spin of the Wheel.

The snarling cries grew louder. Pilar pressed something into Melodía's hand.

"Take this!" she shouted. "Use it—on yourself if you have to."

Melodía lost the stride, slowed, stumbled. She saw she grasped the smooth black wood hilt of Pilar's long-bladed knife.

"The Fae set me to watch over you, Princess," Pilar told her. "I've failed. May they protect you now."

Pilar stopped running. Turning, she walked back toward the pursuing raptors. She spread her arms out to her sides.

"Here I am!" she shouted. "Come take me!"

"Pilar, no!" Melodía screamed.

Behind the horrors, Guilli and his party had slowed to a trot. The Count leaned forward in the saddle. A grin stretched his big face wide. He seemed as avid as the raptors.

Seeing their prey stop and turn back toward them clearly confused the horrors. They slowed, began to chirp to one another, as if in wonder or in warning. They no longer had running prey to chase down. So they began that horrible, characteristic sidle they used when a quarry faced them down. The eerily cunning tactics that did as much to make them feared as claws or cruelty ever did.

Pilar glanced back. "Princess, run!" she shouted.

But Melodía could not. Desperately she looked around for a rock to hurl. But the field had been tended well. Any rocks large enough to make useful missiles had painstakingly been removed by hand from the plow's path generations before.

She hefted the dagger to throw. Then she realized how stupid-futile that would be. *I'll probably miss*, she thought. Even if she cast and killed one, against all odds, that would leave eight or nine more—and her completely unarmed. The one-eyed weapons mistress at the Palace of the Fireflies had taught her better than that.

Pilar kept walking forward. It clearly befuddled the deinonychus. They could be scary-clever, these small, feathered killers. But this was something even they had trouble comprehending: a prey that neither tried to fight nor run, but rather walked straight toward them.

Evidently they decided their customary pincers trick would still serve. The dinosaurs split. One crouched directly in Pilar's path, snarling menace. The others circled left and right.

Pilar never even turned her head to watch as they closed in behind her.

I have to do something, Melodía thought, jittering from foot to foot. But her mind gave her only blankness.

She couldn't bring herself to run. That had nothing to do with the exhaustion that tore her lungs and made her legs feel like boiled noodles. Yet her friend was sacrificing herself so Melodía could do just that.

She thought of throwing herself on one of the horrors that circled Pilar from behind. But what good would that do? If she stabbed one to death, the others would still take down her friend even as she did so.

The raptor on Pilar's right flung wide its arms. It fanned the feathers to show their cream and white undersides. Thrusting forward its big head it opened its jaws wide to shriek. Reflex made Pilar turn toward it.

The horror on her left jumped on her back. She staggered but kept her feet as it sank its teeth in her shoulder. Its killing-claws raked great bloody rips in her loose white blouse. Shouting anger, Pilar smashed its face with her fist.

Light bones crumpled. Blood squirted from flared nostrils. The monster let go and fell back squalling.

But it had done its job. The others charged. One jumped seized her throat in its jaws and hung on as its rear talons tore her belly. The rest darted in snapping.

Pilar fought furiously. But along with outweighing her, the monsters were strong and fast—and sharp. They quickly brought her down. She was screaming now, in what seemed more rage more than pain.

Blood flew like a red fountain in the sun. Pilar stopped struggling. Melodía moaned and swayed.

Then one horror raised its head. It was the one that had spread its arms to draw Pilar's attention: the biggest, the pack-leader. Something hung from its featherless, blood-smeared snout. Something like a softly laden pouch, which dripped red.

The skin crept on the backs of Melodía's hands and neck. Her cheeks tingled. The monster was holding her friend's severed breast in its mouth.

Yellow saucer eyes fixed Melodía. A brilliant blue crest rose in interest.

The prey that wouldn't run away was dead. It wasn't fun anymore. And the raptor pack-leader still wanted to play.

It whipped its face skyward, tossing Pilar's breast in the air. Catching it in its teeth, it chewed twice and swallowed it. Then it uttered a warbling cry.

The other horrors raised their heads. In uncanny unison they turned to stare at Melodía.

The lead horror hopped off Pilar's torn corpse. It minced toward Melodía, head held tipped to the side, as if driven by curiosity, not evil intent.

Melodía wasn't fooled.

Not twenty meters behind her the trees beckoned. She didn't dream of dashing for them. Once she turned her back, the monster would be on her in three strides.

Instead the anger that had smoldered within her for weeks exploded into full flame.

"Come on, you bastard," she yelled, brandishing the knife both-handed in front of her. "I'll teach you what it feels like to be strangled in your own fucking guts!"

The creature reared up in surprise. Its crest rose again. Then it thrust its head forward and screeched again.

It meant to shock her into momentary immobility—then strike. Instead she shrieked back, wordless and raging. It might be futile defiance, but it was born of a fury as terrible as anything that made the horror's heart race.

The pack-leader sprang. Its jaws opened wide to snap off Melodía's face.

Part Three

Redemption

Chapter 17

Corredor de Bosque, Woods-runner, *Coureur de Bois*—A nomadic people who range freely in Telar's Wood in the eastern part of the Empire of Nuevaropa, professing no allegiance to kingdom or county. Skilled trackers, hunters, and archers, the woods-runners tend to be at odds with townsfolk and farmers, whom they disdain as "sitting-folk." Woods-runners regard the "sitting-folk" as arbitrary and mean, and the "sitting-folk" despise the woods-runners as thieves, each with some justice.

—A PRIMER TO PARADISE FOR THE IMPROVEMENT OF YOUNG MINDS

The horror pack leader's open mouth looked huge as castle gates rimmed with swords. Inside it glared bright red and yellow.

Something buzzed past Melodía's left ear like an angry wasp as big as a firefly. She heard *impact*.

The raptor twisted in midleap. Feathers stood out from its arms and body. It dropped, shrieking, two meters away, and rolled almost to her feet.

She stared down at it, not comprehending what had just happened, and why those long, narrow jaws were snapping at a black shaft sticking from its throat instead of on her face.

Something grabbed her arm and yanked her backward so violently she almost fell over. As she did the horror's leg slashed out. The black killing claw scythed air scant centimeters from her belly.

"Don't just stand there!" someone shouted in her ear. "Did you want that thing to gut you?"

Melodía turned her head. A young woman dressed in leather held her. She had an oval face and yellow braids hanging from a browned-iron cap.

"Maybe," she said. She had lost the feeling of reality.

Then more flying things hummed past to either side of the two young women, and reality returned abruptly, snapped back in place by the shrieking and kicking and blood-arcs as more arrows hit the horrors feeding on Pilar's corpse. And not just horrors: a green clad Ranger huntsman fell howling and clutching at his bare belly.

The Crève Coeur hunting party had halted thirty meters back to get a good view of the sport as the pack took Pilar. Guilli stared at the horror now lying dead in front of Melodía with a face mottled and swelling in grief and rage.

"Léonide!" he cried. "My old, my brave!"

The young knight at his right started to draw his sword. "Brigands!" he shouted. "To ar—"

Another black shaft struck his right eye, beneath a square-cut brown bang. His shout cut off and he slumped from the saddle like a bag half-full of laundry.

The hunting party's horses reared and screamed alarm. Another bold young buckethead got his longsword free and charged forward at the archers, male and female, who had suddenly materialized to either side of Melodía as if out of the plowed ground.

A chestnut horse dashed as if to meet him. Instead its rider, a young woman armored like Melodía's rescuer in a light nosehorn leather jack, wheeled the mare broadside to the knight. A twist-dart flew from her hand, spinning as the thong wrapped around its feathered shaft unwound. It struck him in the center of his unarmed chest. He went backward over his grey's cruppers.

A quicker-thinking pair of retainers grabbed their count's reins and turned his horse to flee the ambush. No arrows sought him out.

A man half a head shorter than Melodía stepped up by her side. He drew a heavy recurved hornbow to his ear, loosed. A black arrow struck the temple of one of the nobles who were trying to get their liege out of there.

The archer was Karyl Bogomirskiy, dressed in his usual plain, dark robe with his hair in a topknot.

"Shoot him!" Melodía shrieked. "Shoot him, shoot him, shoot him! Guillaume's right in front of you! Why aren't you shooting him?"

He looked at her with an eye cold as a lizard's. "Guilli I can beat," he said. "Salvateur's actually good."

Guillaume seemed reluctant to quit the field. Eyes rolling, his mare was tossing her head, neighing and sidestepping as the knight pulled the reins one way and her rider another. An arrow hit her white rump. As the Providence scouts and woods-runners laughed, she squealed and took off like a startled bouncer at a dead run back toward the Crève Coeur encampment.

A burly figure trudged past Melodía. It was Rob Korrigan, bearded chin sunk to breastbone and glancing neither left nor right. He walked straight to where Pilar lay. He held his long-hafted dinosaur master's axe in his right hand.

A pair of adolescent blue horrors, bolder than their elders or just stupider, had crept back out of the weeds to snatch a few more mouthfuls of meat from the still-warm body of their victim. One turned to face Rob as he approached. It hissed a warning.

He split its face with a viper-strike blow of his axe. The other lunged for him. He smashed in the side of its skull with the back of his axe-head.

Ignoring the two flopping, dying raptors he stopped and looked down at Pilar.

Rob Korrigan had seen many terrible things. Too many to think it was a good idea to look at what the horror pack had done to his lover.

But he made himself do so.

His vision snapped down to a tube. He wasn't aware of his knees giving way until they jarred against the ground.

He managed just to turn his head aside to avoid defiling Pilar's body with his puke.

Someone laid a hand on Melodía's shoulder. She spun, feeling tears fly off her cheeks but with her knife at the ready. She almost recoiled from what she saw.

A woman stood beside her, taller than she was, dressed in a loincloth and a green scrap wound tightly about her breasts. She had a quiver full of green-fletched arrows slung over her shoulder and a shortbow in her hand. The green and brown paint streaked across her face couldn't mask the hideous knife-scarring beneath.

But Stéphanie's green-flecked amber eyes were gentle, as was her husky contralto voice.

"You were very brave," she said. "You faced the horrors with nothing but a knife, and never flinched."

Tears flooded Melodía's eyes. They stung like scalding water.

"Not so brave as she was." She nodded toward Pilar.

"No," the woods-runner. "But then, who is?"

She turned and went back to the woods. Her friend's final words floated to the surface of Melodía's mind: *"The Fae set me to watch over you, Princess. May they protect you now."*

Melodía didn't believe the Fae—the hada—existed. Any more than she did Grey Angels. Nor the Creators themselves, for that matter.

But the Church taught that they existed—and were demons, enemies of the gods. Could Melodía's lifelong companion, her long-neglected friend, really have been a devil-worshipper?

She gave her life for me, Melodía thought. *Would a demon-lover do that?*

She shook her head. *The only thing that matters is that she was truly my friend. And I let her die.*

The horsewoman who had killed the Crève Coeur knight with her dart rode up leading his horse by the reins.

"Come along, Princess," said the woman who had yanked her away from the horror's death-kick. "We have to go. Guilli won't dawdle any longer than it takes to rally a hundred of his knights before howling back after us with blood in his eye. We're firing the field, but that won't keep him long, as pissed as he is."

Melodía heard crackling and smelled smoke. The breeze wasn't stiff but perceptibly blowing back across the field. The weeds were too green to burn readily. The grain-stalks weren't.

She heard moans and cries from out in the weeds, where injured Rangers lay. No one seemed inclined to go and give them final mercy before the slow-moving flames reached them.

Neither did she.

She looked at her rescuer. "Name?" she croaked. Her throat suddenly felt as dry as kiln-fired clay.

"Pardon, Highness?"

"What's your name?" she managed to say. "Please."

"Valérie."

"Thank you, Valérie," she said.

Hands helped boost her into the saddle of the dead noble's bay. Her years of training and experience as an equestrienne took over. No matter how fast the Providence raiding-party fled Count Guillaume's vengeance, she could keep pace and keep the saddle without conscious thought.

Which was good, because as they set off back through the woods Melodía sank at once into a black abyss of sorrow so profound it swallowed even self-reproach.

Rob's thoughts were black, his heart a lump of lead. He sat his borrowed marchadora in even more sacklike style than usual.

The rescue party rode homeward between ripe-grain fields at an easy walk. Scouts hung back to keep an eye on Guillaume—as they had since the instant he rode into the ford across the Lisette heading east. Even armored in just their shirts his men-at-arms weren't liable to ride as fast as the light horse did. Especially after woods-runners had feathered one or two smartly in shoot-and-go ambushes.

"Are you all right?" asked Karyl, who rode beside him on Asal.

After a moment, Rob stirred himself to lift his chin fractionally from his clavicle. "She was just a girl." His voice grated like a rusty hinge.

Karyl said nothing.

Rob continued to ride. Karyl kept saying nothing. At last Rob growled.

"Damn you," he said.

"That's redundant, I suspect."

"And you claim you aren't good at manipulating others."

"I am good at getting results," Karyl said. "Until I fail horribly, and bring death and devastation to all those around me. Keep that in mind, my friend: if you continue to ride at my side, there's only more misery and loss, and worse, ahead."

But those words no more penetrated Rob's gloom than rain the feathers on a galley-bird's back.

He sucked in a long breath.

"When I was young," Rob said, "I had a sister. Alys was her name. She was older than I by a year and a half. She looked out for me when I was a lad. Whenever my stupid tongue got the rest of me in trouble she came to my defense. And far too often that was, for I had even less sense in those days than I do now.

"She was sweet as well as clever, was Alys. And beautiful as a newborn day. There were no feathers she couldn't smooth, no matter how her scapegrace younger brother ruffled them. Everyone loved her.

"Came a twilight, when I was nineteen and she was twenty-four. I remember it all too clearly. We'd parked the wagons for the night, unhitched our nosehorns and set them to graze. A party of four nobles arrived at our caravan, riding striders. Young bucks, the lot, scarcely older than Alys. They'd been out hunting. And drinking freely, that was clear. Their young buckethead blood ran hot.

"Short story made shorter: they saw my sister. They fancied her. They took her."

He had to squeeze his eyes shut. *I don't know why I don't want Himself to see my tears*, he thought, *but that I do not.*

"They dumped her back by the camp in the wee hours of the morning," he said. "For the brag of it, I suppose. She was . . . they'd used her. Badly. She was bleeding. . . ."

He sighed.

"Bleeding from everywhere was my angel, Alys, my sister dear. And her face all bruised and puffy. Even her nose was broken. She looked me in the eye and said, 'Rob, don't mourn me, please. Find your own beauty in life.'"

They rode a while longer, their horses' hooves clopping out of synchronization. They entered a pine-wood where green- and yellow-feathered climbers chased each other screeching through boughs. The men and women who rode behind stayed oddly silent, their earlier exhilaration subdued by reaction and late-afternoon heat.

"What really happened?" Karyl asked.

"She died thrashing and moaning and never spoke a coherent word that anybody heard," Rob snarled. "What d'you think happened?"

He turned and spat into the brush by the path, where green flies clustered on the body of a small dead thing.

"The rest, though, that was true as Creators' Word, in every syllable," Rob said. "You've no reason to credit that, I know. I've told you many a tall tale of my past, and I'm going to do again. But that was real. That's how it happened with my sister. I loved her, failed her, and lost her. To the stinking nobles."

He shuddered with the effort of holding down the passion that grew huge inside him. "And now I've gone and done it again."

"That's why you hate them," Karyl said.

"Aye. Everything I love, the blue-blood bastards take from me."

"They're good at that. It's what they do."

"And yet you're a noble yourself."

"And you see the good I've done." The bitterness in Karyl's voice matched that in Rob's throat.

Rob shook his head. "Karyl Bogomirskiy, I'll never understand you."

"That makes two of us."

They rode for a time in silence. Karyl had packed Melodía, much chastened, off to the Garden villa—protected by an armed escort, but not under guard. Rob protested: how could they know she hadn't intended to sell them out?

Karyl asked what coin the Count of Crève Coeur could possibly offer an Imperial Princess? Sanctuary, perhaps—but even as naïve as Melodía had proven herself to be, she knew perfectly well that if the Empire demanded Guillaume turn her over, he'd have no choice but comply or face attainder. With the best will in the world—which few had ever accused the Comte Crève Coeur of possessing—there was no way he'd do that for a stranger who was no kin of his.

And the Princess had proven laughably naïve indeed. Had one a sufficiently cruel sense of humor.

Despite her shock and grief at the enormity she had brought upon her friends, Melodía had kept herself under strict control as she replied lucidly and fully to Karyl's interrogation. Nor could even Rob Korrigan, who had slight reason to give her slack, deny her contrition was real.

She had, she explained with her face ashen and fingers writhing together like snakes, intended to try talking to the enemy in hopes of finding common ground; and failing that, to appeal to his better nature.

Unfortunately, Guillaume had none.

Karyl looked to Rob.

"It's time," he said. "Let loose your own human raptor-packs. Have them run down Guillaume's scouts and spies and foragers. Kill them hard, but kill them fast."

"All of them?"

"All. I want Guillaume blind. Completely. We can't stop him foraging altogether. We can make him send out big, slow parties, clanking with armored escorts."

Rob nodded. "My kids'll be glad to hear those orders."

"Well, tell the woods-runners to restrain their more . . . elaborate impulses when it comes to paying off the Rangers. It's not that I'll waste any tears on them, though atrocity isn't how I make war. But we don't have time for games."

"We should be square there, then," Rob said. "Lad Gaétan's been ever so civilizing an influence on Stéphanie. And her brother does what she says, I notice."

"I should talk to the boy, then. I don't want her getting too civilized on me. Otherwise she'll be no more use than that poor pampered little fool of a princess."

Rob started to chuckle. It came out a grunt.

"I still say we rescued the wrong girl."

"Tell your scouts, especially the light-horse, to take as few risks as possible. That said, the more they sting Guilli's broad ass, the better. Have them burn a few tents, run off some coursers, put arrows in a few of his war-duckbills. They won't do much real harm. But that's not the point. The point is, anger makes people stupid."

"Bucketheads are stupid to start with, Captain."

"So they are. But I want them as stupid as theoretically possible. Especially the Count. And don't forget—Salvateur is anything but stupid."

"Oh, aye," Rob said. "That he is, the black Sasanach rogue."

"So then, tell your people that's how much I want them to annoy Count Guillaume," Karyl said. "Until he's angrier than Salvateur's voice of reason is persuasive."

Despite himself Rob found himself laughing. Longer and louder than strictly called for, perhaps.

At last he got hold of himself. Wiping a tear—mostly of mirth—from his eye, he shook his head in admiration.

"Ah, Karyl Bogomirskiy," he said. "They ought to rename the old song for you. *You're* a man you don't meet every day."

"No doubt Paradise is a better place for it," Karyl said. "Now, go. We'll face Crève Coeur tomorrow, most likely. And when we do, I want him mad enough to charge Big Sally head to head."

Chapter 18

***Dinero*, Money**—While regional names vary, our coinage is standardized throughout the Empire of Nuevaropa: trono of 32 grams of gold, equaling 20 pesetas in value; Corona, 16 grams gold, equaling 10 pesetas; Imperial, 8 grams gold equaling 5 pesetas; peseta, 32 grams of silver, valuing 1/20 trono or 4 pesos; peso, 8 grams silver, equaling 1/4 of a peseta; and the Centimo, 8 grams copper, valued at 1/100 of a peso.

—A PRIMER TO PARADISE FOR THE IMPROVEMENT OF YOUNG MINDS

"All right," Rob said in disgust. "You win."

He flipped a silver peso to Karyl. The other caught it without so much as glancing around.

They stood on a low rise with their army around them. Rob's Traveler fancy made it a barrow, soil mounded over some ancient battle's dead. In front of them a valley of tall green grass and blue and purple wildflowers sloped gently down to where a line of tall, feathery-topped reeds marked the course of a small stream half a kilometer away. Then the land angled up again for perhaps eleven hundred more meters to a ridge, taller and sharper than this one.

It was no superstitious fear of ghosts that rippled a chill down Rob's spine. From the woods that crowned the ridgeline dinosaur knights appeared. Steel chamfrons glittered in midmorning sun that already stung Rob's exposed arms through a scrim of cloud. Pennons fluttered from upraised lances, blue and green.

Crève Coeur's colors.

"So you were right, my Captain," Rob said. "It really was that easy to bait Guilli into coming to us."

"So far."

The slaughter of his beloved hunting horror pack, along with a handful of Rangers and some of his favorites—to say nothing of the personal humiliation of having it done right under his tuber-shaped nose—had stung the Count's pride the way a woods-runner arrow had stung his horse's fine white fanny. He had rousted out his army and marched them east toward Providence town straightaway.

They had made slow going. Naturally enough, since the good Count refused to leave the vast unwieldy tail of baggage wagons his buckethead vassals and allies dragged behind them. Rob's scouts had feted them en route with showers of taunts and arrows. Although delivered at such a range that the one did about as much harm as the other, they did what they were meant to do.

No matter how pissed their commander was, the invaders were not about to march all night, especially through the deep forest they found themselves in when the sun sank away in the east. They bivouacked. Not all their sentries had survived the darkness. A dozen or so tents and supply wagons had gone up in flames.

Again, no more than wasp-stings. But Guillaume and his troops had not passed a restful night. Nor was Guilli in a calm, contemplative mood when he marched again in the morning.

Light-horse dart attacks and arrows from covert had promptly met the Brokenhearts. Guillaume pressed with determined fury in the very direction he was stung from the hardest. In his eagerness to get to grips with his foe he even forsook the wide, well-tended Western Road, now two kilometers south, for what was basically a goat track.

"How could he be so easy to bait?" Rob demanded. "Guilli's a dolt, right enough. But Salvateur, now—he's got a long head on him, as our Northmen brothers say."

That was bitter Irlandés irony: the wild Northmen with their sea-serpent drawn dragon-boats were neither subjects of the Empire nor its friends. For the better art of a century they had held the islands north of Ayr-Land, which territory they traded with constantly and raided barely less often. They were as cruel a curse upon the Ayrysh as their Anglysh overlords—almost.

"Crève Coeur's injured pride moans louder than Salvateur can speak wisdom," Karyl said. "Give the Count his due: his best move has always been to find us and destroy us, so totally and viciously the province loses not just the means, but even the will to resist. He wants to fight us, wherever we stand. And after all, he knows in his heart he'll win."

And Karyl smiled. Rob fervently hoped Karyl would never smile that way while thinking of him.

The day was fine. The sun shone halfway up the sky, an intense white round in the overcast. The Shield Mountains made a jagged blue rampart away to their right, seeming deceptively close. The breeze blew stiff and from the north, across the shallow valley, covering most of the army's thousand noises, mutter and rumble and clink of metal, with the rustle of grass and scrub and its own native hiss and boom. It also brought Rob and Karyl the musty smells of the war-dinosaurs mustered to the right of their vantage point. Karyl ran a clean camp, meaning that was the worst smell they were likely to encounter. Until blood and even less savory substances began to spill, of course.

The smell of autumn flowers held a curious note of cinnamon.

"I thought no plan survived first contact with the enemy," Rob said with a certain sourness.

"We've not made contact," Karyl said. "Yet."

He had arrayed the Providential foot in ranks down the valley's gentle slope, athwart the enemy's path. Most sat among the yellow wildflowers with their weapons beside them. A murmur and agitated motion rippled over them like those flowers in the breeze as they saw the enemy knights appear.

His senses honed keen by the need to follow audience reactions, Rob detected both eagerness and apprehension among the waiting men and women. Peasants and townsfolk simply did not stand against noblemen mounted on steel-clad horses. Much less three-tonne armored monsters.

They're a fearful sight, for true, Rob thought, even as his dinosaur master heart thrilled to the beauty of the thirty or so war-duckbills lumbering slowly down the distant ridge toward them at a two-legged walk. The chivalry's coursers, winged out either side, were another thing: heavy cavalry scared him to the marrow. He knew the dinosaurs were deadlier, that a hadrosaur could trample a fully caparisoned warhorse almost as easily as a naked man, and smash them three at a time with its tail.

But war-dinosaurs were to Rob as the sea to a mariner: he knew their dangers, and respected them well. But they were still his element. Horses were alien.

Little Nell stood on the barrow's backslope, cropping ferns beneath the eye of a waifish farm-girl with a mop of brown hair. Rob had a proper staff now, dinosaur-grooms youthful and eager, whom he terrorized joyously, if without the genuine mean-spiritedness that had seemed to animate his own old mentor. Morrison was a Scocés dinosaur master, scarcely older than Rob was now, who had fists like sledgehammers and used them as his primary teaching-tools. Karyl's dinosaurs, at least, were as ready for war as they could be, and Rob knew with certainty that would have soothed him better had he seen any other good news at all.

Rob's axe Wanda, a round shield, and a steel hat hung from either side of the saddle on Nell's steep-sided back. Rob wore a heavy cuirass of sackbut side-leather with rows of black-iron bosses on the front, and divided skirts of enameled leather with smaller bosses on them to cover the fronts of his otherwise bare thighs. They chafed something fierce, especially the breastplate's stiff armholes and the upper ends of his hobnailed boots. But they'd help keep stray bits of metal from wandering into his own personal body when the shitstorm came down. He was just glad he wasn't boiling like the knights in their steel shells.

Absently Karyl tucked the coin Rob had tossed him in a pouch hung from his sword-belt. He wore a stout tan jack of hornface hide and a visorless burgonet, basically an open-faced steel helmet with a bill to protect his eyes from down-bound mischief. A conventional cross-hilted arming-sword rode in a scabbard at his waist. He wore loose white silk trousers and tall boots. In all, he could have been an especially well-off rider in Rob's light-horse scouts.

"You don't really care about the money, do you?" Rob said. "What kind of a mercenary are you, anyway?"

Sergeants began shouting the militia to its feet. On the right flank their meager force of a dozen dinosaur knights bestrode their war-hadrosaurs, which began to bob their gorgeously crested heads and blow booming dulcian greetings to their distant kin. On their left waited fifty men-at-arms on horseback. In between half a thousand pikemen and women rose grumbling and hefting their unwieldy weapons, four meters of sturdy ash haft each tipped with half a meter of polished, pointed steel.

Out front stood a hundred or so men and women with shortbows. Most wore no more than loincloths, and none of them armor. With them waited twenty-five arbalesters, armed with powerful but slow to operate cranequin-cocked heavy crossbows, and fifty house-archers in mail. To guard them a hedge of Faerie-poles had been driven into the turf: stakes with sharpened ends slanted forward.

Behind the main body, on the back of the rise, waited an armored infantry reserve: about a hundred fifty house-shields and mercenaries. Fifty had horses to carry them where they were needed, though they would fight afoot. On the flats beyond the supply wagons were parked in a round mass, with the outermost chained together tongue to tailgate, guarded by camp followers and their own drovers armed with slings, spears, and axes. Though many were children, and none trained combatants, they'd fight with amateur ferocity against any who tried to plunder the baggage.

And in front of all, dead in the middle, stood six mighty dinosaurs with wicker fighting-castles armored with thick leather slabs on their backs, tossing great heads to challenge foes they dimly glimpsed. Wicked steel caps glittered on the tips of their long brow horns. Chamfrons molded of the waxed hides of their smaller hornface cousins protected their faces, as metal ones did warhorse and hadrosaur.

"Shall I give us a song, then?" Rob asked, unlimbering the implement he had slung across his back: his trusty lute.

"If you think it'll do good," Karyl said.

Rob strode out through the stakes to stand beside the three-horns. A strum of his lute brought eyes to him. He began playing and singing "A Rasty Old Bastard Am I." The song was a tavern favorite, penned years ago by one Rob Korrigan. By the time he finished the whole army seemed to be singing and laughing at its ludicrously obscene lyrics.

Rob wasn't sure what the highborn men and women on the mounted flanks made of it—except for Baron Côme, whose lusty baritone rang out clearly across the whole rowdy chorus.

When the song ended, Karyl rode out beside Rob on Asal. He sat for a moment gazing at his little army with those dark, long-flying dragon eyes.

"Men and women," he called. *For such a soft-spoken man*, Rob marveled, *he can surely make his voice ring like trumpets*. "Children of Providence! Today you face great danger—and great opportunity.

"You know what we fight for. Your neighbors and loved ones. Your homes. Your crops and livestock. Your livelihoods. Your lives.

"Some of you live far from this field. Remember that here stands your one and only chance to save everything that you hold dear.

"Not all of us will live to see the sun set in the east. But if you do as we've taught you, and above all, if you fight as if you stood in the doorway of your own house with your children at your backs, then you will prevail. Whether we stand or fall, those we fight for shall live safe and live free!"

The army erupted in wild cheers. Even most of the nobles and their retainers joined in. Only a few sat on their mounts in dour postures.

"So what's it to be, then?" Rob asked softly when the plaudits subsided. The Crève Coeur montadores were less than a kilometer away. They were also, as Karyl had intended, riding well in advance of their own foot, which had just now begun to appear on the far height. "Do we really have a chance, then, Captain?"

"Yes," Karyl said. "Our people protect their own. Crève Coeur only brings serfs, uprooted and unhappy. And mere warriors."

"Mere warriors?"

"A warrior fights for his appetites: lust for loot and rape and blood, the easier, the better. And for his tribal chieftain. No matter how much he tells himself he serves, when his blood runs hot he'll do anything in single-minded pursuit of his own personal glory."

"So what are you, then, if not a warrior?"

"A professional. That's why we always won, the Legion and I."

His voice was haunted. "We fought as the craftsmen and women we were. Until you scattered us with your clever stratagem. And that orange-haired bastard stabbed us in the back."

"So there's a difference, then, between a warrior, and a professional?" Rob asked. He knew his friend for a master of his chosen craft—but all the same, he didn't want him distracted by unhappy memories.

Briskly businesslike again, Karyl uncased his hornbow, already strung and bent into a D-shape, from its sea-monster skin sheath slung from Asal's saddle.

"Professional soldiers fight for their lives and for their comrades. For victory. And for pay."

Slipping a jade ring, worn smooth with use, over his thumb, Karyl tested the tautness of his bowstring evidently he found it to his satisfaction.

"And what of glory, then?" Rob asked.

Karyl laughed. "That's the mark of a professional: to know there's no such thing."

"But pay, then—really? You don't care about gold any more than that coin I threw you. Would you've even noticed if it was copper instead of the promised silver? What kind of mercenary are you, anyway, Karyl Vladevich?"

"There's other coin than gold and silver," Karyl said. "There were things I'd rather have devoted my whole life to, my friend, than perfecting my skills at combat at every scale. But that's where life has brought me.

"Now, to fight with all my will and skill gives purpose to my life. Or its illusion, at any rate. It'll do until I finish my quest."

"And what quest's that?" Even with death literally marching down on him from behind Rob was entranced by this glimpse into his companion's tortured soul. He knew it would be fleeting, and felt compelled to grasp all he could get.

"I seek *answers*," Karyl said softly. "Why am I here? Why are *we* here, men and women, on this world Paradise where we seem as out of place as a titan in a royal hall?"

He shrugged. "Or I seek the peace of death. And that's let me down a few times already."

Shifting the bow to his left he stretched his right hand down toward

Rob. After a blank moment Rob reached out to clasp him forearm to forearm. Karyl's felt as if it were wound in steel wire.

"Now it begins," Karyl said. "May the luck of the Irlandés attend you, my friend."

Rob laughed sourly.

"It's better luck than that we want," he said. "Or it's well and truly fucked we are."

Chapter 19

Gancho, Hook-horn—*Einiosaurus procurvicornis.* A hornface (Ceratopsian dinosaur) of Anglaterra, where they are a popular dray beast: quadrupedal, herbivorous, 6 meters long, 2 meters high, 2 tonnes. Named for their massive forward-hooking nasal armament. Two longer, thinner horns project from the tops of their neck-frills. Placid unless provoked.

—THE BOOK OF TRUE NAMES

As the Crève Coeur knights freshened their pace to a trot, Karyl drew his sword and flourished it high. Red-faced apprentices from Providence town blew trumpets as if trying to make up for lack of skill with sheer enthusiasm. From the woods that anchored either flank of the Providence pikes rode a hundred light-horsemen and women. Forty had woods-runners mounted behind, shortbows in hand. The scouts swarmed toward the enemy like eager bees.

Rob watched from the top of the rise. Beside him stood Gaétan, whose spoke-frill Zhubin was now tethered alongside his boon friend Little Nell with his beak buried in a flowering bush. The young merchant wore a plain cuirass today to guard his still-tender chest. He carried his own hornbow strung, and a quiver slung over his steel-clad back.

Gaétan and Eamonn Copper commanded the foot. The reserve of armored professional infantry was led by Côme's chief lieutenant Mora Regina, a beautiful immigrant from Ruybrasil. She was an aloof one, with skin the color of creamed coffee and sapphire eyes, and not at all impressed with Rob Korrigan's gallantries. Which was just as well, he told himself; she stood a head taller than he on those long, lean legs, and that always made for uncomfortable coupling, in his experience.

Rob's role in the coming battle was to take reports from his scouts, for what use they might be. And, mainly, try not to die.

Thirty Crève Coeur dinosaur knights came on, a hundred heavy cavalry at their backs. Out front rode Count Guillaume, resplendent in gilded plate with his arms on the breast. His dinosaur was a gold-bellied blue sackbut. Beside him Salvateur rode a striking black Parasaurolophus, brindled in cream. His armor was matte natural metal, his insignia black and gold. From the saddle-cantle behind each man rose a standard displaying his arms, and blue and green pennons fidgeted from every upheld lance.

A hundred meters shy of the Crève Coeur dinosaurs' snouts, the light-horse paused. Pillion-riding woods-runners jumped down into waist-high green grass. Rob's mad young riders pressed on.

Flushed and flying high after a night spent massacring the last of the Crève Coeur Rangers and foragers, and a morning harrying the main body, they felt no fatigue. Nor fear, nor—Rob realized with a jolt to his heart—common sense. They were young, and full of themselves, and felt immortal. And due for a hard and sudden dose of reality, his dear, bold boys and girls. Had he the luxury he'd have wept for them in advance.

Time enough for that afterward, he thought, *if the Lady will that I survive.*

The light-horse swarmed up both sides of the enemy column, closing within meters of dinosaur knights to hurl javelins, twist-darts, and mockery. The woods-runners shot their shortbows, taking care not to hit their comrades. The knights had to trust their armor and endure: neither dinosaurs nor the heavy-laden horses behind could catch the impertinent low-born riders.

Crève Coeur house-archers would have slaughtered the light-horse, in their thin leather armor. Too bad for the invaders they were still trudging down the Western Road half a klick behind.

A good terremoto would scatter light-horse and woods-runners—tumble some heels-over-fundament with blood streaming from their ears, maybe even kill a few. But Guillaume wouldn't dignify these vermin with such a noble weapon. Besides, the Cryless Cry was best reserved for a foe that offered more than mere annoyance.

Which was all Rob's riders could muster. Neither javelins nor shortbow-driven arrows could penetrate good steel plate at any range. They couldn't even pierce the war-duckbills' thick hides.

But their barbed heads hurt the monsters. Great-crested war-dinosaurs trumpeted pain. Dinosaur knight ranks churned as mounts flinched and reared.

So huge and powerful were the duckbills that cohesion meant far less to them than even the heaviest cavalry. But disorder put dinosaur knights at a bad disadvantage against other dinosaur knights—and rendered them even more vulnerable to Triceratops horns.

What did tell wasn't minor pangs to sackbuts and morions, but the pricking of the thunder-titan egos of their noble riders. Especially Count Guillaume's. They were the real targets of the barrage, whether pointed with words or metal.

Karyl waved his arming-sword once more. The trumpeters blew a new signal. The shortbow archers with the main body of the Providence army left the safety of their sharpened stakes. They ran out a hundred meters ahead of the three-horns to loose their own volleys of arrows and jeers at the enemy knights.

The missiles fell harmlessly without even reaching the stream, now halfway between the armies. They weren't meant to strike the enemy. Like the pinprick efforts of the scouts, they were sheer effrontery—and that was the point. Rude and ragged boys and girls, town 'prentices alongside peasant farmers, shouldn't dare raise hands against their betters. It was an affront to Nature and to Torrey's sacred Order.

Some turned and bared their rumps to the knights.

The Providence light-horse kept swirling on the Crève Coeur dinosaur-riders' flanks, tantalizingly just out of reach. Rob watched a feathered twist-dart bounce off the shield of no less than Count Guillaume himself.

Meanwhile the woods-runners kept popping up from the grass like inquisitive compitos to shoot and vanish again.

The invading knights' patience snapped. Rob heard Crève Coeur voices shout in fury muffled by visors shut tight against the missiles. Giant-roweled silver spurs raked garish hadrosaur flanks. The duckbills tucked mittenlike paws to their chests and sprang into a bounding bipedal lope.

Baron Salvateur tried to hold his comrades back. Guillaume was having none of that. Bellowing in rage, he almost ran his chief lieutenant's black sackbut down with his blue duckbill in his determination to keep out in front of his rapidly advancing dinosaur knights. Behind them the chivalry urged their horses to a canter.

The Brokenhearts were nearing where a meander of deeper green among the weeds marked the stream's hidden course. Still over five hundred meters from the Providence lines, they were too far away to charge effectively. Their anger drove them to rush straight ahead as fast as they could without spending their mounts. They were panting to get in range where they could charge home against the peasant mass that stood obscenely defying them.

The light-riders pulled away to give the bucketheads ample room. No woods-runners were to be seen. Rob felt no concern for them. They'd practiced hiding from highborn riders since they were weaned.

Terror and exaltation warred inside his chest as the glittering avalanche of steel and scale, color and noise, hurtled toward him. The four ranks of Providence pike-bearers before the barrow shifted and muttered nervously. He hoped they'd stand. He at least had faced the terrible power of armored knights and dinosaurs before. The militia couldn't possibly have imagined what it would really be like.

For their part the shortbow archers laughed and jested with each other as they came trotting back to the shelter of their Faerie-poles. Some kept catcalling at the foe, as if this was all some merry village festival, and the onrushing three-tonne war-dinosaurs no more than pantomimes of sticks and silk with drunken revelers within.

Rob hoped not too many would die of disillusionment.

But the bucketheads have themselves a surprise coming too, so he thought with evil anticipation.

Just as, with a splashing audible above all the colossal hammer and clank and bugling, the proud Count Guillaume and his thirty dinosaur knights plunged into the marsh the tall stream-growth was hiding.

Muck sprayed high as the ramparts of a modest in rainbow-struck arcs. The duckbills reared, threw back gloriously crested heads to bellow their surprise. Several less-alert knights actually bounced against suddenly upraised necks thick as tree trunks.

Though slowed to a plod, the hadrosaurs continued. Despite being weighed-down by a good five hundred kilos of rider and their own armor, either heavy woven caparisons or thick dinosaur-leather plates that guarded breast and sides, a duckbill's big splay-toed hind feet could cope with mud.

Following hotly, the heavy-horse didn't fare so well. Hooves plunged as if pile-driven, deep into mud. Coursers shrieked as legs snapped. Knights tumbled over flying-maned necks to land with slogging splashes.

The rear ranks slammed into the stalled front ones with the sliding crash of two heavy-cavalry armies meeting at full charge. And to much the same effect. More equine legs broke. Horses and men were slammed into the bog. Then the ones who knocked them down tripped over *them*, and all got trampled by following riders who couldn't stop their mounts in time. The marsh erupted in screams and mud and thrashing.

Hornbow in hand, Karyl led his three-horns forward at a walk. The monsters bellowed belligerence. As dinosaurs, they had a simple outlook: *disturbance equaled possible danger.*

In Their wisdom the Creators had not gifted three-horns with a springer's speed, to run away from threats. Nor a tyrant's teeth, nor a titan's impregnable size. They had instead given Triceratops horridus a huge, strong body, equipped with a natural bony shield and lances.

To Rob in the—painfully temporary—safety of his imagined barrow mound, Karyl looked like a child on its stick horse alongside the ten-tonne behemoths.

Karyl drew, aimed, loosed. A dinosaur knight with a red and white lozenge pattern painted on shield and helmet toppled from a sackbut's saddle. With a rattle of steel bows the arbalesters loosed a volley from the fighting castles strapped to the three-horn's three-meter high backs. A grey and gold morion, hit through the brain, toppled thrashing into the swamp.

Lucky shot! thought Rob. *Or not, if it's your leg crushed beneath the beast.*

The Providence heavy riders swept forward to the attack: dinosaurry on Rob's right, cavalry on the left. The hill vibrated beneath his boots. His heart played fanfares in his chest, though his mind knew their numbers were pitifully few to throw against Count Guillaume's might.

The Crève Coeur dinosaurs were beginning to emerge from the marsh onto solid land. But they straggled badly now. With the oncoming three-horns fixing their front, the Providence dinosaur knights had a chance to hit them in the flank.

And unlike the shortbows, Karyl's recurved Ovdan bow and the cross-bows could punch through armor. Rob saw another dinosaur knight fall. Others cried out in pain as bolts struck through plate into their legs, and pinned shields to arms.

Then he saw something he liked a good deal less. That canny goblin Salvateur hadn't joined the headlong race into the quagmire. And now he was using his brindled black sackbut like a herd dog, driving the surviving cavalry out of the marsh, south to where it narrowed down to simple stream. They'd lost over a score of coursers to the inanimate ambush.

Which meant they still outnumbered the Providence men and women at arms three to two.

A fresh and terrible scream brought Rob's attention back to the field's middle. Big Sally, the Triceratops herd-queen, had buried her brow-horns in a morion's unarmored white belly. The duckbill dabbed brown forepaws uselessly at its tormentor's massive head. Its rider toppled backward to the ground. His cries and likely he himself died as a purple and gold dappled sackbut trod promptly on his head.

The three-horns were the most bellicose herd-beasts known, far more than even the wild nosehorns native to the Tyrant's Head. Trikes rejoiced in slaughter as much as any great meat-eater. More: a wild matador or tyrant fought solely to feed. Triceratops fought to defend itself and its herd-mates—and, or so Rob felt sure, for fun.

The other five trikes plodded into the disorganized herd of hadrosaurs, goring legs and spilling guts. Rob's eyes brimmed with tears to see such marvelous beasts suffering so. Yet at the same time his skin seemed to burn, not just from the poorly cloud-filtered sun on his confounded sweaty, chafing armor, but with pride at the sheer power of the living forts he had helped Karyl bring to battle today.

He saw an arbalester lanced by a knight on an ochre morion. She dropped her crossbow to grab at the haft through her belly. The Brokenheart didn't let go of his lance, then, as he should. Instead he thrust it deeper, cruelly driving his victim back against far wicker wall of the fighting-castle. One of her comrades shot the knight; Rob saw him reel. Or her—their breastplates were the same, and a woman's lesser strength was no true disadvantage for a warrior whose weapon was a dinosaur. Another crossbowman took up an axe and began whaling on the lancer's armor with a smithy sound.

Rob's guts seemed to bubble, then, and the skin bunched at the back of his neck. As they closed with the enemy, the Providence war-duckbills had bellowed a mass terremoto. Musician that he was, Rob marveled that a thing could be both unheard and loud: he felt its pressure like palms on his cheeks and thumbs in his eyes, and it was aimed away from him.

The Crève Coeur dinosaurs screamed and shied away from the silent sound-blast. Several toppled kicking and lashing out blindly with their immense tails. The knights' armor protected them from most of the terremoto's force. Small good it did them, with their mounts stunned or thrown into uncontrollable panic.

The Providence dinosaur knights charged home. Butchery ensued. For all their numbers, the Crève Coeur knights were helpless, crushed between plodding trikes and sprinting duckbills.

Not so the chivalry. For all his undoubtedly black character, Salvateur was a wizard field captain: against all odds he had his seventy or eighty heavy-horse forming to meet the fifty Providence lancers closing fast on them.

We've still a chance, though, Rob thought. Once they'd goaded the Crève Coeur bucketheads into a rushing angrily into the hidden marsh, his light-horse had been instructed to keep biting them behind. Cavalry coursers were armored lightly in the rear. A few javelins stuck in equine rumps could go a long way to keeping the Crève Coeur knights in disarray. Which would mean, numerical advantage or no, the concerted Providence charge would shatter them like glass on an anvil.

He looked up and away, past the seethe of dinosaurs and horsemen to his own riders.

Just in time to see them vanish into the trees on the far ridgetop, bound for the Creators alone knew where.

Salvateur's rallied knights counter-charged the Providence horse. Steel masses crashed together. For a moment their impact drowned out the abattoir racket of the dinosaur scrum. Then in what seemed little more than the space of a few heartbeats the Providence knights broke, their horses racing back east with eyes rolled and manes and tails streaming.

Gaétan was yelling at the infantry to make ready. Under-officers ran along the front rank, trying to ensure all the pikes were pointing more-or-less the right way forward. The front rank knelt with the butts of their long spears grounded and the heads angled up. The soldiers behind them held their pikes level at their waists, the third rank at their shoulders, and the last line overhead.

An Imperial tercio would have several more ranks standing behind to take the place of those in front who fell. But a tercio was five or six times as strong, and the Nodosaurs professionals as painstakingly trained to their tasks as any other craftsfolk, carpenters or masons or blacksmiths. Whereas the Providence pikes were handled by hastily schooled amateurs, whose only hope was to stand firm against the terror the wave of armored horsemen bearing down on them sent bursting into every chest and yammering madness into every skull. . . .

Rob ran to Little Nell and climbed aboard. She never paused in her self-appointed task of eating a small spiky-leaved shrub down to the ground. He ran his arm through the leather sleeve fastened to the inside of his round wooden shield, gripped the leather sling. He put his steel hat on his head—swore as sun-heated metal scorched his fingers—and hefted Wanda. He found her weight but moderately reassuring.

Not even Salvateur's skill could get the Crève Coeur chivalry into proper order again after their melee with the Providential gendarmes, brief and victorious as it was. Clearly, they didn't care. Common foot soldiers always ran—the bucketheads made an exception in their minds for the Nodosaurs, Rob knew; something to do with the fact that noble second sons and daughters (a few, anyway) joined the browned-iron Imperial ranks.

They knew they'd win. The bastards always did.

But that doesn't mean I've got to sit by and let them have their way, Rob thought. Sucking down a deep draught of air, he began to bellow the ballad he'd written on the road back from the bloody debacle of Blueflowers, which the minds of the Providence militia-folk had since turned to a song of triumph:

"*Now hear me sing*,

"*Of a wondrous thing—*"

The Providence missileers let fly. Two horses in the front rank went down, the steel peytrels that protected their chests struck through by crossbow quarrels. At least one courser stumbled over a fallen mate, rolling over and over and crushing its rider. Rob thought to see another saddle emptied by the bolts, or even two. But there weren't many arbalesters. And though the archers' arrows fell thickly as raindrops among the gendarmes they did about the same amount of actual damage.

"*When men and women, though their birth was base*,

"*Nevertheless still dared to face—*"

As the knights approached the Faerie poles, archers and arbalesters scattered, streaming north and south across the front of the pike array. They had to flee neither fast nor far; the Crève Coeur chivalry weren't interested in them. A few, perhaps the bolder and the more timid alike, crouched behind the Faerie-poles.

"*The iron knights of Brokenheart*,

"*That day on Blueflowers field!*"

The knights put their coursers to the gallop and dropped their lances level. They wove easily between the stakes, which weren't sown thickly enough to prevent their passing. That hadn't been practicable in the time they had to prepare. It did reduce their cohesion, slowed them ever so slightly. That made them no less terrifying to Rob, whose pulse thundered in his ears.

A few riders speared archers shrieking from behind the Faerie-poles. The rest stayed fixed on the infuriating and inviting target behind: half a thousand mere peasants with long sticks.

Rob heard Gaétan's bow twang. A knight in green-enameled armor dropped from the saddle of a lathered blood bay.

He let his song end. No one was listening to him anymore. Whatever good it could do, it had done.

"This is fucking gonna hurt," he said aloud to no one in particular.

The steel-shod tide reached the pikes.

Chapter 20

Dinosauría, **Dinosaurry**—A military formation of dinosaur knights—as distinct from horse-mounted knights, or cavalry. All but irresistible at the charge, the dinosaurry are the main weapon of decision in Nuevaropan land warfare.

—A PRIMER TO PARADISE FOR THE IMPROVEMENT OF YOUNG MINDS

For the whole ride back to Providence, Melodía's heart had steeped in cold shit, as if sunk to the bottom of a cavern-sized cesspool. But when she saw the whole of the Garden—*what my idiocy's left alive of them*, anyway, she thought in a wail—gathered before the blue château gates in the twilight to greet her, her heart sank and chilled and shriveled even more.

She had scarcely registered when, a few kilometers up the Chausée de l'Ouest from the town, the smallest of her four-rider escort had booted her chestnut gelding to a run to carry word of their coming to the château ahead of them. The other three, two boys and a girl, none older than Melodía if indeed as old, continued at the sedate pace they'd maintained since Karyl had dispatched them. They treated her, as they had all along, as if she was an unfortunate child—possibly one with eggshell skin.

To her relief, one thing they didn't treat her as was a traitor. What they thought her purpose in going to seek audience with Count Guillaume was, she had no notion. They hadn't spoken to her beyond necessities.

From the pitying glances her escorts had cast her way, and the hushed tones in which they conversed on subjects other than how much they hated missing the big fight with Guilli, she gathered that Valérie and the rest who had been in on her rescue had told her of the state they'd found her in, desperately facing down the Count's own horror pack. And of Pilar's horrible death.

The party reined to a halt a few paces short of the quietly waiting crowd. Without anyone saying a word, Melodía swung down from the saddle of her borrowed mount, a buckskin High Ovdan pony, with long black bangs hanging in its eyes and a surprisingly placid disposition. Overhead the clouds were breaking into long horsetail streaks, white or pink, across a sky that shaded east to west from turquoise to a deep blue. The air smelled sweet with freshly cut hay in a nearby field. From somewhere a bird trilled.

It was the hardest thing she ever remembered, making herself stand erect, square her shoulders, and walk right up to the grim-faced Bogardus. Lady Violette stood by his side, the sunset breeze molding her thin white gown to her slim body. Absolon had been her close friend and occasional lover as well as ally, Melodía knew.

I'd rather face the horrors, without even the false hope of Pilar's knife, Melodía thought.

But she made herself do it. Then, face-to-face, she tried to meet Bogardus's gaze. She couldn't. Instead she dropped to a knee and grabbed the purple-trimmed hem of his simple grey smock.

"I'm sorry," she said. "I killed them. I killed them all. It was all my fault."

And the tears erupted, and dissolved her like lava.

She felt two strong hands on her arms. She quailed. What would he do to her? What could he do to her that was one-tenth the punishment she had deserved?

He hoisted her to her feet, with that often-surprising strength of his—she couldn't bear to remember just how she'd learned of it. She raised her face, then, made herself blink away the tears, and look squarely into Bogardus's face.

He smiled.

"We know you acted out of love for us," he said, "however mistakenly you did it. We are in a war, and sadly, there are casualties in war. You are welcome here, as always."

"We're only glad you made it back to us safely," Violette said, with curious intensity.

Melodía scarcely noticed. Because Bogardus enfolded her in his powerful arms, and cradled her against the rock of his chest, and she surrendered to a sorrow that seemed to flow from the coldest depths of Paradise.

Irresistible, an avalanche of muscle and gaily painted steel tipped with fluttering pennons and death, the Crève Coeur cavalry thundered down on the Providence pike-ranks. And stopped.

Neither horses nor dinosaurs were intellectual giants. Rob knew it; everybody knew it. But they were living creatures, and the tendency of such is to do their level best to continue to *go on* living.

Neither horses nor dinosaurs would, unless panicked completely senseless, dash themselves to bags of bone-shards against immovable objects, or what they took for same. Nor were these coursers, exhaustively and expertly war-trained though they were, about to impale themselves on a four-deep hedge of iron thorns.

So . . . they refused.

Of course most of the horses running behind the front couldn't see the obstacle: no one was going to confuse a horse's vision with a long-flying dragon's. So just as had happened when they bogged down in the mire, the rear ranks piled into the ones who had shied and halted meters short of the pike-heads. Which had the effect of driving most of them into the pike-heads.

The force of the impact of dozens of heavy, powerful equine bodies physically drove the Providence line back into an irregular wave. Some of the kneeling front rank had to let go their weapons and jump back to avoid being crushed.

But both sides instantly discovered a very important fact: unlike most weapons, a steel pike-head backed by four meters and four kilos of hardwood shaft would penetrate the finest plate—whether a knight's cuirass or a horse's barding.

Horses and humans screamed as the pikes plunged deep into their torsos. The ones that had been braced against the ground did the worst execution. Not only since they didn't depend on mere human mass and muscle to stay firm, but because some of them actually angled up under the horses' chest-armor.

Perhaps it was Rob's perfervid imagination—which, as a jongleur, was generally his stock in trade, if less in demand for a dinosaur master. But it seemed to him he could literally see a wave of resolution and confidence pass among the ranks of Providence pikes.

They had done the impossible: plain lowborn men and women had stood against the invincibly armored chivalry in full charge. And they not only lived—they were doing the killing.

They liked it. And they began to push back. The impaled mounts began to fall. The pikes of mostly the latter three ranks began to dig into the pushing, milling mob the rest of the Crève Coeur cavalry had become. Pikes thrust through horses' neck-armor and even the chamfrons protecting their faces. They punched holes in knightly steel and the privileged hide—and entrails—behind.

But not all the line had held. And it wasn't the pike-pushers' fault.

Blame momentum: Rob did. A handful of the charging coursers, perhaps slower on the uptake than their kindred, had left it too late to stop. Instead of pulling up before the pikes, they stumbled, and hurtled like living missiles of meat and metal, each weighing just north of a metric ton, screaming and leg-flailing through the foot-soldier ranks. Their riders flew off like discarded dolls.

Rob sucked in his breath as the following knights blasted through the gaps their hapless comrades had made. Though only a dozen or so made it through the painfully thin Providence line, they could now wheel to fall upon the backs of the pike-pushers. Who, engaged from the front already, could do little to protect themselves.

It was one of the most dearly desired outcomes in battle: to strike your foe on the flank, or better from behind. Such attacks struck panic in their victims far out of proportion to their actual danger. Even the hearts of the stoutest veterans—which these Providential amateurs were not—would quail, almost certainly causing them to break and rout in terror as human nature asserted itself.

Instead true buckethead nature reasserted itself. While the peasant infantry's impertinence in defying their betters merited punishment, they remained intrinsically beneath contempt.

Riding equated to nobility. In most tongues the one literally meant the other, hence the use of montador and montadora—"mounted ones"—as the universal Nuevaropan honorifics for knights. Gaétan, who had ridden apart from Rob while rallying the pike to stand firm, was of course a mere merchant. Rob was defiantly proud of being lower-born than *anyone.*

These were peasants mounted. And on *dinosaurs.* Conspicuous horned monsters bigger than any warhorse, even the huge (and currently out-of-vogue) destriers.

So naturally, honor and outrage drew the horse-borne knights to the two men like flies to fresh wounds.

To his eternal if secret pride, Rob's first impulse when three of the knights spurred straight up the barrow at him was to yelp like a dog with a stepped-on tail, wildly think, *What the sod am I doing here?*, and turn Nell's big, frilled head to run away.

But before her ponderous body could start to turn to follow, Rob saw that at least a pair of riders was coming on both flanks. He kept Nell turning left. Then booting her wide sides he sent her bulling toward the rider closing from that side.

The knight rode a white horse and bore a black shield with a raptor's hind foot, gold, complete with upraised killing-claw in silver. A striking design, really. Not that Rob had leisure to appreciate it.

The knight's lance-head glanced off the iron boss of Rob's own shield. The horse shied off from Nell's bizarre stout, front-hooking horn. The Einiosaurus slammed the courser shoulder to shoulder and sent it staggering back on its haunches.

Despite the opening Rob wasn't foolish enough to try making a break for it. While Little Nell was lighter than burly Zhubin, despite being longer she was never built for speed. Much less acceleration. She could no more outpace a galloping warhorse than a springer could a dragon in full dive.

Instead he spun her back clockwise toward the trio he'd first spotted attacking him. Corner-eye motion, reflex, and the Fae's own luck sent his axe wheeling over and down to his right. Its long beard caught the blade of a sword descending toward his own shrinking flesh. The force of his blow knocked the weapon from a gauntleted hand. Then, roaring rage, Rob thrust the spike sticking from the axe's business end into the eye-slits of the knight's armet.

The knight slumped to the ground, as limply as steel carapace allowed.

Then they were all around him. Only the first had used a lance, and that was now discarded for close work. Instead they belabored him with sidearms, swords, and a mace or two.

Individually, afoot or ahorse, any knight would make short shrift of Ma Korrigan's one and only son. They were raised to fight. Along with roistering and hunting, they did almost nothing but.

But they weren't trained to fight *him:* a canny opponent on an entirely unorthodox mount.

Little Nell was snorting and rocking her head side to side. But not in fear. Peaceable soul though she was—lacking the cheerfully murderous belligerence of her gigantic three-horned cousins—she nonetheless reacted to attack with outrage.

She was on her mettle now, and up on her short, thick toes for added traction, as well. The forward-curving tip of her eponymous horn could deliver a fearful downward rip, and drop the entrails of an incautious meat-eater on its hind-feet in an eyeblink. But it would never penetrate a warhorse's steel barding.

Its huge round top made an excellent natural battering ram, however. Little Nell had grown up practicing its use. Plus she weighed easily twice what the biggest courser did, knight, armor, and all.

And unlike Rob, the knights weren't used to *brawling.* Rob knew from literally having it pounded into his skull—or stomped—how to fend off multiple attackers. In particular, how to maneuver them into each other's way. If he used them more with vigor than skill, he did ply axe and shield effectively for offense and defense both.

The code chivalric did not apply to fighting an impudent peasant. The Crève Coeur knights had no compunction about stabbing Rob in the back.

If they only could. While Nell wasn't generally any more agile than she was speedy, she was compact. She could whip around quite smartly. Rob kept her turning this way and that, risking dizziness but keeping his hide unpunctured.

Mostly.

A voice that scarcely seemed his own tolled through Rob's skull as he tried desperately to see a way to stay alive for one more minute, one more second. It cursed him for every sort of fool. *What kind of romantic twaddle ever even brought you here, you git?* it sneered. *You're a performer, not a bloody warrior. Are you as besotted with that fey rogue Karyl as he is with Bogardus? Or it the Garden and its pretty principles you love more than your only begotten arse?*

But Ma Korrigan had also beaten into him the lesson that when needs must, one did what one must. Or had it been life?

. . . The voice's saying *love* brought in his mind a face whose mask of blood had blessed it, by hiding what claws and teeth had done to its loveliness. The mocking voice drowned in the brightness of simple rage.

He ducked beyond a mace's whistling arc, returned a clanging blow on the wielder's upper arm. Metal flexed with a twang. Flecks of blue enamel flew into the air, each glittering like a tiny jewel in Rob's exaggerated perception.

His axe Wanda, with the leverage over a meter of helve gave her, was one of the few weapons on the battlefield privileged to be able to harm an enemy wrapped in full plate. But Rob, naturally strong lad though he was, and kept burly by the hoisting and shoving attendant on a dinosaur master's craft, lacked strength to hack through metal one-handed. He could still deal almighty dents, though—with a lucky hit, enough to break bone beneath.

He handed his enemies whacks that left them reeling. But they were still five, and he just the one. *And while arithmetic was never my strong suit*, he thought, *I'm pretty sure that adds up to me right fucked.*

Amidst his endless evolutions Rob caught glimpse of the Crève Coeur dinosaurs in garish, high-tailed retreat. And Count Guillaume, unmistakable in his gilded armor on his royal-blue mount, either valiantly standing off a pair of trikes or trapped between them. One had lost its fighting-castle and crew; Rob couldn't see a mahout straddling its neck behind the frill. It plainly didn't matter to the beast. The killing-joy was on it.

Exertion burned Rob's arms and shoulders like fire. His lungs tried to turn themselves inside out, tearing themselves to pieces in the process. Metal clanging metal had him half deaf, he choked on the yellow dust their swirling dogfight wound them in, and the rim of his helmet, with the help of a sword-whack or two, had gashed his forehead so he must blink constantly to clear his eyes of blood that both stung and threatened to gum his eyelids shut.

The inevitable happened. From nowhere Rob ever saw a sword-tip raked his axe arm, laying it open wrist to elbow. Blood gushed.

Wanda slipped from his fingers to drop with a shock to her lanyard's short extent. Rob's blood wasn't gushing out that fast—no artery had been cut. But it was as if his energy and strength were air, not fluid; and the gash let all out at once. He slumped in the saddle, so weary and soul-sick he almost welcomed the death-blow by a silver-armored knight who was cocking back beside the scarlet horror tail feathers that sprouted from behind his armet's crown.

Chapter 21

Caracorno Spinoso, **Spike-frill**—*Styracosaurus albertensis.* Ovdan hornface (Ceratopsian) dinosaur. Quadrupedal herbivore with a large nasal horn and four to six large horns protruding from its neck-frill. 5.5 meters long, 1.8 meters tall, 3 tonnes. Mostly shades of yellow and brown in arresting patterns. Favored warmount for heavy *Turano* and *Parso* riders

—THE BOOK OF TRUE NAMES

A fist-sized lump of lead attached to a stout staff slammed down on the crimson-feathered helmet from behind. The knight pitched right out of the saddle.

Where the Brokenheart had been a blink before, Rob saw Gaétan grinning at him from Zhubin's broad back, behind the riderless horse. He'd slung his hornbow. He wore an arming-sword, but for serious socializing he'd equipped himself with a maul.

It was a rough and ready weapon. Archers used them to pound stakes in the ground before whittling sharp the ends with knives and hatchets to make Faerie-poles. The three-horns' fighting-castle crews used versions with hafts two or three meters long. Gaétan's weapon had a haft about the same length as Rob's axe did. While it could righteously bust up an unprotected victim, its main function was to do just what it did: knock an armored rider off his mount.

Now we're outnumbered a paltry two to one, thought Rob. *Joy*. He wheeled a huffing Little Nell to her right.

To see a mace with a proper flanged head smash in the green-enameled side of a burgonet with a gold-inlaid visor worn by the knight he faced. Mora Regina had caught the Crève Coeur horseman with a savage backhand stroke aided by the force of a lunging dapple-grey as leggy and raw as she was. Her own plate was likewise green, with arms in gold and red and the breast.

Through his own pulse roaring in his ears, Rob Korrigan heard a sliding susurration like cicadas in high summer, with metallic music underneath. The Ruybrasiliana knight had brought her mailed-infantry reserve along. Shoulder to shoulder the erstwhile house-shields marched past either side of the barrow.

As Nell faced west again, across the field of battle proper, Rob was astonished to see an orange-maned chestnut rearing against the weight of the knight on its back, rolling its eyes and pawing air with its hooves as nearly naked men and women swarmed up horse and rider like ants on the corpse of a forest-glider. It was a mob of Providence light-archers. Some clung to shield and sword arm. Others stabbed at armor-joints and eye-slits with their daggers. A woman with a wild mat of hair that might have been dark-blond beneath greasy grime actually rode the man-at-arms's back. Her legs wrapped around his cuirass from behind, she wrenched a yellow-and-blue-plumed helmet sideways as if trying to break the wearer's neck.

The last two knights confronting Rob and Gaétan turned their horses and fled. The youthful merchant had clearly dropped another whilst Rob was otherwise occupied. With a nod of her armet to her rescuees, Regina led the reserve forward to bolster the pikes.

The main body of heavy Crève Coeur horse had disengaged from the infantry. The Providential pikes had shifted to fill the holes torn in the ranks by stricken warhorses. At one they used the dead courser itself as a breastwork, crouching to present their long spears over it. The enemy knights stayed close, though, continuing to feint at the pikes, holding their attention.

And whether it was actually their design or not, Rob saw with a belly-kick of horror how they were about to turn the day disastrously against Providence. Because while the knights kept the pikes facing forward, Baron Salvateur was riding his black sackbut at a jarring two-legged run south, around their left flank.

With the unwieldy pikes pointing toward the horse his monster could trample the length of their ranks almost unimpeded. The chivalry, fighting as individuals rather than a unit but full of self-righteous fury, would trample the survivors so completely there'd be nothing for the Crève Coeur infantry to do when it at last arrived.

"Shoot him!" Rob roared to Gaétan.

"Out of arrows," Gaétan said. His big, bluff face had been red with exertion beneath a torrent of sweat. Now the color dropped away, leaving ash.

Swift motion caught the edge of Rob's eyes and drew it 'round. Asal was streaking toward the black dinosaur at a dead run. Karyl leaned forward over her wind-whipped silvery mane. His own bow was cased by his saddle. His arming-sword glinted in his left hand.

"Is he out of his mind?" Gaétan asked.

"Oh, aye," said Rob, almost off-handedly. "But I'd still not bet against him."

It was whistling-past-the-graveyard flippancy. Rob was actually sure he was about to see Karyl's wonderful and terrible song end here.

A normal buckethead would likely not have even noticed a lone, light-armored horseman riding up behind, much less paid attention if he had. But Salvateur, corpse-tearers eat his eyes, showed himself smarter than his brother nobles yet again. Somehow he spotted Karyl and turned to deal with him.

Karyl ducked the Baron's sword-stroke as he rode along the black sackbut's flank. He slashed the beast's huge right thigh, unprotected by its hornface-leather barding, as he passed.

The monster snorted annoyance. Probably at the impact—Rob doubted Karyl had cut through its hide.

Characteristically, the Baron didn't bother with even the semblance of a chivalrous duel. Not that even that could be anything but one-sided, pitting as it did four tonnes of monster, armor, and master against a smallish man mounted on a beast scarcely more than an outsized pony, who massed maybe four hundred kilos with a full belly in drowning rainstorm.

Instead he wheeled his duckbill with that startling quickness the great counterbalancing tail gave to two-legged dinosaurs. Then, as Karyl circled 'round for another futile pass, spun the sackbut rapidly again, looking to smash horse and rider with a sweep of that tail.

No sense of fair play whatever, Rob thought. *Give the devil this, he's a bastard after my own heart.*

Karyl hauled back on the reins. His ill-tempered little mare dug in her forehooves. The tail swept harmlessly by, its tip seemingly no more than a handspan from her flared nostrils.

Then she gathered her haunches and sprang forward like a bouncer. Having missed its target the Parasaurolophus had arched its tail high. Riding beneath it Karyl slashed the duckbill across the rectum.

The monster squealed so loudly Rob tried to cover his ears. Only the mass of the shield still strapped to his left arm kept him braining himself with it.

In its agony the sackbut crow-hopped to the right so violently it fell over. Salvateur, skilled as he was shrewd, jumped free of the saddle in time to land on his feet. He dropped to one knee, putting sword to turf to catch himself. Then he snapped upright as vigorously as if he'd spent all morning resting for just this moment.

Karyl was already on him. Rob thought he might ride the Baron down—which, given his armor, might do the mare more damage than the man. Instead Karyl's sword darted over the top of Salvateur's heater shield as he raised it. Its tip slid precisely into the single slit of the Baron's sallet.

It came back out gleaming wetly red. Salvateur collapsed as if all his bones had been magically dissolved in the instant.

A joyfully belligerent bellowing announced the three-horns' return to the rest of the Providence milita. Their butchery of the Crève Coeur hadrosaurs had barely got them breathing hard; they walked toward the rear of the enemy cavalry at their customary spraddle-elbowed plod. Even the one who had lost his fighting-castle, whom Rob recognized now as Broke-Horn—his namesake, growing slowly back, being concealed by the same steel tip that sheathed its mate. Rob was shocked to see how their flanks ran with blood. Then he realized it mostly couldn't be theirs.

A high and constant keening overrode the other noise of battle. Big Sally marched at the head of her small herd, ignoring the broken-off lance that jutted from one shoulder. Count Guillaume of Crève Coeur writhed on her proudly upheld left horn, whose steel-shod tip was rammed right through the belly of his golden armor. He was screaming without seeming to pause to inhale.

Most of the Providence dinosaurry had gone chasing off after their routed opposite numbers—a pisser, but bucketheads to the life. A couple, though, walked alongside the trikes, clearly winded but still game. Rob recognized Côme, his plain brown plate battered and showing bright streaks of bared metal. His brown and gold morion Bijou hung her round-crested head with fatigue.

Gaétan had sent Zhubin downslope in a lumbering but rapid trot. He already had the pikes advancing on the Crève Coeur chivalry, who were starting to cast worried glances over their shoulders. The infantry shouted in a mix of fury, triumph, and glee fit to congeal Rob's blood, and they were on his side.

It was more than even buckethead bravery could stand: being caught between upper and nether millstones, but with spikes. They broke like a sweat droplet hitting a flagstone. They ran their horses as fast as they'd go around the north and south ends of the approaching monster bloc. The mounts were blown and lathered, and still ran with a will. They were as frightened of the pikes and giant hornfaces as their riders were.

Rob craned to see beyond the war-dinosaurs heading slowly toward him and the horses going rapidly away. His morning's lost wager to Karyl notwithstanding, Rob Korrigan was not a man to lightly gamble coin. Drinking and wenching were vices enough to sop up whatever excess energy and money he may happen to have, thank you very much. But he had a gambler's instincts for odds.

And Providence's were still bad, if the Crève Coeur foot, which had so far done little more than walk in the cloud-strained morning sunshine, fell upon them. They still outnumbered Karyl's infantry. The Providence heavy-hitters were scattered or worn out. The house-shield professional infantry could swarm the handful of three-horns the way the archers had swarmed the Crève Coeur knights, surrounding the beasts and hamstringing them.

"What about their foot, then?" he said to the air.

It was as close to *prayer* as he generally came. He feared the Fae too well to risk drawing their notably trickish attention. And while he had never settled in his own mind whether he believed in the Creators or not, he knew from long experience that if they were there, they were deaf as posts. At least to the importunings of the likes of *him*.

Rob jumped to hear a laugh from right beside him, so dry it was really just a croak with mostly imputed humorous overtones. He turned to see Eamonn Copper. The mercenary captain had lost his helmet, baring red hair starting to curl in rebellion against sweat and the now-absent pressure of his helmet. The plain green surcoat he wore over his armor was splashed with drying blood and torn as if he'd lost a kicking-contest with a horror.

"If any are still hanging about after our duckbills chased theirs right back through the midst of them," Copper said with satisfaction, "having their own chivalry ride them down should set their fookin' minds right, then."

"It's a refreshing draft of home you are, Captain," Rob said, not without either irony or sincerity.

Karyl rode between the pikes, who had halted, and the Providential dinosaurs, who were turning back yet again to march on whatever their own fleeing knights had left of the Crève Coeur infantry. He raised his voice in a clear tenor cry: "Spare the commons; kill the nobles!"

As a hundred throats took up the cry Rob felt his body fill with sudden scalding outrage. *But that's counter to the nature of things!* he thought.

He may've honored the accepted order more in the breach than the observance. But still . . . when all was said, it was an order he accepted no less than any.

His next thought was to wonder how the Providence bucketheads would react. Not just to this affront to their caste, but against their very real pecuniary interests in capturing enemy knights and lords alive to hold for ransom.

Then he heard the unmistakable baritone of Baron Côme take up the call. So did the other dinosaur knights straggling back at last from their pursuit. Not only the lowly had suffered from Crève Coeur depredations. Guillaume's knights hadn't bothered with asking ransoms when they overran the western fiefs. They intended to have it all regardless, and weren't above roasting captives—even ones with blue blood running in their veins—over slow fires to learn the hiding-place of the smallest silver spoon.

The loud and grisly slaughter of the dismounted Crève Coeur knights met head-on inside Rob with reaction to exertion and danger. He slumped from Little Nell's saddle, to stagger several steps on quivering legs. Then he tumbled to his knees and puked lustily into a berry bush.

Chapter 22

***Ballesta*, Crossbow, Arbalest**—Common weapon consisting of a bow, usually of wood or metal, mounted at the end of a stock, which releases a bolt or quarrel. Varieties include light crossbows, which are cocked by hand; medium crossbows, cocked by means of a lever called a springer's-foot; and heavy crossbows, cocked by means of a geared pulley called a cranequin. Increasing power comes at the cost of increasing time to reload, as well as increasing cost. Far more expensive than the common Nuevaropan shortbow, but requires far less training to use effectively.

—**A PRIMER TO PARADISE FOR THE IMPROVEMENT OF YOUNG MINDS**

"I'm sorry, Captain Karyl," Rob said, frowning at the red spot where his arm wound had begun to bleed through the bandages. "I failed you."

The day was done. All that remained was a trickle of light along the eastern horizon, appropriately blood-colored. Rob sat slumped on the well-trodden ground atop the barrow beside a fire that roared head-high, mostly as a beacon shouting victory to the world. Karyl stood nearby. Behind them captured battle standards flapped in the sunset breeze, among them Guilli's golden broken heart, and Salvateur's Creator Torrey in His Glory.

For the moment they had the mound-top to themselves. A party of armored infantry stood watchfully nearby. But Rob wasn't entirely sure what for. They weren't to prevent people from approaching the army commander. Karyl had directed that anyone who wanted was free to speak to him.

As for die-hards looking to avenge the Count and his nobles—Karyl had doffed his armor and longsword, and once more wore his customary hooded robe. More to the point, he held his blackwood staff grounded and cradled between arms folded across his chest, and Rob wouldn't have given the few drops of rancid spit he could muster for the chances of any would-be assassin. Or any six of them.

Out in the dusk cowled figures moved with solemn purpose across the battlefield what everyone was calling the Hidden Marsh. They were sectaries of Maia, Lance, and the Lady Bella, performing their ritual duty of giving final mercy to animals and men too badly injured for even robust Paradise constitutions to heal. There were still enough of them that their moans and cries were constant as the crickets.

It was a duty Rob was glad to have been spared. And indeed, when he quit feeling so sick and doleful, he'd even rejoice over the why. He was taking a sorely needed break from tending to the dinosaurs. Not just his own precious band of six three-horns, none of whom had taken a serious wound despite the loss of fully a third of their crews, dead and injured. Nor even the ten Providence war-duckbills who had survived the battle.

Karyl Bogomirskiy and the Army of Providence were now proud owners of a young herd of war-duckbills, recovered from the routed dinosaur knights. Not all had been captured: a passel of Guilli's bucketheads had sent a squire out beneath the white plume of parley to negotiate surrender, offering to swear fealty and obedience to Karyl.

The killing frenzy had passed, then. If it had ever gripped the enigmatic master of the day, which Rob begged leave to doubt. Several hundred foot, peasant and professional alike, had also surrendered and begged leave to join the victorious army. Karyl had accepted, on the provision that, along with swearing loyalty to Providence, any found guilty of murder, rape, mutilation, or torture would be executed straightaway.

As in all things, Karyl had been true to his word in that. At least a dozen knights and twice as many House troops and mercenaries had been put to death. Not always quickly or cleanly; their surviving victims had got to some of them before the official hangmen could. Nor did Karyl try to interfere with the impromptu justice, or whatever it was. As far as he was concerned they were bandits.

"What?" Karyl asked. "What failure?"

"My light-horse," Rob said.

Karyl grunted.

In midafternoon Rob's prodigal light-horse had come skulking back. They brought fifteen wounded, not including woods-runners, who had taken their hurt to care for in their own way. Eight men and women had been killed. Irate though he was at their unauthorized departure from the battlefield, the losses tore at his heart. These boys and girls had put their trust in him; and if they had let him down, he felt he'd done the worst by the ones he'd lost.

He'd had the story out of them, stammering and shamefaced. Though they had kept well clear of the Crève Coeur archers, they had been shocked to take losses from arbalesters. The mercenaries' medium and heavy crossbows not only had more punch than shortbows did, they considerably outranged them. While Providence had its own, of course, the light-horse hadn't come up against them before, and hadn't fully appreciated the fact.

While they were reeling back from the unexpectedly lethal enemy quarrels, someone had ridden back across the wooded ridge to report seeing a party of knights riding from the west. The light-riders and their woods-runner allies decided to meet this new threat, and rode to try to delay the enemy reinforcements before they could tip the already overloaded scales further in Count Guillaume's favor.

They had forgotten all about their original mission.

The newcomers weren't knights, but house-infantry riding to join the battle. They had quickly dismounted to meet the Providence attack. Neither woods-runners arrows nor cavalry darts proved much use against the mail-clad professionals. And once the house-bows among the party got into action they had quickly driven off the lighter troops.

They'd inflicted most of the losses on Rob's bold children. When the light-horse and woods-runners finished regrouping in some woods to the south, and tending to their injured as best they could, the battle was over.

"That's war," Karyl said. "We're lucky things went as well for us as they did. And we won."

"They serve me well enough, my mad lads and lasses," said Rob, dragging himself back from the verge of a black pit of depression and fatigue he always sank into after battle. Karyl, he knew, would begin to pay his own blood-price tonight, in the form of howling nightmares he could never recall when wakened. "For the most part, very well indeed. But—they're volatile. They're wicked independent, and they don't take to discipline well."

"No," Karyl said. "And that's how we need them to be."

A woman brought Karyl a clay mug. He accepted with a nod and quiet thanks. She wasn't one of Rob's; from her stained leather jack he guessed she'd carried a pike in the third or fourth rank. The first rank had worn waxed and enameled hornface-leather breastplates from the Providence town Armory. The rest had worn whatever was left over.

Rob smelled ale. It was a marvel—or a testimony to the proclivities of his nose—that he smelled anything at all over the terrible residues of slaughter. Which had grown steadily worse all day, for all that decay happened more deliberately here in the relative cool and aridity close to the Shield foothills.

"If I could, lass," he said, around a tongue that suddenly felt as if it belonged to a nosehorn calf and had gotten crammed in his mouth through some misadventure, "I'd trouble you for one of those as well, if you'd be so kind."

She laughed. She had an open face, below the filth, and a shock of brown hair. She might have been quite the pert one, if she hadn't reeked so much of rotting blood herself.

"That's already taken care of," she said, handing him a second mug. The stone grip was cool and somehow reassuring in his hand. "Compliments of Baron Côme. It's his own house-brew, recovered from Guilli's baggage train."

By now Rob had already sloshed half of it down his throat. He finished off the rest, wiped his mouth with the back of his hand—whether putting more ale on his hand in the process than assorted foulness on his beard and lips, he couldn't say—and gave the empty back.

"My thanks to the Baron," he said, feeling like a dry sponge swelling with moisture. "And to you as well."

He did not send his compliments to the Baron, yet. He was sure it was actually fine. Right now Rob was so parched swilling nosehorn piss might have tasted as sweet. He took his ale far too seriously to be handing out compliments for the sake of form.

Karyl sipped more slowly from his mug. "You need to appoint a captain for your light-horse," he told Rob.

It was as if Gaétan's maul clouted Rob behind the ear. His head whirled and his stomach flopped over. A cold feeling crept through his body, supplanting both the cool of the drink and the warmth of the alcohol in the ale.

"So it's sacked I am, then," he said huskily. "Not that I can blame you, after I lost control of my troopers today."

But: *I thought you said I didn't fail!*

At once he cursed himself inside: *Foolish boy! Won't you be happier, sloughing off the woe and hassle? Wouldn't it make you happiest of all to shuck the bloody lot, and hit the free road once more, just you and Nell and no greater burden than pack, axe, and lute?*

Oh, and heart, of course. That's heaviest of all. But there's a burden well-familiar, if not well-loved.

And yet. And yet. There were all those lovely war-dinosaurs to tend and mold into perfect fighting creatures. Not just any dinosaurs: the greatest of war-dinosaurs. The true dinosaur lords, masters of the battlefield. *Triceratops*. And the man who had mastered the use of those living, walking, three-horned fortresses in war as no Nuevaropan had. Nor probably any other in any time or clime.

Rob knew himself a hero-worshipper to the core. In his second and fallback trade as minstrel it made coin clink in the cup, knowing all the hero-songs and ballads, the newest and the oldest, and sing them with heartfelt fervor. He found it harder by far to fake the passion for heroes, and heroines too, than love for any woman.

No matter how painfully that greatest of dreads, responsibility, weighed on his shoulders, Rob could bear to leave neither the monsters nor the man.

Still, he found himself blinking back tears at the hurt of such summary dismissal.

Karyl was staring at him as if he'd sprouted a rack of brow-horns like Big Sally's.

"Of course you're not sacked," he said. "I suspect I need you more than ever. You carry on doing as you've done: tell the scouts where to go and what to do, and take their reports of what they learn. But now we know they need someone to lead them in battle."

"Someone to command them?" Rob asked. At this point the words seemed to make little sense to him; fatigue and adrenaline reaction were turning spring-steel wit to lead.

"We both know they won't put up with being *commanded*," Karyl said. "If they were the sort for that they wouldn't suit as scouts or skirmishers. No, what they want is someone who impresses them. Somebody they can follow as an example, because he's the best. Or she—that cacafuego Stéphanie would serve well, or her brother. As they do, among their own. But they're not horse-people, any more than you, nor have any desire to be. Your wild riders would never accept them as anything but allies."

Some mysteriously still-active part of Rob's mind recalled that was a temperament Karyl understood well. In part he was descended from half-wild horse-nomads. He had spent his first few years of exile among his late mother's Parso clan.

Karyl drained his mug and stooped to set it on the ground by his feet. A skinny youth in a loincloth materialized out of the gloom and scooped it up. Karyl nodded absent thanks as he vanished.

They love him, Rob thought. *And why not? All he's done for them is the impossible.*

"The only way to use the light-horse and not lose them is with the lightest touch," Karyl said. "We just need to find the right person. Someone they'll choose to follow."

"Well, we've time. Today's bought us that. If only a little."

For some mad reason Rob felt abruptly miffed. He got to his feet. It took a bit of struggle.

"Why not me, then?" he demanded, hearing and hating the whine in his voice. "You said yourself I have their trust."

Arching a brow, Karyl ran an eye down his companion's body, which Rob knew to resemble a barrel, and his legs, which were short and bowed.

"You surely don't see yourself bobbing along at half the speed of your light-horse on that fat, outlandish hornface of yours—"

"Nell's not fat. Sturdy built, aye, I grant—"

"—and leading them to attack mounted knights."

"Oh, fuck no!" Rob blurted. Then, "Sorry, Lord! Er—Captain. *Colonel.*"

"I've heard the phrase before," Karyl said.

"I fought today, sure," said Rob. "But that was purely self-defense. I'm not insane. Which you bloody have to be to tackle bloody knights, even hit and run."

It struck him—as usual, too late—that this was not a tactful thing to say to a man who had fought a famous dinosaur knight while tricked out as a light-horseman and riding an ill-tempered mare little larger than a pony. And killed him. Indeed, Rob intended to furiously scribble songs about all Karyl's exploits here at the Marais Caché first chance he got, not just his defeat of Salvateur.

Karyl just laughed and clapped Rob's shoulder. "That's neither your gift nor your temperament, my friend. You serve us best as what you've been: the Master Spider at the center of his web. Whose fangs are deadly, when the prey comes to him. That's the greater part of command, really, finding the right worker for the job. As I've done with you, and you do well in turn.

"Now: I need you to lend me some of your riders. Twenty should do the trick. Plus by your leave I'll take a few woods-runners, if they'll go."

The woods-runners would march through glowing lava if you asked them, Rob thought. *Like pretty much everyone else in the army.*

"What? Lend them to you? For what?"

"I'm off as fast as we can ride, to negotiate the surrender of County Crève Coeur."

"Surrender?" Rob almost stammered the word. "But we don't have siege engines."

"Don't need them. Guillaume died without issue. I'm going to make faces at his court. Believe me, that'll be enough, arriving on the heels of news of this day's doings."

Rob sucked in a deep breath.

"I see that," he said slowly. "Count Guillaume brought an army bigger than yours, better in every way. Now it's dead or scattered or become your own personal property, and Guilli's gone to take his chances on the Wheel."

He uttered a corpse-tearer laugh. "They'll think you're a Faerie yourself."

Karyl's face went ever so slightly pale beneath the orange dance of firelight. His eyes narrowed briefly. Rob reeled, appalled by what he'd said.

At least he'd recovered enough wit not to make things worse by apologizing.

But what Karyl Bogomirskiy didn't kill you for, he got over quickly. *Come to that, if he killed you, he got over that pretty quickly too.*

"We'll ride as soon as I can get some provisions ready," Karyl said. "We need to move fast, though."

"What about me?"

"You'll lead the army back to Providence town," Karyl said. "They need their rest tonight, but get them rolling as soon after dawn as you can."

"Why me? I mean—why not Baron Côme? Or Copper. Or even Gaétan."

"You're my lieutenant," Karyl said. "My second in command. They'll do what you tell them; they swore to do so when they joined. Anyway, literally all you have to do is tell them; they know what to do. And then ride east as fast as the foot can follow."

"So why the rush, then?"

"Don't forget Count Guillaume wasn't the only threat. Métairie Brulée and Castaña have mostly sat things out so far. No doubt they were hoping to help rend the carcass after Crève Coeur killed us.

"Some of Guillaume's scattered knights will no doubt have crossed the Lisette into Métairie Brulée by now. What they have to tell Comtesse Célestine will paralyze her, for the moment. We don't want Don Raúl de Castaña thinking he sniffs opportunity, though. Providence town's a central location. However things break, the sooner you get the army back there, the less likely we are to see rapid trouble."

Karyl started to walk away, briskly as if just risen from a sound night's sleep. But now Rob felt something else sitting in his stomach like a plateful of broken glass.

"How much of it did you contrive?" he called to Karyl's back.

Karyl turned. "How much of which?"

Rob held out an open hand, palm up. "All of it. Since we got to the bloody place, perhaps. The downs as well as the ups. Even the Blueflowers goat-fuck, and our trial for our lives." He shook his head. "All your wizard swordplay and your fine tactics can blind a man to the fact that you're the master strategist, above all. So, my legendary hero—how much did you plan?"

"We've been luckier than any human has a right to expect," Karyl said, "and far luckier than we deserve. On the whole—far less than all, but something over half. That's fair to say."

Rob felt his stomach clench. "Why?"

"I was hired to do a job," Karyl said. "Is it any different for dinosaur masters? Our employers are in many ways a more difficult opponent than the enemy."

"Oh, aye," Rob said, laughing harshly despite the ache. "Your boss you have with you always."

"Precisely. They hire us to perform certain tasks. At some point we inevitably have to choose whether to carry out those tasks, or try to please them."

"True enough. So then?"

"We were brought in to get Providence to defend itself despite itself. We've done so. I have given it the best chance of success it's within my power to. As have you."

Rob stared. The edges of the broken glass stayed sharp.

"If it consoles you at all," Karyl said, "I had no inkling the Princess would do act as she did. A mind like hers, brilliant but driven by naïve idealism and untrammeled by sense, is far less predictable than the shrewdest strategist. That makes for a dangerous foe. And a worse ally."

"So you didn't—truly, you didn't—?"

Karyl met his furnace-vent gaze squarely. "I never foresaw the harm that would come to your woman. Nor the rest of the lot. I sacrifice no life unless I have to. Not even annoying Garden Councilors. I was hired to protect them all."

Rob winched his lips back in something passably a smile. "*We* were hired to protect."

"We were. And that's one of the harshest lessons to learn: you can't protect everyone. No matter how good you are. No matter how hard you try."

To Rob's amazement his voice clotted, as if from emotion. Karyl dropped his gaze.

"No matter how hard I try," he said softly, "everyone who trusts me, dies of it."

Rob gripped his shoulder. "It's only because of you any of us is alive right now."

Karyl lifted his head. He looked at Rob with almost the eyes of a child, glittering with tears.

"For now, my friend," he said. "For now."

After a moment he blinked. His eyes cleared; his shoulders squared.

"And now," he said, almost gaily, "I've got to ride. I've an entire county to intimidate, after all."

Rob watched him stride away until full night swallowed his slight but now-erect figure. He shook his head.

"Who's madder, then?" Rob asked, of the wind and the dead. "Himself? Or me, for following him?"

Chapter 23

Brincador, Bouncer—*Psittacosaurus ordosensis.* Bipedal plant-eating dinosaur, 1.5 meters, 14 kilograms, with a short, powerful beak. Distinguished by quill-like plumes. Common Nuevaropan garden pest.

—THE BOOK OF TRUE NAMES

Providence town's central square bloomed with colors, motions, musics, in early afternoon sunlight gently screened by the clouds. Banners flapped like strips torn from rainbows. Flower petals in lavender, chrome yellow, powder blue, skittered and swirled up around the feet of townsfolk as if joining in their dance. Several competing ensembles performed lively tunes in competition. Though the day was warm the autumn breeze down from the Shield passes hinted with its smell and slight edge of early snow on the cloud-threatening crags.

In the shade of a gaudy temporary awning, Melodía sat by the fountain. Beside her sat Bogardus on the one hand, and Violette on the other. Annoyance pinched the Councilor's fine features into the aspect of a dried fig.

"—should have consulted us first, I tell you," she was saying to Bogardus across Melodía as if the younger woman wasn't there. "Does the Council rule in Providence, or does it not?"

Bogardus smiled placatingly. "We advise, surely," he said. "Guide with a gardener's loving hand."

Melodía wasn't sure why she was here being feted by the crowd. *All I did was bring disaster to these people*, she thought, *and get my best friend killed.* She still alternated bouts of numbness and disconsolate weeping. Right now she felt numb. Mostly. But the other was always there, quivering inside, ready to break forth with neither warning nor apparent provocation.

"Perhaps it's time for our hands to grow more active," Violette said. "Time to shape the unruly growth. And prune away the unsightly."

Something about that tasted bad on the back of Melodía's tongue. Violette's faction already seemed too active to her. But the sensation passed with no more than cursory notice. Her thoughts were too active for ready distraction.

"Karyl removed the greatest threat to our people and our Garden," Bogardus said. "He won a great victory, after all. One that will be commemorated for ages, if the songs sung in the taverns are any indication."

Rob Korrigan had seen to that already, however much Violette sniffed and harrumphed at such vulgarity pretending to be music. To celebrate his bringing the army home he'd got roaringly drunk crawling the town's handful of taverns. Although he'd stayed at the farm—and stayed drunk, Melodía heard—the several days since, he'd been furiously writing songs about the miraculous victory of the Hidden Marsh. Other members of the victorious army had carried them into town, where they became instant sensations.

He deals with grief in the ways he knows best, Melodía thought. *Why don't I have solace like that?*

But she despised the lack of control drunkenness or herbal overindulgence brought. And despite the tutelage of one of the greatest musicians the modern epoch had produced, she never showed sign of musical aptitude aside from a pleasing singing voice. And there was only so much singing she could do. Especially with her throat worn raw from weeping.

The thought of her lost lover—*Did I throw him away as irrevocably as I did Pilar?*—jabbed her like a pin and threatened to set off a fresh sobbing fit. She reined herself viciously in: *I am a Delgao, a noblewoman, a* grande *in my own right. I will not disgrace my family and my title by public weakness.*

"In fact," Bogardus said, with a smile that if Melodía hadn't known him better she would've thought was impish, "I believe this latest group is singing one of Master Korrigan's compositions."

Glad of the distraction, Melodía paid attention to the words as a gaily costumed group of 'prentices march past with arms linked: "On that field was Hope reborn/And tyrant Guilli got the horn. . . ."

Violette sniffed more loudly.

"And we oughtn't forget," Bogardus said, "that he won substantial treasure when he browbeat Crève Coeur's heirs and surviving barons into submission. The coffers we've depleted to pay for the army and its upkeep overflow with silver once more. Our brave warriors enjoyed a reward, the wounded and the families of the fallen are seen to. Karyl's even provided relief for those dispossessed by Count Guillaume's depredations."

He shook his head. "I greatly admire his resourcefulness as well as his nerve. On top of the plunder gained from the baggage train, to auction off the Countship to the highest bidder? And as a condition of the sale compel the winner, Baroness Antoinette, to agree to pay massive reparations?"

Violette cast her gaze sidelong at Melodía. "Perhaps your father might have something to say about that?"

Mention of the Emperor was like a body punch, in Melodía's present state. Words became too curdled in her throat for any to get out.

"The Empire prefers to allow matters of vassalage and succession to sort themselves out on the local level," Bogardus said smoothly. He seemed to sense the question's impact on Melodía. He also had long since shown acquaintance with high-level courts. Although Melodía had never seen him at the Imperial one. She would remember, she was sure.

Violette arched a finely lucked brow. "Wasn't meddling in succession what provoked that nasty little brouhaha in the North, a year or two ago?"

"That involved an Elector," Bogardus said, "not a mere border count. The Princes' Party rebelled because they feared the Emperor choosing one of the very people who'd Elect his successor would grant him too much power."

"But Emperors are always Elected from Torre Delgao. What difference does it make? And who could be so crass as to object if Felipe chose our delightful Melodía to be Empress after him?"

"Offspring can't succeed a parent directly on the Fangèd Throne," said Melodía, momentarily roused from her self-pity. For which she felt a twinge of gratitude to the purple-eyed woman. "Anyway, we're a large familia. It matters to some which branch ascends to the gold and red."

"Come," Bogardus said, squeezing Melodía's arm. The contact was thrilling on her bare arm, even in her current gloom. "We must acknowledge Karyl's genius. Verging on artistry, if not the thing itself."

Melodía was not so sunken in despair that she didn't suspect the Eldest Brother of trying to head off a lengthy disquisition on Imperial dynastic politics. Frankly, she couldn't blame him. She also wasn't so self-consumed as not to realize how quickly the details of Delgao intra-family politics could bore an outsider stupid.

"You must, perhaps," Violette said, crossing her arms pointedly beneath her small breasts. "It's only money. And he should have insisted Crève Coeur embrace the Garden's principles and guidance! Why else did we pay him to win this gaudy slaughter these fools are glorifying?"

Melodía frowned. She liked the Councilor, in a mildly guarded way. Certainly she felt a warmth toward her. She was grateful for the acceptance and affection Violette had shown her. And almost foolishly so, to Bogardus as well, for not rejecting her for what she had done in the name of their Garden, and of love.

Somehow, she felt an impulse to defend Karyl. That shocked her into holding back whatever retort had quickly shaped itself into a dart on her tongue before it was launched. She couldn't despise Karyl anymore for what he stood for—not when he had stood between her and the terrible death she had brought upon Pilar.

How she now felt about him, and whatever he was, she could not say. But what disarmed her vocal weaponry was simply the notion that such a man as Karyl Bogomirskiy could need defending at all.

The apprentices chanted lustily past, no doubt enjoying the day off from their arduous routine as much as they did celebrating their salvation. Melodía turned her head to watch them. As she did she met the sad gaze of the Mayor, his moustaches drooping more pronouncedly than she ever remembered seeing them. He nodded gravely. She nodded back, *noblesse oblige*, and marveled how the two town guards, male and female, who stood flanking him, with cuirass-cased chests pushed out and chins held as high as if they'd had the slightest thing to do with the victory being celebrated, seemed more like wardens than bodyguards.

She felt Violette's thin body stiffen beside her. Melodía looked around to see the Councilor lean forward like a tröodon spotting a bouncer in a berry-bush.

Marching toward them was a phalanx of children, several score, ranging from around twenty—the age at which bodies began to visibly ripen into adulthood—to those who could just toddle unassisted. All wore pure white linen gowns. Each carried in its right hand a thistle, symbol of Providence—Melodía had never figured out why it wasn't a cornucopia or some such; having been raised to the art, she knew heraldry made sense rather less than half the time, and the rest of the time made rather less sense than none at all. In the other hand each child carried a flower, brilliant and gay in scarlet, blue, yellow, white. Their high voices rose in the traditional "Song of Thanksgiving to the Eight" in archaic Spañol.

Hands gripping the arms of her folding wooden chair so tightly the veins stood out blue through milk-white skin, Violette watched the procession go by. *Why such interest?* Melodía wondered.

According to château gossip, Violette had left two grown children behind when she left the land of her birth, a highborn widow dispossessed by a late husband's scheming heirs. Unlike her friends Lupe and Fanny back home, who loved to chat gaily about the day politics would at last let them have babies, Melodía didn't yet see the attraction of spawning. It was a messy, painful business, she knew well enough; and what did you get for all that grunting and screaming? A squirmy, wet-faced bundle of noise and poop. That would, Creators willing, someday grow up into a pest like her little sister. Which, dearly as she loved (and missed) Montse, Montse assuredly was.

Perhaps Violette was feeling the aftershocks of the maternal urge, or missing the presumed grandchildren she might never know—Melodía just had time to think that before homesickness and grief and self-pity rose up in a wet mass to smack her in the face, and she had to snatch out her kerchief and feign a sneezing fit to hide the traitor tears.

Melodía tossed her head on the satin pillow. Her hands clutched clumps of satin sheets. Violette knelt on Bogardus's bedchamber floor with her buttocks, white as Eris, the Moon Visible, in the air and her face pressed between Melodía's wide-spread thighs. After seemingly endless teasing, first of the soft skin of Melodía's inner thighs, then the lips of her sex, Violette's tongue had discovered the center of Melodía's pleasure and now played it like a musical instrument. The tune she played was different from what Jaume might have done—but the pleasure it gave Melodía was no less intense.

It had all happened suddenly, that afternoon when they came back to the Garden villa from the victory parade in Providence town. The three had dined together, quietly, in Bogardus's chambers—simply but beautifully decorated with sprays of flowers in elegant faces, discreet sculptures, and miniature paintings. That was unusual but seemed natural to her, somehow. Or perhaps that had merely been her relief at not having to face the other members of the Garden she had left alive, whose faces would cause her to reproach herself the more that they were smiling and accepting.

When a new Garden acolyte with respectfully downcast eyes had cleared away the dishes, Violette had stood by Melodía and laid a comforting hand on her shoulder. By the time the boy bowed and withdrew with his tray, the Elder Sister was speaking confidentially in her ear.

Melodía could not have said what she had talked about. Because first as if by accident, then with firm purpose, Violette's lips had touched her cheek. She had not resisted when a hand on her chin turned her face toward the other woman's.

And when the kiss came to her mouth, she felt herself responding.

She felt weight shift on the bed beside her. She opened her eyes, shock wide in passion, to see Bogardus kneeling over her. Actually what she saw was his cock by low lamplight, dominating her field of vision like a pink obelisk in the flicker of many candles, and his strong face beaming down on her from beyond her eyes' focus. Love and authority seemed to resonate from his penis. With something like gratitude she reached up to take its hot hardness in her fingers, guide it to her suddenly avid mouth, the salty, meaty taste to her tongue. . . .

Falk had her again. His hands were like manacles, hard and huge. His frenzied thrusting felt like a red-hot spear in her bowels. She was helpless, and violated, and would never be free. . . .

Melodía's own raptor-scream of outrage and anguish snapped her conscious in the act of sitting violently upright. Long, unbound hair whipped her bare shoulders. She was striking out with one forearm to knock away the faint touch that had wakened her.

Freed me from nightmare, she realized suddenly. The panic began to ebb.

Jasmine-scented evening air blew cool on her bare sweat-drenched skin. By the soft yellow glow of candles in brass bowls she saw Bogardus's head on the pillow next to her. His right hand was held open and held away from her, where he had evidently pulled it when she reacted so precipitously to his touch.

His face held an expression just the smiling side of neutral. But concern had stamped the corners of his grey eyes with tiny compito feet.

She studied him. Her hair promptly fell forward to either side of her downturned face like curtains, so that the vertical slice of the world including his face was all she could see. It was a soothing sight, dark and strong and square-jawed.

"This isn't the first time somebody's wakened screaming beside you," she said.

"No."

Deliberately he lowered his hand. He slid it under his own head to meet its mate. His chest rose and fell in a sigh.

"It's a terrible world, this place we call Paradise," he said. "I've seen so much ugliness. It's why I decided to dedicate myself to bringing what beauty I could into the world, to counteract the pervasive ugliness I saw."

That's what I chose too, she thought, *when Violette kissed me this evening.* Hunger for intimacy—for sheer human contact—had flooded her. And even as she let herself yield to the woman's implied request, she had felt defiance.

I won't let Falk define me anymore. Nor the fear he gave me. My life has fallen to ruin again. But I'm going to start rebuilding by taking it back from him.

Bogardus drew in a deep, deliberative breath. "Sometimes I wonder if I haven't come arou . . ."

He stopped the flow midword. His eyelids came down, not quite closing all the way. It seemed to Melodía as if they were trying to shut something in, not vision out.

When his eyes opened they were calm, clear. In a different tone he asked, "Do you want to talk about it?"

"No."

She smoothed the loose hair back over her shoulders. After a moment, accepting that they were both awake now, she crossed her legs and sat gazing at her mentor and lover.

"There's something other than your dream you do want to talk about, though," he said. "What's troubling you?"

Forgiveness, she wanted to say. *It should come harder. I should be made to pay penance.*

But perhaps that was weakness—cowardice. Perhaps she was hoping someone else would exact from her a price less than she was taking on herself.

"I was a fool," she said.

"You're young," he said. "Isn't that what being young's all about? If I recall my own youth correctly. . . ."

She shook him off. "I was desperate when I came here," she saw. "Lost, and—broken. Desperate."

"I know."

"I was like a drowning woman, clutching for something to cling to. Anything. You gave—the Garden gave me that something. I'm still grateful; don't get me wrong. But—I misjudged. Badly. What I seized on most fiercely, most desperately, was love."

"Love? We do teach that, yes. A treasured blossom in our Garden."

She nodded to the edge of convulsively. "Yes. But—I took it for all. The be-all, the end-all. The panacea."

"Ahh." He blew a long breath through pursed lips. "I see."

"It's a lesson we constantly hear from the Church, growing up," she said, "especially Maia's Mother-sectaries. And—well, when I had to leave, when I had to flee for my life and freedom, what saved me then, was love. My sister's love. The love of friends I didn't realize loved me half so well. Pilar's love—"

She choked, then. Squeezing her eyes tight shut, clenching her fists, she willed the sorrow down. Her eyelids were moist when she opened them again and looked at Bogardus.

"Not now," she said. "I need to say this now. It was the thing that caught my eye. The brightest flower in the whole Garden. So I seized on that."

"And?"

She scowled so ferociously he raised both brows. "You know what happened," she grated.

"Yes," he said sadly. "I do." Absolon had been his friend of many years, a friendship never touched by their frequent opposition in Council.

She sighed. "So—I've learned. Love isn't all you need. And it doesn't conquer all. It certainly wasn't what conquered that bastard worm Guilli!"

He waited a moment—to allow the fury-freshet to pass, she realized.

"So you no longer believe in the power of love?" he asked in carefully neutral tones.

She shook her head. "Not that. I—I may be callow, but I'm not that shallow. I love you. I love my fellow Gardeners. I love my sister Montserrat. I love—I love Jaume."

It was hard enough to say that. There was one more name, the object of her longest and most devoted love. But she couldn't bring herself to name person or place, quite now.

"But yes, I see now it isn't what I called it before—panacea."

"If nothing else, we can learn," he said. "Even if that's not enough to atone for our mistakes. I—I like to think of it as the least we can do for those we've wronged, if all else fails: learn to do better the next time."

She sighed. "I hope—" she said.

She sat upright. "I've decided to enlist," she said.

"Enlist?"

"With the militia," she said. "When Karyl returns, I want to join him, if he'll have me. We've still got Métairie Brulée and Castaña to deal with. They may be emboldened to act by a belief we weakened ourselves in taking down Count Guillaume."

He frowned slightly, studying her. She peered hard to try to discern whether what creased his brow was disapproval or merely thoughtfulness. As usual she could see no further than his eyes.

"So, having grown disillusioned with love, you give war a chance?" he asked, not ungently. "Are you sure you're not overdoing in reaction?"

"No," she said. "But isn't that part of finding the Equilibrium the Creators teach us to value above all? Going from one side to the other, from high to low and back? This is what I have to do now. To restore the Equilibrium in myself."

She took his left hand in both of hers, pressed it first to lips, then cheek. "Please," she said, despising herself for how lost and little-girl she sounded. "Please tell me it's all right."

He sat up. Withdrawing his hand, he put it under her chin and raised her face to his.

"You don't need my permission to do what you feel is right," he said. "But you have my blessing."

He smiled, and she thought to read both joy and pain in the expression.

"I think Sister Violette is right," he said softly. "It may soon come time to introduce you to the Mysteries. But now—act as you feel best, dear child. And know we love you too."

Chapter 24

Raptor Irritante, Irritante, Vexer—*Velociraptor mongoliensis.* Nuevaropan raptor, 2 meters long, 50 centimeters high, 15 kilograms. Commonly kept as a pet, though prone to be quarrelsome. Wild vexer-packs are often pests but pose little threat to humans.

—THE BOOK OF TRUE NAMES

Quietly, the great killer arose from her sleeping-covert in dense brush. She was entering more settled country now: the smell of the tailless two-legs and their four-leg plodders grew stronger every step she advanced. It was getting harder to hide her narrow ten-meter length.

But Allosaurs had been hiding from humans for generations. The knowledge dwelt in the marrow of her light, strong bones.

She stretched. Then she scratched her back on a tree bole with hard-scaled bark, grunting at the sheer pleasure of it. Next she found a stout branch at the proper height and scratched between the hornlike projections in front of her eyes, where she was prone to a particularly persistent itch.

The contact reminded the matadora of her mother scratching her there with her tiny, blunt claws. Her loved, lost, longed-for mother, who looked so insignificant, but whom she knew, deep inside, was tall as the sky and mountain-powerful, and would protect her.

She hungered for her mother almost as fiercely as ever she hungered to feed. Although appetite did not gnaw at her this morning. She had gorged well before her latest sleep.

She thrust her muzzle out of the shade and blinked at late-afternoon sunlight, which lightly stung her scaly skin despite the clouds. As her eyes accustomed to the dazzle she scanned the countryside about her. The terrain was broken, brushy in places, wooded in others. She would keep to such country as much as she could. She was less likely to encounter two-legs here than in the open.

Swinging her toothy face toward evening she saw a figure on a ridge, silhouetted against the distant blue mountains. It was clearly a two-legs despite its shrouded outline and bizarrely peaked head; she knew the creatures could change shapes with their strange sorceries. She knew the figure. It never smelled of two-legs. Try as she might to catch its scent, she never sensed any at all.

But sight of it filled her with warm, sweet certainty, like drinking blood spurting from a fresh kill. She was getting closer to her mother. Somehow she knew, as she always did, that this curious figure was guiding her toward reunion. Toward love and shelter.

When she emerged from cover, she stayed wary. A pack of matadores had worked the area, although by the odors of their urine and dung they had moved on suns before. The grass and bushes and low-sprawling clumps of vegetation held a stronger scent of a late-adolescent male. It hunted solo, no doubt driven from the pack by its mother.

The smell caused her no concern. She'd already met him. Two suns ago he had approached her, alternately sidling up to her, then squaring to confront her with his strength and yawning daggered jaws. A mating dance.

She had not been impressed.

She was half again his size, for one thing. He was strong and quick with youth, to be sure. But she was smart and seasoned.

She had roared to tell him she wasn't sexually receptive. He advanced as if intending to force the issue. That angered her.

She was especially outraged by the adolescent's presumption in daring to try to mount her, because he was deformed. His snout had been broken and bent to such an angle that his upper jaw failed to mate properly with the still-straight lower one. He obviously couldn't even take proper prey, but must scavenge, or live on little bouncers.

Either he had been born that way, and was weak, or had suffered some defeat or accident, and was unworthy. To mate with a mighty hunter such as her, in any event.

Yet she recalled the encounter now with pleasure. In the end the avid adolescent had proven himself worthy of a mighty slayer after all.

He had been delicious, if a touch stringy.

All was well with her world. Turning her face to the slanted sun-rays, she raised her head and made the wooded valley ring with a happy challenge: *shiraa!*

"Vexer!"

At the cry, Rob and Karyl turned from the stout piling fence of the three-horns paddock. A young woman had halted her dun pony nearby and swung down from the saddle. Clearly Ovdan, with olive skin and a black topknot sprouting through a brass ring atop her head, she was emphatically built, with broad shoulders and hips, a waist narrow only by comparison. She wore a halter made of some kind of scaly hide, black and brown and shellacked shiny, which might have belonged to a crocodilian of some sort. It had to be padded with something more comfortable, Rob judged, especially considering how heavily freighted it was. She wore a kilt of thinner, softer leather and boots that came almost to her knees. A sword hilt stuck up at an outward angle over either shoulder. A hornbow-case hung by the saddle.

To Rob, her mount, a hammer-headed beast with a roached mane and an evil eye, looked no larger than a big dog. When she'd still been astride it the newcomer had seemed of a size to match it. But when she rolled toward him with the slightly bowlegged gait of someone who spent most of her life on horseback, she seemed at least as tall as he was.

Glancing at his companion, Rob saw something he never thought he'd live to: Karyl Bogomirskiy, the legendary warrior and mystic wanderer, back on his heels and blinking in something very akin to confusion.

"Tir?" he said.

The woman strode up to Karyl and grabbed him around the short ribs. They were bare; despite a cool breeze blowing down from the Shield passes, the noontide sun was warm, and he wore only a hempen kilt and sandals. To Rob's surprise he saw that, short as Karyl was, he stood perceptibly taller than she. Notwithstanding that, with a bend of the knees and only a token grunt of effort, she hoisted his sandaled feet off the ground in a hug.

"Vexer, you little egg-thief!" she yelled, as the breath oofed out of him. "How in the Old Hell are you?"

Rob caught Karyl's eye, which seemed to be rolling slightly in a most uncharacteristic manner. "'Vexer'?" he asked, from the beginnings of a wicked smile.

"A youthful . . . nickname," Karyl said, not without a certain difficulty, as the woman returned him to solid ground and let him go. "From the early days of my exile."

"Little fuck was active as a Velociraptor and twice as pesky, Karyl was," she said. She spoke Francés with a smoky Ovdan accent. "Always sniffing 'round and asking questions, questions, questions. It bothered some of our warriors. Me, I always knew he'd go great places and do great things."

She punched him lightly in the ribs. "And you did! Came back to reconquer your fief and have the head off that frightful cow of a Baroness Stechkina who murdered your dad and exiled you, you did. Right out of the storybooks! So what brings you so far from Misty March, cousin?"

"I died."

She arched a brow. "You're looking pretty hale for a dead man. I'll have to hear that story."

"Long made short," said Rob, "he misplaced it. He seems to find his current situation preferable, so." Karyl seemed happy these days, with challenging work at his craft to do. Rob didn't want to go and stir up painful memories of his betrayal and the destruction of his beloved White River Legion at the Battle of the Hassling. Nor his own role in Karyl's unprecedented defeat.

Tir whipped around to Rob as if meaning to go for his throat. He actually stepped back.

"And who the fuck do you think you are?" she demanded.

"He thinks he's Rob Korrigan," Karyl said, recovering his composure.

"He thinks he's my dinosaur master. And also master of scouts and spies. As it happens he's good at those things, so I let him go on thinking that."

He turned to Rob. "The first thing you need to know about my cousin," he said gravely, "is never to take her seriously."

"Unless I'm naked or holding a weapon in my hand," she agreed, grinning as if her tongue didn't know a word for shame. "Or you can't see my hand. Which comes to the same thing, often enough. So you're a spy, are you?"

Rob swept her a bow so ludicrous-low that he brushed the backs of his knuckles on the ground. *No easy feat when you're built like a cask on legs*, he thought. *Though the somewhat unseemly length of my arms does help.*

"And a bard of some small talents, fair lady," he said, straightening.

"'Fair lady,' my apple-ripe ass," she said. "You're just overimpressed by the size of my boobs."

"It's most impressive they are, for a fact."

By now a crowd had gathered of people Rob was relatively sure had something else they ought be doing. They seemed quite fascinated by the extravagant newcomer. They were mostly male, mixed with a few no less appreciative women.

She turned back to Karyl. "And maybe he's better at singing than spying, if the first you knew I was coming was when I reined up a lance-length from you."

"Don't let her pique you," Karyl said to Rob. "She likes that, as you've possibly noticed. The pickets clearly thought you were no threat. Anyway, this is an army camp, and a growing one. People come and go all the time."

"'No threat'?" she declared in what Rob thought, anyway, was mock outrage. "Perhaps you no longer know me as well as you think, hmm? And why no bodyguards? What if I were an assassin bent on avenging that great fatty Count Guilli?"

"Himself won't have bodyguards," Rob said dryly. "Also, if you think your cousin has much to fear from a common or garden hired killer, it's possible you no longer know him as well as you think."

She turned and cocked an eyebrow at him. She was older than he first thought, from the lining around her eyes and mouth. Possibly even Karyl's own seventy or so. Her firm if well-packed build and gusty exuberance made her seem younger than early middle age.

"What's this? A man who won't take my shit?" She laughed. "I like that. I can always break them to saddle later, if I decide to keep them."

"What are you doing here, Tir?" Karyl asked pointedly.

A rangy bay mare pounded up, sweat-patched and panting. The spectators gave her way.

"Captain," its youthful rider called in a Spañola accent. She was dark, boy-slim, and carried a hunting spear. "There's a herd of three-horns heading this way across the Town Lord Melchor's fallow field west of town! Twenty-three of the beasts, with mahouts, an escort of twenty Ovdan horse-bows, and two baggage-wagons."

"Thank you, Emilia," Karyl said. "You can get back to patrol."

As she rode off Karyl smiled and said, "I notice your pony's still blowing hard, Tir."

She laughed. She had a gusty laugh, to match the rest of her personality. "So the day a lowlander outrides me is the day I shave my head and start spouting *Tianchao-guo* philosophy."

"And who might you be?" Rob asked. "Other than Karyl's cousin, of course."

"Me? He told you. I'm Tir."

"It means 'arrow' in Parsi," Karyl said. "And I'm surprised you left your beasts untended."

"They're hardly untended. See why we called him 'Vexer'? He's a pain in the tits, and likes himself that way. Meantime, if my men can't handle any bandits we encounter by themselves I'll rip their balls off myself. If they're not too small to see."

Rob's mind was moving more slowly than he cared for today. It was hardly surprising: he'd scarcely had a chance to recover from the physical, emotional, and spiritual exhaustion left over from the Battle of Hidden Marsh. He still had to see to the wounds of their war-dinosaurs, and accommodate the bounty of new monsters the victory had won them.

And reports from his far-flung scouts came in at every hour, day or night: of Métairie Brulée mustering forces to the South, Castaña raiding across the Laughing Water. Each neighbor seemed to be waiting for the other to make the first real move. Karyl needed to know the moment one did so—and better, between the decision to lunge at a putatively weakened Providence, and the act itself.

So it took Rob until just now for the real import of Emilia's words to hit him.

"Wait," he said, "three-horns, she said, now? Twenty-three of them? Really?"

Tir laughed again. "A dinosaur master, indeed."

"Our captain sent a message north with one of our caravans for them," said Gaétan, who'd shouldered his way through the still-growing throng.

"And who might this be?" Tir almost purred.

"Gaétan," said Karyl. "Another of my lieutenants. He's scion of a merchant family that trades extensively with Ovda."

Tir ran her fingers down Gaétan's bare chest, tickling across the pale pink pucker of scar left over from the Blueflowers fight.

"Such strapping favorites you choose for yourself, cousin," she said deep in her throat. "I'd think you'd a lovely taste in men, if I didn't know your predilections ran firmly in the female direction. So it must really be their martial skills you choose them for. Tedious as that is."

Gaétan's green-hazel eyes met Rob's own. The young man's cheeks were flushed. Rob felt heat at the roots of his own beard. *This she-raptor's making* me *blush?* he thought in amazement.

"Don't let her bother you," Karyl said. "She was kidnapped as a baby and raised by bandits; her father, the Pasha—my late mother's brother—had only just got her back a year or two before I fled to his satrapy. She still resists the civilizing process, I see. How fares my uncle, Daryush Khan?"

"Still on his pins. And still sniffing his Turanian overlords beneath their scaly tails."

"Why aren't you guiding your herd through the middle of town?" Karyl had relaxed now. In fact he showed his fiery little cousin a casual air Rob had seldom seen in most of an eight-month year. "You used to never be able to resist a chance to show off."

"I've never been overfond of cities, you might recall. Anyway, Providence town's getting a bad reputation, up in Turanistan. Their officials want to poke their noses into too many places; seems they forget how much of their cozy prosperity's always come from smuggling. I hear whispers they've even started grilling outlanders about their beliefs, and leaning hard on those who don't give the right answers. Which is going to start cutting into trade, sooner than later."

"Tell me about it," Gaétan said. "My father's always up before the Garden Council. They treat him like an enemy. People walk the streets with their heads down, and dislike talking where others might overhear. What any of this has to do with 'Truth' and 'Beauty' is a mystery to me. Even my sister Jeannette, who's a Gardener herself, has trouble defending them."

"Sounds as if you've got yourself some doubtful employers, cousin," Tir said.

"They're all doubtful," Karyl said. "As long as they pay, and let us do our work, their politics don't matter much to us. To me."

"If they've taken it into their heads to mind what other people have in theirs," Tir said, "it's just a matter of time before they start trying to pry yours open. And I can't imagine either you or they will enjoy that experience much."

She shrugged. "None of my concern. Been a strange trip overall, though."

"How so?" Karyl asked.

Rob was starting to shift weight from boot to boot; he itched all over with desire to go and see his new acquisitions. All six of his three-horns had survived the Hidden Marsh fight; the two badly hurt had mostly recovered. Like men, the beasts tended to heal fast from wounds that didn't kill them quickly. But as spymaster he wanted to hear Tir's answer too.

"We saw precious few people between the pass through the Shields and Providence town," she said. "It was like a land of ghosts."

"Not that many people live up there, I believe," Karyl said. He glanced at Rob. "Truth is we've been looking hard every way but north. Strange as it is to say it, Ovda's the one neighbor we've not worried about."

She laughed. "Maybe we're growing soft. Nothing against you Nuevoeuros, but we can't let you get too complacent, can we? Anyway, this absence of folk struck me as damned uncanny. And the ones we did encounter were eerie as Fae."

"See anything threatening?" Gaétan asked.

"Not really. No sign of raids, or fighting, or even pestilence, unlikely as that is. Still, I find myself itching to know just why people are making themselves so scarce before I ride back home."

She looked around at the audience. "Say, would one of you yokels standing around with nothing better to do than stare at my boobs be so kind as to take a break to fetch a girl a drink?"

Men darted off in all directions to obey. Smiling smugly she turned back to Karyl and the increasingly impatient Rob.

"I did spy some light cavalry practicing up north of your camp."

"My people," Rob said, ready to defend his boys and girls against what he was sure would be a barrage of insults. Although if this wild nomad woman chose to draw invidious comparisons between his Providential riders and her own people, she could prove them readily enough.

"Well, they don't show too badly," she said, "for lowlanders. "There's one, at least, who can ride halfway decently, though. Mounts a lovely, lively little grey Arabi mare, who's not wholly wasted on her. Who might that be?"

"How would I know?" Rob asked. "It's just a horse."

Tir's brows pushed down hard over her eyes. She gave a Rob a look as if he'd just claimed to have walked here from the Moon Invisible. Turning to Karyl, she shot him a look which said, "Cousin, are you sure about this one?" as loudly as a shout.

"Dinosaur master," Karyl reminded.

"Ah." She brightened. "Fair enough, then. She's a tall girl, not enough meat to her bones, but not a gawk like the one who just rode up. Dark like her, though. Hair cropped short, looks almost black, but when the sun hits right shows highlights red as blood."

"That'd be Melodía Delgao," Rob said. "A new recruit to Rob Korrigan's Highly Irregular Light-Horse."

He could no more repress a grin as he said the name than he could refrain from saying it; he'd coined it himself, on the spur of the moment, when the Delgao girl had finally convinced a skeptical Karyl—and a Rob who teetered on the edge of active hostility—that she was serious about enlisting, and serious about subordinating herself to Karyl and such officers as he chose.

"And an uncommon promising one, honesty compels me to admit," Rob added.

"That a first for you, that honesty thing?" Tir asked with a sidelong smirk.

"I strive to be unpredictable, ever and always."

"The child's a skilled rider," Karyl said. "Not unexpected, given her class and family. She shows a fair grasp of tactics, and flashes of a touch for leadership."

Tir nodded. "If you say that, and I say she's a decent horsewoman, she's a prize indeed. And speaking of family—isn't Delgao what you swamplanders call your Imperial family?"

"Yes," Karyl said.

"And Melodía—isn't she the fugitive Princess who was caught trying to poison her father?"

"She was falsely accused of intriguing against her father, the Emperor," Karyl said. "At least, so she claims."

"She hardly seems the sort for it," Rob said.

Then he faltered, unable to continue for remembering he'd gotten his impression of Melodía—as a sweet, intelligent girl who was spoiled and uncertain as to who she was, but had great potential when she got things sorted out—from her serving-maid Pilar.

"More's the pity, then," Tir said. "If she tried to put an end to an Emperor she'd definitely have the spirit of a horse-nomad. As it is she shows enough potential I should probably provide her some proper horse-warrior kit. No doubt I can scare her up a proper talwar and peaked helmet. And I think I've got a child's bow in my baggage she might learn to bend with practice. It'll still hit harder than the trash they shoot down here. I swear, if all you lowlanders had dicks as short and weak as your bows, I wouldn't cross the passes for gold!"

"And speaking of gold," said Rob, covering a moment's lapse into honest emotion with impudence, "what will this largesse cost us, *Mademoiselle* Arrow?"

"Call it a throw-in." she said, "given what I look to clear on this dinosaur-flesh deal. But if this strapping lad here wants to discuss additional payment, I'm open to private negotiations."

Gaétan's usual cheerful confidence had deserted him, leaving him opening and closing his mouth like a carp.

Rob hoped Stéphanie wasn't the jealous type. He had frankly no idea whether the woods-runners shared the common relaxed Southlander views on sexual fidelity. He did know not everybody happened to feel the way their tribe or nation told them to. Even people with less . . . potentially alarming . . . personalities than Stéphanie.

"You were saying something about us lowlanders and the size of . . . bows," Rob was unable to keep himself from saying.

Tir grinned and hooked her arm through Gaétan's elbow. "This one has strength enough," she said, squeezing a firm biceps. "I think he's worth a trial regardless of the size of his staff!"

The look Gaétan turned over his shoulder as she led him toward the farmhouse was almost pleading.

"Right," Rob said. "That's him seen to, then. Let's go look at our brand-new dinosaurs!"

Chapter 25

Los Libros de la Ley, *The Books of the Law*—The Creators' Own Law. Popularly attributed to Torrey, the Youngest Son, who stands for Order. They are largely filled with explanation and annotation, since the actual laws are few and simple: for example, establishing worship of the Creators as the worldwide faith, although allowing it to take many forms; enjoining people to actively enjoy life; abjuring eternal punishment; mandating proper hygiene; and forbidding slavery and torture.

—A PRIMER TO PARADISE FOR THE IMPROVEMENT OF YOUNG MINDS

"It's a shame what you did to your hair, child," Sister Violette said. Smiling in the light of dozens of candles on the little table around which she, Bogardus, and Melodía sat nude, and in alcoves around Bogardus's chambers, she reached up to run a hand through the brush that remained on Melodía's scalp. "It was so long and beautiful before."

Melodía fought the urge to pull away. *You didn't flinch away from her touch in bed a few minutes ago*, she told herself. *Why now?*

After that first time she realized she had let Violette seduce her after resisting her friends Lupe and Llurdis's incessant attempts because she was more mature, skilled, and—Melodía reckoned—lacking the drama those two brought to sex.

Perhaps she was more irritated now than she wanted to admit to herself by the way the Councilor kept trying to feed her tidbits of cheese and fruit. When Melodía had arrived late that afternoon on an increasingly rare visit to the château, the three had promptly fallen into a protracted lovemaking session. After they exhausted each other, Bogardus had called for acolytes to bring the table, and stools, and food and wine. Now the window stood open to black that shimmered with stars, admitting a breath of cool air that smelled of mountain heights and perpetual snow.

"I wanted to make a . . . break with my earlier life," she said. "Also, it's easier to manage now that I don't—don't have someone to care for it for me."

Don't cry.

"It becomes you," Bogardus said, sipping wine from a pottery cup. "Lovely as your hair was when it was long, this brings forward a different aspect to your beauty."

"I've been elected troop leader," she said, eager despite herself. "I'll have thirty light-horse under my guidance."

"Not command?" Violette asked.

"The *jinetes* don't take well to command," she said. "I've earned their respect. They let me lead them. By example, as much as anything."

"'Jinetes'?" Bogardus asked.

"That's what we call mounted skirmishers. Ah, my mother's people, that is, Catalans. What you might call *gentours*, I think." She paused. "We can't call ourselves 'light-horse' anymore, since some of us ride striders."

He nodded. "You sound proud," he said.

His smile seemed but a shadow of what it had been. *Maybe it's the lamplight*, she reassured herself.

"What's that dour stick Karyl think of it?" Violette asked, stretching like a cat so that her small pink-tipped breasts rode up her ribs.

That irked Melodía. Although not at her.

"He hasn't got anything to do with it," she said. "Master Rob approved my election. Karyl pays little attention to how his lieutenants handle things."

And none at all to her, although everybody else was starry-eyed that an actual princess—the Princesa Imperial, no less—served alongside them, notwithstanding her present legal difficulties. Yet it was Melodía's own ability and charisma that led them to elevate her. That excited her more than almost anything she'd known.

My father rules the Tyrant's Head, she thought, *and I'm thrilled as a schoolgirl at being given command of a handful of commoners who act, moreover, basically like bandits*. And she was, and she would be, and that was all there was to it. So there.

"Master Rob and Karyl want me to lead a patrol east, to sweep our side of the Laughing Water for Castañero raiders. They're getting bolder. Karyl believes they're probing to see if they can get away with a full-fledged invasion, while Métairie Brulée sits by, like a vexer watching horrors feed on a dead duckbill."

She looked anxiously from one face to the other, seeking approval—or its absence. To her surprise it was Bogardus who looked vaguely troubled. Violette smiled and hugged her.

"We're proud of you, Melodía," she said.

"But—I thought you'd be opposed," she said. "You've always stood for a return to the Garden ideal of pacifism."

"And I've realized," Violette said, "we've realized that our ideals are simply that: *ideal*. Goals to strive toward. As long as we keep those ideals pure in our hearts we're sure of doing the right thing."

"I don't understand."

"Your example helped us see the true way to grow. Your experiences, bad as well as good. You rested your hopes on the branch of idealism—and it broke beneath the weight."

Melodía looked down at her plate. She tried not to see dead eyes looking back from among the crumbs.

"The modern world is corrupt," Violette said. "It's too poisonous to nurture the tender shoots of idealism. So we must prepare the soil. Until that's done, we must put aside ideals like pacifism, the pure pursuit of beauty and pleasure, the liberty of actions and desires. Even the indulgence of thoughts at variance with the common good.

"When we have purified our Garden, those ideals can bloom forth once more in all their glorious profusion. Until then, we've got to bind and weed and prune."

Melodía frowned slightly at that. *Bind and prune. Why does that sound sinister? Especially since she smiles so happily as she says it.*

Violette turned to Bogardus. "I think she's ready."

He frowned slightly. "Are you sure, Sister? It's a grave step."

"Don't I know it?" Violette acted chipper, almost giddy. Her lavender eyes were fever-bright. "But you see how receptive the child is. And she'll be going away for who knows how long? Why deny her access to inner Beauty for so long?"

Bogardus sighed. "If you feel so strongly. . . ."

It was Melodía's turn to frown at him. His subdued manner was starting to worry her. His face had a grey cast, and the skin hung slightly loose on his strong bones. He seemed to have declined somehow since her last visit.

This afternoon he had been as thoughtful and proficient a lover as always. Yet Melodía sensed his heart wasn't in it. He seemed vague. Maybe even not as clean as he might be; she had thought to catch just the faintest whiff of decay when Bogardus and Violette squired her into the room. She'd been horny enough to overlook it, after her recent vigorous activity and prolonged abstinence. When he embraced her he smelled fine—faintly of his usual lilac soap, in fact.

But his skin had a curious texture to her touch, partly gritty, partly greasy. *Is he unwell?* she wondered. The thought didn't comfort.

Violette sprang up, sprightly as a child. The candlelight splashed her narrow bare back and backside in yellow shading to burnt orange as she walked for the blue curtain across the doorway at the back of the room.

"We've been discussing this," Violette said excitedly. "We both agree your spiritual development has reached the point where you're ready to ascend."

"'Ascend'?" Melodía said faintly. Her earlier excitement—and later afterglow—had faded. Now she noticed once again that, like Bogardus himself, his bedchamber had changed.

And like Bogardus himself, not for the better. Gone was the brilliant decoration that had enlivened it the first time he brought her here. The cunningly executed paintings were missing from the walls, the sculptures from their stands and niches. The bedclothes were still rich and soft, but their colors were drab.

Most of all she missed the flowers that once filled the room with colors and perfume. There remained nothing living or which had ever been alive between bare whitewashed walls, save for food, furnishings, and themselves. It was as if the Garden's guiding aesthetic was no longer Beauty, but austerity.

The deep blue of silk curtain screening the doorway was the sole touch of color that remained. Violette reached for it. Posing dramatically she looked over her shoulder at Melodía.

"You've heard us speak of Inner Mysteries," the silver-haired woman said, paused with her hand on the curtain. "Now behold the sweetest mystery. Meet our guiding Angel!"

She whipped the curtain open. In the small room beyond Melodía saw what she took for a statue of a seated man. By the candles' faint glow Melodía could make out hints of detail: features and limbs beyond exquisite, curly golden hair. Its face was lowered so that shadows hid the eyes. Even seated, the idol's head rose higher than Bogardus's.

The sculpted beauty seared her soul with its perfection. It exalted and disturbed. *Is this what they've been hiding?* Melodía thought, as her heart hammered at her ribs. *The most perfect work of art ever wrought by human hands?*

The figure raised its head.

It looked at Melodía with pools of blackness for eyes. Slowly it reached a hand toward her. The flesh on the fingers was mottled with discoloration.

The stench of corruption, faint before, now struck her like a breath from a freshly opened grave.

The greatest terror Melodía had ever known seized her. Panic blazed sunlike inside her. She turned and fled, heedless and naked, down echoing corridors and out into the cool autumn night.

"What in the name of the Old Hell is this?" Mor Florian exclaimed, reining in his cream and yellow sackbut atop a stony ridge in the Meseta uplands of western Spaña.

Comte Jaume dels Flors drew Camellia to a halt beside his Companion. He led his fifteen surviving and present Companions to the rendezvous

Felipe had ordered them to make. Close behind them followed their squires and their Brothers-Ordinary men-at-arms. Next, strung out behind them, marched and rode the rest of the Ejército Corregidor, the lesser nobles and knights and their retinues, still grumbling about the plunder and rape and slaughter they'd been denied at Ojonegro. Then came the baggage train, and last tramped the Nodosaurs. They were probably no less disgruntled at missing the fruits of an intaking, but so great had their contempt for the bucketheads become that they wouldn't deign to show it as their supposed betters did, but made sure to keep it among their browned-iron ranks.

The late morning was hot; the year's round of four two-month seasons brought only subtle differences to Spaña, except in the very shade of the lofty Shield Range. Two kilometers west the Grand Imperial Army of Crusade—El Gran Ejército Imperial Cruzador—lay camped by the High Road to rest. Jaume's expedition had just mounted the pass called Gate of the Winds, through the Copper Mountains that screened out most of the rainstorms blowing from the Channel and made La Meseta one of Nuevaropa's driest regions.

Like a great blanket woven of men, monsters, and engines, the Empire of the Fangèd Throne's army lay spread across a dusty dun plain. Skeins of reinforcement, from militant orders and vassal lords summoned from Spaña and nearby Francia to serve their Imperial liege, had expanded it to over twenty thousand strong.

Who now stood in ranks to either side of the gleaming white High Road to await their comrades' arrival: knights on warhorses and hadrosaurs, glittering House troops, peasant levies slouching listlessly, the grim brown block of the Twelfth Tercio of Imperial Nodosaurs. Beyond them a field full of tents and pavilions sprouted like so many gaudy mushrooms. Even at this distance Jaume could see the open red and gold pavilion where Felipe sat between his army and his camp, flanked by his Scarlet Tyrants in their gorgeous figured breastplates and wind-nodding plumes.

That surprised none of the Companions; the riders who had shuttled back and forth between the two armies the last two days had apprised them of the Imperial cantonment's location, as they had the Emperor of their approach. A hill or two back, Jaume and his men had stopped to don armor and swap ambler horses for war-duckbills in order to make a properly grand entrance to their Emperor's camp.

What stopped Jaume and his men with jaws hanging open—and made Jaume's stomach writhe like a spear-spitted bouncer—was the forest that had sprung up along the Camino Alto Imperial.

No natural trees comprised it. And—as the white-blond Brabanter Mor Wouter de Jong had once remarked, in a different setting—these trees bore strange fruit.

They were gibbets. Some bore crossbars from which blackened bodies hung by the necks. Some were simple poles, with strangely nude-looking bodies tied to them, with their flayed skins flapping like flags above them. Some held wagon-wheels, their victims' broken limbs woven among the spokes to increase their final agony. Some were no more than pikes, with heads on top. Others, stouter poles impaled men and women. Or parts of them.

"There must be hundreds of them," murmured Wil Oakheart of Oakheart. "What does this mean?"

"Nothing good," Florian said.

"I fear I am compelled to agree," said Manfredo. The Taliano knight managed to speak normally despite the fact his mouth and entire face were no more mobile than a stone statue's.

Feeling as if his armor had turned to lead around him, Jaume led them down onto the road of horror. Perched atop a tau cross from whose arms two bodies hung by withered necks, a grey-backed flier with a white belly and fanciful yellow and white swirls on its unwieldy-looking crest opened a toothless beak to utter a croak of annoyance at their approach. Spreading wings seven meters wide it flapped slowly away across the scrub-dotted plain.

We were blessed at first, Jaume realized. *The wind's blowing crosswise.* But soon enough and too soon, the Companions were riding between the lines of foul trees.

The stink seemed compounded of more than mere rotting flesh. As if misery and terror and degradation each had a reek of its own.

"Some of them are still alive!" Dieter exclaimed. "They're moving! Oh, Sweet Middle Sister Li, Lady of Beauty, have mercy!"

Tears streamed down his pink cheeks as he looked beseechingly around at his comrades. "Can't we help them?"

"I think they're beyond help," Florian said, without his usual snap.

"But they're not! Some of them are still moving. Look!"

Though he wished he could not do so—though he wished he could do almost anything else, including die—Jaume did look. And he had to admit to himself the young Alemán knight was right. Some of the bodies showed definite movement.

"Look yourself," rumbled Ayaks, his face fisted in a mountainside scowl. "Look close and learn."

He rode Bogdan, his golden morion bull with the cream-colored belly, past Dieter's sackbut into the ditch beneath a breaking-wheel. Drawing his greatsword from its sheath slung over his right shoulder, he gripped the hilt near the butt. Making sure he and his mount stayed well out from beneath he reached up to prod the swollen body hanging there. With a scream that echoed its occupant's agony, the wheel turned. The corpse, which was that of a woman, rotated head-down. Her head swung back, opening her mouth.

A cloud of flies with black furry bodies and opalescent green bodies exploded from her with a buzz like an arrow-volley. The maggots and ants that writhed on every square centimeter of her brown, greasy, naked skin fell like grey living rain.

"See where the dead juices dripped, and killed the grass below?" the weeping blond giant demanded. "See that? But someday flowers will grow here. Tell yourself that, boy: someday, flowers will grow!"

Dieter let his helmet drop from the crook of his arm to cover his face with both hands and cry like a lost child.

The arming-squires had ridden up behind, no doubt closer than protocol would normally allow in their eagerness to see what was happening. Jaume half turned his head toward them and without even looking, said, "If you please."

A brown-haired boy scuttled forward to retrieve the armet. It was Jacques's squire David, not Dieter's Wolfram. Presumably the Alemán was one of those now puking noisily onto the crushed pumice pavement of the High Road.

"The world is an abode of ugliness," the usually taciturn Machtigern said in a voice like an iron wagon tire clattering down a cobbled street. "It's why we seek Beauty, to find and foster it when we can. To fight for it, even. To restore the holy Equilibrium of the World against the likes of this."

"O dear, my lord," someone cried out, "please don't make us do this thing!"

Chapter 26

***Alabarda*, Halberd, Halberd-crest**—*Lambeosaurus magnicristatus.* Bipedal herbivore, 9 meters, 3.5 tonnes. Prized in Nuevaropa as a war-hadrosaur for the showy, bladelike crest that gives it its name. Easily bred for striking coloration, like the more-common Corythosaurus and Parasaurolophus; bulkier than either.

—THE BOOK OF TRUE NAMES

"*Tour*," a voice hissed from the darkness as Melodía picked her barefoot way through the trees and brush toward the light of a campfire belonging, if her somewhat fuddled brain recalled rightly, to one of her jinete contingents. *Tower*, in Francés.

"*Atout*," she answered, the day's challenge-and-reply somehow, fortuitously springing to her mind without conscious effort. It meant, "trump card" in the same language.

"Come ahead on, *jefa*." That last was a Spañol word for "boss," which her light-riders affectionately called her in a nod to her heritage/birthplace.

"Why are you Maia-naked?" asked one of the quartet sitting or squatting around the fire, drinking wine from bouncer-skins and gnawing chunks pulled off the scratcher they had roasted over the fire. This one's name was Magda, Melodía recalled. She was short, barrel-shaped, rode a brown and puce strider, and spoke with an unusual brand of Slava accent.

Melodía frowned.

"I don't actually remember," she said.

"Partied too hearty, back at the château, did you?" said Thom. Who was shorter than Melodía, and also younger. She recalled she often wondered how he kept his brown bangs out of his eyes. "We probably shouldn't offer you any of our wine, then, *hein*?"

"No, thanks."

Melodía felt her frown deepen as she tried to remember anything about the evening just past. She usually avoided the sorts of indulgences, alcoholic or herbal, which might account for her lost time. She recalled setting out for the Garden villa after the end of the day's training and chores. Then, nothing.

Suddenly a memory seized her and shook her like a rat in a vexer's jaws. No sight, nor sound, nor smell. Only fear—terrible, sickening, total fear like nothing she had ever known before.

"Jefa?" Magda stood up, black eyes wide beneath her single brow and the black braid wound into a crown above her forehead. "Are you sick?"

"You look as if you've seen a Faerie," rumbled Gustave, still hunkered by the flames.

The fear left Melodía all at once, body and mind. It was as if something pushed it out. Even the memory of it began to fade, as if she'd dreamt it.

"No," she said. "I'm fine. I must have gotten some bad food."

"Best go get to sleep, then," said the last jinete, Catherine, who looked no bigger than a child. "Tomorrow we ride out before the dawn, to see what mischief Count Raúl's up to."

"You're right," Melodía said. She gave up trying to recall her evening, and immediately felt better. "Sleep will make everything right."

Tormented as that dear, familiar voice sounded, Jaume didn't fool himself that the suffering that elicited it could approach that of even the luckiest of the poor ones who hung dead and stinking around them. His muscles, already wound like lute strings, cranked another twist tighter. He held up a steel-gauntleted hand in front of his face. How strange, he thought, my sinews don't rip themselves free of the bone. It seemed almost unjust.

He turned toward the cry. "My dear Brother Jacques," he said.

And stopped. Nuevaropa's most renowned wordsmith could find, for once, no words.

Despair reddened and deepened the lines in Mor Jacques's prematurely aged face. Jacques, the Brother on whom he relied most of all for the sheer, unaesthetic grind-work of keeping the Order running as an organization in the field. The last of men Jaume might've expected to protest. Should it have been the first? he wondered.

Camellia sidestepped on her vast hind legs and tossed her round-crested head, snorting nervous music at the smell of rotting meat. Spilt man-blood didn't alarm her in her marrow as that of her kind would. But she knew its scent drew big meat-eating dinosaurs as surely as it did eye-harvesters and ants.

"Jacques," he said, "honored friend and advisor. What is this you ask of me?"

The Francés knight wagged his head over his breastplate like a wet dog clearing its ears. His graying flapped lankly at the back of his care-denuded skull.

"Spare me, O Lord," he said. "Spare us. I beg you. This is abomination. It's evil, Captain. If we travel down this road, don't we make ourselves a part of this ugliness?"

"What else do we exist to fight against?" asked Florian, in a quieter tone than customary.

Jacques waved steel fingers at the awful maggot-writhing dangling things that had been born and grown up and lived as men and women.

"What else have we sacrificed so much to oppose?" he asked. "Shed sweat, shed blood, shed limbs and eyes and youth and hope? Lost brothers, lost friends—lost lovers? Please."

Jaume made him meet his friend's tear-filled brown gaze. "I can only ask again: what do you want me to do?"

"Lead us away from here."

This voice was calm and firm. Jaume looked to its source. It surprised him perhaps more than Jacques's outburst.

"We are ordered to present ourselves to our Emperor for service," Jaume said. "Loyalty and love as well as law bind us to this duty. Do you ask us to defy that, Brother Manfredo?"

"Yes," the Taliano said. His beautiful head was high, his jaw squared. "This is crime. Such wholesale murder by torture violates the Empire's own laws as well as the Creators' clear edicts in the *Books of the Law*."

Jaume let his chin hand fall to the sun-heated steel of his cuirass for a moment. He felt the slightly rough texture of the white enamel that coated it against his chin. He drew in deeply and sighed.

"You're right," he said softly. "You're all of you right."

He raised his face to the stinking breeze.

"I cannot deny the truth of what you say," he declared, pitching the words to carry past his too-small circle of Companions on their vast and colorful steeds, and their squires, even to the mailed ranks of Brothers-Ordinary horsemen waiting patiently behind. "I can't gainsay you. Yet I must tell you this: I mean to ride straightaway down this very highway of horror, and make my due obeisance to my master the Emperor."

"But what of our duty to the Lady?" Jacques said.

"What about our duty to preserve the weak and the innocent from the arrogance of birth and might?" asked Florian.

"What about the Rule of Law?" said Manfredo.

"Those are real things we must uphold," Jaume said. "Important things."

He nudged Camellia several tail-swaying steps forward so he could turn her without her knocking into anybody else's mount. Then he faced them all from the front, as was his place, even in this. Especially in this.

The Companions' reaction was plain enough: pain on every strong and beautiful face. Of the squires, the half who weren't still puking into the ditch on either side of the road were green-faced, lips trembling and eyes streaming. The gendarmes, the Ordinaries, kept a watchful air.

Some, like Coronel Alma and his friend the dinosaur master Rupp von Teuzen who sat his horse as always rigidly upright beside him, served Jaume and the Lady because they had found their place upon Paradise, and this was it. They would serve like loyal dogs, or like the gorgeous monsters on whom von Teuzen lavished such expert, tender care. Others served out of hope of so distinguishing themselves as to win elevation to the élite ranks of the Companions themselves—as Florian had. Others were in it for adventure, or hope of loot, or simply pay.

And he must persuade all of them, from the most mercenary Ordinary to his Brothers-Companion of spotless character. At least, most of them, he knew: for in the end, Beauty meant nothing unless grounded in the real world. Or he would prove himself unfit to lead his Order, or serve his uncle as Champion, or carry the polished tyrant forearm-bone baton of Condestable Imperial.

Lady, how I wish I could lay those burdens down.

He had to fight to keep from frowning, then. *Never let it be said Jaume of the Flowers was a coward*, he reproached himself. *Even if such thoughts prove it true, at least have the pride not to show it!*

"This is crime," he declared with all the trumpet-strength he could give his noted golden voice. "This is evil. I tell you only what all of you see in your eyes and hearts.

"And—may I remind you all, that in serving Beauty, we also serve the holy Equilibrium?

"I have sworn an oath. So have we all. We serve Church and the Empire, as well as the Emperor's person. And the Lady. Is it the part of Beauty to turn away from our duty—freely assumed and oath-consecrated—when it becomes unpleasant?"

He drew his longsword, the far-famed Lady's Mirror, and waved it at the corpses festering on their gibbets.

"How can we redress this evil by running away from it, my friends, my comrades, my Brothers? I cannot deny the clear evidence of all our senses: the Empire has strayed from the path of Beauty, of righteousness. Of its own Law, and that of our Creators. Who, if not us, shall lead it back?"

Some of his Brothers had begun to nod, their beautiful faces furrowed in thought. *At least I'm getting through to them*, Jaume thought.

"And I mean"—he let his voice ring out with all its strength and purity—"to dedicate all my efforts, body, mind, and soul, to resorting it to the path of Beauty, and restoring the sacred Equilibrium!"

And with his left hand he traced in air the circle-and-S pattern of the *taiji-tu*, the symbol of holy Equilibrium. The others mirrored him.

But Machtigern scowled. "Captain," he said, "isn't that getting close to the bad Imperial advisors' rationale Falk and his fellow Princes' Party traitors used to excuse their treason?" His countrymen's rebellion had wounded the Alemán knight deeply. That sore still festered.

"He's not wrong, though, our Captain Jaume," Florian said. "We all know Felipe's led by the voice he heard last. I will swallow my pride—and even my conscience—to help our Captain make sure his own voice is heard."

"Thank you," Jaume said. "Thank you as well, Machtigern. Thank you all, for hearing me—for following me this far. Even if none ride a step further at my side."

He lowered his sword and paused to give the words time to soak in. To calm himself he drew a deep abdominal breath from the diaphragm, as prescribed by the Holy Exercises. But the torture his thoughts denied him even the momentary peace of meditation.

"And there you have the choice," he said, "plain as I can lay it forth. Make it as you will—as you must. For my part, I will combat this ugliness in the name of Beauty. Even though it makes me fully complicit in this inexcusable breach of Law."

"I cannot," Manfredo said, meeting Jaume's eyes squarely.

Jaume made himself hold the other's look for as the better part of a minute blew down the breeze. Then he nodded.

"I selected you, my friend," he said, "I selected each every one of you, as my Companions—and your Brothers confirmed you—first and foremost because of your integrity: the content of your soul. If that integrity does not permit you to continue, I honor you and your choice. I absolve you from your oaths and hold you blameless. And Brother Bernat, let the chronicle you so assiduously keep reflect that any of those who choose to part ways with the Order now, do so in all honor, and accord with the highest aspirations and traditions of the Companions of Our Lady of the Mirror!"

"I wish I could in conscience bid you farewell, my lord, my love," said Manfredo. "But I do not see how the path you must choose leads anywhere but to pain and ruin. I wish you the best you can take from what lies ahead. And I must now bid you, bid all of you, good-bye."

He turned and spurred his splendid maroon and gold halberd-crested duckbill Variopinto east across the scrub-pocked plain.

After a moment, Wouter de Jong mumbled something and rode after him.

Mor Wouter's lover Dieter watched him go through pools of tears. He turned his sackbut's long-crested head as if to follow. Then he turned it back toward Jaume, and hung his head, and wept so the tears ran down gleaming across his whiter breastplate and the orange Lady's Mirror painted there.

"The rest of you are with me?" Jaume asked.

"Yes," sobbed Dieter.

"Until the end, Captain," Florian said.

Alma drew his own arming-sword and thrust it high. The whole corps of men-at-arms followed a blink later, joining in one many-throated shout: "For Lord Jaume and the Lady!"

Allowing himself the least of smiles, Jaume looked to the one Companion remaining who had not yet spoken his choice.

"Jacques?" he asked softly.

Jacques squeezed his eyes shut. "I will ride with you to the end of the world, Jaume," he said, "though in so doing I damn myself."

"It will not come to that, my friend," Jaume said. "I swear it. Thank you. Thank you all, my friends."

He stabbed the Lady's Mirror into the heedless, clouded sky. Then he swept it down to point along the befouled lane.

"And now—Companions, we ride!"

"Companions!" they all shouted back. And followed.

Chapter 27

La Vida se Viene, **Life-to-Come**—A radical sect of the Church of Nuevaropa that preached self-denial, holding that the Creators' mandates in *The Books of the Law* were metaphorical, and sometimes even meant the opposite of what they said. Despite its heterodoxy, which crossed the line into heresy when some sectaries claimed that sin could lead to eternal damnation, the Life-to-Come enjoyed a substantial following in the early eighth century.

—LA GRAN HISTORIA DEL IMPERIO DEL TRONO COLMILLADO

The sky on both sides of the Companions was now full of brilliant banners snapping. The bright colors were like nonsense yammering in Jaume's mind.

The peasant-levy masses they rode between were drab, soil-colored. Not unlikely more than a few of the poor tormented victims hung up as road signs came from among their sullen ranks, although Jaume feared the bulk were peasants whose main crime, and greatest misfortune, had simply been to live in the path of an army of badly scared men and women. But the rabble were screened from the arriving champions by cordons of house-soldiers, all gleaming mail and livery in blue and gold and red and green. Their gaiety affronted Jaume's inner darkness as sorely as the banners.

Only the relentless brown and black and silence of the Twelfth Nodosaurs, faceless in their charcoal-scuttle sallets, made sense to his mood.

Perhaps it was that he knew the real authors of the outrage he and his men—champions all—had been degraded by being forced to pass through were to be found among the brilliant colors. The Nodosaurs were about *brutality*—professionally so, and if anything prouder of their ability to absorb it than to dish it out.

But while they might have been tasked with carrying out the atrocities, they did not originate them. Cruelty was something entirely different from brutality. The earlier crimes had sprung from the cultured, the sophisticated, the gay of taste and manner. The natural rulers of Humankind: the nobility.

Jaume's nose told him the doctrines of the world-denying Life-to-Come sect held sway even in the Imperial camp. It was a testimony that he could even detect the unclean smell of the human horde after the abattoir avenue they had been forced to travel.

He led his Companions and their army between the ranks of thousands of men and beasts in unnatural silence. Unless he couldn't hear for the lamentation in his heart. But he did hear the wind: whispering its promises and lies, sighing, moaning, and eventually booming in the silken walls of the Emperor's open-front pavilion.

Jaume forced his gaze to focus on the single figure sitting in the shade—and, most particularly, not to look at the men who stood on the Emperor's either hand. With a plummeting sensation he noted that he didn't find the erstwhile rebel Falk the more unsettling—by a wide margin.

At the tent's peak flapped the Empire's flag, blood-red field bearing a gold imperial tyrant's skull, and beside it the silver key on blue of the Holy Church of Nuevaropa. Flanking them slightly lower were the banners of the Kings of Spaña and Francia. Lower still flew the emblems of the lesser grandes of the Crusading Army, arranged according to strict precedence.

As Camellia drew near the Emperor, Jaume saw he sat in a gilt-wood chair with red velvet padding in lieu of a throne. Felipe wore the simplest of crowns around his close-cropped, greying ginger hair: a gold circlet with the tyrant-skull emblem on the front. A yoke of red and yellow feathers covered his shoulders. He wore a gold-trimmed scarlet kilt of linen clasped by a sword-belt, whose martial effect was somewhat spoiled by the overhanging Imperial paunch. A pair of sturdy marching-buskins wound their straps up his shins.

That surprised Jaume. His uncle usually loved his pomp and display. Now he seemed to hearken back to the more austere days of his youth, when he fought Slavos and Northmen invaders from the sea as a common pikemen in the phalanx his cousin the King of the Alemanes maintained in emulation of the Nodosaurs.

As Jaume halted Camellia the ritually prescribed ten meters from his sovereign, the Imperial Herald cried the approach of the Imperial Champion in a voice scarcely less brassy than the dozen trumpets whose fanfare had preceded him. Jaume bowed in the saddle and touched his brow in salute.

"Your Majesty," he said, "your Constable comes before you, bringing your Army of Correction, obedient to your summons."

Felipe nodded once.

Jaume sent Camellia to her belly. She lowered her beautiful cream-and-butterscotch head, touching her beak daintily to the hard-packed ground as if in submission to the little creature on its chair. Jaume swung down easily, as if the thirty kilos of steel plate stewing his limbs and body were of no more moment than a silken loincloth.

With his right hand he drew his sword. With the left he drew his Constable's baton. Crossing them before his face, he knelt and bowed, so low that his long orange hair fell over the juncture of steel and bone.

"My sword the Mirror and I," he said, "alike at your service, my lord, ever and always."

Felipe laughed. "Of course! Now stand up, dear boy, and come let me embrace you."

Jaume rose. He barely managed to sheath his sword and tuck the baton back in the orange sash wound around the iron waist of his breast-and-back before Felipe jumped up to enfold him in his skinny arms. If the sun-heated armor stung it didn't dim his smile in the least.

"My boy, my boy," the Emperor said, holding Jaume back at arm's length. "So good to have you back with us again!"

"It's good to see you, Uncle."

"Now we shall do great things now in the Creators' name. We'll lay this damned sedition and heresy to rest, and forestall any such terrible thing as a Grey Angel Crusade."

"It's an outcome I fervently desire," said Jaume. Truly: for he didn't want a Grey Angel Crusade. No sane man or woman could.

As for the rest—well, weeks remained of the march to Providence. Maybe he could talk some sanity into his uncle in the interim.

Felipe turned to his right. "You know my new captain of bodyguards, of course."

Felipe said, turning to his right.

"Duke Falk," Jaume said.

"Constable." The black-bearded man stepped forward, extending a forearm thick as a normal man's thigh. Jaume gripped firmly it as Falk took and squeezed his own arm. If Jaume did a thing, he did it without reserve.

It still gave him something of a shock to see the Northerner caparisoned, not in his customary royal-blue plate with the black falcon on its white shield on the breast, but the gilded breastplate figured like a muscular male torso, skirt of leather strips, golden greaves, scarlet cape and red-plumed barbute of the commander of the imperial tyrants. Jaume felt a pang as well. Sieur Duval had never had much use for the Emperor's flamboyant nephew, and had been too bluff and honest to hide the fact. Nonetheless the Riquezo's devotion to the Emperor had been absolute, and his intelligence and vigilance matched his zeal.

Still, Falk von Hornberg was a man of proven ability himself. For all he'd proven most of it fighting against the Empire.

"And I believe you already know the new chaplain of Our Imperial Army," Felipe said. Jaume stepped back. "You'll forgive me, I hope, nephew, for keeping him after he came back to la Merced for poor Pío's funeral. But you'll doubtless be as pleased as I that Leo elevated him to Cardinal, as his predecessor wished."

Jaume could not keep his brow from tensing at he looked at the down-turned red hat that topped the slight figure to Felipe's left. Then the hat raised.

Beneath the flat red brim, black eyes burned into Jaume's from a dark, gaunt face.

"Well met, Count Jaume," said Cardinal Tavares with a smile. "Well met indeed."

"Your Eminence," Jaume said.

"You make grave sacrifice, coming to lead the Crusade against your own adherents."

"Oh, but they've departed far from that," Felipe said cheerfully, "as they have from holy doctrine."

"That remains to be seen," Tavares said.

Jaume set his jaw. *I thought I smelled his unwashed claw behind the horror we rode past*, Jaume thought.

Tavares was a fanatic adherent of La Vida se Viene—the Life-to-Come sect, which preached that the Creators' own doctrine about this world being Paradise meant to give pleasure to its inhabitants was only a metaphor, and that their real Law was stern self-denial, and the unchallengeability of the established order. As Papal Legate to Jaume's Army of Correction, he had encouraged Jaume's already-fractious noble underlings to defy his authority—and, yes, to commit atrocities. Which culminated in the murder of Count Leopoldo of Terraroja and his Countess, after they had surrendered in return for Jaume's grant of parole until Leopoldo could be tried before the Emperor himself.

It had been the greatest blot upon his honor. Until today, at least—an image of his beloved Melodía, naked, tortured, and hung up in the sky filled his mind, and filled his mouth with sour vomit.

But I've still got time, he told himself, *to resolve this madness. Or if I must see my darling spirited away to safety—in Ovda perhaps.*

Thank the Lady she's safe for now!

With a clangor like hammer meeting anvil the longsword struck the flat of Melodía's hastily upflung weapon.

It felt as if Melodía had tried to stop that hammer with her bare hand. The shock that shot up her arm was terrible. It threatened to splinter the bones of her forearm and part her elbow, even bash her shoulder from its socket.

Somehow she managed to keep a grip on the hilt of the talwar Karyl's vulgar but undeniably charismatic cousin had gifted her with. Mirrored in the curved steel of her own blade she glimpsed her own eyes, huge as a frightened cat's. *If I don't do something quick, I'll die!*

The orange dancing light of flames that bellowed as they consumed the farmhouse mere from her lit the Castañero's face sneering at Melodía from his open helmet. Going by his serviceable boiled hornface-leather cuirass and the fact he rode a six-meter-long strider instead of a horse, she guessed he was some hedge knight or mercenary adventurer hoping to steal enough, possibly on this raid, to buy and equip a more potent mount. What mattered most was that being male he was stronger than she was, even if not greatly larger.

And, she was realizing to her dismay, he was *better.* Tir had assured her the long, curved, slightly blade-heavy talwar was every bit as deadly as a longsword, specifically designed for mounted combat. But like most young noblewomen Melodía had trained mainly in missile weapons and spear-fighting, where her upper-body muscle strength would give her less a disadvantage against a male opponent.

Mostly by luck she managed to deflect a backhand cut up over the spired top of her Ovdan helmet. Fortunately her weapons master had not neglected swordplay training for her highborn charges either. Melodía's body remembered what it needed to without the intervention of her brain. So far.

Meravellosa dodged a peck by the raider's Gallimimus. The mare was a shifty beast, agile and sure-footed. But the strider's bipedal build and hefty tail enabled it to spin with alarming speed, and its toothless beak could strike with savage power at serpent speed. Melodía herself was going to have a bone bruise on her right thigh. She found she had almost all she could handle and more just keeping Meravellosa from getting pecked and shying away, giving her adversary a free cut at her.

Battle was turning out to be a lot more complicated than Melodía Estrella Delgao Llobregat, Princesa Imperial, had ever imagined from all her study of book and scroll.

Worst of all, Meravellosa had her tail to the burning farmhouse—and the Castañero's onslaught kept driving them closer. Smoke's scorpion-tails stung Melodía in the eyes and put barbs in her breath that caught in her throat.

A heavy blow rang her blade offline. The longsword darted for her face. Yanking Meravellosa's head aside she flung herself half out of the saddle to avoid the thrust. The sword's tip sliced along her right cheekbone.

The pain was brilliant. Blinding. A scream and hammerblow, all at once. Her nose and mouth filled with the copper tang of fear.

Shock seized Melodía in matador jaws. Brutal as her rape by Falk had been, she'd never been attacked with lethal intent before. As her mind exploded in white panic she somehow managed to send Meravellosa springing forward, away from the blazing building and past her foe.

What will Montse say when she learns I'm killed?

For some reason, thought of her beloved little sister restored a sliver of self-control. Melodía might not know real combat, but she knew riding. And she knew that, though her mare's four legs gave her a fast take-off, the dinosaur's powerful drumsticks would enable it to run Meravellosa down in the sprint.

Without consciously forming a plan she stopped Meravellosa and spun her in place. Her vision was promptly filled was the strider's jaws gaping, stretched right at her to the fullest extent of its long neck. It must have been screeching at her, but she heard nothing.

The fact the beak lacked a single tooth did not make it one Gods-damned bit less scary than the abundantly fanged horror that had sprung at her with every intention of snapping her face off.

As if her body acted on its own, her knees urged her mare forward. Right at the monster and the fire. Melodía felt as if she were observing events from somewhere remote. *I hope when that awful thing bites me*, that *feels as if it's happening to someone else too.*

Meravellosa saved her then. What her mistress asked of her was not simply to launch herself right at an enemy's open mouth, but toward roaring flame. Neither of which was something any horse in possession of its senses would choose to do.

She was a wonderfully intelligent animal, trained as well as the silver a magnate father showered on his daughters in lieu of actual attention could provide. Neither saved Melodía now. It was the love and trust the mare felt toward her.

Plain friendship saved her. That and the fact that, although both mare and dinosaur weighed about the same, Meravellosa's four hooves gave her superior traction to two splay-taloned feet.

Meravellosa put her head down and charged, ramming her left shoulder into the Gallimimus's breastbone. The strider squalled in fury as the horse drove it back. Recovering quickly, the raider shouted something Melodía couldn't make out and raised his sword to cut her down.

Melodía coughed as an acrid, awful stench filled her head and throat. The strider shrieked an octave higher. Frantically the Castañero looked around. His cloak, his mount's tailfeathers, and his own hair had taken fire.

The anger that constantly smoldered inside Melodía roared suddenly to flame, brighter and hotter than the conflagration that was eating some poor peasant's home.

"You fucker!" she shrieked. "*Die!*" Melodía flung herself forward along Meravellosa's neck, and using the last of the mare's momentum and the strength of her own fury, stabbed her sword-tip into the marauder's left armpit. Linked steel rings resisted briefly, parted with a strangely musical tinkle. She felt her blade drive deep.

The man uttered a gargling scream. Feeling the flames bite his mount darted right out from under him. He fell, pulling Melodía's trapped blade with him.

His weight dragged her half out of the saddle. With both hands she yanked the talwar furiously to free it. Fierce heat though not flames stung her cheek and arm. Some still-detached part of her mind thought, *I'm glad I cut my hair short.* Meravellosa snorted, bobbed her head and danced.

A rush of movement brought Melodía's head up. An enemy horseman bore down on her with sword upraised. *I'm dead*, she knew. *Fuck.*

Something blurred in from her left. She heard a wet, peculiar crunch. The swordsman's sudden scream was muffled by the iron shank of the feathered twist-dart that skewered his face from side to side.

As he thrashed backward over his horse's crupper, loudly gargling his own blood, Melodía finally pulled her weapon free of the man on the ground. Meravellosa promptly dashed free of the fire. She almost collided with the chestnut mount of a young blond woman in a leather jack and simple steel cap, who was whipping the thong that had been wrapped around the twist-dart about her right forearm with practiced ease.

"Valérie," Melodía said. Or croaked. "You're getting in the habit of saving me with those darts of yours."

The blond woman grinned. "My pleasure, Día."

Melodía looked around for more foes. None remained in sight. At least none still upright. Survivors of the farm household whose ravaging

Melodía's mixed troop of jinetes and woods-runner had interrupted were noisily finishing off a couple of fallen raiders with farm implements in the yard. Melodía glanced toward them, then hastily away.

When her head stopped turning her brain didn't seem to want to. The whole world whirled around her. She started to topple.

A strong grip on her left arm caught her. She found herself looking at the black beard and gap-toothed grin of the woods-runner 'Tit Jean—short for Petit Jean, or Little John. Naturally he was the biggest person in her scout troop.

The anger that had been tamped by her desperation to free her talwar flared again. Jean's smile faltered as he saw the flash in her eyes.

His look turned to outright worry when she laughed.

"Sorry," she told him, straightening in her saddle. The dizziness had passed. 'Tit Jean let her go and stepped back with manifest relief. "It's just that, when that first man set about me, all I could think at first was, 'How dare he? I'm the Princess of the Empire!' "

At once she regretted the admission, fearing it would make the others think she was giving herself airs. She'd tried so hard to gain the trust, first and foremost, of people who had themselves taken part in rescuing her from a terrible situation none of them would have been foolish to wander within a dozen kilometers of. She measured her success in large part by the fact that Valérie had not only volunteered to join her troop but quickly become her closest friend.

Did I just throw that all away, with a bit of buckethead arrogance? she wondered.

Then 'Tit Jean put his big round catapult-shot head back and bellowed laughter. The other troopers in earshot joined in. Melodía smiled in relief.

Then she swayed again. At once the woods-runner grabbed her once more.

"Best get down while you can," he said. "Better than falling on your snout."

Feebly she nodded. She let him help her, which actually consisted of him taking her about the waist in both hands, lifting her up and pulling her off Meravellosa before setting her daintily on her feet on the hard-stamped ground. She leaned forward, bracing hands on thighs. Melodia fought hard to keep from throwing up, because she didn't want to show that kind of weakness in front of her troop. But mostly because she really, really hated throwing up.

"I never killed anybody before," she said in a small voice.

"It can be hard, Día," 'Tit Jean said. "My first time, I cried for half a week. Of course, I was fifteen."

She didn't glance up to see if he was joking. Mainly because she was fairly sure he wasn't. She'd never encountered woods-runners before joining the militia—scarcely knew they existed. She'd learned they led a hard life.

Her woods-runners were all from the country west of Providence town, or even from Crève Coeur and points father west and north. Although she gathered that they ranged so freely such distinctions mattered little to them, when they were even aware of them. She had a couple who currently lived near Castaña for guides.

Though Raúl's reavers showed the foresters nowhere near the extravagant sadism Count Guillaume's Rangers had—and the farmers and others whom woods-runner called "the sitting folk" bore the brunt of their depredations—a number had rallied to the cause, once their brethren from the west brought word of how Karyl served their great and hated foe Crève Coeur.

"It's the first time anybody ever tried to kill me," she added. "Will I ever get used to it?"

"For some, that is harder to get used to than the other thing," Valérie said.

Melodía found herself laughing again. Even she thought it was crazy, and controlled it quickly. Nonetheless she still shook from its aftereffects when she stood up to say. "I should have said that to him: how dare you try to lay hands on me? It might've shocked the bastard so much I could've finished him right then!"

That sent everyone roaring. 'Tit Jean patted her shoulder.

"You'll do," he said. "You *are* crazy. But it's crazy like the rest of us vagabonds!"

Chapter 28

Guerra Altasanta, High Holy War, *Guerra de Demonios,* Demon War—177 to 210 AP. A global war waged between the Creators, their servitors the Grey Angels, and their human faithful against their archenemies, the hada—or Fae—and their allies. It culminated in Nuevaropa's last Grey Angel Crusade to extirpate Fae-worship. Now widely considered to be a mythic account of the Years of Trouble, from the dawn of human civilization on Paradise in Year Zero to 210 AP, which led to the formation of the Nuevaropan Empire.

—LA GRAN HISTORIA DEL IMPERIO DEL TRONO COLMILLADO

"D'you wonder I drink so much these days? Look at me: I've my hands on nigh thirty of the mightiest war-dinosaurs in all the Tyrant's Head. And Himself without question the Empire's leading expert on the use of three-horns in war—and not just because he's the only one. But do I get to play with my marvelous toys? Do I get to learn how to handle them at the feet of the Master? I do not! All I do is instruct the grooms and order in the feed for the great bloody brutes.

"You think I drink too much, then? Fie on that! Not enough by half! I'm still sober enough to do this bloody job, and that's too sober.

"And a job it's become, this game of spies. A great game it seemed at first. A lark for Master Korrigan, who knows a secret and you do not, by your leave, or not. But it never fucking lets up. Unremitting, it is. Day and night it's roused out of bed or drawn away from my dinosaurs to hear the latest reports I am.

"The bastard Count Raúl is ready to invade. He's trying to get that hunchbacked clown Countess Célestine to attack us too. Will she, won't she, will she, won't she, will she join the dance? Who knows? I don't think the great hornface cow herself does, from this moment to the next!

"So: Himself must know the latest glad tidings from my op'ratives, whatever they may be. At once. If not before. And where do we go now, Master Rob? Whither do we ride? Where do we spy?

"And the Creators will love us more than we deserve what if the Council fools don't buy us fresh trouble in Crève Coeur. We hear naught but unceasing complaints from their shiny new Countess and her lackeys. The Garden's got its missionaries on their tits the whole clock round, nagging them to do this, and refrain from that—worse than they're even after doings in Providence town, to hear 'em go on. And that's bad enough. We're lucky the Councilors fear Karyl well, and rightly so, or it's crawling all over us they'd be like lice, telling us when to go to bed and which side to tuck our tallywhackers away in our scanties.

"And what to do, what to do about the North of Providence? Is it that the no news we get from there is good news? Or is that news itself, and bad, somehow, that we never hear a bloody peep? The merchant caravans are starting to dry up, with the Council at them all the time, telling them what they can sell or carry through Providence—even pestering them as to what they bloody believe. But such as still brave the Council and the snow building in the Shield passes say they see neither teeth nor toenails of a single human between the mountains and the farms just north of Providence town. Nor do we get a bloody useful syllable from our precious woodsrunners. Not that there's much woods there to draw them; but they're afraid to venture there as well. Faugh! Beggars could teach us Travelers a thing or two on the subject of superstition, and that's saying a mighty mouthful. . . .

"What's that? Snort? Aye, snort indeed. It's a hard row I hoe. And now nothing'll do but Karyl the Great decrees we must be ready to march east day after tomorrow; and only by the good grace of our Mother Maia is poor Rob Korrigan able to snatch these few fleeting moments to unburden his soul. But it's a fine listener you are, and that's a fact."

A gusting exhalation, redolent of fennel and new-mown hay engulfed Rob's head in humid warmth. A vast pink and yellow tongue licked him lovingly from beard to brows.

"It's never a bit of back-chat you give me, Little Nell," he said, scratching the hook-horn's sensitive nostrils from where he lay on his back in fresh straw. "Aye, it's the best you are indeed."

"Knock, knock," a sardonic voice came from somewhere over Rob's head.

He rolled an eye back to see a familiar face hanging like a sun-browned moon in the lantern-shine above the gate to Nell's stall, in Séverin farm's restored barn.

"What's that, Gaétan, me lad? Do you know no better than to trouble me in my office, so?"

"What, the bottom of an ale-jug? Up and at 'em, Master Korrigan. Trouble's just exactly what we have."

Rob gave him a one-eyed squint. "Define 'trouble.'"

"A courier just came up the High Road. The Church and the Empire have declared a Crusade against us. They're on the march. Thus: trouble."

"Against—what?" Rob sat up. "Who's 'us,' then?"

"The Garden. Providence. The Emperor Felipe himself leads the Crusading Army hence, bringing fire and sword and all the usual trimmings. Karyl wants to see you five minutes ago."

Rob lay back at full length on straw-covered stone. "Fuck me," he moaned.

"It shall be done," Gaétan said. And laying hard hands upon Rob's ankles he dragged him forthwith into the yard.

"But it's the Empire," Rob Korrigan said.

"So what?" Karyl asked. He kept on walking down the hall of the largely rebuilt villa which now served him as headquarters.

Rob's feet faltered in surprise.

"Perhaps it is the world's end, after all," he said, "when the man who never asks a rhetorical question asks a rhetorical question."

"No such thing. The Crusading Army is far away. Count Raúl is a two-days march down Chestnut Street from this very spot. And that's if he and his toadies weigh themselves down dragging the customary cartloads of whores and other geegaws. I don't see how the news affects our situation, and asked to be enlightened."

Outside in the chill winter evening men bawled and dinosaurs squalled. Wagon-springs groaned as heavy cargoes were loaded and shifted. The Providential army made ready to return to war.

Trotting to catch up with his commander, and feeling like a vexer chick bonded to a farm woman, Rob said, "The proclamations they're sending forth before them say they intend no mercy on the heterodox. Whatever in the name of the Mother Creator and her Three Blessed Daughters *that* might mean. But it's our extermination they plainly speak of, and nothing less."

At the heavy age-darkened oak door to his office, Karyl paused to show Rob a sardonic brow.

"They can't exterminate us if we die before they arrive. Lesson the first: deal with the enemy you have at hand. Let's see off Count Raúl and then see what the Imperials bring us."

He turned the verdigrised bronze latch and opened the door. A slender figure in a leather jack, brown canvas trousers, and jackboots turned with a book open in her hands.

"Ah," Karyl said. "The Short-Haired Horse Captain, then."

"So that's what they call you now?" Rob Korrigan asked, entering the office behind his deceptively slight master.

A thrill went through Melodía, chased by immediate self-anger for being thrilled. Then she decided she should feel good.

It's the first title I've actually earned, she thought. *The first* anything *I've actually earned. Why not get excited that my commander acknowledges it?*

"Yes," she said, successfully fighting back an urge to add a coy, "I guess they do."

She set the book down on a reading-stand. It was an early fifth-century treatise on the Corsair Wars, then still in progress, from the Anglaterrano point of view. It was written in Anglysh, which she read tolerably well.

The room was bare but for a modest writing desk and a few chairs, stained and obviously scavenged. From the mostly empty shelves and the lingering smell of moldy paper, she guessed this had been the landowner's library. What books the Séverin clan had left had surely rotted and been thrown out. The lonely handful of scrolls and bound volumes on the shelves—all military in nature, except one curious, slim book dealing with the Fae, of all things—were in too good a shape to be anything but recent acquisitions. Presumably by the room's present proprietor, Karyl himself.

"You've heard the news?" Karyl said.

"News?" She looked at Rob in confusion. "You mean confirmation Don Raúl is about to invade?" Which news she herself had only just brought back, gleaned from prisoners and confirmed by woods-runners scouting across the river she, a Spañola, thought of as Los Aguasrisueños—the Laughing Water—into Castaña.

"As to that," Karyl said. "I want your troop to scout ahead of the army when we march for the Castaña frontier."

"Really? I mean, it's an honor, sir."

You've dined with the greatest grandes of Nuevaropa, Melodía thought in disgust, *and you sound like a schoolgirl about getting a simple task.*

Then it struck her: "What news, then, please?"

"The Imperial Army is on the march," he said, watching her closely. His eyes, so dark as to be almost black, burned like that of a horror on the hunt. "Here. Against us."

"Here?" Her heart slammed up into her throat and turned the word to a squeak. *They'll take me!* her mind shrilled in terror. *They'll take me and give me back to Falk!*

"It appears they believe they can forestall a Grey Angel Crusade by stamping out the heterodoxy of the Garden of Beauty and Truth," Karyl said, not without irony in his voice.

Her knees went loose. To keep from keeling over she put a steadying hand on the table atop the book she'd been reading.

It wasn't the thought of an Angel Crusade that made her stomach want to leap out of her mouth in fear. She didn't believe in any such thing—no more than she believed in the Creators themselves. To be sure, she had read histories of the Demon War, before the Empire of Nuevaropa was even founded, when the eight Creators and Their Grey Angels had fought alongside faithful men and women against the evil Fae and their worshipers.

She dismissed them, as she did accounts of subsequent Grey Angel Crusades, when the Angels roused uncanny armies to purge the land of sin and error. Just as she dismissed the tales of how Manuel the Great had slain an imperial tyrant—a beast not known before or since—which was ravaging the land, and somehow by virtue of that did established the Empire, with himself and his family to rule it in perpetuity. He had even had the monster's skull cleaned and gilded to serve as his, and his heirs', Fangèd Throne.

Melodía bought none of that. Those stories were all mere propaganda: made up to impress the impressionable.

But Falk, now. Falk was a devil she knew too well.

I can't—won't—believe my father has the slightest inkling what the commander of his bodyguard did to me. But with the Vida se Viene fanatics ascendant in his court, and fear of the legendary horror of a Grey Angel Crusade blazing at inferno heat, what chance had mercy for any of them?

"Melodía?" Rob asked with that strangely musical Irlandés lilt. "Are you ill, then, child?"

She could smell ale sour on his breath. But he acted dead-sober. Unusually so, in fact.

She held up a hand for time. She closed her eyes and pulled in a deep breath. She emptied her mind. Then, slowly, let the breath go, and as it exhausted allowed her mind to speak the single, secret syllable she had been given as a child by a Priest of All Creators.

It was a ritual familiar to anyone born in Nuevaropa. Indeed, everywhere on Paradise Melodía had heard or read of, from Tejas to far Zipangu, folk followed a similar practice. The men waited while she drew two more calming breaths.

When she opened her eyes she felt calm. For the moment, at least. And for the moment, that sufficed.

"What are we going to do about this Crusade?" she asked. Her voice still sounded like a gate hinge wanting oil. But at least it didn't quiver.

"Try to survive long enough to worry about it," Karyl said. "Which entails whipping Conde Raúl back across Les Eaux de Rire in convincing fashion as quickly as possible. Especially since word of this new Imperial adventure may embolden Comtesse Célestine to try to curry the Emperor's favor by smiting the infidel before he can."

Not once had he said, "your father." She appreciated it. She thought.

Then again, there was no reading this strange, and strangely compelling, man.

"We march at dawn, day after tomorrow," Karyl said. "You and your troop get the best rest you can tonight. Be ready to ride out along the Chausée Chastaigne by tomorrow's sunset."

"Yes, sir," she said.

She knew that was the proper response. Still she made no move to go. And not because he hadn't dismissed her; she had already learned that when the fabled Karyl Bogomirskiy gave you an order, you didn't need his permission to carry it out.

But the gaze he held on her was probing, not peremptory. "We will deal with the Imperial Crusade in due turn," he said gently. "Till then, don't let it worry you."

She couldn't help her skepticism from creasing her brow. Instead of reacting with anger, he said, "You're a student of the military arts."

He gestured at the book she'd been reading. "If you learn nothing else about them, learn this: nothing ever happens as expected. Especially in war."

He crooked a smile at Rob. "As your master taught me well, when he stampeded a herd of wild mace-tails under the legs of my three-horns at the Hassling."

"That was you?" she said to Rob.

He shrugged. "A good idea it seemed, at the time."

"A brilliant tactic," Karyl said, "for all it got you sacked."

Questions bubbled to the surface of Melodía's mind. Not least was, *why does Karyl hate my Jaumet then, and not Rob Korrigan?* She decided to ask none of them.

"Strange are the ways of fates and Fae," Rob said lightly. Then he winced. Melodía saw Karyl's brow tense and wondered why.

A hard rap rang from the frame of the open door behind them. Melodía turned to see a stocky, middle-aged woman in a battered drover's hat.

"There's a messenger just down from P-town, Colonel," she said to Karyl. "Says the high-and-mighty Council has their feathers all in a fuss over this news about the Impies. They're demanding you run back to pat their hands and soothe their plumage back in place."

Karyl made a face as if he smelled something worse than mildew in the walls. "Thank you."

"Will you go, then?" Rob asked.

"Not likely. I don't have time for that now."

He frowned and tapped knuckles contemplatively on his desk. Someone had taken it upon him or herself to refinish it with sandpaper and oil. Melodía already knew Karyl well enough to feel sure he'd never ordered such a frivolity for himself.

It's an odd little army I've found myself in, Melodía thought. Karyl didn't demand his underlings truckle to him constantly, like so many nobles she'd known. They treated him almost casually. Yet his least desire was crisply carried out. She'd even seen her near-anarchic jinetes roundly thump a mercenary for speaking ill of their Colonel.

She noticed without marked happiness that he was looking at her.

"You're inward with the Council," he said. "And they can't fault me for sending someone of low rank if it's you."

"For a fact, our employers are uncommon sensitive to social rank, for a passel of egalitarians," Rob said.

"Yes sir," she said. "But—Lord Karyl?"

He raised a brow.

"What do I tell them?"

Karyl smiled. "I leave that to our initiative, Captain. You know our situation. Put all that diplomatic education you got at the Imperial Court to use."

Chapter 29

Raguel, *El Amigo de Dios*, Friend of God—One of the Grey Angels, the fearful Seven who serve as the dispensers of our Creators' ultimate justice. Associated with Maris, the Youngest Daughter, and hence the least of the Angels (as well as reputedly capricious), yet said to help enforce order even among the Seven themselves. A spirit of ice and snow, he is often linked to female Angel and divine messenger Gabriel, as well as the stern Zerachiel.

—A PRIMER TO PARADISE FOR THE IMPROVEMENT OF YOUNG MINDS

Melodía rode a sorrel gelding of dubious antecedents north at a brisk amble along the Rue Impériale. The horse came from the army's general herd. Meravellosa remained behind, resting up from their recent adventures. She'd done most of the actual work, after all.

Full night had descended. The day's continuous cloud cover had broken, but now clotted masses seemed to swoop and collide across the starry sky, as if building to a storm. She smelled the promise of rain, soil still giving the day's warmth back to the night, and early winter crops sprouting in the fields. Off to her left the River Bonté gurgled beyond the trees. Bits of frozen volcanic foam crunched beneath the sorrel's unshod hooves. Moths as big as Melodía's head flapped around her in the middle-twilight, while toothy, tailless fliers squeaked in pursuit. Night insects sawed and trilled in the brush that grew beside the ditch. They gave her a pang of homesickness, specifically for the fireflies with half-meter bodies and meter-long wings that gave La Merced's great coastal fortress its name. They didn't live up here in the cooler piedmont.

She turned off on the unpaved lane to the Garden château east of town. She was surprised to see few lights agleam in Providence; the citizens tended to let go only reluctantly of the day's activities. But a single yellow glow outlined tall, narrow shops and houses as if a huge bonfire blazed in the central plaza. It gave her an eerie feeling.

She shook it off. It was nothing to do with her.

The villa likewise showed few lights. Even in the fitful starlight Melodía could see that the leaves on the trees and the vines drooping over the courtyard walls were curled from neglect and dehydration. She frowned. When she arrived here, scant months before, that garden had seemed a pocket paradise, a microcosm of what the world could be: green, fragrant, vibrant, abundant and inviting. Now it struck her as foreboding.

At least they don't have town guards standing watch outside tonight, she thought. The city soldiery had grown unpleasantly assertive in recent days.

She went inside. The corridors were deserted, dark except for orange light from the dining hall. She made her way toward the bubble of voices by memory, and the feel of fingertips on cool whitewashed walls.

Garden communicants packed the hall to the walls. Bare walls, she saw with a shock: the mural painted by the lost genius of young Lucas, which had once made the room into the semblance of a beautiful garden, had been whitewashed over, and the rafters repainted brown. It was as if the ruling Council of the Garden of Beauty and Truth had determined to purge itself, at least, of every trace of Beauty.

As for Truth, she couldn't yet say.

Torches flickered in black-iron sconces on the denuded walls, red flames giving off more thready, resinous smoke than light. A scatter of oil lamps burned low. Candles glowed everywhere in hundreds: on tables, the bancos, the niches where they emphasized the hollowness where works of beauty, statues and vases of surpassing skill, had recently stood.

Melodía took a seat on a bench built from the wall at the rear. No one paid her any mind. Every other occupant of the hall, even those murmuring to one another, leaned toward the dais where Bogardus presided over the Council of Master Gardeners. She felt as if she occupied her own personal bubble of isolation. *Which suits me fine*, she thought.

She wondered whether it might be residual guilt at having led so many of the Gardeners to terrible deaths, which made her feel so separate from what she had once believed would be her new family. Or was it something . . . here?

Melodía recognized Jeannette, Gaétan's sister, seated nearby toward the rear of the crowd. She had been among those who most warmly welcomed Melodía to the Garden. Ironically, Melodía had felt wounded when Jeannette had smilingly refused to accompany her on her embassy to Count Guillaume of Crève Coeur. At the time made her wonder if the Garden gossip might be true, that her attachment to her merchant family stunted her growth into full spiritual beauty.

Now she reckoned it proved Jeannette had common sense.

The young woman's auburn hair was wound in a severe bun at the back of her head. Her face was pale and strained.

On the dais, Sister Violette leaned toward Bogardus's ear, her face pinched with passion. The Eldest Brother's brow rumpled in an uncharacteristic frown.

The Councilwoman looked up and down the head table, polling the other six men and women with her eyes. Each nodded, some eagerly, some slowly. Bogardus seemed to deflate in his chair. Despite poor light, Melodía thought to see despair engraved in his face.

Violette stood up. Her hair hung unbound about the shoulders of her simple white gown like the ripples of a frozen waterfall. The light of myriad flames turned her hair from ice to blood and fire.

In a throbbing voice she began to preach. It was as if she spoke some language alien to Nuevaropa; Melodía's mind could only accept and parse pieces of it. To the extent she could wring out any sense at all, the sermon was all fire and blood itself, sacrifice and purgation. *What does the Garden grow now?* Melodía wondered, as sickness welled in her soul.

The Gardeners around her, once so soft and sweet and languid, now leaned forward with flame-glittering eyes, keen as raptors. Melodía felt her skin creep. Their quivering eagerness reminded her of Guillaume's horrors.

Bogardus rose. His flesh sagged grey on the strong, square frame of bones his face. His eyes were like caves. His shoulders, once broad and manly, slumped in a linen shift that seemed, even in this orange gloom, slightly grubby. Melodía's heart and gut both clenched to see him this way.

When he spoke his voice was halting, so quiet she had to strain to hear. But as he went on it swelled in volume and conviction, until it rang from the dulled rafters.

"All things that live grow," he said, "or die."

"We grow, and that is good. Plants in our worldly gardens can only wait for our hands, guided by our hearts and minds, to shape them. We alone can shape our own growth.

"Yet how can it be beautiful to try to seize for ourselves the shaping of the growth of our fellow humans? Do they not deserve to exercise their Creator-given ability to grow as they will?

Sister Violette laughed wildly. It shocked Melodía like a blow to the face. Not just because her laughter sounded like the cry of a dragon, kiting above the landscape on colossal wings seeking prey. But because of the sheer disrespect she showed the Eldest Brother.

"How can we not?" the Councilwoman cried. "When we look around at the world what do we see? Weeds, noxious weeds, springing up in profusion!

"What do weeds do? Choke beauty. Weeds leach vital nutrients from the soil, starving beautiful blossoms and healthful fruits and herbs. Does our human Garden differ so much from the world of green growing things?"

"No!" the Gardeners cried.

Frowning, Melodía settled back against the cool wall, with long legs stretched out before her and arms folded tightly beneath her breasts. *What's happening? What* is *this?* Her danger-sense, so late in arriving, began to tingle.

And then the Short-Haired Horse Captain thought, *Well, I've got a good sword and a fast horse. What can a bunch of pacifists do to me?*

Something began to seethe within her mind like a hidden monster in a mire. It wasn't just her perception of a threat that stirred. It was something in her memory.

But something her memory couldn't pull out of the concealing muck. Somehow she felt certainty that she didn't want it to.

She was starting to be damned sure she needed to, though.

Violette stood up smiling. "Bogardus is our Eldest Brother," she told the breathless crowd, "our Master Gardener. As always his words are wise. They grow from the greatest heart in all Providence—in all Nuevaropa. And yet something has misguided that growth. It is the branches of his thought that are twisted, now, and seek to entangle our limbs as we grow to the future. With the greatest of love and admiration I can only say: we must grow past this obstacle, and every obstacle.

"The time has come, my flowers of Beauty and Truth. To sow that Truth far and wide. And to begin the process of weeding and pruning the garden our World cries out for!"

The onlookers took up the cries of "Weed!" and "Prune!" Melodía's lips peeled back from her teeth. She'd heard such terms increasingly tossed around on her recent visits to the Garden. She'd never liked the taste they left on her tongue.

Now they burned like poison.

"Gardeners, hear me!" Violette cried, flinging out her arms in ecstasy. "For months the Eldest Brother and I have been blessed with the guidance of a mystic creature of perfect beauty and grace."

Beside her sat Bogardus, looking bleak. His face was haggard with fatigue spiritual as well as physical. As if he had stayed up late for many nights, listening to awful wisdom poured into his ear by some inhuman being.

"Until now it has been our holy secret," Violette declared. "Now it's secret no more: I bring forth the Blessed One whose hand shall help our Beauty and Truth grow to embrace the world! I bring you our Bright Angel, Raguel!"

At the far ends of the globe, north and south, the maps showed not just constant snow, but ice. Melodía felt as if she had been turned by magic into a block of it.

Nowhere in the Creators word, teachings, books, or legends, was there any mention of such a thing as a Bright Angel. Nor did the histories, however fanciful. She may not have believed them all, as anything but useful if sometimes wishfully thought precepts for a virtuous life. But she had read them, as part of her education.

They spoke only of the Grey Angels, the seven guardians of the sacred Equilibrium between Black and White, whose very touch brought death, their breath terror. Who sometimes sallied forth in Crusade to purge the human world of sin. Largely by purging the world of a large number of humans.

Raguel was one such. In an ancient tongue his name meant, *friend of God*. It did not mean, *friend to mortals*.

Through the entrance to the kitchen stepped a figure bent nearly double. Melodía's eyes went wide.

I've seen him before, she knew with sick certainty. She couldn't breathe.

The being unfolded to its full height. The audience gasped: it stood two and half meters tall or more. It was nude. *He* was nude; obviously, he. His hair was a cap of golden curls, his skin alabaster, his every contour the consummation of Beauty. Yet Melodía thought to see discolored mottling spread across His body like lichen growing on an ancient statue.

The same as before. The growing horror tolled like a bell inside the block of ice her being.

He held out his arms to the Gardeners. They uttered a joint throbbing moan of joy and fear commingled.

It's all true. The words tolled in her brain like funeral bells. The Angels exist. The Creators exist. Those aren't just stories to frighten naughty children. They're true. All true.

And I saw him before. In Bogardus's bedchamber that night I—

That night she stumbled back to camp naked and confused as to why. It wasn't just the existence of the Seven that was abruptly proven true in the face of all her lifelong swaddling disbelief. It was that their fabled powers were real too.

Such as the one to fog minds—and memories. She had been Touched by the Angel. Her memory corrupted.

Violated. Again. Anger began to burn hot inside her.

"Behold transcendent Beauty!" Violette screamed. She threw off her white gown and offered her white nakedness to the Angel.

Catching her frenzy like oil with fire the Gardeners jumped up. They tore their own clothing off and thronged forward. Melodía was gladder than ever she'd sat at the back, with none to push her toward the horror. And with every eye caught by that golden cynosure, no one noticed the way she hung back.

And no one seemed to see what she did: how chunks of rotting flesh fell away from that beautiful body, exposing a shriveled, skeletal frame covered in what looked like maggots solidified in midwrithe.

This is the beginning of a Grey Angel Crusade. This is how the Great Dying begins. The shock and terror still held her limbs as if block-frozen. But a different fear now began to play the bellows to her anger-furnace within.

Naked, Violette straddled a grey and decomposing thigh, grinding her loins against its gnarled hardness and moaning orgasmically. The other Council members gathered 'round, male and female alike, naked and imploring. The other Gardeners flooded around them.

"Wait!" Bogardus's call rang off the repainted rafters. He stood alone on the dais, holding out his hands as if to will the faithful back.

"This isn't right. Don't you see what's happening here? This is a Grey Angel. He'll take your wills, your souls, turn you into mindless creatures who exist for one purpose only: to butcher your fellow humans!"

Violette lolled her head back over her shoulder. "The time has come to prune the Garden of Humanity!" she cried. "I embrace you, Lord Raguel! Take me! Make me your own!"

From the shadows of the Angel's groin his penis arose. When flaccid it was huge, as all of him was, but otherwise not unlike that of a normal Nuevaropan man's. Yet as it stiffened to its full half-meter length the skin split and peeled away like a snake's, revealing a member like decaying granite.

So potent was Bogardus's personality that the audience had actually paused. But sight of that rigid, misshapen cock now seemed to draw them like a magnet. They began to shuffle forward once more, moaning low in throats.

"Is this really what you want?" Bogardus cried. "Where is Beauty in pain and destruction and murder?"

The Grey Angel held out a hand toward Bogardus. Corruption had sloughed half its beautiful face away, leaving skull-like desolation. Something like a thunderclap rocked the chamber, though Melodía's ears heard nothing.

Bogardus stiffened. Stiff as a stick-puppet he turned to face the Angel. Visibly he fought him, muscles bunching, sweat pouring down his face. But step by desperate step he went to Raguel.

The Councilors fell back. Nothing stood between Bogardus and the jutting penis. Even Violette detached herself from Raguel's leg and stepped with head lowered resentfully, peering through tangled white-blond hair with eyes no more human than a matadora's.

Alone and quivering, Bogardus faced the Angel. Raguel rolled his hand palm up. He drew it down. As if attached to it by rods, Bogardus dropped to his knees before him.

He opened his mouth and bent forward. Howling like dogs the Gardeners swarmed forward, hiding his submission from Melodía's view.

The ice shattered. With it the building anger vanished too. What remained in Melodía was *resolution*.

Time to go, she told herself. Well past time, no doubt. Yet despite overwhelming terror that threatened dissolve the bindings of her joints she didn't simply run for her life.

Instead, without quite knowing why, she snatched up her scabbarded talwar from where it rested against the banco she was sitting on dashed to the rear of the howling pack. An auburn-haired woman was ripping the tough green silk of her robe as if it were wet paper with more-than-human strength.

"Jeannette!" Melodía yelled.

Snarling, the girl turned on her. Melodía recoiled at the inhuman hatred that warped her features out of any human semblance.

When she was only a little older than Montse was now, Melodía had briefly been addicted to popular romances, overwrought epics like *Roldán the Doomed* and *The Seven Mystic Warriors*. Remembering them now she slapped Jeannette across the face. Hard.

Jeannette glared in such green-blazing fury that for an instant Melodía feared the might have to cut down the woman she was trying to save.

Then she blinked. "Melodía?" she said. "Did you just hit me?"

"Yes."

Jeannette looked around. "Wait, what's going on? What's wrong with these people?"

Then she saw what loomed above the writhing throng. "Oh, sweet mother Maia!" she exclaimed. "That's a Grey Angel! They're real! They're really real!"

"Yes, they are," Melodía said. She grabbed Jeannette's wrist.

"Run," she suggested.

They ran.

Part Four

Crusade

Chapter 30

Nariz Cornuda, Nosehorn, One-horn—*Centrosaurus apertus.* Quadrupedal herbivore with a toothed beak and a single large nasal horn. 6 meters long, 1.8 meters tall, 3 tonnes. Nuevaropa's most common Ceratopsian (hornface) dinosaur; predominant dray and meat-beast. Wild herds can be destructive and aggressive; popular (if extremely dangerous) to hunt.

—THE BOOK OF TRUE NAMES

With a dinosaurian grunt and a squeal of tortured wood and metal, the harnessed three-horn pulled the wagon off the dirt track that ran through the army camp. Watching by lights of torches and campfires that gilded the great brow-horns and gleamed in its yellow eyes, Rob nodded his satisfaction.

The supply wagon had been badly overloaded; Gaétan's hatchet of a cousin Élodie, who had taken over from Rob as chief quartermaster for the Providential army, would have the hide off someone tonight with her tongue like a dinosaur-drover's whip. No sooner had the wagon's brace of nosehorns hauled it onto the springer-path that led through forests and fields to Chestnut Street than the near front wheel snapped right off the axle.

Because it blocked the way for other wagons there was no time to jack it up and replace the wheel. Especially since clouds were thickening, Rob could feel the imminence of rain on his cheeks. Karyl ordered the wreck hauled to the side, to be repaired if possible, and otherwise abandoned.

The three-horn bull weighed more than the two nosehorns it replaced and their load combined. The professional Ovdan mahouts who had come with the trikes were a surly lot; this one had played no-speak-any-civilized-bloody-language when Rob tried to order him to chain his monster to the wagon and drag it clear. He tried in his rude but fluent Francés, Spañol, his native tongue, and Alemán. His Slavo was limited to a spatter of obscenities. The mahout hadn't responded to those either.

Overhearing Rob's increasingly vociferous efforts, Karyl had brought all the Ovdans together and, in their own language, delivered unto them what Rob reckoned was a truly magisterial ass-chewing. It hadn't made the skinny little man who bestraddled the neck of this particular monster any less sour. But he was more cooperative.

And here out of the night a wild-eyed woman came flying on a lathered horse, with sword in hand and wine-red highlights where firelight touched her short thick hair, screaming, "They're coming!" as if the world was ending.

As she reined up Karyl materialized, hair tied back, stripped to the waist, wearing loose dark trousers and carrying his sword-staff. Light-rider commander Melodía Delgao slipped from the saddle, then turned to help down a second young woman who rode behind her. To his astonishment Rob recognized Jeannette, Gaétan's sister, who had briefly been his lover soon after he and Karyl arrived in Providence. She was naked.

He trotted to help on short, bowed legs. When he put his arm around Jeannette she collapsed against him. He smoothed back sweat-matted hair that had pulled randomly free of her braid and plastered itself to her face like kelp. He felt something stickier than perspiration. When he took his palm away he realized it was coated in half-dried blood.

"By the Eight, girl, who did this to you?" he asked.

"I did," Melodía said.

He stared at her.

"Well, she was about to hurl herself into the flames. So I clipped her with my talwar hilt. I meant to stun her so I could throw her over my horse's rump and escape."

She looked uneasily from one man to the other. "Well, it works in the romances. And slapping her worked the first time."

Rob winced. "How'd it actually work?" He had an excellent idea already, having had more than a few fast-moving bottles and beer-mugs intersect his sconce in his time.

Melodía shrugged. "She doubled over crying and clutching her head instead. But it distracted her, anyway."

"Wait," Rob said, "she meant to throw herself into flames?" He stared at Jeannette. "Where? What flames?"

"At my family's house," she said weakly.

"You have our undivided attention," Karyl told Melodía. "Take a deep breath. Then tell the whole story from the start."

She did. And she did. Karyl's eyes narrowed when she backed up a month to certain events in Bogardus's bedchamber. Then widened at what she had seen and experienced there.

That started whispers scurrying like rats among the crowd assembling about them: Grey Angel. Grey Angel.

Rob began to trace out the S-within-a-circle sign of Equilibrium in air before his chest. Then he stopped. Not the best invocation, he reminded himself. That's their symbol. The whole reason they exist, if they do.

And to his horrid dismay he had a feeling he was about to have the Grey Angels' existence confirmed. In exactly the worst way possible.

"So you're saying this creature squelched your memory of your first encounter with him somehow?" Karyl asked.

Melodía actually faltered. Then she held her head up almost haughtily and said, "Yes," as if daring him to contradict her.

Instead he said, "Go on."

Economically and straightforwardly, she described the unbelievably nightmarish events in the Garden Hall—Rob would have to commend her on her professionalism, from a scouting standpoint. She kept glancing at Karyl as if to see whether he took what she was saying seriously or not. The very fact he failed to bark the listeners back to their tasks told Rob he did.

"Why Jeannette?" Rob asked when she got to the part about the pair fleeing the château.

"She seemed more—savable than the others," Melodía said. "And I knew the Council's harbored an increasing hatred for her family. I didn't like all the talk of pruning."

"So then what?" Karyl asked.

"She snapped out of it."

"It was like waking from a dream," Jeannette said. She looked as wan as she sounded. Rob could tell she hadn't been eating well. Possibly for weeks. But she seemed shrunken in more dimensions than the flesh. "A dream of drowning."

"The Grey Angels' fabled mind control," Karyl said. "You and our horse-captain confirm that it's apparently no more fabulous than they themselves are."

Himself is taking this all quite well, Rob thought. Karyl had spent his whole eventful life firmly disbelieving in the Creators and their mythology, and magic of any sort. The fact that the self-styled witch Aphrodite had regrown his bitten-off hand for him by magic had gone a way to spoiling that part of it for him. But now his entire worldview was getting kicked to pieces.

If it was all true, of course. If it was a lie, these two women were cheating the world of great performances onstage.

Karyl seemed to believe their stories no more than Rob himself. Rob had to credit the man for the steel in his character. Although he was also beginning to suspect with a sinking feeling that Karyl was handling the situation so well because he had already sussed out that he was facing the professional challenge of his life.

And if what I very much dread is coming next, Rob thought, *that means just surviving this night. If we do that things really get bad.*

Jeannette felt gingerly at her head. "I wish you'd found some other way of getting through to me than to keep hitting me, Día," she said mildly.

"Sorry," Melodía said. "She followed me right out of the villa and got on the gelding behind me. We rode into town, to her family's house to warn them."

"What family's house?" a familiar voice demanded. Rob's innards cringed. *Such goings-on*, he thought glumly, *make far better songs than they do livings-through.*

Gaétan swam through the crowd as though breasting surf. "My family? Our family? Jeannette? Baby, what's happened to you?"

She turned to her brother, then clung to him like a handful of mud and wept like a lost child.

"Yours," Melodía said, facing him. To her credit she didn't flinch. She may have been spoiled, the most privileged little girl in all Nuevaropa. But she had stood up to face-to-face combat.

And a Grey Angel, of course. Though Rob's intuition told him that telling the next was worse.

"There was a huge bonfire in the Old Market Square," Melodía said. "A lot of people were there. A man I didn't know was preaching; the listeners showed the strangest mixture of crazy fervor and listlessness. I couldn't understand."

"Grey Angel's spell," someone moaned from the crowd. "It's a Crusade."

"I didn't want to think that," the crop-haired woman said. "I still don't want to. . . . We rode past a procession of blank-faced children carrying candles, flanked by adults with arms and torches. I didn't stay around to watch them. By then we could see the flames.

"A mob was attacking Commerce House. Fire was already streaming out every window and door, and smoke curling up around the roof-beams. Évrard himself stood in front of his house, laying about with a great sword and trying to carve a way to safety for his family and servants."

Gaétan uttered a strangled cry. Jeannette wept in juddering breaths, as if all her ribs were broken.

"Your father gave a good account of himself," Melodía said. "He cut down half a dozen rioters as we approached. But the mob . . . wouldn't stop. Despite their losses, despite the danger, they swarmed him like horrors over a duckbill calf. He did all that a man could. But they brought him down.

"And then—then—" Her voice, steady until now, faltered. "They picked up your youngest sister and threw her into the flames."

"Alive?" blurted Rob.

She nodded. A line of moisture that glowed like molten copper ran down one smooth cheek.

Gaétan's heart-ripped cry reminded Rob of nothing so much as the last great scream Karyl's legendary matadora Shiraa had vented at the Hassling when, her shoulder torn open by Duke Falk's albino tyrant, Snowflake, she had been forced to abandon the being she had bonded to as her mother at the moment when she hatched. That cry had been so full of sorrow and rage it seemed too great for even such a giant beast to emit.

Rob was almost surprised that when this shriek of grief and rage ended, the young man didn't collapse like an empty bladder.

He threw his long arms around Gaétan from behind. Despite the many duties that kept him from playing his beloved lute over the past weeks and even months, Rob Korrigan remained a dinosaur master. He still swung axes and mallets to build paddock fences, hauled cables, tossed fodder bales about. Such a life had made him strong, and kept him that way. His build suggested a beer keg on short legs more than a hero from the ballads. It did not suggest a weakling.

Gaétan struggled. Rob locked hand on wrist, pinning the younger man's arms to his sides. Bending his knees and straightening with a grunt, Rob lifted Gaétan's sandaled feet right off the hard-trampled yard.

"That was when I hit Jeannette with my sword hilt," Melodía said. She couldn't look at the futilely struggling young trader. Rob couldn't blame her. "She tried to hurl herself after her sister."

She pressed her lips together and shook her head. "I wonder if what I did was right. My—that is, Count Jaume always taught that all true virtue begins with personal choice. And when did the Garden lose sight of that? Did they ever even see it? I'm afraid I wronged Jeannette by not honoring her choice to die with her family."

"She can always die," Karyl said. "Nothing easier than that."

Then he spat a harsh laugh. "For most."

"Let me go, you misshapen Irlandés ape!" Gaétan bellowed, kicking and trying to slam the back of his head into Rob's nose. Having had his nose broken by just that trick at least once that he remembered, Rob held his own head back with face averted. "I've got to go back! I have to avenge my family!"

"Will your throwing your life away bring them back, then?" Rob asked. "What kind of trade is that?"

Jeannette reached to stroke her brother's cheek. He turned his face away. He spat curses: at her, at Melodía, at Rob, at Karyl, at the world called Paradise. At the Creators.

At this blasphemy some of the crowd around them began to mutter apprehensively. Rob ignored them, continuing to hold the strapping Gaétan off the ground as though he were a child. Karyl swept the crowd with a gaze like a scythe and the muttering died down.

Jeannette grabbed Gaétan's face with both hands and smothered his outcries with a kiss. "Please, no, brother, no," she said. "I don't want to lose you too. I won't! Curse me if you will. You'll have to knock me down and walk over my body to go into town!!"

He glared at her. Rob felt him tense, and feared for a moment he might try to head-butt her. Then the young man relaxed.

Indeed, not just fight but heart went out of him. His suddenly dead weight forced Rob to let him back onto the ground. He barely managed to keep a hold.

"Very well, Master Korrigan," Gaétan said, his voice almost steady. "You can let me go. Later on you can give me the drubbing I doubtless deserve for the things I said about you. Or Colonel Karyl can have me whipped from the army for disrespect. I won't resist."

Rob let him go and stepped back. "You said something, boy?" he asked, shaking his arms to restore circulation. "I couldn't hear a thing, for your great empty sweaty-haired pumpkin of a head pressed into my face, so."

Gaétan looked at Karyl. Karyl made a brusque dismissive gesture. In a world of touchy nobles who'd call out a peer for the least perceived slight—and ride a whole peasant family into the road for less—Karyl had a hide like an old nosehorn bull. If you could insult him, Rob had seen no evidence of the fact; he had no more amour propre than a corpse.

"What else can you tell us?" Karyl asked the two women.

"There must be a thousand strangers in town," Jeannette said.

"Where did they all come from?" her brother asked.

Rob snapped his fingers. "The north! That's why Karyl's cousin reported it seemed so deserted—and why my woods-runners saw bale-fires, and wouldn't go there." He cut off, frowning. "But the north's sparsely populated. Where'd Raguel go and get a thousand Crusaders?"

"I'm no betting man," Karyl said, "but I'll wager there's not a living soul between Providence town and the passes."

"So they're all dead," Rob said. "Or signed on with this bloody Angel."

"So the evidence suggests," said Karyl. He shook his head and sighed.

"I see no doubt," he announced to the crowd at large. "A Grey Angel Crusade has broken out in our very own dooryard."

"Then let's march on the town and clear them out!" someone yelled. Others shouted aye! Still others muttered nervously of sorcery and blasphemy.

"The townspeople are joining Raguel too," Melodía said. "Those who don't they kill. Horribly."

"So what?" the militant voice cried. Rob craned to see who spoke. But the man stayed lost in numbers and darkness. "Even if they recruit a thousand out of Providence town, we still outnumber them."

Then it came to Rob. "And we've got dinosaurs," he said. To his mind that settled it.

For Gaétan too, apparently. He whipped out his sword and brandished it high. Its blade seemed to catch fire.

"That's enough for me!" he cried. "I'm for going back and recapturing the town! Who's with me?"

Before anyone could offer, Karyl said, "And they've got a Grey Angel." Not loudly; but his words carried.

Gaétan froze.

"How do you fight a Grey Angel?" Karyl asked, his voice still quiet and penetrant as an arrow. "With any chance of winning, I mean? If you think you know how, Gaétan, I surrender command of the army to you on the instant, and shall follow and eagerly learn."

The tip of Gaétan's sword crunched in the dirt. He hung his head. "I'm sorry, Colonel. I wasn't thinking."

"Then gather your wits and start," Karyl said, not unkindly. "We need you, and we need you sharp. We need everybody."

He turned to the onlookers. "If we weren't halfway ready to take the road we'd be doomed," he said. "Take this lesson to heart: sometimes it truly is better to be lucky than good. We march on the hour. Anybody or anything not ready to move then will be left to the horde."

"The horde?" someone asked.

"Did you not hear this woman then, when she rode into camp all in a fuss?" Rob said. "She called out, 'They're coming!' Who do you think she meant, you great git?"

But he looked to Karyl in concern. "We've wounded in the infirmary," he said. Practice, drill, and simple camp routine caused their share of injuries. Anytime you mixed people with big, strong, volatile animals like horses—to say nothing of dinosaurs—they got hurt.

"Load them in wagons," Karyl replied. "Dump food if you have to. There'll be plenty of game and forage along the route, anyway."

"Our route where?" Rob asked.

"South."

"Toward Métairie Brulée?" Rob exclaimed.

"Toward the Imperial Army?" Melodía yelped.

"There's at least a chance we can pass through Métairie Brulée without fighting," Karyl said. "And if we have to fight, I like our chances with Célestine's army better than Raúl's. As for the Imperials, the facts remain the same: they're far. The Angel and his horde are near. And if the Impies are marching to forestall a Grey Angel Crusade—well, they're too late now. Perhaps they'll turn back."

"You don't know my father," Melodía said.

"Better than you might think," Karyl said.

"But what about Count Raúl?" asked Eamonn Copper. Rob hadn't seen him come up. Drink blurred the edges of his words but his eyes were clear. He'll not let a little thing like having a load aboard impair him, thought Rob, good Ayrishmuhn that he is.

"Castaña?" Karyl barked a laugh. "He's Raguel's problem now. May they find great pleasure in getting to know each other."

Then turning at a fresh commotion, he said, "What's this?"

It was a party of jinetes. Rob recognized the picket he'd set to watch in the woods west across the Imperial High Road. They surrounded a rider who wasn't of their troop, who had a flag-bright burn across his face. To Rob's amazement a woods-runner rode beside him. The woods-runners were willing enough to ride pillion with the light-horse, but most insisted they couldn't learn to manage the "great ungainly beasts" themselves.

"They crossed the Lisette last night," the wounded horseman reported, swinging down from the saddle to dump a proffered duckbill-leather bucket of water over his head.

"Who?" Rob demanded. "Not the Crève Coeur army, surely?"

"No army," the rider said. "Not like any I've seen."

"Mad things," said the woods-runner, who had dismounted with evident relief and moved smartly away from the horse as if unwilling to acknowledge the association. "Evil. Like dead men walking. And women, and children. With no more fear to them than logs."

"You couldn't stop them with your bows?" Rob asked.

"There were more of them than we had arrows," the woods-runner said. "More than there are arrows, maybe. They seemed more numerous than the wood's very trees. And the way they treat those who fall into their hands alive makes Count Guilli's Rangers seem like Maia's Mothers of Mercy."

"So that's what the Council's missionaries have really been up to in Crève Coeur," Karyl said in disgust. "Assembling their own Grey Angel horde."

"But how could they . . . *compel* the Brokenhearts, without an Angel's powers?" Rob asked.

"Maybe Raguel visited them himself," Melodía said.

"But it took these men a day's hard ride to get here on horseback!"

"And that awful thing had legs almost as long as I am tall! Who knows how fast it can walk? Or run?"

"Who knows if he needs to run?" someone else shouted. "He's a Grey Angel!"

"I don't care how he did it," Karyl said. "Or how the horde was raised. The fact is: it's raised. It's about to be here. Our only choice now is flight."

"But isn't it our duty to submit to the Grey Angel's will?" a man's voice sobbed from the dark. "They are the Creators' own avengers!"

Karyl gestured in the direction of the town. "Be my guest," he said. "I'm not ready either to become a mindless thing, or a corpse."

The silence that answered was eloquent.

Karyl turned to Melodía. "Are you up to leading your light-horse in a rear-guard action? It will be dangerous. It will also be key to our army's survival."

Melodía's throat seized up. Her pulse hammered. *Face Raguel? Again? I can't!*

She wanted to fall to her knees and beg Karyl to spare her. Even kill her on the spot. Anything but face that horror a third time.

Instead she caught herself on the verge of toppling over. *I'm hyperven-*

tilating, she thought. She forced herself to draw a deep if ragged breath from her diaphragm.

It gave her a little of her mind back. *I wanted to have* consequence, she reminded herself. *I wanted to make a difference in the world. How can I do that, if I give into my fears? Even fear this great?*

"I—" She swallowed. "I'm willing."

"Very well." Karyl nodded. "Get your troop together and ride north as soon as you can to screen our retreat. With your permission, Master Rob."

"But that means fighting our employer!" Rob exclaimed.

All around them men and women rushed this way and that, carrying out assignments barked by their superiors. In the torchlight Karyl's smile could have looked no more ghastly had his mouth been filled with blood.

"I'm surprised a dinosaur master as seasoned as you forgets the Mercenary's Second Rule."

"And what might that be?"

"When your employer turns on you, the contract's canceled. Of course."

He turned away. Feeling a jongleur's professional awareness of playing the straight man, Rob called after him, "But what's the Mercenary's First Rule?"

Karyl looked back. It looked as if every nightmare that had wakened him screaming on the road and in the first months in Providence, the night-terrors that went away once campaigning began in earnest, had all come back on him at once like a cloud of corpse-ripping fliers.

"They always turn on you," he said. "As I was taught at Gunters Moll."

Chapter 31

Jinete, **Light-rider**—Skirmishers and scouts, often women, who ride horses and striders. They wear no armor, or at most a light nosehorn-leather jerkin, with sometimes a leather or metal cap. They use javelins or feathered twist-darts, and a sword. Some also carry a light lance and a buckler. A few shoot shortbows or light crossbows, but mounted archery is very difficult, and not much practiced in Nuevaropa.

—A PRIMER TO PARADISE FOR THE IMPROVEMENT OF YOUNG MINDS

"Don't get your weapons stuck in an enemy," Melodía told her jinetes in the cool and pregnant dark. "Edge over point. If you have to thrust with sword or lance, don't be afraid to let it go. You can replace a weapon easier than you can replace you."

They were mustered in the Séverin farmhouse foreyard beside the elevated Imperial Road. Volunteers had swelled her troop to nearly fifty. But they were all she had to stall whatever awfulness was coming, and give the army time to get underway.

"Use your darts and javelins when you can. That's why you have them; that's why the Colonel sent a whole wagonload more along with us. Questions?"

"None," called out Valérie, her lieutenant and now best friend. Slender, deceptively delicate-looking, Valérie was a town girl of some means who joined up after the first successful ambush looking for adventure and had distinguished herself in action. She was popular, and could easily have been elected troop-commander. But she preferred to play second-in-command.

Melodía drew sword and signaled the advance. The jinetes followed her across the ditch, whose weedy bottom already ran in a trickle from the rain that had begun to spit down intermittently, then up the berm onto the roadway. Turning right to tunk across a plank bridge over the stream that angled through camp they set out north at the trot.

Providence town burned. In places orange flames shot higher than the peaked roofs. Smoke rolled up to meld with forge-hued clouds. Melodía imagined she heard screaming.

I hope it's my imagination, she thought.

Half a kilometer up the Chausée Imperial, they met a hundred refugees streaming south. Grey-faced in diffuse light of stars and Eris and reflected fire-glow, gasping in their terror and fatigue, most carried nothing but the clothes on their backs. Without need for orders the troop split to either side of the road, flowing back together when they passed the dispirited gaggle.

Halfway to town the road climbed a long, slow hill. Hellish yellow glow silhouetted a wagon piled high with household goods, drawn by a single plodding nosehorn. Melodía signaled her riders to go slow. Karyl had ordered that refugees be allowed to join the army if they agreed to follow instructions—and showed no signs of Raguel's madness. She wasn't sure that was wise. But it wasn't her problem; she put it from her mind.

Then she saw that shadow figures swarmed over the wagon to grapple with people perched atop the cargo-mound. A woman ran toward them, eyes wild, smock ripped to bare a swinging breast, pleading for help. Her cries rose to wordless shrieking as she was tackled to the pumice from behind.

"They're here!" Melodía shouted, thankful that tedious years of singing-lessons by a fussy, overly perfumed Taliano had taught her to project her voice like a brass trumpet. "Troop, skirmish forward!"

She charged on Meravellosa, lashing out with her talwar. She used the curved blade's flat to beat back the people piling onto the fallen woman. But although in her excitement, and with her height advantage, she struck so hard it hurt her whole arm and shoulder, her blows did no more than momentarily distract the attackers.

Even as she'd ridden out of Providence town with a bloody-faced and moaning Jeannette behind—was it really just an hour before?—Melodía wondered if she could bring herself to kill members of the Grey Angel horde. The man she had fought in the valley of the Laughing Water was a professional warrior, and a raider to boot—no more than a violent criminal, really. Although once she would have thought him nothing worse than a member of her own class who exercised his privileges to excess; maybe she would've nodded with appropriately furrowed brow as Josefina Serena wept for his cruelty.

Instead she'd killed him. And, after her purely physical reflex, felt nothing but justified. She'd dreamed of the confrontation since, to be sure. And in those nightmares seen, not herself killing him, but what he would have done to her and her friends if she hadn't.

But could she kill mere . . . people? Innocents caught up by an irresistible force?

Then a woman raised a face whose bottom half was masked in blood from her still-screaming victim's back to snarl at Melodía. And suddenly all Melodía could see were the red-dripping muzzles of Count Guillaume's horrors as they ripped her best friend to death.

She slashed the face apart with her backhand, screaming louder than the woman she cut down.

Belatedly remembering her own instructions, Melodía darted Meravellosa ten meters back down the hill. Slamming her Ovdan sword into the pebbled duckbill-leather scabbard hanging from her pommel, she snatched a javelin from a pannier behind her right leg.

The refugee woman's struggles subsided to twitches, and her shrieks to moans. A pool of darkness grew around her quicker than the porous tufa and well-drained roadbed could suck it down. A man stood up from his victim with an air of satisfaction. Melodía flung the javelin into his capacious belly.

Jinetes rode up beside her. A strider, worse-tempered than a horse, squalled rage. A horde member howled as a lightning peck burst his eye in its socket.

Quickly slaughtering the blood-soaked pack, the riders showered darts at the figures who still clung to the wagon like baby sea-scorpions to their three-meter-long mother's back. Melodía hung back to pant for breath. Her body ran with unpleasantly slick sweat inside her fatty-leather jack.

A farm boy named Marc rode up on a bay gelding, carrying a hunting spear. He looked down at the fallen fugitive, then at Melodía. She nodded. Face wrenched by emotion, he drove the spear down hard between the prone woman's shoulder blades. Her limbs and head starfished backward up off the gravel. Then she went limp.

The jinetes regrouped. To Melodía's relief they hadn't lost anybody, and suffered no hurts worse than scratches and bruises. She wished it would last, knew it couldn't.

"The road ahead's clear almost to the outskirts," Valérie reported. She shook her head, making her braids swing beneath her steel cap. "They—the—the hordelings, they won't run. All we can do is kill them."

Her voice held a leaden quality to it, not the usual light and bright of a naturally high spirit exalted by the fierce pleasure of fighting deadly danger and winning. Melodía understood.

Melodía's troopers trotted back to the supply wagon to replenish their missiles. Some who had experience with wagon-handling beseeched and bullied the thoroughly terrified nosehorn into dragging the refugee wagon athwart the road, then released it from its harness. With its long tongue the vehicle more than served to block the thoroughfare. It wouldn't stop the horde, especially not afoot—as all the hordelings Melodía had so far seen had been. But her job wasn't to defeat Raguel's host, nor even turn it back. It was to buy time for Providence's army to get away as cleanly as possible. Any slight delay helped.

A couple of riders Melodía detailed to drive the liberated nosehorn back to Séverin farm. Karyl could use every dray beast he could get. She led the rest, panniers filled with fresh darts, north along the High Road toward the glow of a burning town.

A few hundred meters to the east a farmhouse blazed. West by the river flames shot from the top of the old stone water-mill. Melodía hoped all the occupants were safely away.

I wish I could believe it.

The jinetes were spread out across open country to either side of the Chausée Imperial. The horde had spread out even farther to advance cross-country, over fields and through woods.

A flurry of brief, bloody skirmishes had confirmed what she never doubted: Valérie reported truly. The hordelings, as they had fallen to calling them—wouldn't flee. They showed an almost complete lack of sense of self-preservation or will—except to kill. Most walked at a slow and mindless shamble. Until they spotted prey: then they pounced with the swift savagery of dromaeosaurs.

They might not rout, Melodía and her riders had learned, but they could be discouraged, even stopped. When jinetes stood off from a mob of them and pelted it with darts, it would come apart like a dirt clod in a hard rain. But they soon discovered that not all the Angel's followers lacked volition. They regrouped quickly, and sought ways to bypass her pitifully small blocking force. Some intelligence guided their actions.

That Raguel himself might be near hit Melodía like a gulp of cold sewage: it sickened and chilled her at once. But she kept the panic that yammered and fought like a penned beast to escape and devour her mind under control, by focusing on keeping her people alive.

As many as I can. As long as I can.

"*Bluhdi Hel!*" Rob Korrigan roared in Anglysh, waving his dinosaur master's axe Wanda for emphasis. Then in the Francés his listeners might actually comprehend: "They're your brothers and sisters, not clotting sacks of grain!"

Soldiers carried wounded from Séverin farm's main house and loaded them aboard a wagon. Its drover had tied bandannas around the eyes of its two yoked nosehorns to keep them from stampeding; as it was they tossed their great-horned snouts in panic and added their bawling to the general pandemonium. Rob knew the need for speed, but the crew was getting a little enthusiastic about slinging the injured into the bed.

Screams rising behind made him turn. A man ran at him across the yard. He wore a leather apron of some sort. Rob's first, mad thought was, *An awfully incautious dyer he must be: not only are his arms stained halfway past the elbows, he's splashed his fool face as well.*

Then he saw the way the man's eyes rolled in his face and his mouth gaped unnaturally wide. He reached hands that were wet with something that definitely wasn't dye for Rob.

His head burst like an overripe melon when Rob slammed his axe both-handed into the side of it.

"Shit," Rob said. All around him he saw people grappling.

I hope I haven't lost the Short-Haired Horse Captain and her whole troop. Karyl expected they'd never hold the horde, just delay it as long as they could. Which was exactly this long, it seemed.

He even found himself hoping the Imperial chit had survived. Aye, she had cost him dear; yet she showed promise. And he was no man to take lightly the loss of such a beautiful girl.

He spun and waved his bloody axe in the air. "To arms!" he shouted. "The bastards are upon us."

To their credit the burly pair handing up a sheet-wrapped woman didn't simply drop her. They did however sling her right past the pair of attendants standing in the wagon-bed—like, yes, a grain sack. Rob hadn't the heart to yell at them.

Nor the breath. He set off at a lumbering run toward the nearest knot of combat.

As if waiting for this moment the rain burst down in torrents. It chilled Rob to the core. *No matter*, he thought. *The work'll warm me, quick enough.* He was more concerned that he'd be fighting in treacherous footing.

Most invaders fought unarmed. The rest sported a bizarre assortment of weapons, from hoes and kitchen knives and crafters' hammers, to swords and halberds likely looted from the arsenal. All attacked amateurishly, but with as much straight-ahead ferocity as any house-shield armored cap-a-pie.

As he came up on the rear of a mob assailing a cart stacked high with casks, Rob saw Karyl. The Colonel stood alone in the midst of a circle of hordelings. Rain streaming down bearded face and bare chest, his single-edged staff-sword in his left hand, staff-sheath in his right, he faced a dozen attackers with his customary battle calm.

Right, then, he's got the blighters just where he wants them, Rob thought, and began to chop flesh and bone like cordwood.

They fought in driving rain, amidst a black confusion of brush and trees. Chance had set Valérie at Melodía's side. She had lost her helmet. By the scattered, shifting light of a wood-cutter's cot burning off to the right Melodía could see her lieutenant's blond hair was a seaweed mat of blood and sweat. Her features, so pertly pretty Melodía felt pangs of jealousy at times, were smeared with dark muck whose composition Melodía didn't care to guess.

It was all either woman could do to keep her legs clamped around the heaving, rain and sweat-slick barrel of her horse. Melodía's arms felt as if their skin was filled with embers, and every slight motion drove spikes into elbows and shoulders.

Unfortunately, staying alive required constant movement that was anything but slight.

She heard her friend call, "*Sacrée Maia Mère*, it's a little girl! Come here, child."

As she drew her talwar once more, having exhausted her supply of darts, once more—how many trips she'd made to the steadily retreating wagon, she couldn't count—Melodía saw Valérie urge her chestnut mare several splashing paces forward. Leaning from her saddle, she reached down to a child with long dark hair falling in her face and over the shoulders of a grubby sleeping-shift. She couldn't have been twelve.

The girl grabbed Valérie's wrist with both hands and bit hard on her forearm. She clung single-mindedly as the horsewoman cried out more in surprise than pain.

After the night's exertions the scout lacked strength to pull away. From the brush a swarm of hordelings boiled like flat-nose fliers from a barn loft at sunset, shrilling with blood-hunger. Before Melodía could do more than blink, they engulfed her friend.

Melodía charged Meravellosa into them, slashing with renewed energy. Blood flew at her like reverse black rain. But there were already too many to cut through. More crazed people swarmed to surround Melodía. Dozens of them, faces blood-smeared and contorted, eyes standing out as if grown too big for the sockets.

Even as Valérie's mare sent one flying with a kick that audibly broke his pelvis, the hordelings pulled her down. Somehow she managed to land on her feet, striking out with a fist and the hilt of her arming-sword.

Her blue eyes met Melodía's. She flung out her free hand. "Go!" she shouted. "Get away!"

Melodía faced a choice: die, or do as her doomed friend said. Wheeling Meravellosa about, she hacked her way free. At least there was this: fresh hot tears as well as raindrops cleansed her eyes of spattered blood.

All around her she could hear brush crackling and shouts and screams as her jinetes battled the fresh onslaught. Marc appeared at her side, clutching his spear. Blood ran from its head, over its crossbar, up its haft and halfway up his bare arm. He looked as if he'd seen ghosts.

"Give me your spear!" Melodía shrieked. He didn't so much obey as gape blankly at her. She grabbed the weapon from his hand.

Somehow Valérie still kept her feet. But the hordelings had her hair, had her arms, pulling in either direction as if to rip them off her body. They screeched like feeding fliers.

The spear was heavy, balanced for thrusting, not throwing. But her one-eyed arms-mistress had taught Melodía well. She reversed it, hefted it once to get the feel, and threw.

It struck Valérie in the sternum, and punched through thin bouncer leather, bone, and heart. Despite the hands yanking at her braids that heartbreakingly pretty face turned toward Melodía. She smiled a last red smile.

Then she was gone, down and hidden by a seethe of madness.

"Fall back!" Melodía screamed. Marc at least followed her as she crashed blind into the undergrowth. She had no aim in mind but to increase distance between herself and the inexorable monster tide. Then rally her riders—such as remained—and go at them again.

Another one! the voice of the child within her wailed. *I lost another friend! I got her killed too!*

With an act of coldest will, Melodía sealed memory and heart behind an iron door. She had a duty—to her troop, to Rob Korrigan, to Karyl and the people of his army. To all the people of Nuevaropa, perhaps—since who knew how many lives Raguel intended to reap? She couldn't let anything hinder her carrying out that obligation.

It might not be my duty to survive, she thought. *But it is my duty to sell my life as dearly as possible.*

In a small clearing she stopped and turned. *I'll pay in pain for you later, Valérie*, she told her friend's memory. *I credit Pilar for teaching me to choke down emotion with survival on the line.*

With a raw hunting-dragon cry, she raised her sword to rally her riders to her for yet another attack.

The prone man's legs kicked when Rob split his close-cropped skull with his axe.

The attack was over. All the hordelings who'd entered the cantonment were down. The dawn blushed red in the west as though in shame at the butchery that greeted it.

The army hadn't lost many to the unskilled yet ferocious assault. Bone-tired and cold from the rain that only lifted when the battle ended, some had complained aggrievedly when Karyl ordered that each and every fallen horde member's head be crushed, stabbed through, or severed. Until a man whose guts hopelessly entwined his own legs, and had already been trampled into the muck all around him besides, tripped a mailed soldier—and a woman showing bone from a dozen deep cuts tore out the house-shield's throat with a single bite.

Seeing no other prospects awaiting his axe nearby, Rob thrust her spiked head into the mud and leaned against the butt, almost too tired to think.

Something made him look around. Riders filed around the farmhouse's field-stone flank from the west. Melodía Delgao rode in the lead, slumping in the saddle as if barely conscious. A mere dozen jinetes followed her into the bloody mud of the yard. All of them showed hastily bandaged wounds.

Rob moaned aloud in mingled relief and grief.

Twenty minutes later, mounted on Little Nell, he followed the last of the Providential army onto the High Road. South, marching toward the Laughing Water's juncture with the River Bountiful, and on to where the Lisette marked the border with Métairie Brulée.

Chapter 32

Dragón Grancrestado, **Great-Crested Dragon**—*Quetzalcoatlus northropi*. The largest of all the *Azhdarchids*, which are in turn the greatest of the furred, flying reptiles called *fliers* or *pterosaurs*. Wingspan 11 meters, stands 6 meters tall, weighs as much as 250 kilograms. Known for flying vast distances; feared as a major threat to both livestock and humans, whom it lands to stalk and kill with its swordlike beak.

—THE BOOK OF TRUE NAMES

Despite a lack of signs of pursuit, Karyl drove his refugee army for two days without respite, though torrential rains that turned even the exquisitely engineered and scrupulously maintained Rue Imperial into a white-mud river. Those who had exhausted themselves in the fighting—like Melodía Delgao and her sad scrap of survivors—were simply stacked in wagons like the wounded to sleep. So was anyone who faltered on the road. Animals that broke down were slaughtered, efficiently butchered by the roadside, and continued the journey as meat.

While they weren't yet followed by what the army had generally started calling hordelings or hordelings, they were continually overtaken. Refugees caught them up singly or in haggard clumps. And not just from the Lisette Valley and Providence town.

The second evening after the flight from Séverin farm a party of eastern woods-runners arrived. Castaña had invaded, they said, looking to take advantage of Providence's upheaval. Raguel himself, mounted on a big black stallion, had led his Horde to meet them. He cut the round-crested head off Count Raúl's glorious scarlet Corythosaurus with a single sweep of his strange weapon: a sort of scythe attached like a spearhead to a halberd haft that legends called a soul-reaper.

When the Conde fell the Grey Angel's followers swarmed him, shucked him out of his armor like a crayfish, and stripped the living flesh from his bones with their teeth.

Tales of Raguel's reign continued to reach the army from Providence town. They were no more pleasant than Count Raúl's end.

The rain broke the night before the army reached the great granite bridge across the Lisette into Métairie Brulée—a blessing too small for Rob, for one, to appreciate too hugely. His scouts told him that Comtesse Célestine had nervously withdrawn her assembled army to her seat of Belle Perspective about twenty kilometers southwest along the High Road from the frontier.

A barricade made of a giant tree trunk blocked the Métairie Brulée end of the bridge. Two weather-beaten stone towers flanked it. Not just the two formerly listless guards manning the barrier but the entire detachment of a score or so house-shields and bows who occupied the towers fled promptly south at first sight of Karyl leading his ragged-assed cavalcade out of the woods two hundred meters from the river.

Rob sent light-riders galloping in pursuit. As the army began trudging across the bridge they brought back a pair of House troops who had skinned out of their hauberks and fled in their linens. After Karyl expended considerable patient effort convincing them he didn't mean to have them, or indeed anybody, roasted over slow fires, they calmed down enough to listen to the message he wanted them to take to their Countess: *We mean you no harm. We have no choice. We're fleeing a great and terrible danger. Join us if you will, but please let us pass through your lands unmolested.* Then he gave them horses and sent them on their way.

Though it was only noon Karyl had the army camp on the Métairie Brulée side of the river to rest. The Lisette would serve as a moat should the horde be chasing them after all.

The next morning they hit the road early. Also armed, armored, and ready to deploy from the march into battle. Never expecting the Countess to accept his reassurance, and simply stand aside to let his army pass through her domain, Karyl had told Rob to set scouts watching her army around the clock.

As usual, he was right.

"You did well," Karyl said to Melodía. On her return he had assembled his chief lieutenants at a campfire council of war in the middle of the camp.

She felt like purring.

Belle Perspective's curtain walls were imposing—but in a picture-pretty way, more than serious defensive works. Even Melodía, who'd never had near her baby sister's fascination with siegecraft, could see how easily they'd be brought down by a little judicious application of dinosaur muscle. Or even some brisk pick-work.

And the walls did little to reassure Comtesse Célestine and her surviving lords when they huddled in her throne room to receive Karyl's appointed delegate. Not after the hiding his army had dealt her blocking force that day on the road north of her keep.

Melodía didn't even know if the portly Countess recognized her as the Princesa Imperial. She suspected not. If it miffed Célestine to be sent a mere captain of light-horse—which would seem by definition to mean *lowborn*—to negotiate her surrender, she didn't show it. The remorseless efficiency of the Providential army, its otherworldly monsters, and most of all its legendary commander, left those who had experienced it (or even watched from safety, as the Countess had) shaking with terror hours later.

Light-horse captain or not, Melodía had shown the Countess her finest Corte Imperial hauteur. Not rudeness—Melodía hadn't enjoyed her etiquette lessons any more than Montserrat did, but both were good students, and learned. Instead she showed the simple, invincible assumption that anything she asked for would without question be granted.

It was. Before Melodía could so much as ask, Célestine offered a tribute in silver that forced even the Emperor's elder daughter to exert great will to keep her eyes from popping.

Boggled or not, Melodía had wit to ask for twice the sum. The Countess folded like a badly set up tent, causing Melodía to curse herself silently for not asking three times as much.

Still, Karyl expressed himself well pleased at what she got.

"That and the ransom of the knights we took will go a long way toward keeping us in supplies," he told his captains.

"Supplies?" asked Luc Garamond, with the huskiness of vocal cords as scarred as his broad sword-slashed face. "We won't just take what we need?"

"But why pay?" asked Élodie, the merchant Gaétan's cousin who had signed on as Quartermaster-General. A slip of a woman, she kept sharp features crowded onto the front of her unusually large head, whose size was emphasized by the severe ponytail into which she drew her blond hair. She was competent, unusually honest, and even personable—for a quartermaster. Or so she struck Melodía, who'd seen the breed before at her father's courts, in La Merced, La Majestad, and back home in Los Almendros.

"Normally I'm in favor of paying for what one takes," Élodie said. "But in this case, what can it matter? Soon or late, the horde will come after us. Then the inhabitants of this land we've passed will lose everything, lives included. They'd do better to pitch everything portable in the pot and join us."

Karyl scratched at a corner of his eye. "Perhaps. But for that very reason we've got to keep moving. We'll find our road much smoother if we don't have to fight guerrillas for every step. Or worse, find our way blocked by refugees, who've left all the land burnt bare and the wells poisoned."

Even Garamond, murky green eyes glowering beneath his square-cut black hair, nodded at that.

"Even so," Élodie said, "with all the expenses we face"—she flicked blue eyes at Garamond—"can we afford the outlay?"

"I intend to pay as much as I can, as long as I can," Karyl said. "After that—"

He shrugged. "People will have to decide whether they'd rather take their chances with us or the horde."

"Or the Imperials," Côme said.

That evoked a general growl of resentment. Melodía frowned. *They blame the Empire for their problems*, she thought. *It isn't fair.*

The truth, it had sickened her to see, was that those at the Corte Imperial who'd feared a Grey Angel Crusade had been right. And it sprang indeed from the soil of the Garden of Beauty and Truth—if not from any seeds obtained from her lover Jaume. Although having held the Grey Angel in her own eyes, and felt his awful power in her mind and soul, she couldn't doubt he'd played Bogardus and Violette like puppets all along. He had come to them, for reasons of his own.

She didn't say any of that. Of course. Recent experiences had taught her better respect for the concept of futility.

"Seems to me," Côme drawled, "the real question right now is, where are we going?"

That caused a nervous look to pass around the bonfire like a yawn. "That's in the Creators' hands now," said Gaétan.

He spoke in a heavier voice than he ever had since Melodía joined the army. Events had baked ebullient youth into maturity. And somberness, at least for now.

He now commanded all the foot-archers, erstwhile House troops as well as peasants. Under Karyl's keen but calm black eyes the highborn took orders from the low when called upon to do so.

That tickled the underbelly of Melodía's own class-consciousness in a most uncomfortable way. Too well she recalled how Imperial Court gossip held out the egalitarianism of Voyvod Karyl's own March as proof of his deadly perfidy when her father employed him as mercenary captain. And she herself had spouted her share of fashionable leveling rot to her ladies-in-waiting. Yet here and now she plainly saw it worked—at least for Karyl Bogomirskiy. And she had also learned a hearty respect for that.

Birth-blind the army may have been, but it acted with one will. Melodía now fully believed what her beloved Jaume told her in despair: Karyl never intended treachery against her father. Any compact he made he would honor to the death. But as for the potential of Karyl's ability and personal force—the advisors who had prevailed upon Felipe to order Jaume to strike down his own ally had been right to fear him.

"Or at least in Raguel's hands," said Karyl. "We go where he drives us."

"To what purpose?" Garamond asked gloomily.

"One thing we know: Grey Angel Crusades come to an end. Or there'd be no one left on Paradise."

"The last Crusade in Nuevaropa ended five hundred years ago, at the end of the Demon War," Melodía said.

That brought her some hard looks. Raguel was the blade hanging over everybody's necks, but the Empire and Torre Delgao were far from popular. There was still that *other* Crusade to fear.

Besides, as mere troop-leader she was much the junior here. But though she'd accepted her humble rank—she'd signed on as a simple trooper, after all—if she knew something relevant, she was going to speak right up. *What can they do*, she thought, *bust me back to the ranks?*

"That's history," Garamond said, "and that's just dust."

"I want to hear her," said Côme, taking a pull from a bouncer-skin of Métairie Brulée's famous wine and wiping his mouth with his hand. "All I know about these cursed Grey Angels are the stories my mother told me when I was small, to frighten me out of misbehaving."

He laughed. "Of course, I heard those stories a lot."

Karyl looked to Melodía. "Tell us more."

"The Crusade that ended the Demon War lasted over a year," she said, "but that was a unique circumstance. The Empire's had reports of Crusades in other lands. They seem to last anywhere from a few days to several months. But no credible accounts of any have come in the lifetime of anyone living, except my grandmother, Doña Rosamaría."

And *she* was head of Torre Delgao, and over half as old as the Imperio itself. "Most people now just think they're legends. Or at any rate, things that only happened in the past."

"Well, the past has bloody risen up to haunt us now," said Rob.

"I don't really even know why the news of what had to be Raguel's Emergence in Providence caused such immediate panic in La Merced," Melodía said. "Why would so many people believe it? There must have been forces at work there I still don't comprehend. For that matter—why didn't anyone hear about Raguel Emerging here? Or—in Providence, anyway. Where it happened?"

Everyone looked at everyone else, but no one brought forth an answer.

"That much makes no difference to us now," Karyl said. "What does is knowing that our task is simply to keep clear of the Grey Angel Crusade until it's over. Which I've no doubt we'll find an easier thing to say than do."

"What happens then?" Élodie asked.

Karyl uttered a soft laugh. "I believe in planning," he said, "but that risks taxing our powers of prophecy into penury. Let's survive the end, and make assessment then."

"If there's aught left to assess," Rob said.

"There's that," Karyl said.

The shadow Melodía thought to see cross his martyr's face seemed darker even to her than the Irlandés's words would merit. She wondered at that.

But the war-council began breaking up, and her people and animals needed her. Plenty of healing remained to do, and not just to wounds of the body. Taking herself as dismissed she left to hurry to them.

As the captains returned to their own fires Rob stood up from his squat. He picked up his lute, which lay beside him, by its slim crooked neck.

"A word with you, Master Korrigan," Karyl said softly.

Rob cocked a brow. The others dissolved into the night. Karyl stood quiet, compact, dark and self-contained, until they were out of earshot.

"What do you think of her?"

"Beg pardon, Colonel?"

"Our fugitive Princess. Melodía. Though I suppose we're all a legion of fugitives now."

Rob laughed. "Truth to tell, I hardly think of her as that at all anymore. Everyone calls her the Short-Haired Horse Captain now. I guess I do too."

"What about the job she does for you?"

Rob laughed. "She's a marvel, and I don't lie. She's taken to the light horse like a great-crested dragon to the air. And they to her. Spoiled princess or not, there's nothing at all, no matter how dangerous, dirty, or arduous, she'll ask her troop to do that she doesn't jump to do herself. If anything she's a bit too heedless of her own safety. And that works wholly to her favor with the sort of mad things who are Travelers, or become jinetes."

Karyl nodded briskly. "What would you say to giving her your light-horse, then?"

"Beg pardon?" Rob said again.

"Put her in command of all mounted scouts."

"The little Princess? You can't be serious?"

Karyl cocked a brow at him.

"Think back on what you just said, my friend. It seems to me you made her case most compellingly."

"Huh," Rob grunted. "Ah. Well. So I did. And given they all clamor to ride with her, even after she lost so many of them fighting to keep the horde off our backsides, I'd say she has the lot in her well-bred palm already."

"Splendid. Give her the news yourself."

"Gladly, Lord. Gladly indeed."

Something about the way Karyl continued to look at him held him longer.

"What will you do now?" Karyl asked.

Rob laughed. "Find a rousing song circle and some beer, get me inside the one and the other inside of me, soonest. Then off to bed to snatch what poor rest I can before some messenger lout awakens me to the latest catastrophe."

"Ah," Karyl said. "I—wish I had your easy facility with others."

"What on Paradise can you mean, man? You've wandered the length and breadth of Aphrodite Terra, rubbed elbows with paupers and emperors. What's a bunch of your own people?"

Especially ones who'd throw themselves in molten lava if you so much as crooked your little finger, he added mentally.

"I have. I've even passed time with rogues like Travelers and dinosaur masters. But easy camaraderie—" He shook his head. "I seem to lack that gift."

"Gift? It's the same gift as falling backward drunk off a rock. It's not something you do, it's something that happens. Come on. Join me. You'll be welcome, and that's an evil understatement, so; your men and women think you float two meters in the air and glow all on your own, and that's plain fact."

"I'd be like a matador peering in the window at a banquet. Not for me, I fear. You go and enjoy."

"You, fear?" Rob scoffed.

"I fear," Karyl said. "More than I hope you ever know."

He turned and walked away. Rob thought him the loneliest thing he'd ever seen.

Chapter 33

Hogar, **Home, Old Home**—When they were done making Paradise, and found it good, the Creators brought humans, their Five Friends, and certain useful crops and herbs here from the world we call Home. Ancient accounts teach us it is a strange place. It is cold, and we would feel heavier there, and find the air much thinner. The year is 1.6 times as long as ours. We must admire the fortitude of our ancestors in dwelling on such an inhospitable world, and always praise the Creators for bringing us to our true Paradise!

—A PRIMER TO PARADISE FOR THE IMPROVEMENT OF YOUNG MINDS

"All these kids in the procession wore white," Little Pigeon said between horror-sized bites of a meat pie. "They all had candles. They all looked . . . funny. Some had frozen faces, some looked crazy-happy."

In the shade of an ancient spreading oak, the child sat on a camp stool at one end of a heavy table of well-polished walnut. Scouts had found it tipped in a ditch up the High Road from Belle Perspective, where the army continued to rest, recover, and assimilate the volunteers who kept streaming in to join. Nobody knew whether it had been looted from some abandoned manor, or carried by its fleeing rightful owners until they saw fit to abandon it. Rob couldn't quite fit his mind around why anyone would dream of lugging the great brute along in the first place.

At that, it was easier than shaping his mind to fit the tale his former chief spy in Providence town unfurled.

"There were like forty of them, walking in pairs. The oldest were just shy of fully grown—twenty-five, maybe twenty-six. The youngest could barely toddle. I was hiding out in Mare's Alley next to the old counting-house when I saw them march down Peacock Walk. I wondered what was going on, so I followed them."

Little Pigeon had arrived in early afternoon on a farm wagon with ten other children piled into the bed. When Karyl heard his first uncharacteristically halting words about what he'd witnessed in the province's capital—Rob was thinking of the androgynous child as "he" today—Karyl had convened an immediate council of war.

"I didn't know what was happening—it all seemed just a lark, at first. But then I started feeling like a weight pressing on my mind. Like a hand pushing me to join the parade.

"They went from house to house down the street. At each door a child would knock. When the door opened, the child demanded the householders let them in to look for signs of sin."

"This was just children?" asked Melodía. Since she'd been named field captain of all the light-horse no one questioned her right to sit in council. Not that Rob thought anybody'd incline to, since the tribute she'd wrung out of Métairie Brulée had begun to roll in.

"No. They had some adults along too. Like, I don't know, fatty-herders or something. If somebody resisted letting the kids in, they dealt with it pretty mean. Some of the grown-ups walked as if they were asleep. But they pounced quick as vexers if anybody pushed back."

"How long are we going to waste listening to these childish fantasies?" demanded Garamond, who'd been hitting the ale a little hard this morning.

Baron Côme had his elbows on the table and he pressed either side of chin to prop up his face. He cocked a brow at the mercenary man-at-arms.

"We're up against a Grey Angel Crusade, here, Luc," he said. "I don't know about you, but that makes me uncomfortable calling anything 'fantasy' anymore. I want to hear what he says. Uh—her. Whichever. Anything that might keep the horde from peeling and eating me like a shrimp, the way they did Count Raúl, I'm interested in."

"I'm listening," Karyl said directly to Petit Pigeon. "What happened when the children entered a house?"

"I couldn't really see. I was trying to hang in the shadows. Not as if anybody was looking around or anything. Stuff they found they didn't like they passed outside. It got carried off and thrown on the big bonfire in the Old Market Square. Like I said, anybody resisted got beaten down pretty hard. But that wasn't the worst. That was when we came to this house—nice house it was too. Simon and his wife Mathi, the silk sellers, lived there. Their youngest daughter Nicole accused her elder sister Muriel of sin. Muriel wasn't even twenty yet, but what they did to her—"

Little Pigeon looked at Rob with black eyes brimming with tears. "Do I have to tell that part, Master Rob? I don't want to. I so don't want to."

Rob glanced to Karyl, who shook his head once. "No," Rob said gently, letting relief hum in his voice. "You don't have to tell any more about that."

Melodía went to kneel by the child, to wipe his eyes and cheeks with a handkerchief.

"Who did these bad things?" Gaétan asked. As usual since their escape Jeannette haunted his shoulder silently from behind. "Not the children, surely?"

"Uh-huh." Little Pigeon nodded. "But it was the preachers who told them what to do."

"Preachers?" Rob said. "Who were these, now?"

"Two of them. A man and a woman, both stiff necks from that Garden Council. They were encouraging the kids, spouting all that crazy-talk the Gardeners have been shouting all over town for weeks. Self-denial, purity, pruning the world of wickedness, on and on. That kinda shit."

"'Pruning,'" echoed Melodía faintly.

"Weeks, you said," Karyl said.

"Oh, yes. It got really bad when the Princess went over to the army. They got all upset. As if scared they were losing ground. Their sermons started getting shriller and fiercer."

Rob frowned at Melodía. She shook her head. "I never knew anything about this," she said. "Bogardus and Sister Violette were pleased when I told them I wanted to join you."

She seemed to deflate. "Acted pleased. I guess."

"So why didn't you tell us all this, then?" Rob asked the child.

His eyes got huge. "But I did, Master Rob! I did too!"

Rob rocked back on his own salvaged milking-stool. "Did you, for a fact? How could I've missed it?"

"Reports go astray," Karyl said. "You've seen that often enough by now. Probably you disregarded such reports—I confess I might have done. With Castaña pressing against the border like a titan on a village fence, and Célestine lurking in the weeds awaiting her chance to pounce, our employer's noisy rhetoric was the last thing on our minds."

He sighed. "After all, it was a foregone conclusion they'd betray us."

Rob frowned again. It came to him to wonder if his friend's very fatalism on the subject might have hindered them getting a *trifle* more warning of catastrophe rushing down on them like a volcano's glowing cloud.

"It's all right, Little Pigeon," he said. "You did your best. What happened next?"

"I ran away. Nobody noticed me. Nobody followed me, anyway. They couldn't stay with me in the alleys if they did. Especially not the adults. Adults are stupid and clumsy."

Gaétan had risen and begun to pace. He was too full of frustrated energy, barely contained rage and grief and the Lady of the Mirror knew what else crackling inside him like static in a fleece cloth, to sit still for any length of time.

"So this Angel . . . controlled them all?" he asked.

The child shook his mop of black hair, which looked to Rob as if he haggled it off with a dagger whenever it bothered him. Which was no doubt the case.

"No," he said. "I never saw any Angel. Everybody was talking about him, though. Some of them were so scared they could barely stand up. Others seemed . . . all happy, I guess. Excited."

Rob cocked a brow at Melodía. Her cinnamon skin looked overlaid with ash.

"I hid out in this place I know," Petit Pigeon went on. "Stayed there three days. Lived on scraps I stole from busted-open houses. Lots of the people didn't even seem to care about stuff like eating. I saw . . . things. Horrible things. They kept the bonfire burning all the time in the Square. It smelled awful. I could see . . . people in it, all burned up and black and all."

Élodie turned away, gagging.

"The Old Market was always full of people, all listening to that silver-haired lady from the Garden. The real hoity-toity one, used to be some kind of noble."

"Violette," Melodía said, in a tone that suggested spitting out a bite of rotten meat.

"Finally I figured things were just too crazy, and not gonna get better. By then I'd pulled in some other kids I found wandering. Some of them had managed to get away from the crazies, some hid out all along. We snuck out by night. By then I heard you guys had hit the road south. So we followed you. It was pretty tough; the crazy people're everywhere, eating up all they can and burning the rest. But we're pretty good scroungers, and sly. And here we are."

"You didn't see the Angel," Melodía said, picking words as if they burned her fingers. "But I think you felt his power touch you, when you were watching that children's parade. I felt it too, just a little. It was—terrifying. How did you manage to keep free?"

Little Pigeon shook his head. "It was like it was trying to own me. Nobody owns me but me. So I made it stop. Which it did when I ran away from the parade. I was ready to fight like a cornered alley cat if anybody tried to stop me. But nobody noticed I was gone."

"So the horde's begun moving south in force?" Karyl asked.

"Oh, yes." The child nodded emphatically. "They can move wicked fast when they want to. You don't want to hang out around here too long. Believe me, you don't."

"You're right." Karyl leaned back. He looked troubled. The child picked up on it right away.

"Did I say something wrong, Lord?"

"What? No. Not at all. You've done very well indeed. What can we do for you?"

"Well, feed me, for a start." He stuffed the last of his meat pie in his mouth and brushed crumbs from his hands. "Well, more. I'm starving. My friends are too. And—and if you could let us stay with you, please? We won't make no trouble. Won't steal or nothin'."

"I doubt that," Rob said. The child gave him a stricken look. He chuckled.

"I'm counting on you to keep the theft petty and the mischief minimal, my boy."

Little Pigeon drew himself up indignantly. "I'm a girl," he said.

"Oh. Well. Of course you are, lass. Any rate, take your friends 'round to the kitchen tents and tell them I told them to feed you all you can hold. We'll find something useful for you and your friends to do."

Little Pigeon jumped up and hugged him. To Rob's surprise his—her—cheeks were wet. "Thank you, Master Rob! And you, Lord Karyl! Thank you!"

She set off at a brisk scuttle across the green and lavender ground cover. Garamond glared after her. He clacked his pewter mug down on the table and wiped his lips with the back of his hand.

"Are we an army or a rolling charity?" he demanded. "Do you mean to take in every rag-tag starveling that wanders in, Colonel?"

"If they swear to follow my rules and serve as we tell them to," Karyl said, "yes. I do."

"Sentiment?" Melodía asked. Rob thought her more surprised at the fearful king tyrant Karyl showing compassion, than objecting herself. *Or maybe I'm just a sucker for a pretty face*, he thought. *Well, I am that that, surely.*

"By no means. We can't run forever. We'll have to fight—certainly the horde, all too likely the Empire. We'll need every pair of hands we can muster then."

"But—children and untrained peasants?" Côme said. "I'm all for saving those we can. But they're not going to be of much use in battle, surely?"

Karyl smiled. "I can use them."

Côme raised his brows, pulled his chin up and the corners of his mouth down, in an almost-comical look of surprise. *Another noble*, Rob reflected, *might've taken immediate and violent exception to Karyl's flat contradiction.*

Of course any grande who responded that way would be doing very well indeed to live long enough to feel his own steel clear its sheath. Côme was a formidable fighter even for one of his class. Karyl was . . . unique.

But there was a reason Karyl had set the displaced Baron to command his dinosaur knights. His often deliberate clowning notwithstanding, Côme was no fool. Scarcely a buckethead at all, really.

He rubbed his chin and nodded thoughtfully. "I'll happily learn the trick of using them, then."

Karyl stood up sharply.

"Very well. The horde's following us now. We've got to move with a purpose. Ladies, gentlemen: you know your tasks. Do them."

Screams grabbed Rob by the scruff and yanked him up from the depths of sleep.

Dressed only in a soft linen loincloth, he tumbled from his tent. He had his axe Wanda in hand. At once he felt self-conscious about it.

I'll not be needing you after all, love, he thought. *I know that sound.*

As he expected the cries issued from the humble tent next to Rob's and no larger than it.

He grabbed a passing arm. "Steady," he said to the wide-eyed look its owner, a woman dressed like him and carrying a dirk, gave him. "Himself is having his bad dreams. It's that and nothing more. Pass the word, there's a love: there's no threat to the camp. Only nightmares."

"Nightmares? But it sounds like a man being eaten by a matador!" she said.

She must be a newcomer, Rob thought. *We've plenty of those, and more every day.*

He tipped his head and listened. "Close, aye. But not altogether. Now—away with you!"

They had marched a few hours southwest along La Rue Imperial, then halted to laager in for the night. Now the whole camp was roused. Men and women jumped up from beside fires or poured from tents, ready to make their final stand against the whole of the Grey Angel horde.

But Rob heard older hands, veterans who'd joined in early days, already spreading the message had given the mostly naked woman: "Relax. It's just the voyvod's nightmares." Behind Karyl's back they called him by his outlandish noble title, Slavo, for a warlord who ruled a March.

They remembered such dreams from before the first time they ambushed a Crève Coeur raiding party, back even before the Blueflowers. Once action began, the nightmares stopped.

What worried Rob, who'd endured Karyl's screaming dreams and night-fears and bouts of black depression far longer than any soul in the refugee army, was the question of why they'd commenced again.

As he walked through the camp helping pouring oil on troubled water he heard a greybeard who'd joined the army in Métairie Brulée addressing a rapt circle of listeners.

"The Fae caught our lord when he fell from the cliff with a mortal wound," he said, "and bore him to the Land Below. There they saved his life and healed his hurts."

He shook his hoary head. "But it's a terrible price they exact. One he ain't done payin', yet. But he pays in pieces, each night in dreams."

That went right down Rob's spine, hitting every vertebra.

"I thought nobody remembered what happened to them in the Venusberg," a young Castañera said.

"Why d'you think it haunts him when he sleeps? That's when the bodies buried deep in your mind and soul get up and walk around."

Feeling as if his skin were trying to crawl off his body and creep away, Rob confronted the tale-teller.

"Where did you hear that bloody twaddle, you old rogue?" he demanded.

The oldster shrugged. "Here and there. In the wind."

Rob frowned. It was the sort of answer a Traveler might give. Then again, the man was clearly a caravaneer. That breed had much the same lives as the Irlandés-gitano Travelers, rootless and wandering, hence had much the same attitudes. And superstitions.

He also knew he'd get no more specific answer. "You're just confusing his tale with the old song 'Tam Lin,'" he said.

He sang a few bars: "I forbid ye maidens all, who wear gold in your hair/To travel to Carter Hall, for young Tam Lin is there."

To his annoyance the old man laughed. He was missing teeth. Rob felt tempted to loosen a few more.

"Aye. And the Queen of Faeries caught him as from his horse he fell. My eyes are old and weak, and my mind wanders further afield than my aching feet can. But I know the difference between a horse and a three-hundred meter cliff. Voyvod Karyl had his sword hand bit off by a horror, he did; and fell toward the surface of the Tyrant's Eye. How did he come to live, then, I wonder? If the fall didn't kill him, blood loss would've, sure.

"Yet there he lies not fifty paces from us, alive as you or me. And with a sword hand as good as any man's. And better, on the evidence!"

"That's nothing to do with the Fae!" Rob said hotly. Then shut up. That Karyl had lost a hand—and more to the point, regained it—wasn't a story he wanted noised around any more than Karyl himself did. He wasn't sure why. He just knew it would be no good thing.

"And what's a man named Korrigan think he's about, anyway, doubting Faerie deeds?" the old man asked.

That took Rob aback. "'Touched by the Fae,' the name means," the old caravaneer said. "Does it not?"

"How'd you know that?"

The old man cackled. "You think my travels haven't taken me across Anglaterra, and even Irlanda? A caravaneer goes where wind and whim drive him. Just like a Traveler, lad."

"Then I'll tell you why I don't like hearing talk of the Faerie Folk bandied about," Rob said in hot Anglés, reading in the other's eyes that he understood full well—as hardly anyone else in camp would. "It's no healthy thing to speak of them, for body or soul. And whatever do you think you're about, to go on so with a Grey Angel abroad in the world working his great mischief?"

But the old rogue was nothing daunted. "What better time to invoke the Fae" he said softly—and blessedly, still in Anglysh—"than when the Creators' retribution stalks us all? Who better to give us hope against the Seven, than enemies sworn of the Eight?"

Rob stared at him. His bearded jaws worked futilely. That enraged him more than anything: this daft old bugger had robbed him, Rob Korrigan, of words. He thought of striking the caravaneer down for his truly terrifying blasphemy—and even more terrifying knowledge.

But while Rob Korrigan did not imagine himself a good man, he knew he wasn't that man.

Instead he made the cross-and-circle sign of the Lady's Mirror, the evil-averting gesture he hoped was most remote from Grey Angel malice. Then he turned and stalked away.

He crawled back into his tent and bedroll, and pulled his vexer-down pillow over his ears.

Chapter 34

Tiranes Escarlatos, Scarlet Tyrants (singular *Tirán Escarlato*)—The Imperial bodyguard. They are easily recognized by their gilded armor—their breastplates usually figured to resemble muscular human torsos—and their barbute helmets with red or gold crests of feathers or horsehair. They are handpicked, mainly from among the minority peoples of the Torre Menor or Lesser Tower, for loyalty to the Fangèd Throne regardless of who occupies it.

—A PRIMER TO PARADISE FOR THE IMPROVEMENT OF YOUNG MINDS

As Duke Falk von Hornberg entered his gold-and-scarlet silk pavilion pitched next to the Emperor's similarly colored but much grander one, he tore his barbute helmet from his sweat-curled hair and threw it across the room without regard to its fancy, imported Ridiculous-reaper plumes.

"Fae eat that fool of a priest! His madness gels my blood. And he only makes that infernal caterwauling worse."

"What do you expect, your Grace?" said Bergdahl, who sat astride a stool examining the armor the Duke had brought from the North for chips in its royal-blue enamel, or signs of rust. On court occasions, such as tonight's, Falk wore the armor of the commander of the Imperial bodyguard, not his personal harness. "Off they've marched to war to prevent a Grey Angel Crusade. And here they've just learned it's all in vain: a Grey

Angel has raised a horde anyway, and marches now to meet them. Their worst childhood nightmares have been realized."

He cocked a sly brow at his master. "Haven't yours?"

Falk made a clotted sound and dropped onto a sturdy camp chair. Up here on Nuevaropa's central massif the night was neither especially hot nor humid, any more than winter chill reached here from the mountains. Yet his body stewed beneath his gambeson, and his thighs, bare between figured gilt greaves and the red metal-studded strips of boiled duckbill-leather that made up his kilt, ran with perspiration.

The fact was, he hadn't himself yet truly absorbed the news that arrived that afternoon with a messenger whose eyes rolled as madly as her near-foundered horse's. He held himself devout, at least in relation to these slack Southerners. Perhaps precisely for that reason, he'd never even in his nightmares anticipated that he might someday find himself facing the Creators' fearful justice, in the form of a Grey Angel horde.

There was that within him that understood too well the almost-animal fear and grief of the mob that howled outside his silken walls. It wanted to cast the shackles of *mind* aside and join the ululation.

There's the virtue of the discipline you've devoted your life to, he reminded himself sternly. *Sacred Order begins within one's own head. And heart.*

Outside in torch-lit night his recently minted Eminence, Cardinal Tavares, preached in a voice thin and cutting as a whip. He praised the Creators and their servants the Grey Angels, thanking the latter for their mercy in purging Paradise, or at least this part of it, of sin. He urged the mob to confess, repent, and beg forgiveness.

He certainly wasn't soothing them.

"A wonder Jaume doesn't cut the imbecile down himself, after the grief he's given him," Falk said, pouring a goblet full of wine from an ewer and draining it at a tilt.

"Highly profitable grief to us, though, wasn't it, your Grace?" Bergdahl said.

"He was useful undermining Jaume when his only game was bringing naughty lordlings to heel. Now everything's at stake, and if Tavares hasn't become an active liability, he's at least a thrice-damned pest. Why does Felipe stomach that noise, anyway? It walks perilously near sedition."

"Yet Tavares may serve us."

"Will he? His cant's weakening the army, not strengthening it. How will that help us fight this horde?"

Bergdahl pretended busyness and said nothing.

With lowered head and lower brows, the young Duke regarded his shadow, his servant and master.

"Is this part of my mother's plan? A Grey Angel Crusade? She sent me to return order to a decadent Empire, and bring glory to it and ourselves. What glory is there in this? What honor? Is it an honor, to survive what the Church teaches is the Creators' righteous punishment?"

"If you know a man who sincerely apologizes for surviving," Bergdahl said, "send him my way by all means, your Grace. I'd like to study such a sport of nature.

"As for glory and honor—those're just made-up, anyway. Whoever survives this shitstorm will make up plenty to go around after the fact, *because* of his doubts and sins."

With a growl Falk turned away. The most damnable thing about this creature was that his very worst impertinences often contained kernels of truth Falk knew, in mind and belly, he could never refute.

"Come now, your Grace," Bergdahl said, putting down one darkly gleaming vambrace blue and picking up the other. "Weren't you even the least bit pleased to see the look on Jaume's pretty face when Tavares commenced his yowling? Calling on lords and lowborn alike to show this Angel they know how to punish, so that His wrath will pass us by?"

Falk made a rumbling in the top of his wide chest that maybe only he could hear. It was true. He did feel a certain satisfaction.

Which stabbed him through with guilt. *What knight is truer, nobler, or more capable than the Constable? Don't we all need his skill and heroism now more than ever before?*

He had felt just such a roil of love and hate for the Princess Melodía before—he pushed that thought away like a plateful of offal.

"I wonder, now," Bergdahl said, filing smooth a nicked edge, "what look Don Jaume will have on his face when you tell him how you took his woman in the ass by force?"

Falk felt as if an iron mask had been forge-heated red and clamped on his face. He had to fight to draw in a breath.

"Never mention that again," he managed to say at last. "Not to me. Not to anybody."

Bergdahl gave a one-shouldered shrug and a single chuckle of amusement. "As you wish, your Grace. As you know, I exist only to serve your true will."

Outside a man screamed. For a moment Falk dared hope somebody, perhaps even Jaume himself, had stuck a sword through the unwashed middle of Cardinal Tavares. But then he heard the voice he had come to hate hissing right along. Apparently His Eminence's bloody eloquence had momentarily overwhelmed some particularly susceptible listener.

"Don't you see what he's doing?" Falk asked. Whether of the air or Bergdahl hardly mattered; his servant heard everything in any event. "He's tearing the army apart! I believe in the firm hand. The iron hand, when called for. And I believe in the absolute right of blood; how could I not? We have to keep the common ruck in their place, for their good as well as ours.

"But this goblin Tavares preaches cruelty for its own sake. The things some of the magnates and their knights do turn my stomach. And it'll all turn 'round to bite us like a stepped-on adder, if the people between us and the horde come to fear us more than them."

"Some have tried to bite the Imperial ankle already," Bergdahl observed dryly. "Their bodies form peculiarly baroque roadside decorations, do they not?"

"Bad as it's been, Tavares is making it worse. And that's not the only thing. It's hard enough to control the nobles at the best of times. Their knights—they're scarcely better than horrors. They need a harder hand to keep them in line than any serfs. But torture, rape, and murder can't be controlled. They're chaotic by nature."

"The knights and nobles did the same to Jaume in the Army of Correction," Bergdahl said. "With Tavares egging them on. And didn't we encourage him to do so, if only by sly suggestions that the Emperor pay more heed to his mad friend the Pope than his kinsman and champion?"

Falk sighed heavily. "And I'm beginning to repent it now. Especially since that damned red-wrapped priest is beginning to really get on my nerves. He's got a voice like fingernails on a slate-board."

"Yet who, after His Majesty himself and the Constable, might be the

Imperial Army's third most powerful man, if not the head of the Scarlet Tyrants in their pretty feathers and red skirts and all? Pity you're so helpless to do anything about Tavares's noise. What with the Empire crying out for strong men and all."

Falk glared at him a moment. As always Bergdahl ignored his heated look. His certain knowledge that Bergdahl was quite aware of it—as he was of every detail around him—only made Falk the angrier. Though not as mad as the realization that the bastard was right. Again.

He slapped hands on his thighs and stood.

"Time for a last turn around the camp," he said. "And while I'm at it, I believe I'll detail some squads to beat the more enthusiastic whiners and screechers unconscious if they won't shut up. I may not be able to put a rag in Tavares's reeking gob. But nobody from Duke to dung-shoveler's got the right to defy the Tyrants."

"Hmm," Bergdahl said. "Decisive. Your mother would be so proud."

Falk had collected his helmet, straightened the golden plumes—now he was glad they were merely disarrayed, not broken—and started for the door. He halted turned back frowning.

"How does this insanity advance my mother's plan?"

Bergdahl shrugged. "Who can say? Who can say? Kiloliters of blood will spill before this game plays out. Rivers of red stuff. Who knows what doors will be left open to a strong man when the last drop is sucked down by the thirsty soil of this shithole called Paradise?"

"But what if I fall? Gods, what will be left?"

Bergdahl shook his head and smiled a brown-toothed smile. "As to that, not even the Creators can say. But if you're the man you ought to be, the man to bring the Empire to new heights and order to the world, won't you survive? If you don't, what kind of world-bestriding hero are you?"

"One thinking more about what kind of world might be left for me to bestride," Falk said.

"Faugh." Bergdahl made a gesture like scraping an evil taste from his grey-pink tongue on his upper teeth, which thoroughly revolted Falk. "Some men would whine if they were hung with a golden rope."

"What's the meaning of this?"

Sitting in the box of the lead wagon of the baggage train, whose drivers had fled when her jinete troop appeared out of the woods to both sides of the road, Melodía took a meditative bite from an apple before answering. The fruit was late-harvest, gold, and piled high in the bed. The nosehorns who had pulled the wagon stood in the ditch, nipping off mouthfuls of hock-high green weeds in their beaks and grinding them happily in their teeth. Her exotic upland sword lay in its scabbard by her right hand, her pointed steel cap on her left.

The challenge had emitted from a broad, florid face with iron-grey side-whiskers sweeping out to the sides like wings. The face perched without a neck's apparent intervention atop a black breastplate painted with a fisted black gauntlet on a golden shield. Its owner bestrode a night-black sackbut with a yellow throat and underbelly.

"It means," Melodía said, "you should have accepted our offer to parley for safe-passage through your county. It means now my light-horse has ridden all the way around your army."

With a broad smile she gestured at the two score lightly armored riders who sat horses and striders in the grass on both sides of the right-of-way, and the woods-runners who stood among them with bows held casually ready.

"It means, in fine, you're fucking surrounded."

Alerted by panicked messengers—Melodía extrapolated; they'd certainly been panicked when she let them go—that raiders had materialized behind them to capture a wagon train, County Fleur's three leading nobles had ridden post-haste back through the army they'd thrown across the road to block the fugitives' progress. A dozen men-at-arms supported them.

These latter looked nervously toward the brushy woods to either side, clearly suspecting more enemies lurked there than stood in plain sight. Melodía was amused. *Someone on their side is thinking straight, at least.*

"This is an intolerable provocation!" the stout black-armored man shouted.

From intelligence gathered by Rob's spies, Melodía knew him for Vicomte Eudes. He was in the process of giving up the power he'd held as regent to his late sister's son, Morgain, who had just attained majority at twenty-seven and ascended to full Countship. He wasn't best pleased, as her friend Fanny would say.

Hoping to take itself out of the Grey Angel Crusade's path, the fugitive army had veered off the High Road down a tributary, west into Métairie Brulée's neighboring province. The Shield Mountains stood far enough away now that winter held little sway here, felt mainly as a perceptible drop in air temperature by night. Flies in their usual cohorts buzzed around the beasts and their droppings. Birds and fliers squabbled in the brush and trees. The hardwoods here had adapted to a yearlong cycle, leaves browning and falling off and being replaced constantly, instead of dumping them in fall as their higher-up cousins in Providence did.

"If we wanted to fight with you," Melodía said cheerfully, "your baggage would be charcoal now. Voyvod Karyl's crossbows would be turning your breastplates into colanders. And let's not even *talk* about what his three-horns would do to those pretty duckbills of yours."

Speaking of *not talking*, Melodía didn't even want to think about Karyl. On the march from Belle Perspective he had retreated completely into himself. Rob Korrigan, who'd been with him the best part of a year, said he'd seen these black fits before. But nothing like this. Always before Karyl, managed to function. Not now.

At least the Colonel had chosen his captains well. His army worked fine without his active participation. His mere presence, riding each day at their head on his surly little grey bruja of a mare, seemed sufficient to inspire his troops, and keep them acting as one. For the moment.

The red-haired boy in the middle of the noble trio blanched at the vividness of Melodía's description. He clearly didn't care to envision his gorgeous, long-crested green and yellow duckbill eviscerated by brow horns tipped with filed iron. Count Morgain looked gangly even in his gilded plate armor with three green Fleur-de-Lys on the breast. He had high cheekbones, straight nose, and a prominent jaw. His green eyes resembled those of a horse confronting an open-jawed matador.

I kind of like producing that effect, Melodía thought. She took another bite of apple. Although it was hardly sporting of her; he was two whole years younger than she.

"What can we do?" Morgain stammered, looking nervously around.

He had noticed how close the trees grew to the road here. Perhaps at last it occurred to him Melodía might not be showing all her hand.

He'd addressed the question to his elders. But Melodía answered.

"Join us," she said. "We'll give you a fighting chance against the Grey Angel horde. If not—"

She shrugged. "Best thing to do is ride right off and get to packing. Clear out as quickly as you can. The horde follows hard. You've got no time."

"Nonsense!" barked the Vicomte. "Grey Angels and their Crusades are mere legends. Bogeyman stories to frighten naughty children."

"Now, Eudes," said the man who sat a beautiful white ambler on the young Count's left. "Let's be wary of blasphemy. It might be unwise, if the young lady speaks truly."

He wore a green gown fringed in purple. The trim signified he was a bishop—Archbishop of Fleur, in fact, Toville by name. The main color signified allegiance to the Creator Adán, the Oldest Son, as did the symbol on his breast, of two broken lines stacked atop an intact third. Notwithstanding that the sackbuts in their splendid barding dwarfed his unarmored mount, and he himself was slight and balding, he held stage, as it were, as well as the others and considerably better than his liege. He was fellow—some said rival—to Vicomte Eudes as counselor to the bewildered young count.

"There's not a peep about the Angels in the *Books of the Law*," rasped Eudes, showing more erudition than Melodía expected. "They're not canonical. I've a hard time believing in superhuman beings and soulless armies."

"But what about the refugees streaming over our borders from Métairie Brulée, Lord?" asked a knight.

Eudes's face purpled. Not a good shade for him, Melodía thought. Apparently he wasn't accustomed to contradiction and had no intention of becoming so.

"What could be clearer? They're fleeing the freebooters who've invaded our land!"

"We've done nothing more than exercise our rights of the Imperial roads," Melodía said. She knew full well that stretched the truth. Imperial law did allow free travel among domains. But it placed some pretty clear constraints on exercising those rights with large armed bands. "You'll find out for yourselves in a few days whether we're telling the truth or not. In the meantime, what do you lose by letting us pass?"

"But you'll ravage the countryside!" Morgain managed to get out.

"We're prepared to pay for whatever we consume."

Adán's purview was Commerce. The word *pay* put a sparkle in his prelate's eye.

"If you've silver to pay for supplies, surely you can pay for your passage," Toville said.

"Our payment for our passage," said Melodía, "is that you get to keep your lives, your lands, and your play-pretties. At least until Raguel shows up to take them from you."

At the name a shudder ran though the Fleuries. Several made the sign of Equilibrium. The Archbishop not least among them.

It quite pleased Melodía she was able to think of the Grey Angel, and even speak His name aloud, without shaking.

"Try to chisel us or hinder us in any way, and we'll kill you," she said. "Then we'll take what we can carry from your estates, burn your lands black, and poison every well in the county to keep the horde off our backs."

The three grandes exchanged uneasy looks. They'd ridden too close to Melodía to consult unheard. And they weren't about to lose face by backing away from a slender young woman armored only in a light jack, brown linen trousers, and high-topped cavalry boots.

"What if we win?" Toville asked slyly.

"You've already lost. You're caught between fires. And make no mistake, my lord Archbishop: we're desperate. Not for fear of you, but of what follows snapping at our heels. Standing against us, you'll find, is as wise as standing in the way of a titan herd fleeing a forest fire."

That hit home, she saw. But young Morgain looked as if he doubted his own name, right now; and the men-at-arms didn't count. The men who did, Archbishop and uncle, still looked stubborn.

"Let's say you do win," she said. "What then? In a matter of days your battle-weakened army will face the horde. And you die."

She took an emphatic bite. "Horribly."

Eudes's beard bristled as he set his jaw. The Archbishop pursed lips as if adding sums. Morgain dangled from uncertainty as from hooks through his cheeks.

"Listen to the lady," a voice called.

A young man with brown hair held back from his face by a dark-green band leaned on his shortbow in front of a berry-bush, whose branches currently bore neither flower nor fruit, but only thorns. The Fleury blue bloods looked offended that a mere commoner—and a half animal woods-runner at that—would dare to speak. Being a woods-runner, he spoke right on with fine unconcern.

"My name's Henri," he said. "I am a coureur de bois, as you can plainly tell, and proud as any king, though I own only what I carry and don't want more. I was born in the land you sitting-folk call Métairie Brulée. I ask you now: would I have left the trees and soil that make up my very flesh and bones for a mere Faerie-tale?"

To Melodía's surprise, none of the nobles barked at him for silence. Apparently a few rats of doubt had crept in to gnaw the roots of their certainties. *Good*, she thought. *Perhaps they aren't too stupid to live.*

"Our captain has seen this awful thing, this Angel, with her own good eyes," Henri said. "I've fought the creatures He commands. As have we all."

Which also strained fact a bit—the army swore in fresh recruits day and night from the refugee-streams, men and women looking for slightly improved chances of sustenance, to say nothing of survival. At least a quarter of Melodía's detachment had joined since the flight from Séverin farm. But woods-runners, she'd noticed, were generally concerned with higher truths than the merely literal.

"Creatures?" said Toville doubtfully.

"These are surely men and women you're talking about!" snapped Eudes.

"Have you seen them then, fine lord that you are? I have. I told you. I've seen the terrible fervor with which they fight. How they show no fear of death or wounds. How they're bent only on slaughter and destruction.

"And I've heard the captives we've taken speak. Most say they felt some power take hold of their minds like a fist, and squeeze out all their will. Those who resist—" He shrugged. "The hordelings kill them in such a way as to encourage the others, if you take my meaning."

"Why do we sit and listen—" Eudes began.

"Shut up, uncle!" Morgain snapped. His eyes and cheeks burned fever-bright. "I want to hear this."

That so shocked the Vicomte that he did.

"Some of the ones we capture," Henri said, "act like dead men walking—aye, and women too. Listless they are, responding to no argument or sentiment or even threat, refusing food and water till they die. Others rage like rabid dogs until exhaustion kills them. Some speak and act like ones awakened from a dream.

"These last—the ones who can talk, and will—tell of lights and colors and strange swirlings in their minds. Of storms of fear and exaltation they can't describe or account for. Some of these folk accept Colonel Karyl's articles and join the army, where they serve as well as any other. Others simply wander off and are seen no more.

"But the worst aren't aught of those, my fine *monteurs*. No, not by half. Worst by far are the ones who join the horde willingly. Who butcher and torture and burn, either to expiate their sins—or because the Angel gives them license to give into them.

"Them we slay."

He stood a moment, chin held high as any grande's. It amused Melodía to think how once she—even long-ago's spoiled, sheltered princess full of fellowship for the downtrodden—would have reacted with instant fury to that presumption. Now she felt pleased at his defiance—and proud.

"Here's one truth greater than any other you've heard or ever will," Henri continued. "The Grey Angel horde devours everything, like a swarm of soldier-ants. It's coming here. It will devour you. Raguel comes."

"What should I do?" the boy Count asked the air, eyes overflowing tears.

"Either fight the Angel," Melodía said, "or flee him. Decide fast. Above all, do not oppose us. For your sakes as well as ours."

She extended a finger of the hand that held the half-eaten apple and ticked it at them.

"Everything you've known is about to change. For the worse. Worse than you can imagine. So don't try to cling to what you have. Or even what you know.

"Or Raguel will take it all. And you."

Chapter 35

Morión, Morion—Corythosaurus casuarius. A high-backed hadrosaur, 9 meters long, 3 meters high at shoulder, 3 tonnes. A favored Nuevaropan war-mount, named for the resemblance between its round crest and that of a morion helmet.

—THE BOOK OF TRUE NAMES

Like battling bull sackbuts, two nude giants slammed together. Jaume's sandals slapped hard yellow soil as he ran up, alerted by a frantic Bartomeu. Ignoring him, Timaeos and Ayaks continued to grapple, grunt, and pummel each other with fists the size of springer-hams.

Without hesitation Jaume flung himself into the scrum.

By midafternoon the great Imperial Army had laagered-down on a dusty plain—ironic in a county called Bois Profond, meaning Deepwood. In fact the province occupied the transition zone between La Meseta and the moister country rising to the Shield foothills. They were approaching Telar's Wood, the forest that spanned the Tyrant's Head from north to south.

As they neared Métairie Brulée, the army had cause to move cautiously. They had to contend with an unceasing torrent of humans, beasts, and overloaded wagons fleeing a province now completely overrun by Raguel's

Horde. But ultimately their lack of progress had little to do with caution or refugees either one. Despite the best efforts of Jaume and a handful of competent sub-commanders—like the officers of the two Nodosaur tercios—the Ejército Imperial was rolling pandemonium.

Though Jaume was no small man, Ayaks and Timaeos together could easily make three of him. Using their freely flowing sweat as lubricant he managed to wedge himself sideways between them, chest to chest with the red-bearded Griego, his face turned to his right. A musk of dust and man-sweat filled his head. Both fighters did keep scrupulously clean, as the *Books of the Law* mandated.

The enormous pair now held one another's shoulders with their left hands and hammered each other obliviously with their right. Stars shot behind Jaume's eyes as a misaimed fist clipped him. The watching knights growled.

No, my friends, he thought as loudly as he could, though he'd never shown any sign of the rare and dangerous gift of psi. *I've got to handle this myself. Or we're lost—and with us, hope.*

Resetting his legs beneath him, Jaume inhaled, tightened his belly on the breath, and, bending his knees deeply, sank his *qi*. He placed a palm beneath each fighter's left elbow. He exhaled, retaining a bit of breath deep down to support his spine. Then sucking in hard he drove powerfully upward with his legs.

Though neither huge nor bulky, Jaume was strong. He was also as skilled a wrestler as the Order could boast, except perhaps the deceptively dainty-looking Florian. In a one-on-one match, of course, either the Griego giant or the Ruso might easily throw Jaume by the simple expedient of picking him up and dropping him to the ground. Here, with each man focused entirely on the other, that trick wasn't available.

He knew better than to push straight outward, opposing strength to strength. So he pushed perpendicular to the grunting, straining pair. In just such a way, the *Classic of the Holy Exercises* claimed, a force of a scant few grams could deflect a force of half a tonne. . . .

Timaeos's and Ayaks's hands lost their grips and slid upward. Their huge, naked bodies crashed together, sandwiching Jaume in a way in which, in other circumstances, he might even enjoy. Now only the fact he had his gut muscles clenched on a bellyful of air kept them from crushing the wind straight out of him. As it was he felt his ribs flex alarmingly, actually heard them creak with the strain.

Lowering both hands he pushed out his elbows. Then, employing the connectedness of body and limbs the Exercises taught, he twisted with all the force of his hips and legs.

Already off-balance, the two giants fell straightaway on their faces.

The circle of knights applauded. Jaume stepped clear in case the two decided to go for each other again right off.

But they'd had enough. Ayaks lay prone with arms and legs splayed, gasping like a fish. Timaeos rolled over, sat up on his broad bottom, and burst into tears.

Jaume swayed. Florian was instantly at his side. He grabbed Jaume's arm to steady him.

"I'm all right," Jaume said. "Thank you, my friend."

Timaeos's Taliano arming-squire Luigi was beside his master, trying to get him to his feet. A slight, olive-skinned boy, with a mop of black curls and black eyes, he looked like a mouse trying to coax a thunder-titan.

Jaume felt his face settling into the unfamiliar contours of a frown. He let it. *Is it really so unfamiliar, these days?* It was hard even for a man as philosophically determined to see beauty everywhere as he was to find much to smile at.

"What's caused this," he asked softly. "Brother fighting brother?"

The two giants had clambered to their feet. They faced him, so slouched and abject they barely overtopped him. Jaume raised an eyebrow. "Well? Anybody?"

"It was Jacques's arming-squire David," Ayaks said heavily. Timaeos snuffled like a nosehorn at a drinking trough. "We both . . . fancy him."

"You're sleeping with a squire?" Jaume demanded. "You both swore a mighty oath on acceptance as knights-brother not to do that very thing. Even the attempt is a violation."

The boy in question himself ran up. He flung himself at Jaume's feet and clung to his shins, weeping and gazing beseechingly up at Jaume with enormous blue eyes.

"Please, Lord," he blubbered, "it's my fault! I encouraged them both! I was so flattered such mighty men were interested in me. . . ."

Jaume knelt, helped the brown-haired boy to his feet. Although "helped" was something of a euphemism. David was limp as kelp. Jaume's blood still sizzled with adrenaline. It was all he could do to keep from yanking him upright.

"It's not your fault," he said, voice buzzing with passion and exertion. "You made choices. You've got to live with them, good or bad. You're young: that's a time for learning, and no better teacher than mistakes. Jacques, my brother?"

The eldest Companion approached quickly from the direction of his own tent. As always these days Jaume was shocked to see just how haggard his friend was. His hair was grey and straggling, his cheeks sunken, his eyes seemed to stare out of brown pits.

"Take him somewhere else," Jaume said, gently steering David to his master. "And maybe keep a better eye on him, hein?"

Jacques gave him a stricken look. Jaume's heart fell. He anticipated the words about to spill from the moustached lips. "No, it's not your fault either. Now go. I'll talk to you soon."

He turned back to the repentant giants. "As for you: you are the ones most responsible. Grown men. Men of unparalleled strength. Champions. Knights. *Companions.* Whatever the boy said or did, you are responsible for what took place.

"You raised your hands against each other. Don't you see, that's one of the very reasons we prohibit romance with servants and Ordinaries? That, and to spare all parties from the ugliness of exploitation."

He swung an arm in an arc encompassing the bulk of the Imperial Army—no longer calling itself a Crusade, since a Grey Angel had preempted the word. Shouts, screams, the clash of arms floated on a wind that stank of wastes human and animal. And blood, mostly human.

"And *that.* Random duels aren't enough for our fellow nobles anymore. Now they fight melees to the size of minor battles, while wallowing in their own filth—and wondering why they sicken and die in droves, as if the Creators themselves didn't promise just that punishment for disobeying their Laws of hygiene. Do we want to let that inside? Do we want to give it entry into the sacred circle of our Order and the Lady?"

He exhaled heavily.

"It's my fault. The disorder, the murder and atrocity, the plague. I am

Marshal and Constable; I command the army. Yet I don't know how to control it. It's the greatest defeat of my life. But I do not have to let the general foulness and discord breaks our ranks. And I will not. Especially as we're called to the most vital service to Empire and people of all our lives!"

"They don't let you bring the blue bloods to heel," said Machtigern. "It's not your fault at all."

A ripple of consent ran around the circle of watchers. It held an ugly undertone. Everyone knew whom the Alemán meant by "they."

Jaume held up a hand. The muttering stopped.

"I command," he repeated. "What happens in the army is my responsibility. Leave that for now. Brother Ayaks, Brother Timaeos, you have broken not just our law, but your faith with one another. What have you to say for yourselves?"

"Kill me," Ayaks said, his voice more a tyrant-growl than usual with his chin pressed to his clavicle. "Or . . . exile me. I deserve no better."

Timaeos emitted a startlingly shrill whinny of despair. Mor Dieter stood near him. With a speed that had fatally surprised many foes from a man his size, Timaeos snatched the dagger from the young Alemán's belt, held it out at the extent of both his tree-trunk arms, and aimed its point at his heart.

Then he fell forward on his face. His vast body actually bounced a couple of centimeters back into the air amidst a cloud of khaki dust. He made gobbling sounds.

Behind him stood Machtigern. No small man himself, the taciturn and practical Companion had clipped the suicidal giant behind the ear with the flat of his war-hammer.

"Is that Beauty, to deny a man's choice to take his own life?" Florian asked.

Machtigern shrugged gallows shoulders. "He can always kill himself later, when he gets his wits back. Such as they are."

Florian laughed and clapped his shoulder. "Fair enough, my friend."

His cheeks flushing pinker than normal Dieter retrieved his poignard. Timaeos picked himself up. He made himself meet Jaume's gaze.

"I'm sorry, Captain," he said. "I've failed you and all our brothers. I accept your judgement. Whatever the punishment, I've earned it."

Jaume stared at them a moment. They wilted beneath the unaccustomed heat of his gaze.

"We know from the poor refugees that we've two days, three at most, before the Grey Angel horde lands on us. They've got three times our numbers, at least. And you've all heard the stories again and again: that they think of neither survival, nor avoiding pain, nor least of all of pity, but only of destroying every living thing in their path. What greater dereliction could you perform, than to deny us your strength in the battle to come?"

As if two could make a difference against such a horde, he thought with a spasm of bitterness. *Or all of us, knights and Ordinaries together. Against pure horror.*

"So hear my judgement: I do not permit that you die, nor go into exile. Clearly, you've too much time on your hands and minds: you will busy yourselves from waking to sleep. At exercise, at drill, at your art—which, now of all times, we must not neglect—and barring those things, at mucking the duckbill paddocks! And when you go to bed, it will be alone. For one year you shall remain celibate.

"Above all: you will continue to serve. And you will *fight*. The horde, not one another!"

They started to respond. He stilled them with upraised palms.

"Understand: there are no more chances. Fail again of your oaths, any of them, and you will be cast out. Let your eyes linger too long on one of your juniors, and out you go.

"You are good men. You will redeem yourselves, and atone for your actions, and heal our sacred circle of Companionship, in the name of the Empire and of the Lady. Do you understand me, brothers?"

Both of them looked at him squarely. "Yes, Captain," they said, a beat apart.

Their very bluntness heartened him. He'd suspect a greater display of emotion as mere histrionics.

"Then turn, apologize to each other as brothers, clasp arms and embrace. And then get busy, in Bella's holy Name! The battle of our lives awaits."

He found Jacques standing apart, on the brow of the hill where they'd made camp, hugging himself tightly and weeping like a lost child. He looked up at Jaume's firm grasp on his shoulder.

"Come back to us, old friend," Jaume said softly. "We can't afford to do without you. Now less than ever."

Jacques shook his head violently. A teardrop flew from lank greying locks, struck Jaume's upper lip and ran into his mouth. It tasted of salt and sorrow.

"What's the use?" Jacques said. Not very far away, in the turbulent camp below, somebody screamed in bubbling final agony. "Isn't it all lost already? The ugliness wins at the end. It always does."

Jaume put back his head and laughed. It was a full laugh, a hearty laugh that belied his lean frame and often-languid manner. Jacques blinked his brown eyes clear to stare at his lord in bewilderment.

"Why else do we fight?" Jaume asked. "Why continue to *live*, when death inevitably waits? Both for the same reason: to keep a little spark of life, and Beauty, alive against the black."

Jacques still frowned. But he stood a bit straighter.

"Thank you for reminding me, my friend," Jaume said.

But when he was alone in the paddock of handspan-thick pilings he himself had helped to cut and drive, Jaume let his own tears flow.

"I know how badly I've failed my Companions and my Lady," he said as he brushed the supple pebbled skin of Camellia's graceful neck with soapy water. "I thought I'd picked men who wouldn't need to be commanded. Then I'm placed in charge of men who refuse to be commanded by anything but their impulses. Men who think they have the right to rule everything but themselves."

He dumped a hornface-leather bucket of pure water over the dinosaur. She bobbed her cream and butterscotch–crested head with pleasure.

"I've no right feeling sorry for myself," he said. "But sorrow has its beauties too, I suppose."

And he wept freely, standing beside his morion's comforting immensity.

She nuzzled his ear with her broad blunt beak, then rested her chin on his shoulder while he scratched her cheek.

They stood that way, man and dinosaur, until Jaume's arming-squire Bartomeu found them and told Jaume he was summoned at once to the Imperial presence.

Chapter 36

Orden Militar, **Military Order**—An Order chartered by the Church of Nuevaropa to defend the Faith, the Church, and the Empire. Usually small, élite military formations, usually, devoted to a single Creator, whose deeds range from individual feats of daring to acts of charity to decisive battlefield maneuvers. Most, such as the all-female Sisters of the Wind and the Knights of the Yellow Tower, consist wholly of knights. A few, like the mercenary Struthio Lancers, refuse to accept knights, and their members defiantly refuse knighthood. Many Orders are famous, most are rich, and some are powerful. Imperial Champion Jaume's all-male Companions of Our Lady of the Mirror may be the most of all three—occasioning resentment inside the Church and out.

—A PRIMER TO PARADISE FOR THE IMPROVEMENT OF YOUNG MINDS

"Voyvod Karyl Bogomirskiy's still alive?" Jaume repeated in astonishment.

A curious sense of relief flooded his belly. Not that this in any way alleviates my guilt, he told himself. And many others certainly aren't, good men and women.

And good beasts too: a lover of war-hadrosaurs, he tended to deplore Karyl's living fortresses with their terrible goring horns. Yet they were living things as well, with beauties of their own, and not to be destroyed without cause. *In the name of duty I committed a great crime*, he thought. *I can't help feeling a certain gratification that my intended victim survived.*

The color fell from Duke Falk's face like sand from an upturned glass jar. "Impossible! I killed the man myself."

"Apparently not enough, your Grace," Jaume said with a small smile.

That got him a blue-hot glare. Instead of bursting out further the commander of the Imperial bodyguard slouched down with arms crossed over his gilded breastplate, with his massive bearded chin sunk to its rolled upper rim.

The Imperial council of war was gathered in a large chamber in the Emperor's personal pavilion. The morning sun laid red and yellow tints across the drawn faces gathered around the long oaken table. Vents near the roof let in sultry air from outside. Despite them the walls of bright cloth kept the worst stinks of the camp at bay.

But certain of the grandes assembled seemed to be trying to take up the slack. As for Tavares . . . *Does the man even deign to wipe himself when he shits?*

"You're telling us a dead man's up and walking again?" asked Duque Francisco de Mandar. He sketched the symbol of Equilibrium before him, then touched forehead, loins, shoulders, the sides of his rib cage, and hips in the Creators' sign.

His Duchy contained the Spañol royal capital, La Fuerza. He had come in place of his cousin the King. He commanded a sizable force of vassal lords, *hombres armaos*, House troops, and peasant levies.

"Truly," he said, "it's a sign of judgement upon us." An immensely tall man, cadaverously thin, Francisco had short black hair, drooping moustaches, and a blue undertone to his skin which Jaume found off-putting. Jaume had heard it said he looked as if he were mourning when he was getting a blow job from one of his innumerable mistresses; his expression today was fit to sour milk.

"Or shocking bad management on somebody's part," muttered Graf Rurik.

The beefy Rurik, noted for gruffness, valor, and a majestic tawny moustache, had brought his Knights of the Yellow Tower, an Order-Military devoted to Torrey, to serve the Emperor. So had Lady Janice Tisdell and her Telar-worshipping Sisters of the Wind. Neither Captain-General looked with particular favor on the upstart Companions, nor on Jaume's jumped-up status as Condestable. Still, Rurik manifestly thought even less of his countryman Falk's elevation.

"Can we really fight this horde?" asked a worried-looking Maxence. The Count of a neighboring province of Collines Argentées, he had arrived just today. Indeed, he had brought the news of Karyl's astonishing survival—along with regrets from his liege, the Duke de Haut-Pays, unavoidably detained by warding off the incursion of a whole army Karyl had somehow raised in Providence.

"A better question is how?" said Rurik.

Maxence shook lank brown locks. He was no devotee of the Life-to-Come Sect: in fact his hair was wet because the Imperial summons had reached him in the middle of his bath.

"I didn't mean that. I mean, is it morally permissible? Spiritually? Raguel is the Creators' holy servant. He works Their will. Can we resist that, except at risk to our souls?"

"Of course we cannot!" Tavares brayed.

His pet nobles bobbed grubby heads in agreement. The outburst made Duke Francisco start. Though he smelled too good to be a Life-to-Come votary, he deferred to the cardinal too much for Jaume's liking.

"Rather we should submit meekly to the just punishment our Creators have decreed for the wickedness we have wrongly permitted in Their names!"

Felipe frowned. "I disagree," he said mildly.

It was as if he'd scuffed up a flier pelt and touched a spark from it to everyone in the room. Felipe the pious, the great friend of Tavares's late patron Pío, contradicting a man of the cloth? A man he himself had seen given the red hat despite the known distaste of Pío's successor for him—had hand-selected as the Imperial Army's chaplain?

It was so unexpected that instead of his usual theatrics Tavares simply blinked at Felipe as if he had spoken in the tongue of far Vareta.

"I have taken counsel," Felipe went on, voice strengthening as he went along. "Of my prayers, and of course of my faithful and pious confessor, Fray Jerónimo, who as you all know is an exceedingly holy man."

That sent a certain look scurrying around the table like a mouse. *None of us knows that*, Jaume thought, covering his own skepticism by lifting a goblet of rather sour local wine to his lips. Because so far as I know, no living soul other than His Majesty has ever so much as seen this holy man. Not even his own chief bodyguard.

"Fray Jerónimo has shared with me this wisdom," Felipe said, eyes shining with eagerness. "As is well known, the Grey Angels exist to maintain the Equilibrium of the World: the smooth and regular turning of the Wheel. A Grey Angel Crusade hasn't got destruction as its end, although it may employ such means. So my confessor asked me, is it not possible that this Crusade is ultimately meant as much as a test as chastisement? To discover whether the Imperio is fit to persist—and I to rule it?"

He paused. The expressions Jaume saw around the long table ranged from blankness to shock to anger-flush growing behind Tavares's surprisingly trim beard—and coating of grime. Jaume hoped his own habitual soft smile hadn't frozen too hard.

Felipe noticed none of the reactions. That was nothing exceptional: he was a man who didn't take hints. Instead he warbled on, happy as a child opening his Creators' Day gifts:

"'Should the Emperador'—my confessor said—'confront and defeat the Grey Angel Crusade, that will signify, not blasphemous thwarting of the Creators' will, but rather irrefutable demonstration that he and his dreams of centralizing power unto the Fangèd Throne enjoy the purest favor of the Eight. Win, and you win their imprimatur.'"

Felipe sat back beaming all over his pudgy face. "Now that I know it's all a test of my worthiness—*our* worthiness, my friends!—I await the contest with eagerness!"

You're the only one. Even as he thought it, Jaume could read the words on several of his fellow-captains' faces as plainly as if they were block-printed there.

He looked to Tavares. The cardinal's face was like a skull without the grin. For once the chaplain could find no words.

With an anything but congenial grin of his own, Jaume leaned forward. He had not beaten the brutal miquelet mountain bandits of his native Catalunya as a child, or won countless duels and battles since, by lacking a matador's instinct for the kill.

"If we wish for signs of our Creators' judgement," he said, "we need look no further than the plagues that stalk the camp, carrying away hundreds and weakening thousands to the point of uselessness. In very face of the battle, which, as your Majesty says, will determine the fate of the Empire."

"They are themselves judgements for sin!" Tavares declaimed. At once his narrow jaw clamped shut, and his eyes went wide. For all his obduracy, he wasn't stupid. He knew he'd said too much already.

Jaume smiled sweetly. "For once," he purred, "I agree with His Eminence. By defying their Creators' explicit commands on cleanliness we have broken Divine law. This hideous pestilence is the very punishment they decree for that crime."

"The *Books of the Law* are allegorical!" Tavares cried. "To take them literally is to be found wanting. And wanton!"

"Rubbish," the tall and ice-blond Lady Janice said. "The outbreak proves the literal interpretation's correct—to anyone impious enough to doubt them in the first place."

Tavares's eyes shot black fire at her. But he said nothing. Like Rurik and Jaume, as leader of an Order Military the Anglesa was a cardinal in the Holy Church. And all three were considerably senior to Tavares.

Felipe nodded. "True, true. What the *Books* predict is what we're suffering. Falk, my boy: see to it that full compliance with Holy Teaching on cleanliness is promulgated as army regulation, and rigorously enforced."

Falk's smile reminded Jaume of the Duke's albino war-mount, Snowflake. "It will be a pleasure, Majesty."

Tavares glared through knife-slit eyes. "Softly, my lord. Softly. We already face the wrath of our Creators."

"I won't surrender my Empire or my people to destruction, no matter how righteous it's supposed to be!" Felipe said. "I have served the Empire as well as my Creators loyally for all my life. I cannot believe they would damn me for doing what they Created me to do."

"They don't damn at all," Jaume said—softly. "As they also make clear in the *Books of the Law*."

"Lies!" Tavares almost screeched the word. Spittle flew from his mouth. Jaume recoiled. Did the man think that was persuasive?

Ah, no, he rebuked himself. *The fanatic doesn't seek to persuade. He wants only to punish disbelief.*

The chaplain inflated his narrow chest for another outburst. But Felipe held up his hand.

"Enough," he said. "I don't have the stomach for theological debate right now. If nothing else, it would seem to be rather after the fact at this point. The hay is in the barn, the Slayer's in the herd, the Grey Angel Crusade has begun.

"I am not asking for *discussion*, gentlemen, ladies. I see a threat to my people and my throne. Wherever it originates I intend to fight it.

"Therefore I command: let anyone who cannot in good conscience fight leave the army at once. Because from this very instant any who resist, sow dissension, or even hang back from the fight once joined, will be hanged forthwith as a mutineer and traitor!"

"You risk your very soul," Tavares said, his voice now low and deadly as a venomous snake.

"Yes," Felipe said. "Well. It's my own to risk. And if there's sin, let it be mine alone, as the decision to fight is mine alone."

"So be it."

Tavares stood. He turned a mad glare from Felipe to Jaume, who forced himself to meet it with calm. The chaplain spun toward the door in a crimson swirl.

"One moment, Eminence." The Emperor's quiet words snapped the Cardinal back around. "You were wished upon me by my late friend, Pío. For his sake I've put up with you, though I've found you quite as insufferable as Jaume reported you were with his Army of Correction.

"And now I've done all I can for Pío's blessed memory. If you think yourself exempt from any decree I have made or shall make, you are sadly mistaken. Do you understand me? One word of doubt preached to my warriors, and I will request the captain of my bodyguard to remove your Eminence's head from your shoulders with that pet axe of his. One word."

Stiffly, Tavares bowed and left.

"What is it you need to tell us, and us alone, your Majesty?" Jaume asked.

Emperor Felipe sat silent a moment in the gilded folding chair he'd had made up in case he ever got to lead the army on campaign, as if to ensure the dismissed conferees had gotten fully out of earshot of the chamber in his sprawling and elaborate pavilion. Then he looked at Jaume and Falk, and the broadness of his grin and the joy in his sea-green eyes startled Jaume almost to the point of shock.

"Gentlemen," he said. "My good, loyal boys. Maxence brought further news, which he wisely chose to impart to me alone. My daughter escaped the fall of Providence town."

"Bella!" Jaume exclaimed. He flung himself on one knee beside the Emperor, clung to him, and gave way to heartfelt sobs of relief and joy.

Felipe's arms grasped him clumsily from above. Jaume felt him shake as he cried too. The Emperor pressed his cheek against Jaume's head; Jaume felt hot tears drip hot onto his scalp and run down his cheek.

But Jaume's duty would not permit him to indulge himself too long, even in the pure and simple beauty of his passion. He forced himself back into control and pulled away, blinking his eyes clear.

The Emperor's own eyes still swam, and tear trails glittered down his cheek. Tears dewed his Imperial beard.

"But there's worse news too," Felipe said in a clotted voice.

"Majesty?" Jaume's own voice was clear.

"She's with Bogomirskiy's rebel army."

Jaume's soul was a blade red from the forge, plunged into icy water. *I knew the moment His Majesty's words reached my ears, of course. How else could my beloved have escaped the rise of Raguel in Providence town?*

"She's safe, at least?" he asked.

The Emperor nodded. Tears dripped from the end of his goatee.

"The last anyone has heard. But Maxence also says that his Grace the Duke of Haut-Pays has heard claims from refugees that she serves him, riding with his scout cavalry."

Which, given that Voyvod Karyl was engaged to fight for our declared enemies in Providence . . .

He stood.

"What will you do?" Felipe asked him, almost beseechingly.

"What my Emperor directs," Jaume replied. "As always. Majesty?"

He could not trust his self-control anymore. Barely waiting for Felipe's answering nod he spun to the door-flap.

To find himself looking into Duke Falk's sapphire eyes. Being who he was, Jaume could not help but feel a flash of admiration for the masculine beauty of the powerfully built young man.

But it was more elusive beauty than usual. Because the taut alabaster skin of Falk's face had gone an unhealthy grey and sagged most alarmingly, and those long-lashed, lovely eyes were wide as a startled matador's.

He's as stricken by the cruelty of His Majesty's dilemma as I am! Jaume thought.

"Your Grace," he managed not to mumble, and fled back to his encampment and his private grief with as much dignity as he could.

As the silken flap swished shut behind the departed Condestable Imperial, Falk turned to follow. His face and chest burned with shame at having witnessed the spectacle of two men—important men, *leaders*—weeping openly. He already felt ambivalent about Jaume. But he could afford no such confusion with regard to his liege the Emperor. Could he?

"Your Grace," Felipe said from behind. His voice still trembled unmanfully. Falk gritted his jaw, then composed himself and turned.

He bowed, both to show respect—*I must respect the Emperor!*—and to hide the last of scrubbing his face of emotion.

"How may I serve your Majesty?" he asked.

He meant it. *All my life,* he thought, *I've been groomed to serve Chian, and his principle of power. I admit I've wondered whether Felipe truly was the strong man the Empire needs. He shown my doubts were pointless.*

"I thought I—I thought we'd saved Melodía by getting her away from La Merced," Felipe said haltingly. "Now she seems likely to be crushed like a grain of millet between the millstones of our armies and Raguel's Crusade. Events both vast and unforeseeable."

Not altogether unforeseeable, Falk allowed himself to think sardonically. *Not to me.*

But I must admit I never foresaw an actual Grey Angel Crusade. He was a believer in the True Faith of the Creators, as mandated for all human inhabitants of Paradise. But he had not expected the tenets of his religion to manifest in quite such concrete ways. To say nothing of such appalling ones.

The Emperor hung and shook his head. "I don't see what better I could have done. Yet I feel that I've failed her."

For an agonizing moment Falk sat frozen. *Does he know? Is this a test? Some subtle torture, before he summons my own men to hale me off to the more overt kind?*

But Felipe simply sat, head down, shoulders slumped, looking prematurely aged by care. He didn't have much guile in him in any event. Witness the ease with which Falk had persuaded him that allowing Melodía's escape was the Emperor's own idea, weeks before.

"I cannot call her back," Felipe said in a way that showed how he fought to keep the tears from surging back. "Not after all . . . all that's happened. Nor can I treat this unexpected revenant Karyl or his host as anything but enemies. Since, ultimately, they're the enemy we marched out on Crusade against."

"I see your Majesty's dilemma."

"What am I to do, boy?" Felipe blinked rapidly at Falk. "What am I to do for my poor baby girl?"

Inspiration came. "Wouldn't Fray Jerónimo tell you to bide? Wouldn't he say that all things happen for a purpose? Be patient, he'd say. And rest easy about your daughter's fate."

The clever devil's managed to keep his true identity and even his face secret from me, the chief of the Scarlet Tyrants. And more than that, from Bergdahl's best efforts, at the Palace of the Fireflies *and on the march. I might as well at least have use of him.*

Felipe's head snapped up. His eyes glittered so sharply Falk feared he'd overplayed his hand.

But the Emperor just sighed and subsided back in his chair. "Melodía's fate rests in the Creators' hands," he said. "As do all our fates. You're right."

He reached out to take Falk's huge hand, white scarred with lighter white, with his own. It was soft as a baby's. The pikeman's calluses he'd earned in youth had long since worn away.

"You have my gratitude," Felipe said. "Go now, boy. Tend to your duties and then get what rest you can. You'll need it.

"You've put my mind at ease. Now leave a tired old man to his prayers."

But instead of rest, when Falk entered his own tent after nightfall, he found Bergdahl, sitting and sharpening his big peasant's knife on a stone.

"See to my armor," said the Duke, naked and dripping from his bath outside. "It got somewhat blood-splashed."

"So some of the nobles resisted his Majesty's edicts about cleanliness being next to holiness, did they?"

"Briefly."

"Isn't cleanup your arming-squire Albrecht's job?"

"I'm telling you to do it."

"Well, I'm pleased to say I've long since given up all pretense to holiness," the servant said, tucking away stone and knife and rising.

"One thing," said Falk as Bergdahl headed out to fetch the armor from its rack outside the tent.

He turned back with a brown-toothed smile. "Your Grace commands me."

"As a matter of fact, I do. As I traveled the camp, delivering the Emperor's edicts—and enforcing them on those who weren't quick enough on the uptake—I encountered rumors flying everywhere. Remarkable rumors. Rumors concerning the Voyvod Karyl Bogomirskiy. The ostensibly late Karyl Bogomirskiy."

"Ahh." Bergdahl shrugged. For once he actually looked abashed. "Well. Like your Grace, I'm used to those I kill staying that way. Gave me quite a turn, it did, to hear he's turned up alive and well—and with a brand-new army. But I swear on my life—which I'll be damned lucky of your lady mother leaves me—I saw him go over the cliff, clutching that horror and bleeding out from the stump of his sword-arm, with nothing beneath him but three hundred meters of air and the surface of the Eye."

Falk waved that away. "What troubles me are these rumors I'm hearing that Karyl never intended any treachery—that Count Jaume stabbed an innocent man in the back."

"Why, those are surely true—as who knows better than your Grace? After all, didn't I deliver the Princes' peace terms, requiring Karyl's destruction, to his Highness Marshal von Rundstedt with my own hand? Which he viewed with manifest distaste, I'll add. And unhesitatingly carried out, as Jaume himself did, loyal little lapdogs that they are.

"Not that Felipe found putting the wood to Karyl any great hardship.

That bastard Slavo's unbroken chain of victories scared his own masters as badly as they did us in the Princes' Party."

"All that aside, such rumors now serve only to discredit our Constable."

Bergdahl snapped dirty-nailed fingers.

"Ah! Why, I believe—yes, they were calculated to do that very thing. By me, as it happens. And spread by the selfsame party." He showed awful brown teeth in his goblin grin.

"What on Paradise for?"

"Have you forgotten? The stress of being in charge of the Scarlet Tyrants is weakening your mind. He's your rival, of course. He stands between you and the Fangèd Throne."

"He's also a military genius," Falk said, "whose skill might be the only thing standing between us and annihilation."

"You discount your own gifts. I never thought I'd live to see it."

With one hand Falk grabbed the front of Bergdahl's soiled tunic. Although his servant was no small man, and fully as tall as the young Duke's one hundred ninety centimeters, he hoisted him straight off the ground so far his sandals dangled.

"Don't you understand, you damned fool?" Falk roared. "We don't dare weaken the army now, staring a Grey Angel in the face! If Jaume loses any more control of this army, we lose everything."

Despite the huge fist knotted beneath his chin Bergdahl sneered down his long, bent nose. "You truly don't understand the game you play here, do you, young master? Good thing your mother had sense to set me to provide sense for you."

"It stops now. The rumors. The scheming. You will obey me, or I'll wring your head off like a scratcher for the pot."

He dropped his manservant. Bergdahl caught himself from falling and stood as tall as he ever did.

"What would your dowager mother say?" he asked, massaging his throat.

"If we don't stop this," Falk said, "not a blessed thing. She'll die. You will die, and I will die. Everyone will die. We're fighting for our lives as much as for Empire. If you hamper that fight in any way, you're my enemy. And I will treat you as such."

That made Bergdahl blink. Falk felt grim satisfaction. It was the closest he'd come to getting the better of the villein.

"Don't say anything," he said. "Just nod your head and walk away. Or run very far and very fast."

Bergdahl nodded his head. And walked away.

If we survive, the goblin will make me suffer, the young Duke thought. *But first—we must survive.*

Chapter 37

Troodón, Tröodon—*Troodon formosus.* Pack-predator raptor, 2.5 meters long, 50 kilograms. Sometimes imported to Nuevaropa as pets or hunting beasts. Like ferrets, tröodons are clever, loyal, and given to mischief. Vengeful if abused.

—THE BOOK OF TRUE NAMES

"Ho, there, Horse Captain!"

Melodía led her troop into the village of Florimel off a sweep to make sure the army's rear was clear of the Grey Angel horde. She found the fugitive army already halfway through the little settlement snuggled deep in Telar's Wood. She trotted Meravellosa down a line of three-horns rumbling along nosehorn to tail, grumbling softly in their throats, following their own shadows cast well before the by the setting sun. They were hungry and cranky; even horse-aficionada Melodía, who knew little and cared less about dinosaurs, could tell that much.

She had to trust her mare's cleverness and sure-footedness to thread a path between marching monsters and gaping locals. Apparently unaware of Triceratops's belligerent nature, the good inhabitants of Florimel, adults as slack-jawed rapt as children, lined the main lane to watch the fantastic enormous three-horned dinosaurs go by. Nor was that the only danger they seemed oblivious to.

Why are you just standing around? Melodía wanted to scream at them. *The Grey Angel is coming. You should be running for your souls!*

At the cheerful, boozy call Melodía looked right. An inn, its façade whitewashed and half-timbered, fronted right on the road. A shingle hung by the door featured the legend, *The Purple Horror*, and an appropriately colored painting of a deinonychus rampant. Feeling less than charitable, Melodía suspected that was a truthful portrayal of the effects of taking on too much of their home brew.

On a half-log bench beside the sign, Rob Korrigan leaned back against the narrow building with bandy legs crossed. He had his long, thin-stemmed clay pipe in one hand, a blue and white ceramic liter mug in the other. Little Nell, hitched to a stone post nearby, had her beak in a bucket hung from the two long horns that topped her frill, happily ignoring the world and munching grain.

Melodía envied the hook-horn her obliviousness.

"Master Korrigan?" she called.

He hoisted his mug in salute. "The same it is, my charming captain."

"You're drunk!"

He waved the pipe. "And getting stoned too, I'll add."

She turned Meravellosa off the road and reined to a stop before him. "How can you do that, at a time like this?"

"Can ye name me a better time?"

She frowned. She knew he'd been finding shelter in bottle and herb more and more of late. Most frequently after another screaming fight in Karyl's tent.

Rob did all the screaming. If Karyl had uttered a word in days, Melodía didn't know the person who'd heard it.

"I can't imagine you unfitting yourself for duty with your precious dinosaurs to be tended to," she said sternly.

He shrugged and swilled. Wiping his beard with the back of his pipe-hand, he said, "Little enough you know of dinosaur masters, then. It's more often drunk we work than sober. Easier to face the horns and fangs and tonnes that way, don't you see? Anyway, I've a staff of grooms well trained and hopping. When I inspect these beauties in their paddock southwest of town in an hour or two, they'll be spotless, with every little nick and scrape anointed."

"What about your job as chief of intelligence?"

He sighed, put down the mug, dropped his boots to the yellow soil, and leaned forward.

"And there we get to chasing our own tails, lass, as to whether it's the news that drives me to drink, or I need to drink to digest what you and the rest of our fine scouts tell me."

Melodía blinked. Then again, formal logic was never the Irlandés's strong suit in the soberest times.

"Or haven't you heard?" he said. "Duke Eric of Haut-Pays has raised his vassals on the northwest side of the Petits Voleurs. Even if he doesn't know his business—and the talk is all that he does, distressing well—he could hold the ridges against our lot forever, with a few handfuls of peasants with sticks, commanded by pages with cook-pots on their heads. It's caught between the matador and the horror-pack we find ourselves. And, giving all respect to your Imperial daddy, I'm hard-pressed to decide which is which."

He turned his mug upside-down and shook the last drops onto the sparse and battered green and purple ferns by his boots.

"Then I know something you don't know." Melodía could have stopped herself from saying it. She chose not to. "We might not be caught at all. The horde's turned off our trail. That's what I'm here to report. And there's room between the Little Flier ridges and the Imperial Army for even a force as big as ours to slip between, especially with the horde occupying the army's attention. Given sufficient skill, that is. And luck."

He blinked at her, then narrowed hazel eyes that currently showed mainly green with a shrewdness that belied his self-professed state. "*You're* lucky," he said. "And surprising skillful, for one so young, raised so soft."

"I learned on the job," she said, with an equanimity that surprised her. He was right. As was she: this minstrel-turned-spymaster, deliberately loutish and deliberately fey as he liked to play, had taught her surpassing well.

"The question then being, are you lucky and skillful enough?"

"No. But I know someone who is."

"Himself?" Rob sat back, gusting laughter like a volcano rousing itself to a real full-bore eruption. "It's all your luck and more you'll need for that! Me, I doubt the Creators themselves could rouse him from his sulks. The Fae, now—"

"Superstition."

"Ha! You say that, who twice clapped eyes on Raguel His own fearful self? Ah, the certainty of youth. Deliver me from same."

What hair she'd left herself, she tossed. "I'm off."

She turned Meravellosa back to the road and nudged with her heels.

"And that, lass," he called after, "is why Ma Korrigan's son was always wise, when wise enough he was to evade *responsibility*.

"It's not just that it's wicked heavy. In the end it always turns to sand, and runs out through your fingers."

Two male woods-runners guarded Karyl's tent. It was a largish affair, although nothing to compare with the complex and palatial pavilions most grandes affected. Melodía knew he'd have settled for a one-man shelter, but for the need to hold occasional council under cover. Especially with winter rains come to the highland forests.

Melodía was in no mood to brook interference, and ready to pluck every string to get in to see the moody master of this traveling circus. Even the Daughter of the Emperor string: her need, and theirs, was that great.

But the woods-runners, who worshipped Karyl no matter what, also held her in high esteem. Ironically, given their disdain for authority and class distinctions, the more so because of her birth. That the Emperor's own heir treated them as equals and even friends made them think she must have a proper heart in her, unlike most of her kind.

Besides, she'd earned enough rank in this ragtag yet efficient army to justify the guards admitting her. As they promptly did. *Let no one in* surely couldn't apply to the Short-Haired Horse Captain herself, now, could it?

With only such sun as filtered through cloud and canvas, the tent's interior looked big as a cave and only marginally better lit. The only objects were Karyl's bedroll and cloak, rolled against one wall with his walking-stick propped against them, and the mat on which the man himself sat cross-legged, eyes shut, and dressed only in a loincloth.

He showed no sign of noticing her. She sat down facing him.

"You can play dead, like a tröodon waiting for an unwary eye-harvester to hop in range of an easy chomp, as long as you wish, my lord," she said. "I'm quite prepared to wait you out."

He opened one eye. "If you weren't determined and resourceful I never would've given you the light-horse," he said with a theatric sigh. "I shouldn't have expected to keep you out."

"No."

He face looked ghastly: cheeks hollow, eyes sunk deeply into dark grey pits. The bone looked ready to split the skin of his broad forehead at any second.

"What made you so determined to override my wish to be left alone?" he asked. "It's not the fact your father's outlawed me, is it?"

"Old news. I know Rob gives you regular reports. Although you don't respond."

The odd thing was, those tidings had arrived with a large number of Imperial deserters begging to join the newly minted outlaw.

"What, then?" he asked.

"Rob and I have been doing your job for you."

"And a splendid job you've done," he said. "Especially bringing Fleur around."

She grunted in a fashion that would've made her dueña Doña Carlota screech like a Pteranodon chased from its perch. The success in Fleur, such as it was, seemed to belong to a bygone age, though it happened only a week ago. In the end the peasantry and a few barons and knights roused themselves to flee, most joining the refugee army.

Poor befuddled Count Morgain, though, died for a crime usually absolved by time: adolescence. He was too young and uncertain to extract himself from the tug-of-war between his uncle and Archbishop Toville before the Grey Angel Crusade consumed them all.

"Or is it that Haut-Pays holds the Little Fliers against us?" Karyl asked. "I heard that too. The walls of my tent don't keep out much sound, sadly."

"Not that either. What I come to tell you is: the horde no longer pursues us."

"So Raguel scents bigger prey," Karyl said softly.

"Yes. My patrols report the Imperials have taken up positions on high ground athwart the Imperial Road, just this side of the town of Canterville. The horde should hit them no later than midmorning tomorrow."

Karyl raised a brow. "And?"

She flushed. "I was getting to that. The Imperial Army has the Fortunate River to secure its right flank. But there's a good ten kilometers between their left and Duke Eric's ridges. We might—might—be able to slip through. If someone led us with enough daring and skill."

"You forgot luck," he said in a dry whisper.

"That too."

Karyl hung his head.

"What's happening to you?" she asked.

"Didn't Rob tell you?"

"No matter how much you exasperate him, he'd die before betraying your confidence. I doubt I could say that about another human being, alive or dead. He worships you."

Looking up, Karyl touched the right side of his forehead, where a faint blue discoloration peeked out of the grey-streaked brown hairline. "The young hotspur Duke Falk von Hornberg dented my skull with his axe at the Hassling. Since then I've suffered terrible headaches off and on."

"But you're not suffering one now."

"No." A corner of his bearded mouth twitched. "Although you may be about to change that."

"If you're trying to make me feel guilty, Voyvod, it won't work. Is that why you cry out at night, the headaches?"

"It's the dreams. I've experienced them ever since I . . . returned. They abated for a while after we reached Providence and began raising the militia. Now they've returned with unholy fervor."

"What do you dream?" She was beyond tact now. Anyway she doubted she could outflank this man with words any more than troops.

"Well, there's going over the edge of the Eye Cliffs, with a horror trying to gut me with its killing claws and my life pumping away out the stump of my sword-arm," he said. "Nothing like reliving certain death to add a touch of terror to one's nights."

"That happened? Really? I thought it was just another part of your legend, like defeating a full-grown matadora single-handedly as a stripling, and then having her egg hatch out that famous mount of yours so she bonded to you forever."

He smiled sadly. "I wasn't really alone," he said. "I had my faithful duckbill mount. Who sadly didn't survive the encounter. How I miss sweet Shiraa."

"'Sweet'?" Melodía blinked. "An Allosaurus?"

"She accompanied me throughout my travels. I hope she's made her way well in the wild; she was always clever. And I trained her to kill better than her real mother ever could."

Melodía was shaking her head incredulously. "But that other? How can that be true? As you say: certain death. In at least two ways, falling and bleeding."

"I often wonder that myself."

"And your hand—you've uh, *got* a sword hand. And everyone knows it functions very well. You can't regrow a severed limb."

"That's what I said when the witch who hired us on Bogardus's behalf cast her spell over my stump," he said. "Along with, 'there's no such thing as sorcery.' If I can't rely on my disbelief, what certainty is there? Precious little, I find."

"But that's not all that haunts your dreams?"

"No. I get visions—flashes—of incredible beauty. The pain of separation from it is as great as any pains of the body I've known. But there's real pain too. And terror, and despair like an infinite well. A sense of helplessness—of being toyed with. And a sense that . . . it's not over. That I've never truly escaped."

"I can . . . see that would be disconcerting."

"But you don't see that it's reason to sulk in my tent."

"Well—I know it wakes you screaming most nights, lately. I definitely know how you used to sneak off by yourself so your cries won't waken the camp. It was damned obnoxious, frankly, having my people keep watch over you in your nocturnal hidey-holes."

Especially since I won't ask them to do anything I don't do.

He smiled like a slit throat. "That isn't all."

"What more?"

"Guilt," he said.

She drew her head back in surprise. "Guilt? What do you mean?"

"You've heard the story, I suppose, how I was driven into exile by my own father? How I wandered Aphrodite Terra for ten years and more, until I acquired the skills and means to return, punish the wicked, and reclaim my birthright?"

"Your legend I spoke of." She couldn't help a passing smile. "No getting away from it in camp."

"So you know the rest: I achieved my goal—the goal of every dispossessed hero in every bedtime story and tavern song. My quest ended. I won. And what I won, was ashes."

It was growing dark inside the tent as day settled with illusionary ease into twilight. "I was . . . overwhelmed by my victory," he said. "It took so long. My struggle so great—both exile and the day's battle.

"As I sat on the throne I'd regained my first coherent thought was, Why?"

"I don't understand," Melodía said.

"It all made no sense to me, suddenly. All the years, all the tears. I realized that I hadn't wanted the damned throne so much as I felt obligated to win it back. Not because I had any reason, or any desire. Maybe . . . a last attempt to please my father. Who'd betrayed me, and been betrayed and murdered by his own mistress, years before.

"That was when the grief hit me. It seemed as if everyone I'd known and loved, cared for, even liked, had died to win this . . . chair. Oh, to be sure, some I cared about got merely been left behind, like my cousin Tir. But of course I'd lost her too, in a way.

"I had killed my loved ones, my friends, thousands who trusted me. With my ambition. Which wasn't even mine.

"The grief crushed me. Almost physically. It was all I could do to go though the motions of setting things in order.

"It was after that, when the blackness lifted—a little—I determined to expunge *passion*. From myself, and—this sounds crazy, no doubt; it does to me, now—from my realm. As if I could force my subjects to put aside all feelings in favor of the coldest calculation.

"I failed. Mostly because—well, because it can't be done; it's insane. But beyond that, I never really got around to trying to enforce it. There were too many other things for me to be doing. And my secret police."

"But you feel now," Melodía said.

"Yes. So much that every emotion, however fleeting, is like a reopened wound. Even happiness. It makes me think that my resolve to purge myself of passion was really nothing but an attempt to hide from pain. The pain of feeling."

"How did you get your feelings back?"

"I don't know. I suspect it's twisted in with the source of my nightmares. It's as if somebody, some thing, gave me back the capacity to feel."

"Isn't that a great gift?"

His laugh was raw as the edge of a freshly sharpened sword. "Is it? Or the subtlest of tortures?"

"So what you're really telling me is, you're crippled by feeling sorry for yourself."

He laughed again. "Perhaps I am. But listen: just as I've been betrayed at every turn—at home, at the Hassling, in Providence—so I have betrayed all those who relied upon me to their own destruction."

He blew a sigh through pursed lips. "With the sanctuary of death denied me, when I came here—when I came to Providence—well, I drew courage to put faith in myself and others from my hope I'd found a cause worth living for. Embodied in a single man."

"Bogardus!" Melodía blurted before she could stop herself. "You were as smitten with him as I was!"

He's tipped his head forward. Now he regarded her through the curtain his hair.

"Yes. As good a way to put it as any, I suppose."

"But you spent so little time at the villa," she said. "At least, I only saw you there when you came to make reports or requests."

"But Bogardus had given me that greatest gift: a task. A challenge. It took away my pain, the headaches and the nightmares. And I suppose I feared to look too closely at my idol, lest I see imperfections."

She sat back. "As did I," she whispered.

"We both sought badly needed shelter," he said. "We both thought we'd found it. And we both were wrong.

"Bogardus's betrayal hammered one more spike into my soul. And, as it were, my head."

Empathy filled Melodía's soul and heated her cheeks like fever. *He's so strong*, she thought, *simply to have survived such horrible things. And yet so vulnerable.*

She stepped hard on her feelings, then. She knew them too well. The last thing she needed now was another attachment. Especially to their fugitive army's reluctant commander. And the last thing she wanted was a sexual entanglement.

It wasn't just her rape by Falk—she felt anger stir within her. It wouldn't leave, but she'd learned to keep it on a short chain. But it never slept.

It was also her own betrayal by Bogardus and Violette. She recognized that now as another violation. No matter that her body still craved their touch.

That much is easy to dispel at least, when it becomes a distraction, she thought. All she had to do was remember the terrible voyeur, sitting in His alcove a few meters away during all their lovemaking. . . .

"And this gift—" She made herself focus on what Karyl was saying. "—if that's what it is, of having my feelings back. I've come to suspect that's addition by subtraction: somehow my head lost the ability to rule my heart."

"I can't address any of that," Melodía said. "I only know that your army, your *people* have a need. They need leadership."

"Haven't you heard a word I said?" he said without heat. "Everyone who follows me, I lead to devastation, emotional if not physical. It's happening again. How does that differ from me betraying them?"

"Well—it does. You don't intend to."

"But I keep doing it. Am I not culpable? What betrayal will I bring us next?"

"You don't have to carry the weight of the whole world on your shoulders! If you set that down, maybe you wouldn't feel so—crushed."

"But I carry the whole army on my shoulders," he said quietly. "You said so yourself."

Melodía glared at him a moment. "Well—it's smaller."

They both laughed. Too long, too loud. In the end laboriously, until tears began. It wasn't that funny; nothing could have been. Still, that was how they laughed, until they couldn't anymore.

"Suppose I do carry the army's weight on my shoulders," Karyl said.

"And perhaps the weight of the world as well. Have I the right to lay them aside? Apart from that—can I?"

"You certainly can't lay down the army! We all depend on you."

He squeezed a bitter laugh out his nose. "There's your first mistake. You need to learn to rely on yourselves. The desire to be led is the betrayal of self."

She frowned. She believed with all her being in the principle of leadership. And not because she'd been raised to it. She was sure.

"Well," he said wearily, "my people, as you call them, won't learn to rely on themselves between now and sunup, will they? For good or ill I've let them come to depend on me. And at least we face the kind of technical challenge I've the skills to meet."

It struck her as odd that he'd equate an existential threat to a challenge. But whatever he said, it didn't matter. So long as he picked up the reins again.

"Considering the problem might even alleviate the blackness," he said with a wry smile. "For a while, anyway."

She blinked at tears. Her skin prickled. *Is this victory?* she wondered.

"So," he said, sitting straighter and putting more snap in his words. "You've proven yourself competent in large-scale maneuver as well as tactics. Sum up our options as you see them, Captain."

"We can get away clean," she said. "If we act decisively and at once. Otherwise—"

She shrugged. "It's stand and fight, or move and fight. The only other choices—"

"Die passively," Karyl said, "or join the horde. Yes. I think we can discard those. So what would you do? Leave the Imperials and the horde to one another's good graces?"

Daddy! the little girl within her cried. She tried to moisten her lips. But her mouth was dry.

She looked at him helplessly and spread her hands. "I can't make that choice. I don't have the . . . standing. I don't have the right. People have flocked to join this, this agglomeration because you command. We don't have a banner of our own. Not even a name. And we haven't needed those things. Because you're our beacon. You define us. Karyl, the hero of legend."

He winced. "The very burdens I've tried to shed."

"You admitted that wasn't an option right now. Please, Colonel. We'll follow you no matter what. Only, command us!"

He deflated. Seemed actually to shrink. Her heart stopped soaring like a bird hitting a high tower window, and plummeted. Then, as if his head weighed as much as a mountain, he looked up at her.

In the near-dark of the tent his eyes were black beacons of despair.

Chapter 38

Gordito, Fatty—*Protoceratops andrewsi*. A small Ceratopsian dinosaur: a frilled, plant-eating quadruped, 2.5 meters long, 400 kilograms, 1 meter high, with a powerful toothed beak. The only "hornface" to lack horns. A ubiquitous domestic herd beast, not found wild in Nuevaropa. Timid by nature.

—THE BOOK OF TRUE NAMES

The Allosaurus woke to the smell of something good: a hadrosaur haunch, roasting over flames.

She stirred herself, then slipped from the bed she had made in a patch of nettle scrub, to which her pebble-scaled hide was impervious, in a wood of fragrant spruce—not too close to a game trail to a small stream, but not too far either. As was her custom, she made little noise or commotion for an unfriendly eye to see, despite her size.

She knew the smell from being raised by her mother. She was normally fed fresh flesh of plant-eating dinosaurs. Or at least dead. Occasionally she was allowed to hunt her own prey, under her mother's supervision. But sometimes she got to eat cooked meat, fresh off a fire placed in a big pit the two-legs had dug for the purpose. Which was how she knew which smell went to which beast.

Her stomach rumbled. She had not eaten in suns. How many—more than her mind would hold. Such details concerned her little, anyway. Hunger, however. . . .

She smelled the breeze cautiously. It came from up the trail. She would have to be careful approaching the stream, lest she run into two-legs or another great meat-eater. But that didn't bother her much. She could give them slip. Or if not, kill them, for then they'd threaten her.

She had the brook to herself, except for a scurry of the usual small forest creatures, all hurrying to be elsewhere. After drinking her fill she followed the aroma. She felt uneasy doing so. Her mother had taught her to avoid two-legs whenever possible, as well as to refrain from killing the small, vulnerable, so-tasty creatures, without her mother's express command. Or when she had no choice.

She knew the smell of that much flesh roasting meant many two-legs gathered together in one of their camps, or the clusters of above-ground dens of wood and stone they liked to raise for themselves. That meant added danger.

But hunger drove her. And not for tasty Hadrosaurus alone.

She was lonely. She had been with her mother constantly from the moment of her hatching on—her mother was the very first thing she had laid eyes on, emerging from her egg. Which of course was how she knew that was her mother. They had never been parted for very long—until that terrible day, now seasons past, when a cowardly sneak-attack by a white Tyrannosaurus bull and the two-legs who rode him left both Shiraa and her mother wounded.

The sneak who had struck down her mother had too many two-legs mounted on war-hadrosaurs and horses with him for Shiraa to contend with. She had been forced to flee splashing through the water, which was rich with the smells of blood and fresh shit, while her mother floated helplessly away downstream, stunned.

She had laid up until she healed, then come out and fed. Her mind was fixed on one thing: reunion with her mother.

And lucky matadora that she was, she had smelled faint traces of her mother and begun to follow them. That had begun even longer ago than her last meal—much longer, she felt—but her determination never faltered. Her love was too great.

In time she learned to associate a strange two-legs, silent and peculiar of head, with the wisps of scent that led her on. She sensed, somehow, it was steering her toward her mother. That was enough for her, though not for the ache in her loving heart.

That tantalizing food-cooking smell led her out of her thicket and around the hip of a gentle swell of the ground. The land fell away before her, flattening into a shallow valley, natural meadows interspersed with the oddly regular ones with all the same kinds of plants in them that she knew the tailless ones tended to live next to.

Sure enough, not far away lay a cluster of the boulders made of wood and stone she knew she would see. Even more curiously regular than the one-plant meadows, though far from uniform, their mostly peaked shapes resembled rock crystals. Yet they were hollow, she knew. The tailless two-legs dwelt in them.

As her mother had. Except when they were traveling on the great, noisy hunts her mother took her on, filled with metal clashing and screams. Then her mother lived in an angular shelter made of plant matter.

Turning her head from side to side, she tested the air. As expected, the scent of roasting meat came from the cluster. She could see smoke rise from several of the crystal-like outcroppings, as often happened when the air was as cool as it was today.

She was pleased that the wind blew toward her. The two-legs had little sense of smell. But they kept beasts, especially the small, baying four-legs, whose hides bore small filaments like the ones on two-legs' heads, instead of feathers or scales. They had keen noses indeed.

She made her way down toward the cluster. On the fringe of a field a field where a flock of fatties browsed on dry stubble, she flattened herself among weeds, waited. After bit the pair of small two-legs who tended the plant-eaters turned away to look at something. She slipped by them downwind, and in among the hollow, peaked-top boulders.

A broad path ran through the midst of them. She stayed away from that, though her senses told her no two-legs moved abroad through the gathering twilight. Until by lesser ways she reached a boulder larger than the rest, whose sides were as if made of lesser stones, smooth-polished as if by running water, of dark and pale grey, and dark blue.

Tall, narrow openings with pointed tops pierced its sides. From its pinnacle smoke flowed up into the cloudy sky, as though it were a miniature volcano. This was what she smelled: not a stink like rotting nosehorn eggs, but succulent roasting dinosaur-flesh.

She pressed her snout to one of the arched openings. A lattice, cool, hard, and grey, blocked it from poking inside. Some kind of clear but slightly sight-distorting membrane like a bubble's skin was stretched across the aperture behind it.

Nonetheless she could see well enough, by the glows of the small, pet fires the two-legs liked to keep in clear objects near them, and the bigger fire-cave by a far wall. There were propped-up slabs and a pack of two-legs sitting at them, making happy noises at each other while some of their young moved among them with high-heaped platters.

Some of these held merely heated plants, and as such had no interest to her. But then she saw one, so huge it had to be upheld by four two-legs spratlings, which carried a whole roast thigh of duckbill. She thought she could smell it growing nearer. She could definitely hear the crackle of hot grease.

Her stomach growled. *I'm starving!*

But she could not burst in and take the food by force. Her mother would disapprove most strongly. And she was a good Allosaurus.

Anyway, if she did that, she'd have to fight them. Aside from having been strictly trained not to do that, she didn't *want* to. Almost as fierce as the emptiness in her belly was the emptiness inside her. It hurt her now as much as the pangs in her stomach.

She knew the hole could only be filled by soft words and stroking by their oddly smooth, soft hands. She missed, then, not just her loving mother, but the friendly attention of the grooms and others who had helped care for her.

Maybe they'll be nice two-legs, she thought. *Maybe they will give me food and pet me. Like my mother and her friends.*

She heard a high, shrill sound: a two-legs' mouth-noise of distress. A male rounder than most, sitting at the farthest table, was pointing an arm at her. His eyes and mouth were circles of fear.

More two-legs turned to look at her. They uttered many terror-cries. Even through the thick, hard membrane and the tang of smoke and roasted meat, she could smell their fear.

She turned and fled.

She felt mostly sorrow. *Why are they so mean to me?* She only wanted to be friends. She hadn't even eaten any of their fatties, though they were delicious, and could see that these in particular lived up to their name.

But two-legs were dangerous. She rejoiced in fighting and killing, when the time came. That was the way she was, just as she ate and drank and voided. But she had a keen sense of self-preservation. She was no foolish hatchling.

Despite their puny size and strength, the two-legs when aroused could swarm even a mighty hunter such as herself, like ants devouring a fat grub. And she knew especially to fear the way they could even sting her at a distance.

So without hesitation—nor further attempts as stealth—she ran through the rest of the boulder-cluster as fast as her powerful hind legs could drive her. From behind her came sharp ringing that stabbed at her ear-membranes. She recognized a distress call often made by tailless two-leg flocks from their hollow-rock huddles.

It spurred her on even faster. It might bright out a pack of two-legs encased in metal and carrying long stings to chase her on the backs of their four-legged beasts, which had smooth hair like fliers. She wanted no part of them. Nor of their weird ability to sting at a distance.

I don't want to leave! But she had to. And so she did, racing on with the sun lowering beyond her left shoulder, out into the fields that lay outside the cluster. As she made her escape, she cried out a bitter and triumphant "*Shiraa!*"

As she passed through a grassy meadow she did veer aside to make a quick dash through another fatty flock on the far side of the village. Initially frozen by sight of the giant meat-eater thundering toward them, they scattered too late. Her jaws snapped shut behind a yearling's frill. She carried it, not slowed at all by her burden as it thrashed futilely against the poignard teeth clamped on its neck and bleated through a wide-open beak.

She spied another pair of two-legs young. They were running away as fast as their spindly little legs would bear them.

Serves you right for being so mean! she thought.

She slid through the brush of a woodlot and away over small hills until she reached an opening on the flank of a wooded ridge that felt safe enough. She killed the feebly struggling fatty with a quick head shake, dropped it, and pinned it among the low plants with a hind foot on its shoulder. In case some impudent tröodon or horror tried to snatch her prize away.

She turned her head from side to side, senses questing. She could found no sign the two-legs had pursued her.

But on a ridgetop the way she had run, the way the low sun was casting her shadow, she saw a solitary shape that might be the strange-headed two-legs she had so often seen. She smelled her mother's scent, then.

It was stronger than it had been since she lost her mother, that bad day.

Mommy close! she knew with ferocious joy. *See Mommy soon!* She raised her head and roared the only thing she said, or ever had: her name, *Shiraa*.

This time it meant, "Shiraa coming, Mommy! Shiraa good!"

Then she dropped her head. Not all hungers could be assuaged by dining on a fresh-killed fatty calf.

But then, some could.

Part Five

Dubious Battle

Chapter 39

Nodosaurios Imperiales, **Imperial Nodosaurs,** ***Infantería Imperial*** **(Official), Imperial Infantry**—Élite armored infantry, backbone of the Empire of Nuevaropa. Their colors are brown, black, and silver. Their basic formation is the *tercio,* a phalanx of three thousand pikes supported by more lightly armored hamstringers, arbalesters, artillerists, and pioneers. *Tercios* have died in battle to the last man and woman, but never broken.

—A PRIMER TO PARADISE FOR THE IMPROVEMENT OF YOUNG MINDS

Like a lake of flesh the Grey Angel horde seethed, half a kilometer distant across a field of gently waving brown grass. A human cataract poured continuously from the north over a forested rise to join it.

If they can be called human, thought Jaume, Comte dels Flors, Constable of the Imperial Army, as he stood watching from the brow of the low, loaf-shaped ridge called La Miche that stood between the Fortunate River and the High Road. Around him his fourteen remaining Companions stood in their beautiful white plate, with the Lady's Mirror red on their breasts.

"In the name of our Lady and all the Eight!" Dieter von Grosskammer exclaimed.

Machtigern laid a big, square hand on the younger Alemán's shoulder. "Steady."

Jaume stood with arms folded across his breastplate. The sun, just-risen over the forested Petits Voleurs ridges to the west, had already perceptibly heated the steel despite dense black-hearted clouds. The wind ruffled his long hair. Around him stood the pitiful handful that remained of his Companions, their white-enameled armor shining.

"One thing we can be grateful for," Florian said.

"What?" asked Ayaks.

"The wind's not blowing in our faces."

Ayaks's frown turned into a disgusted grimace. If some of the Emperor's grandes were indifferent to the Creators' commandments on hygiene, the horde seemed to have abandoned them entirely.

"One other thing," said Wil Oakheart of Oakheart dryly.

"So many blessings," Florian murmured.

"Raguel seems in no damned hurry."

That being so, Jaume took stock of his preparations. Fifty meters away, across the High Road, a lone hill rose to a height of about thirty meters, somewhat taller than La Miche. It was known as Le Boule. At its crown a great banner snapped defiance at the Grey Angel and his Crusade: the Imperial flag, golden tyrant skull on a field of blood.

Beneath an open tent stood like a red-and-yellow mushroom. In its shade sat His Imperial Majesty Felipe. He wore plain armor of polished, clear-enameled steel with the Imperial arms, colors reversed from the flag—red skull, gold shield—painted on the breastplate. A bare longsword lay across his knees. Pages and squires hovered around, waiting to run messages to his commanders. A score of Scarlet Tyrants guarded him.

Lower down the hill Falk stood like an ancient monolith. He wore his personal harness of royal blue, silver, and black armor today, not Tyrant gold and scarlet. Beside him Snowflake squatted like a broody scratcher, glowering in red-eyed malice held in check by his master's will.

The bulk of the Tyrants stood at the hill's base: five hundred élite Imperial bodyguards in gilt cuirasses and pot-helmets with tails of overlapped plates. Each held a curved, oblong shield and a spear with a short heavy haft, a long skinny black-iron neck and an evilly barbed head. A short sword rode in a scabbard at each man's hip. Each would die fighting before he allowed an enemy near the Emperador's person. Even Raguel himself.

Off on the army's left waited a wing of two hundred dinosaur knights with a thousand heavy cavalry behind, commanded by the youthful Archiduc Antoine de la Lumière. His uncle the Francés King had sent him to serve in the campaign against Providence—reluctantly, the rumor ran.

To Antoine's right stood the three thousand pikemen and -women of the Twelfth Tercio of the Brown Nodosaurs, the "Steel Wall," who had marched with Felipe from La Merced. Their hamstringers, arbalesters, and stingers were arranged in front of them. From their right to the High Road stood, sat, or shifted nervously in place the bulk of the Imperial foot: seven thousand peasant levies, all that remained of a high of over ten thousand. The army had lost some conscripts to the rampaging passions of their ostensible betters, and far more to desertion, including several hundred who had sneaked through the pickets the night before, apparently to join the enemy horde. In front of them stood a bloc of three to four hundred armored house-bows, and another of around five hundred common archers.

Across the Chausée Imperial the Third Tercio, "Imperial Will," was arrayed in the same way as the Twelfth. Between them and the riverbank's steep drop one hundred and fifty war-duckbills, steel chamfrons, and rainbow caparisons shifted from hind foot to hind foot, muttering to one another in low dulcian hoots and farting. Another thousand gendarmes on coursers waited behind. Duque Francisco de Mandar commanded that wing.

The peasant mass, no more happy than their kind ever were, were stiffened by the presence right behind them of a short, wide wedge of two thousand five hundred house-shields—like the armored archers, retainers of the various lords taking part in the campaign. A second formation of five hundred backed up the Third Tercio.

Behind the two heights waited the reserve: Jaume and his fourteen remaining Companions, their five hundred Ordinary men-at-arms, and six hundred cavalry in plate and chain. These latter were adventurers, second sons and daughters or hedge-knights, too poor to afford full plate. Two hundred fifty more House infantry lounged on both sides of the road to the south, their spears and shields beside them in the grass.

Past them the Imperial wagon train had been drawn into an immense circle on the road's west side. The wagons were chained together tail to tongue to form a rough-and-ready wood-walled fort. The drovers and wagoneers and camp followers within could be relied upon to put up a stout defense of themselves and their livelihoods.

Out in front of the army were ranged artillery engines: mostly the Nodosaur stingers and some others, plus some catapults. Four trebuchets Jaume had brought with his Ejército Corregidor stood with long arms poking toward the overcast. They reminded him most unpleasantly of gibbets.

Jaume drew a deep breath and willed his heart to slow. It had a tendency today to race far out in advance of the rest of him.

He had an excellent anchor for his right flank in the Fortunate River. But his left flank was up in the air. Dense forest stood five hundred to a thousand meters off to the west; beyond it he could he could see the blue line of the Petits Voleurs. If he'd tried to stretch his forces to cover the distance they'd be thin as an embezzler's excuse; the horde could blow through them and scarcely break stride.

He felt a pat on the pauldron that guarded his left shoulder. He turned to see Jacques smiling sadly at him.

"Leave it, Jaumet," the lank-haired knight said. "What humans can do, you've done. We couldn't find better ground to fight on, in the time the Angel left us."

"Mor Jacques, the pessimist eternal, telling me not to worry?" He laughed in genuine delight. "A miracle!"

The Francés shrugged steel shoulders. "Don't count on us getting another."

Still, he stood straighter than Jaume had seen him do in months. That reassured Jaume—some. His old friend's air of resolute resignation would serve everyone better than despair.

"They're deployed in conventional array," Florian said. "Infantry in the middle, dinosaurry and cavalry on both wings."

In battles of this scale mounted wings customarily consisted of dinosaur knights before, heavy-horse behind, rather than each constituting a single wing. Just as with horses, war-duckbills required a certain concentration to be effective.

"Where did they get so many dinosaur knights?" asked Owain de Galés. He carried his longbow strung. A quiver of meter-long arrows in a flier-skin quiver rode his back.

"They've cleared the provinces between here and the mountains," Jacques said. He stood taller than Jaume had seen him do in months. Jaume was little reassured. His old friend's air was one of resolute resignation. Still, it would serve everyone better than despair.

Including, Jaume hoped, the man himself.

"But knights?" persisted Ayaks. "Why would they join in such abomination?"

"Nobles certainly aren't any less susceptible to a Grey Angel's compulsion than common folk," Florian said. "And as for evil natures, have you forgotten the Via Dolorosa we rode down to join our Emperor? Terraroja's fate, and the murder and disorder every day in our army's camp?"

"I remember," the blond-bearded Ruso rumbled. "Too well to sleep well."

"We're their equal in armored riders, anyway," Machtigern said. "Or superior even."

"If only there," Wil said. "Even allowing for defeat-induced exaggeration, refugee reports make Raguel's Horde a hundred thousand strong."

Felipe fielded a vast army by Nuevaropan standards: almost twenty-two thousand fighters, as nearly as Jaume could reckon. Notwithstanding their own unhappy residue of peasant infantry, they probably had more well-trained and equipped fighters than the whole Grey Angel Crusade. And those were interspersed among half-starved, half-naked lunatics armed with hands and teeth. Yet even though the enemy captain—Jaume had to guess that was Raguel himself—had deployed mounted wings like a proper army, the legends, and ancient histories everyone including Jaume had assumed were legendary, said that a Grey Angel horde relied on size, speed, and ferocity instead of tactics.

The point of a Grey Angel Crusade, after all, was the wholesale destruction of human life. Raguel's casualties would gratify his unknowable desires scarcely less than his enemies'.

"Wait, now" called Jacques.

Jaume shook his head, smiling with gratitude for his friend snatching him back from an abyss of black despair.

The Francés knight had a shiny brass spyglass pressed to one eye. "Something's happening. The mob is clearing a path."

The horde's front ranks flowed apart like the early morning river-mist that was slowly yielding to the feeble sunlight. A figure rode between them on a pure-white sackbut. It was a woman with a wild mane of silver-white hair. She was naked except for a cape of white feathers thrown back to lie over her back like folded wings.

Bartomeu cleared his throat. He stood holding his mare nearby. He and the Companions' other arming-squires waited to serve as message-runners.

Jaume shook his head. He didn't need to send a message for his commanders to hold in place. They had orders too clear for even the most willful buckethead to misconstrue. Also the Emperor's personal assurance that anyone who disobeyed would be relieved of his command at once, as well as his head.

Down the road the white Parasaurolophus trotted on its hind legs, holding its pawlike fore-hooves daintily to its chest. It was a huge animal, Jaume saw, bigger than any sackbut bred for war. Midway between the armies its rider reined it to a stop.

"I am the Herald of the Grey Angel Raguel of the Ice, Bringer of Divine Justice, Scourge of the Impure," she called, brandishing a metallic staff that bore a circular emblem like a grey mirror at its top.

Her words carried clearly to La Miche despite the distance. "She has a loud voice even for a woman," Timaeos muttered. Though the Griego was a confirmed misogynist, no Companion was more devoted to the Lady's service. Not even Jaume.

"No doubt her patron gives her help with some Angel trick," said Florian.

Several Companions made the sign of the Lady's Mirror at their comrade's flippancy. Even Jaume felt a thrill of dismay.

"You have offended the Creators," the nude woman cried. "You must submit now to the will of great Raguel, or else expiate your sins in blood."

Jaume looked to Le Boule. Felipe signaled. The Imperial Herald mounted his white marchador and rode past the nodding Scarlet Tyrants' plumes to the road. Spearmen rolled aside the wagons that blocked it. He set forth at an amble with bare head held high.

"He's got stone," Machtigern said, rubbing his chin. Like most Companions he shaved clean.

"Heralds are protected by convention," said Dieter.

"And do Grey Angels feel bound by our conventions, I wonder," murmured Florian, "any more than we do by compacts made by ants?"

"Oh," said the youngest Companion.

The Imperial Herald stopped twenty meters from his opposite number. All Jaume could hear was the fact of his voice, no words. "It seems you're right about Raguel helping the woman," he told Florian.

"That brings me little enough pleasure. As usual."

"*Then look and see your fate!*" Raguel's Herald cried in response to the Imperial envoy.

She turned and gestured dramatically at the heights behind her.

"Behold the Angel Raguel. Behold your doom!"

"Trite," grumbled Bernat, who was scribbling furiously on a piece of paper he held pinned to a slate with his thumb. "But you can't expect any better from fanatics, I suppose."

Through the trees on the far heights emerged a colossal silvery-grey shape. Even the Companions gaped: it was a Tirán Rey, a bull Tyrannosaurus rex, most feared of all Aphrodite Terra's dinosaurs. Even at this range Jaume could see the monster dwarfed Falk's albino adolescent Snowflake.

"Beautiful," murmured Rupp. "He must weigh seven tonnes!"

Jaume found a smile inside himself. "You shame us, my friend, finding Beauty where even we find only terror."

The slight Alemán shrugged. "I'm a dinosaur master," he said simply, as if that explained it. Which it did.

"And only a dinosaur master," muttered Wil, "would notice the bloody beast first."

A thing that looked like little more than a grey skeleton straddled the tyrant's back. By proportion to its monstrous mount Jaume guessed it would stand nearly three meters tall. It held a curious weapon, a meter of haft with a meter-and-a-half scythe-blade the same length fixed in line with it, like the head of a glaive.

"So that's a Grey Angel," Florian said. "Why did the Creators choose such an ugly brute for a servant?"

"Perhaps they have other canons of beauty than we do," said Bernat. He barely glanced up.

"Why make ours different, then?" Florian asked.

A commotion from the hill across the road interrupted the discussion.

"Tavares," Florian muttered as if cursing. He wasn't the only one.

The Imperial chaplain's red robes fluttered about him in a rising breeze. He had thrown his hat away. His heavy, unwashed hair stood up in a skewed shock from a narrow, passion-twisted face.

"Sinners!" he screeched, a cry as penetrant and chilling as that of a long-flying dragon on the hunt. The Boule was close enough for Jaume to hear every hateful syllable. "You have all sinned in the eyes of our holy Creators! And you all must atone."

Felipe sat rigid. Jaume saw that his round face was strained and color-drained. Falk stood at his side, hefting his axe in blue steel hands.

"The Creators' Avenger stands before you. Submit to him! Submit to judgement. A heartbeat, and it will be too late. You must serve, or perish."

Felipe said something low enough that Jaume couldn't hear. The Emperor shook his head.

Tavares flung fists in the air. "You dare defy the will of the Creators? Blasphemer! Sinner!"

Falk started forward. Felipe thrust himself up out of his chair and stalked forward, all but brushing the huge armored man aside.

"You have abused my tolerance for the last time, priest," he said, gesturing with his sword. These words were clearly audible on La Miche. "Go now, and never return. Or I'll send your head, limbs, and torso to your Angel on six different fatties!"

The prelate's eyes shot wide. His dark face paled. For a moment he stood as if expecting the undistinguished-looking man with the steel-clad paunch to soften. But not even Falk showed less *yield* than the Emperor.

Tavares turned and walked down the slope. Stiffly he mounted his own waiting ambler and trotted around the Scarlet Tyrant ranks to the road.

Dieter stared openmouthed, his cheeks a brighter pink than usual. "But he's just a middle-aged fat man!" he blurted. "How could he stand up to the Cardinal under Raguel's eye?"

Florian laid a hand his armored arm. "The Emperor is a middle-aged fat man who has a gift of making everyone underestimate him."

The guards on the High Road let the Cardinal pass. Without a backward glance, Tavares rode out of the Imperial Army. A knight on a blue and yellow sackbut rode to join him from the left wing. A dinosaur knight and several men-at-arms followed him.

"Look at that," Florian said. "Our dear friend Montañazul, with vassals."

"They increase our strength by subtracting themselves from it," Machtigern said.

Others broke from the Imperial ranks, peasant pikemen, House soldiers, gendarmes, even two more dinosaur knights. Jaume saw briefly violence flurry as some were discouraged by their comrades, mostly among the lowborn conscripts.

Owain and Will Oakheart of Oakheart, the Companions' expert longbowmen, looked expectantly at Jaume. Both had arrows nocked. He saw leaders among the shortbows and even the Nodosaur crossbows turned toward him for instruction.

Jaume looked in turn to the Emperor: this was policy, not tactics. Felipe shook his head. Then he turned, went back to his humble chair, and sat down as if already overcome by weariness. Jaume signaled for the missile troops to hold their shots.

As Tavares and fifty or sixty followers approached the horde, the Imperial Herald backed his mount off the road. Herald or not, he was unwilling to contest passage with that many heavily armed knights. To say nothing of dinosaurs.

The white-haired woman turned to Raguel, who sat immobile on his strange grey tyrant as it squatted on the hillside, switching its long tail. The Angel made no sign that Jaume could see. But the Angel's Herald backed her white sackbut off the road as well.

Tavares's party approached the horde's silent ranks. "I don't like waiting like this," Dieter said. "I want something to happen."

"Patience, boy," said Pedro the Lesser.

Dieter turned in surprise. The diminutive weapons-master seldom spoke. Not with words, anyway. He preferred to let his arts, whether the intricate engravings and miniature paintings he created, or arms, talk for him.

"They'll come to us soon enough," he said, digging at an ear with his thumbnail. "Then we'll fight rested, and they'll tire."

"They are the Grey Angel's slaves," Timaeos said in a hollow voice. "They don't tire, any more than they fear."

The distant Angel waved a grey claw. His Crusaders opened ranks. Without hesitation Tavares rode into the avenue they cleared. His followers trooped after.

When the last of the defectors was at least fifty yards up that corridor of living bodies, Raguel slowly raised his arm. He clenched his claw into a fist.

The corridor closed.

The Crusaders rolled over the defectors like a returning tide. Tavares turned in his saddle. Jaume thought he could see the outrage and anger on his face.

He also thought he saw the Cardinal's expression turn to fear as a score of hands reached for him. A woman scaled Tavares's right leg and sank her teeth into his neck. Dark spray flew from her jaws.

"Well, his robes won't show the blood much," Wil Oakheart said.

Screams floated up as from a distant rookery of sea-fliers as the others were submerged. Montañazul, taken by surprise, was toppled from his saddle immediately. The other three dinosaur knights bolted in different directions, trampling Crusaders by the score, laying about madly with their swords. The Crusaders didn't flinch from the basso-bugling monsters. They attacked.

"They're swarming them like ants on a grasshopper," said Bernat. "Fascinating." He wrote furiously.

Retching, Dieter turned away. He covered his face with his hands. "No one deserves that!"

"I disagree," said Florian, shaking back golden locks. "I think Tavares and his filthy friends have earned precisely what they're getting. The Angel has a sense of justice, at least. And more than a touch of humor."

"I wouldn't rely too much on either quality to help us today," said Machtigern.

Florian leaned against the taller man and rested his head on a pauldron. "I'm not, friend; believe it. But then, we've always known there was little justice in this world, save what we make for ourselves."

Dieter turned a red and tear-streaked face toward Jaume. "How can our Lady sanction such horror?"

"The Creators are different from us," Jaume said. "And yes: I know that's no answer. All I can do is say what my heart tells me: whatever lies behind this Raguel's Crusade, Our Lady Bella has no part in it."

The shrieking died away. Hamstrung, the war-hadrosaurs fell thrashing, crushing dozens, smashing dozens more with their tails. The flesh-waves closed over them as well. In a matter of moments they were quiescent, no more than prominences on which the Crusaders stood, eerily silent, waiting.

As for Tavares and his companions, it was as if they had never been.

"You couldn't want a better tonic for the troops," Wil Oakheart said. "Nobody who saw that's about to shirk."

Raguel's Herald urged her white duckbill back up onto the High Road to face the Imperial ranks.

"Your submission does not suffice," she declaimed. Again her words rang in Jaume's ears as if from mere meters away. "You continue to defy the will of the Angel Raguel. So be it. You all are judged. Now you will suffer."

The wind veered to blow toward the Imperials from the hordeling. It brought with it the stench of a vast open sewer and ten thousand open graves combined. Men long grown inured to the reek of their own unwashed bodies and those of thousands around them recoiled, gagging and retching at the smell. The Companions, prepared, brought forth handkerchiefs doused in essence to mask mouths and noses. Jaume's smelled of lilacs.

On Le Boule, Snowflake looked up. His red eyes glared. He rose and shook himself, wagging his big white head. Apparently what the fortune of the wind had brought *him* was scent of the grey Tyrannosaurus. He thrust his face forward, opened jaws armed with teeth like daggers, and uttered a roar of fury that made even the red and gold ranks of the Imperial bodyguard flinch away.

Raguel's mount heard. Leaning far forward he opened jaws armed with teeth like shortswords. His bellow of answer rang like a thousand trumpets. The ground vibrated beneath Jaume's feet. Everywhere among the Imperial ranks men pressed hands to ears against that awful sound.

The horde charged. But not even a hundred thousand throats howling at once could drown the final peals of the grey monster's challenge.

Chapter 40

Terremoto, Earthquake—A call too low for humans to hear, employed as a weapon by crested hadrosaurs such as halberds, morions, and sackbuts. Can panic or stun; a mass terremoto, properly focused, can deal lethal damage to the largest meat-eater, and instantly kill a human. Effective to 30 meters, 40 en masse. Favored ranged weapon of Nuevaropan dinosaur knights, whose armor and training help them resist its effects. As it takes a hadrosaur several minutes to recover from giving a terremoto, it can normally be used only once per battle, to disrupt an enemy formation during a charge.

—THE BOOK OF TRUE NAMES

With a groan like a constipated thunder-titan a trebuchet swung its long arm up into the sky. A hundred-kilo stone, knocked roughly 'round by artillerist chisels, soared off against the dark grey clouds.

Falk watched its flight intently. A trebuchet was a true siege engine, fixed in place and slow to reload, even with nosehorns harnessed to draw back its arm against a massive counterweight. It served best against a big, stationary target, like a castle. The projectiles moved with a slow majesty, and were large enough to easily track by eye—and clear the way for. Though they could be wicked accurate, they usually required one or more shots to find the range. Even massed troop formations could usually find a way to get out of the beaten zone before taking too much punishment.

But the Grey Angel horde was by far the largest army Falk had ever seen. It was the largest army anyone had ever seen, so far as he knew. At least on the Tyrant's Head, only the colossal forces employed in the Demon War of half a millennium ago approached it. And until now, he'd taken for granted that the accounts exaggerated the numbers involved.

And the Grey Angel's soldiers didn't bother to dodge. They cared nothing for their own deaths. Only others'.

The stone struck well back in the advancing wave of bodies. It bounced high in amidst dark spray. When it fell again Falk saw bodies tumbled like duckbill-pins. It struck at least three times more before he lost sight of it, smashing bones and mangling flesh.

The horde flowed instantly to fill the gapes it left. Like water.

The lesser engines raked the enemy. Stinger-shafts impaled rank after rank of Crusaders armored lightly if at all. Tar-balls bounced, leaving pools of black-smoking fire that gyrated, screamed, and spread.

Undeterred the horde came on. Falk expected nothing else. These were mere preliminaries, albeit hard enough on the impaled and ignited. History judged causes' greatness proportionally by how many individuals, themselves powerless to affect any outcomes of consequence, suffered and died in their service.

Human history was known to stretch back for millennia before Creation, although its details were lost in clouds of myth. Duke Falk wondered if things had always been so. He suspected they had.

Trumpets blew discordant signals from the Imperial lines. The engine crews were hard at it. Hands cranked stinger windlasses. Grunting nosehorn teams hauled back catapult and trebuchet arms. Iron darts were dropped in slots. Heavy round stones were placed lovingly in slings, and tar-balls in cups. Falk heard a *whump* as one was lit in front of his position.

Nodosaur crossbows launched a withering volley as the Crusader wave rolled within range. Archers swarmed forward to loose their shortbows. The infantry waited, the peasant levies restless and uncertain, the House troops almost eager, the Nodosaurs silent and grim.

Without awaiting orders, Archiduc Antoine led the Imperial left wing forward at the trot. They promptly masked the aim of the Nodosaur engineers who had just turned their stingers to engage the oncoming enemy dinosaur knights. Falk imagined the artillerists cursing savagely as they swung their ballistas back to bear on the horde infantry.

On the right the Third Tercio stingers loosed a volley into the war-dinosaurs bearing down on them. No armor could stop the black darts. Two war-duckbills tumbled into avalanches of flailing tails and giant bodies. A second pair stumbled over them, fluting in pain and dismay. A dart shot transfixed a dinosaur knight on a mostly orange sackbut, pinning shield to chest.

Seeing his left move prematurely, Jaume ordered the Imperial right wing forward. Pennons fluttering from upraised lances, the dinosaur knights sent their duckbills jogging after the Duque de Mandar, followed by the men-at-arms on their coursers.

As the west wings of the two armies closed, each let go a terremoto that raised the hair on the Duke's nape. He could see no effects from the inaudible hadrosaur killing-cries before Antoine's dinosaur knights and their enemies spurred to the charge.

They met with a terrific crash. Squealing morions slammed breastbone to breastbone against sackbuts. Lances splintered. Knights hurtled from high-cantled saddles. Breast-and-backs crumpled beneath monstrous feet with weird musical warbles.

Masses of war-dinosaurs interpenetrated with a sliding clangor of sword on shield and plate. Screams skirled to Falk down the stinking wind. The heavy-horse swung wide of the monster scrum to replicate their battle in miniature.

To Falk's right, the Crusader dinosaur knights struck the Duque de Mandar's duckbills between the High Road and the Fortunate River cut in a sustained thunderclap.

A cloud of feathered shafts rose hissing from the Imperial shortbows. They fell like steel rain among the scarcely protected Crusaders. They ignored the arrows as they did the quarrels and bounding boulders and fireballs. Those who fell or even faltered were crushed without qualm. The wounded screamed no more loudly than the unharmed.

A cheer rose up from the Imperial foot ranks as the whole of the horde's first several ranks fell. And died away as the horde swept forward, heedless as surf.

Seemingly as little concerned with their own survival as Raguel's slaves, the Imperial artillery crews and missileers shot, reloaded calmly, and shot again as the horde rolled down on them. But though hundreds were killed, the Grey Angel Crusaders showed that reports of their fanatical ferocity were if anything understatements.

Yet as Falk watched his fear turned to terrible exaltation. So fiercely did the pre-battle energy surge within him that he tapped his horseman's axe against his greave like a drumstick. Despite the fact that he was about to fight against an undeniable servant of the Creators, a sense of righteousness filled him.

Whatever else is happening, he thought, *I am defending the principle of Order. It's what I was raised to do.*

If Raguel wants to use disorder to His ends . . . so much the worse for Raguel.

Imperial pikes swung down in a ripple. At last the archers and arbalesters turned from their Faerie-poles to race for the safety of the heavy infantry lines. The trebuchet crews unhitched their beasts and joined them, driving the nosehorns before them. Those serving the lighter engines hitched them to horse-teams waiting in harness. Jumping on the animals' backs and clinging to catapults and stingers they rode the wheeled weapons-carriage for shelter.

One catapult's wheel hit a rock hidden by a low bush and overturned. Most of its passengers sprang free; a woman shrieked as the frame crushed her leg. The crew halted the horses long enough to uncouple them. Then as the riders whipped them on the other artillerists hoisted the upset carriage enough to yank the victim free. With two of them holding her under the arms they all ran on. She howled as each step jarred her broken limb. But Falk felt sure she'd rather that than what the horde would do to her. . . .

Coming hard after them the horde hit the Imperial line. Falk clearly heard the Emperor grunt in sympathy. Snowflake growled. He smelled blood.

Once more the enemy front ranks died in droves. Some silently, some shrieking and wriggling like hooked worms on the pikes. Those behind kept running as if to a combined feast and orgy.

For the moment even the Imperial peasant ranks looked steady; all they had to do was hold up their five-meter polearms and lean forward.

Reassured, Falk looked to his left to see the outnumbered horde riders had broken before Archiduc Antoine and were streaming back north as fast as horses and hadrosaurs could run. Grey Angel Crusaders might not flee—but clearly that didn't apply to their mounts.

In any battle, war-beasts formed factions of their own. Whether mammalian or dinosaurian, most were herd animals, and all had keen senses of self-preservation. If they suffered enough casualties they'd run away, no matter exhaustively and expensively trained they were.

Behind Falk, the runners clumped around the Emperor suddenly twittered like a flock of frightened fliers. The Imperial Herald, who had somehow returned virtually intact to Felipe's side, shouted at them to be still in a voice as loud as any trumpet. He failed to silence them.

Falk quickly saw why: The Imperial right had routed. Its beasts ran flat-out along the riverbank. Some toppled over screaming. The great duckbills ran down and crushed any horse or human that got in their way.

Felipe rose, looking aghast. Falk trudged up the hill to his side, hoping to reassure his liege with his own blue-armored bulk. "Wait, your Majesty," he said through a throat dry as a chimney. "Your Constable will handle it."

As if his full suit of plate hampered him no more than a silken breechclout, Jaume had raced to the east end of La Miche. He shouted instructions and pointed with his famous longsword, the Lady's Mirror. Over the epic noise of battle Falk could no more hear his rival's words than if he had shouted them from the far side of the moon Eris.

But at this moment they were rivals no more. Felipe himself had overridden Jaume's insistence on serving in the forefront: el Condestable was needed to command the reserve—and the battle itself, as long as he was allowed. Certain nobles had subsequently muttered about the too-nice Jaume and his pretty-boy Companions hanging back from the fight.

It had pleased Falk greatly to inform them that, if they uttered another such syllable, they could try speaking their minds around a rope dangling them by their throats.

For all that had passed between them, Falk all but worshipped Jaume, as warrior and war captain. No better man existed in all Nuevaropa to lead the brutally outnumbered Imperial Army against the Crusade and its superhuman Master. In any event the plain fact Jaume was the battle leader, as Felipe was the spiritual, was enough to earn Falk's whole obedience. For now.

There was no turning a rout of dinosaurs. Not before they ran themselves out. Jaume didn't try. Instead he called into motion the plans he'd laid for just such a necessity.

The defeated wing fled out of Falk's sight, around the far end of the loaf-shaped rise. As soon as they went by, nosehorns lunged to pull wagons to block the gap between ridge and riverbank. Some drovers released the animals and led them back behind La Miche, as others wrestled the wagons into a makeshift wall of several layers. A body of the mailed spearmen in reserve took up position a few cautious paces in back of them.

The brunt of the horde's foot-charge had so far landed on the Twelfth Tercio and the peasant pikes. They hadn't yet flowed around the Third's currently unprotected right flank. Had the Crusaders tried to rush through the opening left by Mandar's advance, house-shields stood ready to stop them.

As the pursuing enemy bore down, dinosaur knights precariously mingled with gendarmes, whistles shrilled from the Nodosaurs' brown ranks. With practiced precision the right end of the Third Tercio phalanx pivoted back to anchor against the foot of La Miche, forming two sides of a bristling pike-box.

Nodosaur crossbows pumped bolts into the onrushing dinosaurs. A splendid green and scarlet sackbut with yellow speckles on flanks and belly took a lucky hit the right eyehole of its chamfron and went down. The horde riders were able to swing around the ten-meter monster's death thrashing, but inevitably lost momentum. Some swerved toward the tercio. Others continued rushing upon the wagon-wall.

But neither warhorse nor dinosaur would willingly impale itself on a hedge of long spikes, or crush itself against an apparently impenetrable barrier. The charging duckbills stopped short, shying and crying alarm, when they saw what awaited them.

Unfortunately for everyone concerned, dinosaurs weren't terribly precise judges of their own momentum. And even in a cloth caparison in lieu of metal and hornface-leather armor, with a saddle and steel-clad rider on its back, a war-hadrosaur weighed almost four tonnes.

Even as they dropped thick tails as drags to help slow them down, duckbills crashed into wagons. Shattering wood squealed as deafeningly as the monsters themselves. Splinters whirled upward in a cloud of yellow dust. Wagons flew up like kicked toys.

Meanwhile the dinosaurs who had refused before the four-deep array of browned-iron pike-heads were rammed from behind by their fellows and impaled regardless. They fell among the Nodosaurs like flailing, bellowing trebuchet stones.

Three-deep, the wagon-wall buckled but held. And the Nodosaurs knew what to expect from a charge of dinosaur knights. Though scores of pike-wielders were squashed to crunchy brown-and-red pulp, the Imperial phalanx stood firm. The ranks behind lowered their pikes and pushed forward to fill the gaps.

Blocked by walls of pikes and wood, what had been victorious pursuit decayed into a vast and noisy traffic jam. The house-shields waiting behind the Third Tercio charged out to strike the stalled knights, jabbing duckbill bellies and courser flanks with their spears. Beasts and riders alike wailed as they tumbled over the seven-meter drop to the river below.

Nodosaur auxiliaries in light dinosaur-leather tunics and browned-iron caps, with bucklers strapped to their forearms, darted among milling warbeasts to hamstring them with their hatchets. It was risky work. Many were ridden down, smashed to rag dolls by frantically swinging duckbill tails, or crushed beneath massive falling bodies. But they fought with the same fatalistic fury as their fellows in the phalanx: they were all Nodosaurs.

When he knew the right would hold, Falk ran his eyes back along the lines. Against general expectations the peasant masses of the Imperial center not only held, but fought. The terror inspired by a Grey Angel and his horde could take two forms: panic or desperate resistance. The latter emotion prevailed among the hard-pressed Imperials.

So far.

On the west the Twelfth Tercio stood like its namesake: a Steel Wall in truth. They had killed a whole rampart before them. Screaming as though afire, the Crusaders swarmed over their fallen comrades, to die in their turns on the obdurate pike-heads.

Beyond the Nodosaurs and their artificial berm of bodies a less pleasant sight met Falk's gaze. Archduke Antoine had chased the horde riders from the field. Unfortunately his force had also slowed, tired, and gotten strung out, as pursuing riders always did. Crusaders afoot attacked the knights in soldier-ant swarms. Falk saw a yellow and blue morion pulled down by barehanded men and women. Their easy victory had put the Imperial dinosaur knights and gendarmes in deadly trouble.

Men- and women-at-arms in plate and chain rode from the left to aid their bogged-down heavy brethren. Jaume had thrown his cavalry reserve into the fight. Falk expected to see him lead his own Companions and Ordinaries shortly to support them.

Four men in gashed plate and bloodied rags of feather capes trudged up the back of Le Boule. Sweat-lank hair framed grimy, sagging faces. Falk recognized the Conde de la Estrella del Hierro and several others from the quickly defeated Imperial right wing. They dropped to their knees to kiss Felipe's hands, sniveling excuses and pleas for forgiveness.

Sneering at their disgrace, the Duke turned his attention back to the battle as an outcry rose from the Imperial ranks. Tall as a two-story barn on the back of his tyrant, his soul-reaper poised at his side, the Grey Angel Raguel had begun to ride forward. His curiously colored monster walked with the characteristic tail-swinging gait of a big flesh-eater.

Screams of unmistakable horror made Falk snap his head left. To his surprise the horde on that side had pulled back fifty meters from the corpse-rampart the Twelfth Tercio had made of their brothers and sisters. *I thought the horde never quit coming*, he thought, *much less retreated.*

The flesh-floodwaters parted. Out ran two hundred horrors. Bodies streaked green and brown, wide-open mouths pink and rimmed with yellow saw-teeth, they sprang forth with their killing-claws daintily upheld.

On each feathered back rode a young child.

Chapter 41

Guerrero de Casa, **House-soldier**—Professional soldiers, usually well-armored infantry, who fight for a lord as retainers. Most are either *Scuderos de Casa* (house-shields), armed with spear and shield; or *Arcos de Casa* (house-bows), armed with shortbows or occasionally crossbows. Most are commoners. Widely hated because unscrupulous lords often use them to bully their serfs most cruelly.

—A PRIMER TO PARADISE FOR THE IMPROVEMENT OF YOUNG MINDS

The deinonychus-riding children had solemn faces. Their mouths were tightly shut. Each clutched a spear or dagger in chubby hands.

Over his left shoulder, from just behind his line of sight, Duke Falk heard Count Ironstar begin a high-pitched litany of terror: "It is a judgement on our wickedness, that even children raise their hands against us! We're all going to die! All going to die! All going to—"

Falk transferred his axe to his left hand. Without looking around he swung backhand. He put broad hips and strong legs fully into it.

"All going—" The words stopped suddenly. Falk felt resistance. Then parting. Then shock.

Then nothing. Something bounced heavily on the turf behind him.

"Perhaps the rest of you gentlemen will do a better job of keeping your heads," Felipe said dryly, as Falk heard a second, weightier thud. He brought the axe back around to ground before him. Crimson dripped from the blade into the grass by the shiny blue toes of his sabatons.

To Falk's alarm, he realized the Nodosaurs' own lethal efficiency might undo them. The Crusaders unflaggingly continued clambering up the berm of dead bodies the terciaries had built before them, even as more were added to it. Now the wall rose higher than the tallest Nodosaur. It totally masked the Twelfth's view of the abomination rushing toward them.

Until the horrors themselves, frightfully agile despite their burdens, reached the top of the grisly pile.

For a moment each froze to regard the other: the ravening pack-hunters and their stiff-faced riders; gazing back up at them, their attitudes eloquent of shock despite the brown sallets that hid their faces, the Nodosaurs.

Not even in the gruesomest bedtime stories his nannies, encouraged a moral instruction by his mutually antagonistic and lethally capricious parents, had told him had Falk ever heard of such a thing. And while those in his earshot were careful to control their reactions better than the unfortunate and now considerably shorter Estrella del Hierro, from the gasps from close at hand and the outright screams from farther, he reckoned no one else had either.

With a many-voiced screech of rage the raptors flung themselves on the pikes. Some were held in the air, impaled alongside children who still eerily made no sound as they wiggled futile arms and legs. Some ran down the inner slope of the flesh-mound to dart among the Nodosaurs' legs. Some ran up the shafts of the very pikes that transfixed them to snap at exposed chins and throats.

Not even a seasoned veteran in helmet and half-armor could stand for long against a man-sized meat-eater that hung on with fore-claws, raking for any gap in protection at body and thighs with the huge rear talons that gave them their True Name, which translated to "terrible claw." As the Nodosaurs wrestled with squalling horrors, children ran among them slashing and stabbing until they were swatted down.

There weren't enough of them together to defeat a tercio three thousand strong. Far from it. But a pike formation lived on its solidity as much or more as a mounted charge did. The handful of dinosaurs and children spread disorder fast and wide.

Falk had just a sense of the Steel Wall beginning to waver at this attack from within. Then the horde, which had held back to allow the spectacle of the raptor-riders to take full effect, surged forward. They rolled over the wall of bodies like a flood tide to smash down on the disordered Imperials.

Falk would never get the chance to ask any man or woman of the Twelfth whether they stayed their hands for ever so-slight a fraction of a moment from unwillingness to slaughter children wholesale, or from the unexpected, mind-bending awfulness of the sight. In the proudest tradition of the Imperial heavy infantry the Tercio Duodécimo had stood and fought unyielding. Now in the proudest tradition of the Nodosaurs it stood and died in place. The lightly armored hamstringers and arbalesters, the engineers and artillerists who had retreated into the phalanx for shelter, fell alongside the browned-iron pike-wielders to the swords and spears, the axes and clubs, the bare hands and crimsoned teeth of the Grey Angel horde.

Through eyelashes laden with unabashed tears Falk watched the Companions, resplendent in their white armor, trot around Le Boule to rescue the embattled remnants of the Imperial left. Their half-thousand Ordinary cavalry thundered behind. Falk bellowed to the spear-and-shield men who waited behind the peasant center to advance; his bull nosehorn build gave him the volume to make himself heard over the racket. The Imperial Heralds, hearing his commands, relayed them with blasts on their long brass horns.

Falk shouted new commands. The Scarlet Tyrants at the foot of the hill braced. Each man plucked the pair of heavy throwing-spears from the turf where it was planted before him.

The Duke ran the few steps to Snowflake. His arming-squire Albrecht waited with a stepladder to help him mount the restless Snowflake. His eyes wider and wiry hair wilder than usual, the boy handed Falk up first his helmet, which Falk placed over his head and cinched beneath his broad chin, and then his heater shield with its blue border, white field, and black two-headed falcon. Last, Falk accepted his horseman's axe, taking the lanyard loop about his right wrist.

When Falk had last glanced toward the Imperial center the peasants held their own and more, despite being shoved back step by step by the sheer weight of bodies in the scores of thousands. But their fear had grown like a tinder-pile.

The Twelfth Tercio's death gave it the spark.

The levies' morale went up in a flash. Throwing down their pikes they ran for the rear with piss and shit streaming down bare legs. Here was why Jaume had deployed the professional household troops behind them: the fleeing mass shied like warhorses from their shields and spear points, then flowed to either side of their wide wedge formation. Which channeled them around Le Boule as well—instead of them stampeding up it to trample the Emperor himself.

Snowflake rose to his feet. His heavily muscled white sides trembled with anticipation. Falk gave him a special press of armored heels. The Tyrannosaurus roared.

It was no terremoto. But then, it was the hunting cry of a monster scarcely less mythically terrifying to Nuevaropans than the Grey Angel Himself. It halted not just many fleeing peasants but a number of the Crusaders who chased them.

The house-shields yelled and charged, battering through the last of the broken commoners. The Imperial archers, who like the Nodosaur missile troops had pulled back among their better-armored comrades as the enemy closed, added a quick shower of arrows. Then the mailed foot waded into the horde, bashing with shields, jabbing with spears.

They killed their way deep into the howling mob. They were no Nodosaurs, whose skills at fighting and shoulder-to-shoulder maneuver were as matchless as their courage. The bulk of the House troops' experience no doubt came from brutalizing unarmed and unarmored serfs. Then again, that described the vast majority of Raguel's shrieking minions. The mailed soldiers fought professionally and well, and worked terrific execution.

But they had never faced an enemy like this one. No one had, for half a millennium. Their butchery, while exemplary, won no more than the pause of a few breaths.

As Falk rode past the splendid red and gold ranks of his Tyrants, he signaled with his axe for them to hold in place. They needed no orders to kill any Crusaders who got past the spearmen. Their one overriding imperative was to protect the Emperor himself.

Behind Le Boule, or so Falk both hoped and expected, the several hundred household foot who formed the final Imperial reserve would be corralling and rallying as many fleeing conscripts as they could to return to the fight.

The horde was already beginning to flow around the flanks of the house-shields' wedge to surround them. Falk knew it showed no conscious tactics. Only the brute nature of mob and flow.

He smiled. Letting his axe dangle momentarily by its lanyard, he leaned forward to pat his mount's thick neck.

"Time to show what we can do, eh, boy?"

Snowflake roared again. He, at least, was happy.

Then with a mighty thrust of his hind-limbs the tyrant was among the hordelings, his great jaws tossing men and women like screaming mice.

"Oh, those children! They're children!" cried Jacques, riding at Jaume's right hand.

"We have to forget them!" Jaume yelled back. "We're on the enemy!"

Whether driven by Raguel's malevolent will or their own, a dozen Crusader dinosaur knights and several dozen gendarmes had returned from their rout to the fight. They beset an Imperial left wing stalled and losing the battle against the nominally human flood of the horde. Or they were reinforcements; either way, to throw them in piecemeal was poor tactics. Jaume already knew Raguel didn't care.

He waggled his upraised lance side to side. The Companions winged out to either side into a chevron. Then he dipped the pennon-tipped lance head briefly forward.

As one the trotting duckbills stretched their gloriously crested heads out and uttered their inaudible death cry.

A few of the enemy duckbill-riders had turned to face the new threat. It didn't help. Though their armor saved the knights from most of the terremoto's effects, their mounts took it all. Some reared and plunged, trumpeted pain and fear. Two fell over kicking.

The Companions couched lances and charged home. Of all the good works they meant to do for their Lady today, mercy was not among them.

A knight in clear-enameled plate tried to wrestle his brilliant blue sackbut back under control. Its tube-crested head wagged frantically left and right; its eyes rolled as if loosened in their sockets. Jaume lifted his lance to let Camellia plow into the beast with her massive keelbone.

The Parasaurolophus had no chance. The impact rocked it back so hard Jaume heard its tailbone break in a thunderclap. The dinosaur shrieked so shrilly it broke out of Jaume's hearing-range as the beast toppled with a crash and a cloud of yellow dust.

Ribs broke loudly as Camellia ran over her fallen foe. The rider's armet-encased skull popped like an overripe berry as her right foot came down squarely on it.

Another Crusader knight managed to wheel his buff and green morion toward Jaume. Though blood ran from a ruptured right tympanum, the hadrosaur coiled back onto huge haunches to spring. It didn't get time. Jaume had time to register that the trim of his enemy's green shield and breastplate was real gold. Then his lance took him in the gorget and knocked him right over his cantle to tumble down his monster's tail.

Camellia bulled the morion aside. Its rider squealed like a scalded fatty as she trampled his armored thighs.

She bore down on a bay courser. Agile as a springer, the warhorse leapt out of her way. Jaume's lance crunched through the mail guarding the pit of its rider's upraised swordarm. He let the lance fall with its victim and drew the Lady's Mirror.

His main weapon now was still Camellia herself. Her rampaging bulk scattered coursers like straw dogs.

The Companions' rush had hammered down the Crusader dinosaur knights and blown right through the men-at-arms. But it wasn't without cost.

To his right Jaume saw Persephone, Timaeos's sackbut, hurtle to the ground. Her breastbone threw up a bow-wave of dust and well-minced vegetation. Blood pulsed dark red from the lance broken-off through segmented gorget and cream-and-rust neck.

Timaeos flew over her neck. The giant Griego had presence of mind to cast his shield, which bore his device of a red lantern, away in midair. Then he tucked his armeted head and rolled.

The helmet was ripped away. Timaeos sprang to his feet as if nothing had happened. His bronze hair and beard blazed defiantly even in the feeble sun.

Ayaks rode toward him. He held out a hand to swing Timaeos aboard his morion Bogdan. But Timaeos waved him off.

"Go!" he roared. "Ride like Hell! I follow on foot!" And turning he smashed the head of a charging courser with his maul. The rider's neck broke with an audible crack as he was thrown free.

Jaume turned his attention forward again. He and Camellia were now plunging into the horde. Men and women burst beneath her feet like blood-filled bladders. Blood spattered Jaume like unceasing rain.

Somehow Jacques had forged forty meters ahead of his Captain-General. Now the Francés knight stood at bay on his white female sackbut Puretée. Hooting plangently, she reared, pawing air. Jacques slashed longsword at Crusaders clinging to his chain-and-leather reins.

Screaming, the hordelings swarmed up the sackbut's sides, climbing each other in their eagerness to come to grips with her rider. A woman jumped up behind Jacques and wrapped her arms around his armet. He hacked up and back with his shield. Its rim caved in the woman's left cheek. She fell away—but pulled the helmet off as she did.

Jaume urged Camellia to a two-legged run through the throng. For a moment a seethe of filthy bodies hid Jacques from his view. Then he saw his friend dragged from the saddle. Puretée spun squealing. Her tail knocked Crusaders broken and kicking through the air.

But the mob closed over Jacques as seamlessly as water over a pebble tossed in a pond, and almost as quickly. Hooting in panic and despair, his sackbut fled through the horde.

Desperately Jaume steered Camellia toward his fallen friend. As he approached the place where Jacques had vanished a woman jumped up, holding a white-armor encased leg above her head and screeching triumph. She was so drenched in blood and filth that Jaume couldn't tell whether she was nude or not beneath hair that hung matted to her thighs. He split her head in passage with his sword.

Weeping, Jaume drove on past. The unceasing squelch of bones and flesh at every step was like a gauntleted fist punching his soul. But the only hope he or any of his Companions had—to say nothing of the horse-mounted Ordinaries following them—was to *keep moving.*

Never before had he encountered enemies who refused to flee when confronted with war-dinosaurs trampling them to ruptured bags of shard and juice. But not only didn't the horde run, it *attacked.*

Cutting left and right at snarling faces that leapt at him, severing hands that clutched for legs and reins, scarcely able to breathe for the unbelievable reek of filth and piss and ruptured guts, Jaume rode Camellia all-out across the very floor of Hell.

Blowing a sigh of complete exhaustion, Snowflake sank to the hilltop just left of Felipe's tent. Red threads twined his head, his tail, his vast powerful body. Not all of the gore was human. He'd suffered at least a dozen gashes.

Albrecht helped Falk down from the white Tyrannosaurus's saddle. Falk sat down heavily on the grass. He barely noticed when his arming-squire unstrapped his helmet and took it off. He only roused when the boy offered a bucket of water, which he gratefully seized and dumped over his head.

Nearby a naked woman lay on her side, pinned by a Tyrant pilum through the belly to a man behind her in a terrible parody of sodomy. Her fingers and toes twitched. If still conscious she must be suffering unendurably.

Falk threw her instantly from his mind. He had run out of compassion for Raguel's killers long before he ran out of strength to kill them.

Albrecht had thoughtfully brought more buckets. Falk drank deep from a second, then poured the rest of that one over his head. Pink runlets streamed down his armor into the soil.

His shield was gone, torn away by enemies who showed neither fear nor fatigue. His armor was dented, his arrogant two-headed toothed falcon insignia almost effaced. The curved blade of his axe was notched and dulled. Though it weighed no more than an arming-sword, between the mass of its head and Falk's strength it crushed skulls and smashed bones even without a keen edge. But there were so many of them, attacking so relentlessly, that he'd blunted and notched his axe so badly on foes—few of whom wore armor, and not all even wore clothes—that it was little more than a steel club.

Jaume's drive through the Crusaders' right flank had at least slowed their onslaught. But though the Companions and their Ordinaries had ridden clean through to the riverbank, losing at least half their numbers but killing a thousand and more, still the horde came on, undiminished.

Falk had fought as long as he could. Then he'd fallen back up the Emperor's hill to catch his breath. He reckoned conservatively that together he and Snowflake had killed over a hundred men and women. And some had arms, and knew how to use them.

It was a feat of legend. He doubted it even came close to being the day's most remarkable one. That, he suspected, belonged to the Companions on their epic hellride.

The problem, of course, was that the only witnesses who might have interest in commemorating all that skill and insane bravery would probably not survive to do so.

Falk could literally not raise his arm to strike again. His body throbbed in a discord of a hundred aches. *I wonder, would Father at last be proud of me?* he thought. *Would Mother?* As greatly as such questions had tormented him day and night throughout his life, right now he couldn't rouse himself to really care.

Yet he knew he'd get little respite. Already his Scarlet Tyrants were hard-pressed by the flesh-flood, falling step by step back up Le Boule's base. From up the slope crossbows and shortbows loosed ceaselessly over their heads. The Imperial Army missileers were resupplied by a constant stream of wagons full of arrows and quarrels. Which barely slowed before they were emptied.

By now the Grey Angel Crusade must have lost tens of thousands dead and wounded. It made no difference Falk could see. It was like trying to bail the ocean with his hat.

Someone shouted alarm from nearby. Falk raised his lead head.

Raguel, who had sat watching the battle like a statue, was riding his monstrous bull tyrant slowly forward again. And thirty dinosaur knights and a hundred heavy-horse had just trotted from the wooded rise to the west, along the horde's right flank.

Falk sighed. "That's it," he said aloud despite himself. "We're done."

Anchored on the Fortunate River, the Imperial right held firm despite awful losses. But on the other wing the Imperial Army had nothing left that would slow so much as a procession of cripples on crutches. Much less that many fresh riders on fresh mounts.

He felt a pat on his right pauldron. He looked around. For the first time he noticed that the vambrace and rerebraces protecting that arm had been stripped away, leaving a torn silk gambeson sleeve and steel gauntlet.

The Emperor stood beside him, smiling down on Falk like a benign bearded moon. He held his longsword in his right hand.

"The time has come to show these madmen how Nuevaropan grandes can die," he said, holding out his left arm to allow an ashen-faced page to strap a heater shield to it.

"No, Majesty," Falk said. He tried to stand. Felipe held him down with unexpected strength.

"Rest, son," the Emperor said. "Conserve your strength. They'll come to us, you know."

Sighing, Falk slumped. There was no denying the truth. The Tyrants were being driven up the hill. They'd soon be overrun.

Snowflake lay on his belly with blood-red eyes closed and the tip of his snout resting on the sod. A change of the humid breeze wind brought coolness and a waft of forest smell. The contrast to the hot abattoir stink shocked Falk. Its freshness was a taunt, reminding him of what he was about to lose—hope; the world; all—in a few more inhalations.

Snowflake whuffed. His eyes opened. Despite his own killing exhaustion he raised his great head to stare toward the newcomers.

The messenger boys pointed that way, shouting. Some cheered. Others danced and laughed, mad as hordelings, tears gleaming on their cheeks.

Falk looked. For a moment his brain flatly refused to make sense of what he saw.

A kilometer to his left, monsters were emerging from the trees. Monsters that walked on four columnar legs. Monsters with horns like lances on their brows, who wore steel on their faces and castles on their backs.

Triceratops horridus came to war. They bellowed gleeful belligerence as they trundled toward the horde.

Beside them marched infantry with spears and shields and bows.

Before them rode a single lonely figure on a grey horse, followed closely by a man on a curious and much smaller hornface.

"And so my enemy comes to join the battle," Felipe murmured. "Will you help them, Voyvod Karyl? Or us?"

He shook his head sadly. "It will hardly make a difference either way."

Chapter 42

Hombre armao, Man-at-arms, *Gendarme*—Warriors who fight on horseback, whether knightly or not: cavalry, as opposed to dinosaurry. Unlike dinosaur knights, they are overwhelmingly male. Heavy cavalry wear full-plate armor; the medium cavalry, plate-and-mail or nosehorn leather armor.

—A PRIMER TO PARADISE FOR THE IMPROVEMENT OF YOUNG MINDS

"So," Rob said, peering through the screen of brush at the forest's edge at a turbulent grey sea of humanity, "are you sure this is a good idea, then?"

Tiny, colorful fliers chattered at each other among the branches all around, incongruous highlights to the constant mutter of clatter, shouts, and screams from below. Rob was on his hook-horn, Little Nell. Karyl sat Asal at his side. Despite the greatest bloodletting in five centuries taking place practically at their feet, the hook-horn was clearly more nervous about a mare half her weigh.

Rob wore a pot-helm and a mail coat, and carried his dinosaur master's axe, Wanda. A white-painted round shield hung by his left knee. It bore a blue Triceratops head, which someone had started using as the badge of what someone else had dubbed the Fugitive Legion. Both had spread through the army like dirty limericks.

"Of course it isn't," said Karyl. He had his imperturbability back. "But we're going to do it anyway."

He wore a peaked Ovdan cap with an aventail of overlapping steel plates protecting his neck, and his usual buff strider-leather jack. A buckler rode his saddle's right side, his cross-hilt longsword at his right hip. He carried an arrow-quiver slung, and others more arrows in the saddle panniers. He held his recurved Ovdan hornbow in his right hand.

He nudged the mare to a walk. Bobbing her head ill-naturedly she crackled through the thin leafy branches into the sunlight. Such as it was on this dark and dreary day.

"But why?" Rob called after. "Why are we doing this? Why are *you* doing this? The Impies betrayed you, stabbed you in the back. Now they've put a price on your head. Why court death to rescue them?"

"Because I find, after everything, I'm still human," Karyl said without glancing back.

Tree limbs splintered around Rob as twenty-nine armored monsters rumbled out of the woods. Shaking his head, muttering curses not even he could hear above their noise, he booted Nell's stout sides and rode bouncing and trotting after his Fae-touched master.

"We're alive, Lord."

The usually matter-of-fact Machtigern spoke in tones of wonder.

The Companions and their Ordinaries had come to rest on the bank of the Fortunate River. They had ridden clean through the Grey Angel horde. The surviving Ordinaries had arrayed themselves in a semicircle facing outward, guarding the remnants of the medium cavalry and the knights-brother.

Jaume and men slumped in the saddle of duckbills whose gloriously crested heads hung in exhaustion, and whose sides pumped like vast bellows. The men had stripped off their helmets to pour water over heads steaming from confinement in steel cans, then drank cautiously.

For the moment the horde passed them by. It focused with inhuman single-mindedness on throwing itself against the last stout defenses on La

Miche and Le Boule. Battered and spent, Jaume could barely stand to look around and take stock of what they'd paid the butcher.

But how can one see beauty, if one never confronts its opposite? he asked himself. Not even the Lady's truth could do much to ease his pain at the loss of his beautiful brothers and their auxiliaries.

When he did look what he saw was ugly enough. Only Florian, Ayaks, solid Bernat, Machtigern, and the two Anglaterranos, Owain and Wil Oakheart, remained of their sweet brotherhood.

"What about Timaeos?" he asked.

Oh, Melodía, my love, he thought. *How I pray to the Lady that you're safe away from here!*

But he didn't dare reflect too deeply on the likelihood of that. Even his soul had a breaking-point.

Ayaks shook his sweat-drenched blond head. "Gone. He waded through devils for two hundred meters before they brought him down."

"Another epic feat's going to go begging for lack of tongues to sing it," said Florian lightly. He had clambered down a collapsed section of bank to refill the Companions' water gourds from the river. He tossed one up. Owain caught it with one hand and tipped it into his upturned mouth.

"I'm writing down as much as I can," said Bernat. He flashed a rare smile. "Maybe someone will find my chronicle on my body and see fit to preserve it, when this madness is over."

Jaume grimaced. "I saw poor Jacques die. And so we've lost Iñigo Etchegaray and István—"

"And both Pedros, yes," Florian said. "And Dieter."

Jaume shook his head. "A shame. The boy never had a chance to show the world what he could do."

"He died well," Ayaks said. "I saw it happen." He didn't elaborate.

"I can only hope to do as well," Jaume said. "I saw Rupp die too. At least our good Coronel Alma survived. The Ordinaries are in good hands."

"What now?" Ayaks asked.

"We can die standing," said Florian, "or die riding. Other than that—" He frowned thoughtfully. "That's it."

"Mounted troops are always at their weakest standing to await attack," Machtigern said.

"So do we try to fight back to the lines, or charge back into the thick of things?" Owain asked.

"I say we hit the horde squarely," said Wil. "Say we reach the lines: doesn't that merely defer the 'dying standing,' then?"

He shrugged. "I hope none of you'll think the less of me, that I'd rather not wait any longer. If die we're going to, let's get after it!"

"I'm with you," Owain said. The others agreed.

"What about the Ordinaries?" Machtigern asked. "They deserve a choice. And the poor bastards from the reserve."

"They're cavalrymen," Florian said. "Dare I suggest when they chose that occupation they made their choice?"

He threw a final filled gourd to Wil Oakheart, then climbed up the bank with the aid of some tough soda-brush roots. While well-made plate—and the Companions wore the best—distributed its weight so well it didn't much impair its wearer's movement, Florian's agility was striking.

"*Morte à cheval à gallop*," Jaume said: Death on horseback at the gallop. It was every mounted warrior's creed—and professed desire.

"So that's it, then," said Wil tucking his gourd in his remaining pannier on the back of his resting green-eyed red sackbut, Red Dragon. "Shall we dance, then, mates?"

"Wait."

Florian had stopped half over the edge of the cave-in. He got to his feet and pointed west, past the protective ring of Ordinaries and the horde rolling relentlessly south.

Machtigern cursed. "More dinosaur knights."

"Wouldn't you rather die cleanly on their steel," asked Ayaks, "than torn limb from limb?"

"You make a good point, brother," Wil said.

"Not them," said Florian. "There—beyond. Look, my friends!"

Huge dinosaurs were striding from the distant forest. Horned dinosaurs, with fighting-castles swaying on their backs.

"Three-horns!" exclaimed Ayaks. He said something in his own native Slavo.

Jaume didn't know the tongue, but caught the words "Voyvoda Karyl Vladevich." He began to laugh.

"Before the Hassling I never committed treachery and murder before," he said. "Now for the first time in my life I'm pleased to be reminded of a job poorly done. Gentlemen, get ready. We ride!"

Twisting sideways in Meravellosa's saddle, Melodía hurled a javelin. It struck a sackbut's haunch through a green and white lozenged caparison and bounced back to hang by its barbs. Her missile had failed to pierce thick hide beneath the quilted cloth.

She led her jinetes north, sweeping in to almost touch range of about thirty dinosaur knights who plodded beside the horde's west flank. As long as they stayed beyond reach of a quick-pivoting tail-sweep it was as safe as anything you could do on an actual battlefield; if the horde bothered using missile weapons she'd seen no evidence of it.

Of course, with sheer mind-numbing numbers like these, the Grey Angel Crusade had little need of darts or arrows or even engines. It surprised Melodía mildly they even used armored riders in conventional blocks. *It amuses Raguel to degrade his highborn slaves by flaunting his mastery of them, I guess,* she thought.

She breathed through open mouth. Though the breeze blew from the north, the horde's reek of filth and decay was a miasma so dense it had hit her in the face like a sandbag when she came within a hundred meters.

Duckbills bugled as darts hit home. Some reared. One javelin, lucky for the caster, less so for its recipient, had struck the unarmored back of a sackbut's neck. The beast turned in vast circles, shaking its steel-encased head as if to rid itself of the pain and blowing cacophonous chords through the horn its head. Knights behind had to veer well wide to avoid its scything tail.

Melodía heard tormented howling as several of the duckbills waded right into the mass of Crusaders afoot. Raguel's bucketheads cared even less about their inferiors than regular ones, it seemed.

Hand-hurled missiles couldn't much harm steel-shelled riders. But even stinging their monster mounts helped. To the extent anything could, in such unequal battle.

She passed the last swaying hadrosaur tail. As she did she heard whistles shrill from the Legion's ranks, each blowing three sharp blasts. *Time to lead my kids clear*, she thought. *Karyl's three-horns are coming into crossbow range.*

She turned her mare's head and set her at an easy lope to pass around the dinosaur knights and gendarmes on the Legion's left flank. She heard a ringing clatter as steel bows cut loose, then a rippling hiss as feathered quarrels flew past her riders in a hornet swarm. Louder twangs resounded as the two trike-mounted stingers shot.

Karyl's mounted artillerists weren't yet adept at aiming from the backs of moving beasts. Both darts went high. Which meant only they sailed over the high backs of the war-dinosaurs to do unseen carnage among the trudging hordelings.

Which, of course, would have the same net effect as spitting in the Océano Guenevere.

Melodía glanced back over her left shoulder. The arbalesters had learned the knack of shooting from howdahs. She saw two empty saddles. A morion toppled majestically forward like a felled tree, evidently chance-struck in the head.

She turned her face forward. Meravellosa was smart and keen-eyed but it paid to have an extra set of eyes scouting for holes made by small burrowing mammals or dinosaurs. A hoof dropped inadvertently down one could snap a horse's leg beyond healing—and possibly an unwary rider's neck when she went flying over her hapless animal's neck.

Archers and arbalesters on foot had trotted out in front of the three-horns to shoot at the horde. The ones who carried the heaviest crossbows shot and then ran back; they had the only real chance to do more damage to the enemy knights—and simply didn't have time to cock their weapons again with gear-and-pulley cranequins. The lighter crossbows and short-bows, though, could do the same as the jinetes' hand-thrown projectiles had: prick the enemy duckbills and disorder them further, rendering them more vulnerable to the charge when Karyl's duckbills and terrible trikes closed in.

As she passed back Legion montadores riding the other way, Melodía found space to think of something besides striking the enemy and not dying. It was an uncomfortable place to be. She was deliberately bringing herself closer to the two greatest nightmare-sources of her young life: Falk, and Raguel.

Each, in her mind and belly, monstrous.

But what can I do? she asked herself for the hundredth time in the last night and day. *What choice do I really have?*

She had braced the tyrant brooding in his den to force him to act—to command. He had. Now, if Karyl could help the Imperial Constable, the man he saw as his betrayer, for sake of being human, could she hold back? Abandon her new friends in the Fugitive Legion who relied on her? Her father? Her own true love, Jaume, whom she'd spurned in what she now knew was a fit of childish petulance for not doing what she wanted and for defying her father's command?

She hoped that even as the spoiled, sheltered twit she had been, she would not have been that person. But she certainly wasn't now.

Jaumet, forgive me! she wailed in her own mind.

And then: *No. I can't do that now.*

She led her squadron around the northern flank of the Legion heavy riders. Wagons followed close behind, carrying bundles of fresh twist-darts and javelins. She and her command had mostly depleted what they carried.

It wouldn't be the last time, she reckoned.

Not without pride Rob watched his Short-Haired Horse Captain lead her wild riders back to the wagons to reload. She'd topped her helmet with a red-dyed horsetail to make her easier for her troops to spot in combat. It streamed grandly behind her now, lending her an even more imposingly heathen, Ovdan look.

Karyl's she-hada cousin was right about her, he thought. *Pampered princess or not, she does have the spirit of a horse barbarian.*

He wondered briefly how that would play when she became an archduchess and took her place among the Empire's high grandes. Then he laughed.

"As if that's likely to happen," he said aloud. "She's destined to end the day in a hordeling's belly, same as me."

He scratched Little Nell behind her neck-frill. "Maia grant I give the foul things indigestion." She tossed her head and snorted.

The hook-horn jounced along just out of kicking-range from Karyl's cantankerous mare. They in turn rode just before and to the left of the block of advancing three-horns. Normally, of course, the fighting-castle crews would shoot their crossbows over the heads of anyone so close, even mounted on horseback—or, like Rob, on a much-smaller cousin of Triceratops. But Karyl had not survived decades of lurid romance-novel adventures by taking things like marksmanship for granted. For which Ma Korrigan's only acknowledged son was duly glad.

He refused to let his mind linger on the question of whether the kindest fate the day could offer might be a chisel-pointed quarrel through the back of his fool head. . . .

Regular as clockwork, Karyl loosed shots from his hornbow. Rob's eyeballs were rattling in their sockets so hard he had trouble focusing, but if he knew Karyl—and to the extent any living creature could, he did—his arrows were regularly reaping Crusader lives. From the rising ruction out ahead he gathered the Legion's shooters were likewise doing their customary bloody work.

Heavy footfalls drummed from Rob's left. He looked to see Baron Côme leading the dinosaurry past the trikes on his brown-backed morion Bijou. Behind them rode the heavy cavalry. To the south the right wing did the same. They were commanded by the youthful Baron of Fond-Étang, Ismaël, who, much chastened, had joined the fugitive army with a few retainers in Métairie Brulée shortly after it saw off Célestine's troops. Like so many others he had seen his fief overrun by the horde, and barely escaped.

Karyl's army today was the largest and most powerful he'd fielded since he and Rob had arrived in Providence with little more than what they carried on their backs. Well, and Little Nell's back. As close as Rob could reckon—admittedly not much; numbers didn't sing to him as they did to Élodie, say—they brought six thousand fighting men and women against the horde. Many had been battle-seasoned into veterans in a sprinkle of days.

None of which meant a nosehorn-fly bite on a thunder-titan's ass against that endless flood of malice. "What am I even doing here," he muttered to Nell. "Not much call for a spymaster in a headlong charge to certain doom."

He sighed theatrically, even though he was pretty sure no one was paying any attention to him. He was always his own best audience, anyway.

"Probably because at this point I couldn't bear to be left out. Even of this grand self-immolation on which Himself and His whole army seem bent."

The hook-horn snorted again.

"Aye and you're right, Nell," he said. "Think of the songs I'll sing of this day if by some fool's chance I happen to survive it? Oh, and the glorious palace I'll build us when you learn to shit gold, a thing roughly as likely."

The Legion duckbills commenced a ground-shaking trot. Something drew Rob's eye far to his left, above the heads of Côme's dinosaur-riders. Up by the ridge's treeline five hundred meters away stood a lone figure, cloaked and hooded.

The Witness, Rob knew, and his throat seized up. *Karyl was right. She's real too. And why should you, of all people, wonder at things legendary rising up to walk the world?*

He thought of calling her to Karyl's attention. Then he thought better of it. *Precious little goes on that Karyl misses. And right now I fancy he's a few better things to think on.*

The archers and lighter arbalesters came streaming back between the trikes. And the mounted Legion wings charged home against the head and tail of the column of dinosaur knights and men-at-arms.

Karyl slowed Asal. Rob hastily followed suit, reining Little Nell to her easygoing walk. The three-horns plodded on.

And, lowering their huge horned heads, dug into the Grey Angel's war-dinosaurs.

Refugees and prisoners alike had told the Fugitive Legion that the bulk of the Crusading knights had joined of their own choice, not Raguel's talons sunk in their brains. Some did it for fear for their families, or themselves. Others took up the Grey Angel's cause for loot and glory or to be on the winning side. Some even came over from religious zeal: the Grey Angel Crusade must be carrying out the Creators' divine judgement.

But some knights came willingly to Raguel for the pleasure of blood and torture.

Little of which accounted to Rob for the fact the Crusader knights continued riding toward the Imperial lines until the very moment the Triceratops commenced their lumbering attack. Raguel must have laid that much compulsion on them, he thought, to ignore the approach of a threat so dire. To say nothing of so massive.

At last the Crusaders spun their duckbills to counter-charge the walking fortresses. Launching off their tremendous drumsticks, war-hadrosaurs got off the mark a good deal quicker than coursers did.

Now it only meant the monsters and their riders died that much sooner.

Triceratops could build up fair speed of their own. Karyl seldom used them that way. It jostled the fighting-castles something fierce, threatening to pitch their crews clean out or even jar the hornface-leather reinforced wicker baskets free. And was unnecessary besides: the trikes were at their most brutally effective when they lowered their enormous heads, dug upward, and simply walked.

So close at hand it took Rob's breath away, Mañana, one of the youngest bulls brought down from Ovda by Karyl's cacafuego cousin, slid his steel-capped horns beneath a charging sackbut's buffy chest. Ignoring the lance that glanced sparking off his steel chamfron, he used his horns like a giant hayfork. With a heave of massive neck muscles he raised the hadrosaur upright. Then he drove home the horns in the sackbut's belly.

Rob winced in sympathy at the Parasaurolophus's symphony of pain. Blood squirted over Mañana's face. Purple-grey loops of gut as big around as Rob's thigh plopped into the yellow calcite dust. Squealing, the beast fell onto its side. Its three-toed feet kicked its own viscera to shreds.

Rob felt as if the horns were spearing his own belly. That was ever and always the dilemma of his foremost trade as dinosaur master: to love and nurture and coddle and train the huge beasts that dominated the Paraíso landscape—for just this: to kill and be killed by each other.

Well, and men, of course. To any dinosaur master worth his or her silver, that was a side issue. You'd never endure the risks and drudging and heartache entailed by the trade if you didn't at base prefer dinosaurs to humans.

And Raguel's war-duckbills were magnificent. The strange, will-less hordelings made only the scantest effort to care for themselves. They often dropped dead on the march from hunger and dehydration. Not because food—if of often terrible nature—and water weren't available, but merely because, in whatever fearful ecstasy gripped their minds and souls (if they still happened to have them; a point unclear), they simply forgot to drink or eat.

But no one, not even a Grey Angel, could treat war-beasts that way, equine or dinosaurian. Not and get use out of them. Somebody had been found to care for them. And their riders' armor, by appearances.

Which confirms these bucketheads have voluntarily joined in this great evil, thought Rob. *More's the pity our trikes can't get at the bastards directly, and spare their lovely dinosaurs.*

In a shockingly short time it was over. None of the three-horns were seriously hurt. They spread out slightly to avoid the kicking bodies of those they'd felled. The duckbills, anyway; they didn't deign to notice when grounded riders got in their way.

Led by their dinosaur knights, the Legion wings had already plunged among the Crusader foot. The coursers in the three-horns' path took one look at the ten-tonne monsters and bolted. Most stampeded straight into the horde themselves, disregarding their riders' efforts to control them.

Gaétan rode past Rob on Zhubin, waving his sword and whooping. Behind them marched the Legion pikes—no hapless conscripts but volunteers, well-trained and respected, and leavened with veterans. With what Rob thought more courage than sense Gaétan's spear-and-shield men ran forward with mail jingling to form a buffer between the horde and the vulnerable trike legs and bellies. Archers launched arrows over their comrades' heads and even fighting castles rising two stories in the air; they could flight-shoot at absurdly high angles and be sure of finding plenty of targets when their arrows stormed down. Rob heard their feathers hissing over even the demon-chorus of screaming and bugling and banging.

Rob reined his hook-horn to a stop. *By your leave, Karyl dear,* he thought, *Nell and I'll just stay back here and wait for the goblins to come to me. Not as if I've long to wait.*

Not long enough. . . .

He slipped his arm into the leather sleeve on the back of his round shield. As he picked it up and wiggled it down his arm to where he could grasp the leather-wrapped wood handle, the hordelings turned to attack their new tormentors.

"The Eight make us fucking grateful," he croaked through a throat dry as High Ovdan desert, "for what we are about to fucking receive."

Chapter 43

Montador, Montadora—To honor knights we give them the title of *Montador* or *Montadora*, meaning a man or woman who rides in battle, on horse or dinosaur. Usually we call them *Mor* or *Mora* for short.

—A PRIMER TO PARADISE FOR THE IMPROVEMENT OF YOUNG MINDS

Shock ran up Melodía's arm as she slashed her talwar across the back of a hordeling's neck. As the middle-aged woman pitched soundlessly onto her face, Melodía tried not to think how she resembled her long-dead mother, Marisol. Or what the pink scrap was that she'd been masticating as mindlessly as a duckbill with a mouthful of weeds when Melodía cut her down. . . .

She wheeled Meravellosa away from the mob. Karyl's three-horns and montadores had already vanished into the horde's main stream. She and her jinetes were now slashing at the rear of the colossal mob trying to overpower the Legion's peasant pikes.

The temptation was simply to wade into them, laying about with her curved blade. But she'd watched two hadrosaurs and a Triceratops brought down by nothing more than human swarms already. The horde was itself a monster, knowing nothing of pity or remorse. Only rage. And hunger. It would swallow her and all her riders at a single gulp, and not slow down. . . .

So she had to lead her jinetes in doing what they usually did: hit. Run. Ride back in to hit again. She knew she'd lost some of her laughing boys and girls already.

If we weren't all lost the instant the sun rose on this horrible day.

She turned in the saddle to check her panniers. Just a single meter-long dart remained, a three-meter leather thong wound down it to impart a stabilizing spin when hurled. Time to head back to restock. There were no signs the supply wagons running dry of missiles, in any event. Melodía could only marvel at where Karyl had laid hands on them all.

She looked back around. And reined Meravellosa to a sudden stop.

She found herself facing a black cliff of sackbut. The hornface-leather barding that guarded chest and flanks, the steel chamfron on its face and segmented gorget down its throat, all gleamed the same black as its hide. The armor and shield of the rider who stared down at her past its shoulder were likewise all of black, as was the plume that nodded at the nape of the crested armet.

"Fuck," she said.

She might have darted clear. Instead some impulse made her lean forward to pat her mare's neck soothingly. It ran with sweat that was hot to her palm.

Leaving his lance upright in its socket by his right leg, the knight reached a black gauntlet up to open a black visor. From all that blackness gazed the sad, lost eyes of Bogardus, sunken in purplish-brown pits of flesh.

What she saw there was the darkest black of all.

"Melodía, my love," he said.

"Don't call me that!" she screamed. "You lost the right to call me that when you stabbed us in the back!"

He shook his head. "But you were there. Didn't you see? Yes, I betrayed you. I betrayed everyone. Most of all myself. But at the end I fought him. You saw."

She sucked in a shuddering breath. "Yes. I did. You failed. But you did try."

"And only when it was much, much too late. I can hear it in your eyes. Melodía—Día, will you believe me when I say I'm sorry?"

"If you were to turn now and join us, I might."

Nervously she looked around. Nobody paid them any mind. The

hordelings were preoccupied throwing themselves at the Imperial pikemen and -women, who had managed to form themselves into a circle. The other light-riders continued to pick at the Crusaders. Most kept flowing on south as mindlessly as a river.

"I would," Bogardus said, "if only I could. I cannot. Raguel controls my actions."

"He's making you say that?"

"He allows me to. I can control my speech. Only that—I think it amuses Him."

"Why is He doing this to you? Why is He doing this to us—all this cruelty and horror?"

"To punish me. To punish us."

"Couldn't He do it—I don't know—more cleanly?"

"He hates us," Bogardus said. "They all hate us, His kind—the Seven who remain. He belongs to a faction who thinks the Angels need only wipe out *most* of us humans for the sake of Paradise.

"They're the merciful ones. Their rivals want to erase us all and start from a clean slate."

That rocked her back in her saddle. "But why?"

"I don't know. They feel it's the Creators' will."

"They *feel* it? They don't know? The Creators didn't tell Raguel to unleash a Crusade?"

"No. That much I know. Apparently the Grey Angels are allowed substantial . . . latitude in how They discharge Their duties."

"Wiping out the people the Creators went to so much trouble to put here—I'd call that too much latitude!"

There was a dispassionate-observer part of her, which often drew closer to the fore at times of intolerable stress, like this. Now it was amused at the way a lifelong agnostic was talking about the Creators as established facts.

Well, if Grey Angels exist . . . her usual self admitted.

"Now what?" she asked the sad thing that had been her lover. "What do you want of me?"

He grimaced as if in hideous pain. Apparently he had to fight to get the next words out.

"Kill me."

He slammed the visor down.

Rob slammed his axe deep between the shoulder blades of a pallid woman trying to pull herself up Big Sally's barding. The fighting-castle crew was preoccupied battling hordelings attacking from the far side with half-pikes and axes.

The woman screeched. Rob wrenched the axe-head free. Something fluttered and stank at him from her shoulders as she fell.

"Sweet Maia, Mother of Mercy," he moaned, "please tell me what she was wearing for cape and cowl was not a flayed human skin!"

Ducked low along Meravellosa's outstretched neck, Melodía thought, *That was much too close*, as she raced beneath the sackbut's fast-moving tail as it swept at a rising angle. It had come within a scale's thickness of breaking her and her mare like a bundle of dry sticks. She was so focused on dodging Bogardus's lance that the monster's sudden spin almost caught her.

She rode fifteen meters straight to get well clear of the black sackbut. *I never appreciated how agile a big two-legged dinosaur could be before.*

Gazing up at the blank black visor she wondered how much of the man she once adored still lived behind it. And what Paradisiacal good he could possibly do her.

Bogardus's mount pirouetted to face Melodía. From her training she knew nothing drained a human like combat. Horses too, to judge from the way Meravellosa stood panting, with legs braced wide and head hung low. She marveled that she could stay in the saddle. How the poor souls in the Imperial lines still fought on after hours of combat was more than she could fathom, though she supposed necessity had something to do with it. She struggled to keep breathing slowly and deeply, despite the way her lungs burned.

The battle raged without her. That didn't matter. She faced the black dinosaur and its black rider alone; her jinetes were doing their duty, trying to keep their foot-bound fellows from getting swamped . . . as long as possible, anyway.

And that was fine. This was her fight. She'd prefer a quick death under the sackbut's feet—or if she were truly blessed, a clean stroke of her former lover's longsword—to the fates of the scores she'd seen beaten or mauled or bitten to death. Or disjointed like a scratcher for the pot, but still alive.

She did feel a stab of apprehension about Karyl. *Is he still alive?* Then wondered why she felt such concern.

Probably he did. Because as long as he lived, so did his army. So did hope . . . somehow.

The thought stoked that always-anger to a rising a rage blaze.

"How?" she screamed at Bogardus. "How can I kill you? I can't cut through your armor with my sword, even if I could reach you! Help me, damn it—if there's really anything still human in there, and it isn't just that goat-fucker Raguel playing with me!"

He gazed at her, eyes invisible through the narrow gap in his visor.

Slamming her talwar into its sheath, Melodía grabbed the final dart from her pack. Slipping the end-loop over her right wrist she tested the feathered missile's weight and balance.

Can I hit that eye-slit? she asked herself. She knew: she couldn't. Her arm trembled just holding the dart. Besides, even if she hit the mark precisely, its iron tip was too wide to fit through the slit. She couldn't throw it fast enough to punch its way inside.

"Or are you just playing with me? Using me again the way you and Violette did?"

Bogardus dropped his lance. He unstrapped his black shield and let it fall. Moving as if underwater he raised gauntleted hands. They grappled with his midnight helmet as if it were a living thing.

Somehow unwilling fingers fumbled the catches open. He tossed the armet away.

His hair hung damp and lifeless around his slack-skinned face. It had all gone a leaden grey, like the clouds that threatened overhead.

His features clenched in a look of agony. "He's punishing me for my defiance," he forced through locked jaws.

His longsword sang free of its black-enameled scabbard. A black gauntlet flourished it high.

"Defend yourself, my love!" Bogardus screamed. "I can't do any more—"

Melodía nudged Meravellosa to gallop left at an angle that would bring her hard along the sackbut's glistening black flank. And within easy range of its rider's meter-long blade.

As she came level with the dinosaur's blunt beak, Melodía threw her dart. The longsword whistled down. Then she ducked down beside Meravellosa's neck. It rang off the peak of her cap and sliced away the horse-tail.

She hauled left hard on the reins and pressed with her heels. Meravellosa spun as if she had her own giant counter-balance tail, gathered herself like a bouncer, and shot away.

At twenty meters Melodía slowed the mare. Her poor, faithful girl was stumbling on the stumps of trampled weeds now.

Melodía looked back. Bogardus sat motionless in the black sackbut's saddle. His arms hung by his sides.

His dark eyes met hers. Somehow they seemed less black.

"Thank you," he mouthed.

But no sound came from his mouth. Just blood gushing from the dart through his throat.

He fell to the ground. So did a princess's tears.

As the three-horn went over with a crash, hot tears blurred Rob Korrigan's eyes. It was Broke-Horn, ever ill-fated: one of their original six, brought low by nothing more than the hands and malice of a mob of creatures with scarcely more claim on humanity than the Triceratops himself.

The great beast, the four men and women of its crew, and its mahout were all Rob's friends. To see them swarmed by these unclean things made him clench his fists on axe-haft and shield-grip in impotent fury.

Gaétan, who was closer than Rob, led a dozen house-shields to try to rescue the fallen monster's crew. Zhubin was limping. He had a javelin-shaft broken-off in his left haunch. A true hornface, the spike-frill didn't hold back from a fight, even hurt.

It was futile. The flesh-torrent forced the rescuers back. Not even Karyl's transcendent genius could transcend the sheer overwhelming numbers of the Grey Angel Crusade.

We've worked a frightful execution today, Rob thought. Wanda's head, his shield, and even his face dripped with blood. It itched most abominably, drying on his skin and in his beard. *Much good it's done us.*

For the moment he was left alone with his weariness and sickness of heart. Behind him the Legion pikes were stalled into bristling circles. The rest of the infantry and the surviving cavalry all moved together in a clump with the trikes. They were still mostly alive; they killed so effectively that the horde now tended to steer clear of them. Raguel, it seemed, had some desire to preserve his awful engine—at least until He was done with it.

Had the horde been any natural army it would have run screaming back up the Imperial High Road . . . probably hours ago, from the hurting the Impies had laid on it. Rob could see occasional hints of a great commotion away off to the southeast, where he could see a handful of war-duckbills and a substantial body of cavalry carving their way through the horde toward Karyl's band. *Jaume Orange-Hair and his pretty pals, or I miss my guess*, Rob thought. *And what would I give to see* that *reunion?*

He laughed aloud, causing several house-shields nearby to stare at him as if he'd bid sense farewell. Which no doubt he had—since after all, to see a reunion between Karyl and the man who had literally lanced his White River Legion in the back would require them all to live that long. Which Rob counted slightly less likely than the sun setting in the west this evening.

Vast as it was, the horde had taken vast casualties. But of course it didn't have scores of thousands of merely human wills. It only had one single and thoroughly inhuman Will directing it. And that Will, it seemed, was still fixed on bringing down that gold and scarlet Tyrant's-Head flag, flapping from the top of a distant hill.

Rob sighed. Little Nell reeled beneath him. Wanda felt as if she weighed as much as the dead Triceratops. His shield might have been an anvil. His muscles ached so badly he couldn't feel what had to be a score of minor wounds—not all the blood spread so liberally across his and Nell's persons originated in other bodies. Not that it mattered.

"Once more into the breach," he muttered, forcing the axe to rise again by sheer force of will. Or cussedness, more like. Will's *never been me strong suit*, he thought. *Perversity, now. . . .*

An eerie stillness dropped over the entire battlefield like a blanket. The Crusaders all stopped where they were and turned their heads to stare back toward the center of the horde. Rob saw a gangly man turn away heedless of Gaétan's arming-sword swinging down at his head. It split his skull from behind.

Rob felt his own limbs go limp. It was as if something had reached inside him to drain the last of what little strength they had. His own head swiveled the same way as the Crusaders' had. His comrades' heads did too.

"Raguel!" he croaked, awed and terrified by the creature's power.

Then he saw what it was the Grey Angel wanted all to witness. And gave a wordless raptor-scream of denial and fear.

Raguel of the Ice rode his king tyrant in the midst of a clear space a good fifty meters across. It traveled with him: some force compelled his servants to stay well away from their dreadful master. Not that anyone with even the slightest spark of sanity, even the most skilled and seasoned dinosaur master, would care to approach any nearer to the seven tonnes of rage and terror the Grey Angel rode.

Yet someone did.

Hornbow in hand, arrow nocked, Karyl Bogomirskiy galloped straight toward the looming horror, and the greater horror on its back.

Chapter 44

***Tirán Imperial,* Imperial Tyrant**—*Tyrannosaurus imperator. Tyrannosaurus rex*'s big brother: 20 meters long, 10 tonnes. According to the histories, Manuel the Great, founder of the Empire of Nuevaropa and its ruling Torre Delgao, killed an imperial tyrant that was ravaging Nuevaropa in the wake of the *High Holy War,* and had its colossal skull made into the Emperor's Fangèd Throne. Curiously for such a large and terrible creature, none have been seen anywhere on Paradise since.

—THE BOOK OF TRUE NAMES

"Oh, no, my lord," Rob moaned. "This is too mad even for you. Are you that eager to die, then? You did not have a prayer against that behemoth on your poor lost Shiraa, and it's three times her size. How can you hope to win on that bloody-minded nag?"

The unseen grip on his volition went away. But now even Raguel would have been hard-pressed to force Rob *not* to watch.

The giant grey tyrant noticed that some pitiful creature had the impertinence to approach. It turned smartly about, thrust forward its face, opened an abyss, and roared through swords.

Karyl's reply was pointed, and to the point. An arrow's black fletching stood suddenly from the tyrant's right eye.

Its left looked quite surprised.

The monster shuddered. Rob half fancied he could feel it quiver, through the ground and up Nell's thick legs.

The silver-grey Tyrannosaurus reared as high as its none-too-flexible tail would let it. The colossal head lolled to one side. The monster collapsed.

Into dust. Grey dust that sparkled as it swirled away down the wind.

Raguel landed standing.

"Holy shit," Rob said reverently to Gaétan, who had ridden his spike-frill up by Rob's side. "There's something you'll not see every day."

"Maia," Gaétan croaked. "The Angel looks pissed!"

A moan arose from the horde. The free humans around Rob cheered lustily. A similar sound rose from the distant doomed ranks of the Imperials.

Rob slumped. "And then, a man on horseback can't face a Grey Angel afoot either," he said.

"No one's ever fought one alone and lived," said Gaétan. He sounded as if he were about to cry.

"Ahh, well, then," Rob said, "if we credit the songs and fancy-stories—and what better source might there be on mythical creatures?—nobody's fought an Angel and lived at all."

Gaétan shot him a nasty look. "Quit being encouraging."

Fearlessly, Asal raced toward the Grey Angel. Raguel raised his soul reaper. Karyl drew and shot again.

The Angel lowered its long grey badlands of a face down to stare at the shaft through its stomach. Then it raised its head and looked at Karyl with empty-looking sockets. It didn't even bother plucking the arrow out.

Twenty meters from the Grey Angel, Karyl halted his mare. She snorted and tossed her mane defiantly. "Show heart like that, and I might forgive you, you evil little witch," Rob said. "Not Nell; but she could never see that far, withal."

For a moment that stretched into agony the two antagonists faced each other. Karyl slung his bow. Then, drawing his arming-sword, he set Asal in a slow counterclockwise walk around his two and a half meter tall opponent. Raguel stood unmoving. He didn't stir even when Karyl rode clear behind him.

Himself must know it's a trap, Rob thought. But seizing as near a thing to an advantage as he was liable to get, Karyl wheeled his mare and charged the Grey Angel back.

Snake-fast Raguel spun, his soul-reaper slashing a high arc. Karyl swung his sword. In a flash Rob knew his aim: to deflect the blow, then cut backhand.

But the Angel didn't strike at Karyl. His blade swept through Asal's neck as if though it were made of mist. Her head flew away end for end.

The mare tumbled hooves-over-spurting stump. Karyl threw himself clear. Putting a shoulder down, he rolled through the dust with all the aplomb of his horse-barbarian kinsfolk.

But he too had been driven near exhaustion from fighting his way through the horde to his appointment with embodied Death. He was slow to rise. His hair had come undone during his fall, and now hung in his face and to just above his shoulders in lank strands.

"Are you injured, man?" Rob asked the air.

Though he'd lost the bow, Karyl still gripped his sword hilt. Holding it two-handed, down and to his left, he began to pace. He spiraled closer to Raguel.

As before, Raguel stood rigid and let him come. Rob thought with a shiver of a cat and a mouse. By all reports, in this the Grey Angel's true form, his face could show no more expression than the hideous and none-too-expertly carven idol he so resembled. Yet his attitude spoke fluent cruel triumph.

No more slowly than the Angel had, Karyl attacked. Steel rang off—whatever undoubtedly invulnerable mystic metal the soul-reaper was made of. Karyl and his foe passed each other by.

Ten meters apart they turned about to face off again. Raguel's posture changed; now Rob thought to see puzzlement that this impertinent human wasn't holding a metal stub. Karyl's sword was intact.

Rob laughed out loud. Gaétan stared at him as if he were mad. *I am, and what of that?*

"Don't you see?" he told his comrade. "Our voyvod didn't let that monster's edge catch his blade. It's that skillful he is: he caught that evil thing on its flat and guided it safely past."

Gaétan shook his head. "I don't think I've even heard of anyone surviving a single passage of arms with a Grey Angel."

"Don't fret yourself, lad," Rob said. "I doubt Raguel has either."

Raguel waited for his human foe to come to him. And come Karyl did. Time and again metal sang its sliding song. Yet Raguel could score no solid cut against either sword or wielder.

But neither was Karyl able to strike the Angel's rotted-rock-looking flesh. And one of them was mortal. However fierce the will that drove it, Rob reckoned, Karyl's body must have reached its limits long since. Karyl could not keep fighting long.

Visibly he began to slow. Still the Grey Angel was able to sever neither his steel nor the silver cord his life. But each time He came closer.

Rob had to keep reminding himself to breathe.

At last the duelists stopped facing each other from five meters away. Karyl sagged as if only strings hooked to his shoulder blades from the clouds held him up. Sweat dripped from the ends of his hair. His sword tip dragged in the dust.

Raguel awaited, all supreme assurance once more. His foe had put up a fight that was literally unparalleled. But now he was done.

Voicing a wheezing cry that by dint of Angel magic Rob clearly heard, Karyl raised his sword and staggered forward. His dark eyes glared madly between sodden kelp-streamers of hair.

Rob's lips twisted behind a beard caked with mud made of what he daren't think about; behind them gullet and gut twisted too. *A shame to see such a gorgeous battle end on such a desperate unskillful note*, he thought. Though thinking so seemed to betray the fight Karyl had fought.

It ought to form the greatest legend of a man who had lived many of them. But alas none would live to sing it.

Almost casually Raguel flicked the soul-reaper horizontally at his opponent.

With a burst of vexer speed, Karyl plunged into a forward roll. The scythe-blade hissed harmlessly over him. He came up slicing at the long grey arm that held it.

Raguel's forearm parted. The hand whirled away, claws still clutching the soul-reaper, to fall in the dust fifteen meters off.

Raguel threw back his head, opened his jaws, and vomited a cry of cosmic rage. Rob clapped hands to ears. He saw hordelings fall to the ground by the hundreds, stunned or killed by the Grey Angel's wrath.

Karyl wheeled and flung himself at Raguel's back. His arming-sword cut an arc of brightness in the face of the gloom.

Raguel spun widdershins. His intact left arm backhanded Karyl into a backward flip. The man's peaked helmet tumbled away. He landed heavily on his back.

He didn't move.

Rob moaned. The hordelings hissed in triumph.

"No," screamed Melodía. "Not possible!'

But of course it was. What wasn't possible was the fight this lone man had put up against the Creators' own Avenging Angel.

And what wasn't possible was saving Karyl now.

She swayed in Meravellosa's saddle. When she killed Bogardus a desolation had fallen upon her, as if she had killed the last other soul in her world. And then when Karyl rode to challenge the Angel, it was as if a shaft of bright light pierced the black abyss within her.

Now she was about to lose Karyl too. And with him she, and the world, would lose even the hope of hope.

Summoning everything she had and more, she hauled Meravellosa's head up from where the mare scrabbled for bits of trampled vegetation to nourish her exhausted body. "Please, girl," she whispered hoarsely, leaning forward to pat her friend's neck. "Do this for me now."

Meravellosa snorted and tossed her pale mane. She began to run as if she'd just sprung up from the sweetest rest of her life.

We can't reach him in time. The words rang like a dirge in Melodía's brain. *And even if we could, what can I do?*

But she had to try. *If nothing else, I'd rather die at the gallop than standing still.* Even if that meant galloping toward one of her two greatest nightmares, the Grey Angel Raguel.

As if from the very soil of Paradise a huge and sinuous shape arose, a javelin-cast to Melodía's left. Ten meters long, vertically striped from near-black back to tawny underside, it was unmistakably an Allosaurus. It had lain in cover Melodía would have sworn would scarcely hide a housecat.

Lifting its head it uttered a ferocious, pealing cry: *shiraa!*

No one but Melodía seemed to hear. The great meat-eater's sudden apparition almost at her side would have scared her mindless, if she wasn't already as scared as she could be.

With vast springing strides the monster ran toward the unequal combat. Though Meravellosa was running as fast as Melodía had ever known her to, the meat-eater effortlessly outdistanced her, lancing straight through the middle of the horde.

To Shiraa, the tailless two-legs made a ridiculous amount of fuss killing one another. Given that they hardly ever seemed to eat each other.

Climbing a ridge through a hardwood forest she had spied the two-legs with the weird head standing at its edge. Pulse quickening she ran toward it.

Before she even reached the brushy verge the wonderful smell reached her nostrils: *Mommy!*

But Shiraa was a good Allosaurus. And her mother had taught her well. She smelled a lot of other tailless two-legs, and a whole lot of blood. It made her tummy rumble.

Remembering both her natural guile and her lessons she had looked for cover. She crawled down a little crack of gulley right into the heart of the slaughter-field. Of course, it did help that everyone else was paying attention to everything else than the possibility a tonne-and-a-half predatory dinosaur was sneaking into the middle of their war.

Driven by a growing sense of urgency, Shiraa had not fed in days. Now her stomach seemed to be eating itself, driven mad by the succulent smells of torn flesh.

But more compelling than the pains of hunger was that smell. The smell of her mother. Who loved her, who took care of her, and who had been stolen from her by bad things.

Mommy! Shiraa comes! Shiraa good girl!

As she crept forward she saw her mother fighting. She fought well, as the mother of a matadora naturally would. She killed a terrible, grey Great Hunger that must have been twice the size of its albino cousin who had blindsided Shiraa that awful day, hurt Shiraa, and taken away her mother.

She smelled that one too. The coward. But vengeance would wait. Only Mommy mattered now.

But now her mother faced a great big tailless two-legs. She showed no fear. Yet something about that tall, grey two-legs caused fear to trickle from Shiraa's spine down into her belly.

Her mother kept fighting. She bit one hand clean off the tall, scary two-legs.

The bad grey thing struck her. *Struck her mother.*

That shit was *not* happening. Roaring her own name, Shiraa rose from covert and charged in loving, white-hot rage.

He's taking his sweet time about, is Raguel, Bringer of Divine Justice, Scourge of the Impure, thought Rob in a fever of despair. Clearly he wanted everyone, followers and enemies alike, to see the futility of human resistance to the will of a Grey Angel played out in terrible detail.

The Angel held up his remaining hand. It seemed to take fire with black flame.

"The Hand of Death!" Rob yelled excitedly to Gaétan. "No one's seen it used before and lived to tell of it."

A heartbeat and he shrugged. "Nor is that likely to change today."

Then something like a tawny, black-striped, ten-meter stinger-bolt on legs flashed into the circle of death.

"Shiraa!" Rob Korrigan shouted in astonishment. In unison the running monster voiced the same cry, magnified a hundredfold.

Raguel began to turn. Without breaking stride, the matadora darted her head and snatched up the Grey Angel in her teeth. She held him up against the cloudy sky. Long, bony arms and legs waved uselessly.

Shiraa bit down with all her strength. With a sky-split crack, the Grey Angel's body fell in two halves.

It reached the soil of Paradise as a rain of glittering grey dust.

At one side of the circle, Sister Violette sat astride a white sackbut, mother-stark naked but for a white feather cape. No sooner had the ash that had been Raguel vanished into the hard-stamped ground than her own three-tonne dinosaur disintegrated.

From the resultant cloud of white powder she ran, shrieking like a woman on fire. She brandished a longsword over her head.

"Blasphemer!" she screamed. "I'll send you back to Hell!"

She made straight for the still-unmoving Karyl. Somehow she managed to overlook so trifling a detail as three thousand scarlet-eyed kilos of Nuevaropa's best-feared killer, bending solicitously over Karyl with the tip of her snout a handspan from his face.

"A wonderful thing, fanaticism," Rob said, as Karyl reached weakly up to touch the nose of his long-lost friend.

Her mother's breath blowing into her distended nostrils was the sweetest thing Shiraa had ever smelled. Her fleeting touch made her quiver with joy. *Mommy back! Mommy!*

A strange cry reached her ears. She turned her head.

She saw a tailless two-legs, pale as a cloud. Running right at her. It waved a hurt-stick in the air.

Abruptly Shiraa remembered how fearfully hungry she was.

Mommy safe, she told herself above the rising rumble of her belly. *Shiraa can eat now. Shiraa good Allosaurus.*

And looky-look! Food comes to good Shiraa.

Part Six

Just Deserts

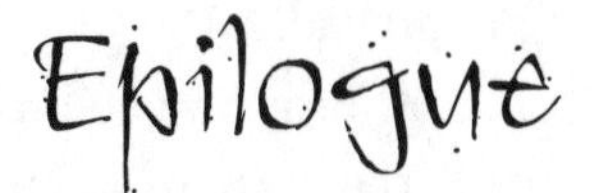

Epilogue

Uriel, ***El Fuego de Dios,*** **Fire of God**—One of the Grey Angels, the Creators' Own Seven servitors and vindicators of Their divine justice. A fire spirit, linked to the Oldest Daughter, Telar, and imbued especially with Her Attributes of both creation and impermanence. He is said to be allied with Raphael the Healing-spirit, and Remiel the Merciful, hence among the more approachable of the Seven. It is wise to remember that such things are relative, since the Angels' ministrations are seldom gentle.

—A PRIMER TO PARADISE FOR THE IMPROVEMENT OF YOUNG MINDS

"Father," Melodía said. She made herself smile as he swept her into his arms. His embrace was stronger than she remembered.

All she could think was, *He looks so small.* But maybe it was because that was all she could permit herself to think.

He held her out to arm's length. "It's so wonderful to see you again, my daughter. I've missed you terribly."

"I missed you too, Father." She wondered if that were a lie. She thought she could trust the fatigue that weighed down her words to keep anyone from sensing any falsity to them.

Felipe stepped back and beamed around at the small group gathered on the hill before the Imperial tent. Sun stung Melodía's cheeks. The overcast had begun to thin when Raguel fell.

The horde's will to fight had vanished with him.

The buzzing of flies on thousands of bodies heaped nearby was almost lulling in the noonday heat. The smell of the ocean of blood they'd spilled was far less so. Melodía wondered if she'd ever stop smelling it.

"So these are your friends." The Imperial head nodded at them in turn: Gaétan. Garamond. Côme. Rob Korrigan. All sweaty and bloody and swaying in their armor. And Karyl who, despite cracked ribs and other injuries, insisted on facing the Emperor of the Fangèd Throne on his own feet, unassisted. They all looked as if they'd bathed in blood, which was now caking and beginning to go bad.

As Melodía knew she herself did. She could hear her absent dueña's clucking outrage at her getting the nasty mess all over her father. It might in fact have bothered her—if his breastplate didn't already look as if a butcher's-bucket had been splashed across it. Red traces lingered in the crannies of his round smiling face, at the roots of his short ginger hair and Imperial beard. The Emperor of Nuevaropa had not stood or sat idly by while others defended him. Not at the end, anyway.

Maybe she'd feel proud, someday.

She felt the absences too, like missing teeth. The turbulent Eamonn Copper. Baron Ismaël. And so many of her own laughing wild children: Marc, Arianne, 'Tit Jean. Henri the woods-runner. There'd be no honors for them save the memories of friends and comrades.

Melodía would not let herself look past her father toward one who stood right behind him, though she felt his presence like sunlight. The need to see that beautiful face, to meet those long green-turquoise eyes with her own, burned inside her like a white-hot iron.

Yet she couldn't bring herself to risk seeing the man who stood *beside* the one she longed for, as though her dream lover and her greatest remaining nightmare had become close comrades. As indeed, apparently, they were.

Karyl raised his head and shook back his long dark-brown and silver hair. "Don't you remember, Majesty? You outlawed us. Although in view of current circumstances I'll ask you please to overlook that fact in the matter of my comrades. It's me you want, and I'll gladly stand for them."

"Tush, son," Felipe said, "don't talk nonsense. It's unfitting in a Duque Imperial."

"A what?"

Karyl hadn't just faced a Grey Angel riding a supernatural outsized Tyrannosaurus rex without flinching, he'd *charged* them. Now he looked nonplussed.

"I think it's a rank suitable to the service you performed today," Felipe said, "inasmuch as without your intervention we'd all be dead now. For the moment it's purely titular; no lands or income come with it. But they will."

He stepped back and swept the group with weary yet calculating pale-green eyes.

"As of this moment all of you are nobles of the Empire. Every man and woman who fought beside us this day is a knight at least. Chián, but I'd make that matadora of yours a duchess if I thought she'd comprehend it, Duke Karyl. If only to see the faces on those mealy worms in the Diet when I went before them in the People's Hall to have them confirm it."

He smiled thinly. "I don't doubt I'll find fiefs for you and all your officers and more. Some seem to have fallen vacant of late."

He looked to his right. "As for you: Falk von Hornberg, you are created Imperial Duke as well. And you, nephew—congratulations: you're now an Imperial Prince. If anything, that honor's overdue. But then nothing can recompense you two for what you've done, and suffered, today. The same for all of you."

With a clack of poleyn on hard dirt, Jaume dropped to a knee. "Majesty, Uncle, I can't accept—"

"Nonsense again. You'll do your duty. Just as you always do."

"Majesty, wait—if you please!"

Felipe frowned at the interruption, timid though it was. Melodía's heart sank. Rob was a strange man, to be sure, but he'd treated her well. And he'd really loved Pilar, it seemed. He deserved a better fate than to be shortened by a head now for lèse-majesté.

"Begging your pardon, please, Majesty, but you don't mean to include me among such a glittering crew, surely? I'm no noble, Majesty, but plain Rob Korrigan, dinosaur master, minstrel, Traveler, and rogue thoroughgoing, if I don't repeat myself. By very definition and grace of the Creators the lowest of the low. Your Majesty. Sir."

Felipe raised a brow. "So? Well, you're Baron Korrigan now, lad, so stand up straight. There're eyes upon you. And if you're near the greatest rogue among my vassals I'll eat a dung-wagon, cargo, tongue, and tires."

Rob stared at him with what resembled scratcher eggs with green-hazel eyes painted on the narrow ends. He stood up straighter.

"Understand, my friends, that your accomplishments this day have earned you any reward it's within my and the Empire's power to bestow," Felipe said. "Please also understand that it is necessity as well as justice that impels my largesse. For as things stand I have to reward you all—or hang every one of you for the blackest blasphemy imaginable. And myself right alongside.

"So go. Clean yourselves up. Drink something, for Maia's sake. And tonight at the great feast of thanksgiving for our deliverance I'll proclaim your elevations. And we'll all celebrate until we're too drunk to stand. What say you?"

A hefty clatter told Melodía that Falk had gone to his knees. Beside Jaume. She hunched her head down between shoulders drawn unbearably tight against her body.

Don't let them see it, she ordered herself.

He had violated her in a terrible and secret way. Had destroyed her life and falsely accused her of treason, although those seemed petty things next to his great crime. She had longed for months for the moment when she'd face him again.

Preferably looking into those deep-blue eyes as she drove her talwar slowly into his belly.

And yet here he was, a hero of the day. And she couldn't doubt he had done heroic things. She'd heard the surviving Scarlet Tyrants' awestruck whispering as Companions-Ordinary escorted her and the other Fugitive Legion captains up the round hill. He'd saved her father's life, again and again, they said, though her father fought well.

So I'll kill him quickly, then. She burned to point at the bastard and scream, *He raped me! He's a monster!*

But she could do no such thing. For the Empire's sake. For her family's sake.

She could no more accuse him, here and now, than she could stab him here in front of her father and the entire Imperial Army. Her accusations would be dismissed as the delirious ravings of a mind temporarily unhinged by more of horror and exhaustion than any human being should endure, anyway.

I have to hang on, she told herself. *Have to swallow my pride and anger. For now.*

Because she saw her duty clearly now. To herself, to her family, to the Empire. She must root out the rot that allowed a cancer like Falk to take hold so near the very heart of power. And she would have her vengeance on Falk von Hornberg.

How, she had no idea. But she swore to herself she'd find a way.

Karyl had taught her that: until you're dead, there's always a way.

Baron Côme knelt next, his smile even wrier than usual. Then Luc Garamond, and Gaétan, looking bemused. And Rob, who looked as if he'd been hit in the head with the haft of his own axe.

Melodía wondered if Karyl would bend the knee, even now, to the man who had ordered his betrayal and his outlawry. And what her father might do to him—even to Raguel's conqueror—if he refused.

Karyl Bogomirskiy did not bend the knee to El Emperador de Nuevaropa.

He fainted and fell on his face.

Falk von Hornberg felt his head yanked rudely up away from the bucket he'd been puking in by the hair on the front of his head.

"D'you think you could stop now, your Grace?" his servant, Bergdahl, asked, his goblin face hanging centimeters above Falk's own like a misshapen moon. "It's a good job you ate hours ago and not bloody much. Still, best get control of yourself, unless you crave seeing the color of your own lungs in there with the slop."

Falk gagged. Then he fought down the urge to throw up more emptiness. He nodded despite the tight clutch on his hair. The motion stung his scalp.

Despite the servant's wiry strength, he'd never have been able to haul his master's head up against the strength of Falk's neck the way he had when Falk was a child, if Falk hadn't been so utterly spent from exertion. And vomiting.

Bergdahl let him go. Falk's head lolled forward toward the wooden bucket, which fortunately wasn't very full, before he managed to stop it.

"And when did you grow such a fine sense of squeamishness, my lord? Slaughter's seldom troubled you before. Either as participant or spectator."

"I've never seen that scale of slaughter before," Falk said, his voice hoarse from corrosive bile. "Much less killed so many at one time."

Bergdahl began wiping Falk's mouth and beard roughly with a rag. "I know even the truly manly can find themselves unmanned after the fighting-fury's abandoned them, at the end of the day. But I've never seen you react in this particular weak way."

As Falk began to grow aware once more of something beyond the wracking nausea and the terror yammering inside his own skull, he heard ladles clanging in pots, soldiers on patrol exchanging banter with servants preparing the evening's impending feast, a woman's voice singing beautifully in Francés, and other random sounds of work around the Imperial tent cluster atop Le Boule. It seemed jarringly commonplace, after a day like today.

"And did you fail to notice the Princess herself going into the Emperor's big tent?" Falk asked, sitting up straighter on his camp stool. "Or did you just not recognize her with short hair and blood splashed all over her light-horse armor?"

Bergdahl laughed his corpse-tearer caw of a laugh. "Your wits aren't that addled, that you'd really believe I'd miss any such thing."

"Don't you see, you damned fool? She could expose me at any time. What would that do to my mother's precious plans? Much less her only living child?"

"If the Dowager Duchess were here, your Grace, she'd remind you that you are the hero of the hour, since you and that red-eyed white nightmare of yours very publicly butchered a truly exemplary number of unwashed lunatics whilst carrying out your duty to preserve the Emperor's saggy ass."

He picked up the puke bucket, glanced inside, gave his master a cocked-eyebrow look. Then he shrugged.

"The little quim's cleverer than I gave her credit for, that much is clear. Or she wouldn't be here now playing at soldiers. But she's still a grande bred and brought up. She knows full well there's not a thing she can do or say right now without causing a crisis when the Empire and her precious family can least afford it. Since her daddy and all the rest of you just thwarted the Creators' own Will made flesh, and all. And that's if her wild tale's even believed. Which it won't be."

Falk wiped his mouth. "By the same token," he said, aware of the fact the hada's gibes had indeed shocked him back into a measure of self-control, and burning with humiliation over that fact, "she's grown up with intrigue. She'll bend every effort to give us the full Triceratops horn with pointed steel cap and all behind the scenes, first chance she gets."

Bergdahl spat in the puke-bucket, which made his master's stomach turn over anew.

"If she was so fucking good at intrigue, she'd never have gotten her ass locked up so you were in a position to fuck it, your Grace."

"She strikes me as the sort who learns fast. Remember how her father pays the most attention to whoever talked to him last. She'll have plenty of opportunities to get in the last word. All it takes is him to sniff the truth. And then even you can't hope to escape the impaling stake."

"What about the Creators' precious Law forbidding our rulers creative pastimes like that?"

Falk grunted. "Even with that two-legged dung beetle Tavares sent to Old Hell by his hordeling friends, don't forget all the atrocities he talked the army into on the march here. Without Felipe saying him nay, mind. I'm guessing that's all broken Creators' Law on the subject comprehensively enough for His Majesty to lose precious little sleep about overlooking its niceties in paying us off for his daughter."

"I was born to be hanged, my mother always said," Bergdahl said dismissively. "And she wouldn't lie to me. That once, at least.

"But you do have a point for once, in spite of fatigue and fear addling your brain more than usual. We are in the shit for a very fact, and it's clearly closing over even my head."

Falk glared at him through matter-crusted lids.

"You're not—"

"Oh, yes, your Grace," Bergdahl said with a horror smirk, "I am. I'm calling in your lady mother."

"You wouldn't. Not so soon."

Bergdahl croaked another laugh. "You think I like it any more than you do? She's a less unsettling master by far when I'm at least out of the immediate reach of her arm."

"You sound as if you're afraid of her."

"Only a fool doesn't fear your mother. She's like the Fae in that."

"There's no such thing as the Fae."

"There was no such thing as a Grey Angel to you either, before you found yourself staring one in the face. But enjoy your comforting disbelief a while longer, boy; for once your ignorance isn't likely to cost us much of value."

"But bringing her together with Felipe?" Falk shook his head. Which was a mistake. It made him so dizzy he almost pitched over sideways. "That sounds like a recipe for trouble."

"Oh, it is," said Bergdahl. "But if we get better than we deserve, it'll bring more trouble to others than to us. If it makes you feel any better, that's been her plan all along. For now, what's important is that if anyone can pitchfork us out of the latrine, it's her. She can deal with that vengeful little slut of a princess.

"And her whole high-and-mighty family!"

Maids she didn't know had bathed her, anointed her in scented oils, dressed her in soft silks. Soft, *clean* silks.

Someday soon Melodía would learn their names. Who they were, who their families were. Whom they loved and what they desired from life. She wouldn't take servants for granted again. Not after Pilar. Or what the servants in the Palace of the Fireflies had done and risked for her.

But that was for later. Right now she was all but overwhelmed by the sheer existential joy of no longer being blood-sticky and smelling like seven kinds of shit. Literally.

Anointed with oils whose delicious aromas almost didn't make sense to her in her present state, gown clinging to her still-damp body, she started from the tent's bathing chamber.

And stopped dead. She sensed a presence looming in the main room. A tall and distinctly masculine presence.

She stopped dead just short of the curtain across the doorway. Her eyes cast frantically about. No weapon lay to hand. She pressed her lips together hard, thinking of her talwar waiting in its sheath in the other room. It might as well be in La Merced.

Then: "Melodía? Beloved?"

The voice was music, the words honeyed wine. She pushed through the silken curtain. He had bathed and changed to a fresh silk blouse and trousers of white and butterscotch. A thin circlet of braided gold held his fine orange hair back from his dear, perfectly sculpted face.

As she flowed into his arms she could feel the way exhaustion slackened his normally taut muscles. It didn't matter. All that mattered in all the world was that he was here.

"My love," she whispered. "Jaume." And tipped back her head so that her still-wet hair cascaded down the back of her gown.

Their mouths met in a kiss like that first long drink of water at battle's end. And if he still carried a hint of the smell of death about him . . . so did she.

Melodía wriggled herself free enough in his arms to shed her robe. He was pulling off his clothes as well, still holding her. Then she forgot everything but him, and the two-souled and single-minded worship of Beauty and the Lady.

"Welcome, Duke Karyl of the Empire of the Fangèd Throne. I salute you."

Karyl's sword slid from its walking-stick sheath. That voice haunted with familiarity.

Then he caught it. "Aphrodite?"

It was the sorceress—so-called and, he supposed, proven. The woman had hired him and Rob Korrigan to take the road to Providence, so many lives ago.

Who gave me back my sword hand.

He still wore battle-garb and the attendant coating of battle-filth. He had been out seeing as best he could to the needs of the people and animals he'd led into the fight before he'd consent to bathing and changing clothes. The toll on them weighed on his soul like mountains.

Gloom filled the tent assigned him. It had been pitched on the west slope of the round hill the Imperials called Le Boule. The sun had descended far enough to throw it into shade.

Aphrodite stepped into a shaft of residue light that fell through a mesh patch high up in the tent. Motes swam in it. Karyl's sword, which had begun to droop as weariness won out again, snapped up to guard.

The sorceress wore a dark brown robe and cowl. Karyl frowned.

"Wait," he said hesitantly. "Why do you look just like the Witness?"

She drew back her cowl, revealing hair that fell like living lava down her back.

"Because I am the Witness, Karyl."

"But you're young," he said. "The Witness is old as the world. She told me."

"Silly boy," the uninvited guest said, "I am the world."

"You're a monster!" he screamed. He slashed at her.

The sword cut only air. Dust danced. He overbalanced and fell flat on his belly.

"What evil magic's this?" he cried, coming desperately back to one knee.

"I'm not here," she said. "This is only my likeness. A projection."

"A what?"

"An illusion, then. You can hear me and see me. But I'm not here. Or rather, I am—I'm everywhere. But not in any form you'd recognize."

"You heartless monster," he said. Then he burst into tears.

How long he sobbed on his knees with his face cradled in his hands, Karyl couldn't tell. When he looked up, spent at last, she stood over him, smiling gently down.

"I wish I could take you in my arms," she said, extending a hand above his head.

"What's changed now?" he demanded. He swiped at the hand, forgetting his would go right through. It did. "Why didn't you feel that way when I was naked and desperate at the Hassling? Why haven't you—why haven't you helped any of us? Why have you watched us suffer and die for centuries? Cheap amusement?"

"No." She knelt by his side. "Now get up and into a chair, at least."

"Why should I?" he said, knowing it was petulant.

She laughed like gentle rain. "I'll tell you things," she said. "That's what you really want."

Painfully he climbed up to fall into a camp stool. He had cracked ribs, he knew; those had their way of reminding you they were there. The Emperor had had his personal physicians tend to Karyl, over Karyl's objections that there were hundreds with real injuries awaiting care. The doctors had anointed his rib cage with pain-reducing salves, and wrapped him tightly with bandages. They had also offered him herbal decoctions to take the edge of the still not-inconsiderable pain he experienced whenever he found himself having to do something like breathe. These he declined. He didn't want to dull his wits or reflexes any more than fatigue had done already. He knew that deadly danger was always near on Paradise. And pain he'd learned to live with.

Otherwise his bones, miraculously, seemed intact. If there was a square centimeter of him that wasn't bruised to the bone, though, it wasn't making its presence known.

"You have me at your mercy, then," he said. "I've nothing left to fight you with."

She laughed again, louder this time. "This from the man who defeated Raguel single-handedly?"

"I didn't; that was my Shiraa."

He was so exhausted that even his joy at being reunited with his oldest friend felt muffled. His good girl herself lay gorged and asleep in an especially stout pen south between the battlefield and the nearby town of Canterville. She'd been so worn out that a mere dozen handlers had been able to restrain her when she went snarling and snapping at Snowflake. Who was himself so tired he could barely lift his head to blink a ruby eye at her.

"You fought him. Hand to hand, and *made* it a fight. No other man in the whole history of this world has done so. Some especially brave or rash souls have tried. They died instantly. Believe me: I know."

He waved wearily at her. "As you say. You have things to tell me, you say. But I'll bet you're not going to tell me what I really want to know."

"What?" she asked. "Why you're still alive, you mean? Where you spent those months between the time you fell from the cliff above the Eye with your life's-blood bursting out of your severed left arm and a live horror clutched to your breast like a child's doll, to when you found yourself tramping a nosehorn wagon track in Sansamour? Or do you mean, why you humans exist on this world? Why, indeed, the world exists?"

"Yes."

"You're right. I won't tell you that."

He blinked. She consistently managed to surprise him. He didn't like that.

"Then what?"

"I can tell you that your fervent and frequently expressed disbelief in the Creators is mistaken. The Creators are real, the stories of Creation true. Substantially."

He held up his left hand, flexed filthy fingers. "So much I surmised," he said. "And something about facing a Grey Angel in single combat tended to dispel any last lingering doubts I had, I must admit. So, who are you? *What* are you? Will you tell me that, at least?"

"I am the Soul of the World," she said. "Paradise is I. I am she. I was Created at the same time as the world, and observed the final shaping of it. Now I am its caretaker. The Creators' major-domo, as it were."

"So why don't you just strike me down and finish the job your fellow-servitors the Angels failed to?"

She shook her head. "We are . . . separate. We were created for separate tasks."

"Was it you who resurrected me?"

"No. I told you: I cannot directly intervene in human affairs. If you ask, can I make a rainstorm—yes. I can. If you ask, can I make it rain to help you—or to hinder you—no, I cannot. Healing you was the outermost limit of what I am allowed to do. And even that entailed fearful risks which you cannot be allowed to understand.

"The Creators . . . limited and bound me. The truth is they exerted far more effort ensuring that she—like the Grey Angels—should never become too powerful, than in making them powerful. And they were wise to do so."

"Even in your case?"

"Especially mine," she said sadly.

"Can you be killed, like Raguel?"

"I don't know. I suspect so. Angels die. But make no mistake: Raguel is far from dead. What your loyal and lovely friend destroyed in such a timely way was no more him than this illusion is me. His essence was safe, unreachably distant from the battlefield. He's merely . . . inconvenienced."

"What's to keep him coming back to finish, then, even angrier than before?" Karyl asked in real alarm.

"He won't," the World-Soul said. "The Seven Grey Angels have their own hierarchy, their own culture, their own conflicts, their own rivalries—politics, if you will. Having failed this time, Raguel will be a long while trying again. Even as you reckon."

"But other Angels will?" asked Karyl, not hugely reassured.

"Rest assured they shall."

He blew out a long breath. "You oppose them, though?"

"In this," she said, "yes. They mean to wipe out humanity. I've come to love your kind, Karyl. And beyond that, I believe the Angels have come to misinterpret the Creators' desires."

"Why don't the Creators set them straight?"

"The Eight have their own agendas, let's say."

"So what do you want with me?"

"Remember that I told you, that day on the Hassling, that I thought I sensed something special about you? Some kind of destiny?"

His fingers clenched on the camp chair's arms. His overtaxed hands promptly knotted in cramps. He bent over, wincing, prying the fingers loose by sheer will.

"I doubted my perception then, I admit," Aphrodite said. "You proved my doubts wrong. You possess unusual gifts, not least of survival. And so I have chosen you."

"Chosen me for what?"

"My champion."

"What does that mean?"

She smiled. "As with your other questions, that awaits you learning enough that you can understand the answer."

She leaned toward him, pursing her lips as in a kiss. Where the phantom mouth touched his forehead, he felt a tingle.

"Wait!" he cried. He lunged for her.

His arms wrapped air. She vanished. He fell on his face.

He was still weeping broken-heartedly when servants came to ready him for the great thanksgiving feast.

Rob Korrigan—Sir Rob, now, Baron Rob If-You-Please—was drunk.

Not just drunk. Not tipsy. Not shitfaced. Gloriously, rousingly, thunderously drunk. As only a goblin-brew of fatigue poisons, the exhilaration of sheer unexpected survival, and liters of better booze than he'd ever dreamed existed could make him drunk.

And, well, he thought, *I am shitfaced. That too.*

When a body sucked down such pelagic quantities of alcohol in many forms, particularly the Emp's own beer and ale (ambrosia!), there were certain regular and predictable consequences. And so Rob, cut loose after the great banquet broke up, was stumbling about the dark Imperial camp behind Le Boule in search of a place to pee.

Having found a tent grand enough to conceal him from wandering eyes, he took himself in hand. He was experiencing relief so pure and profound he was surprised he didn't just deflate like an air-filled strider bladder and fall flat down, when he heard voices close by. One voice, in particular, seemed familiar. If only of recent acquaintance.

It came through the tent wall, he realized. He noticed, then, as the release of pressure on his bladder allowed blood to flow to his brain again what he had failed to mark before. By the light of the rising Eris, the tent showed distinct broad stripes. Of red and gold.

Well, Rob lad, and isn't that you all over? he told himself. *No sooner made a noble you are, than you go and piss behind the Emperor's very tent.*

Or, to give the Truth more service than is your custom, piss on *it.*

The voices murmured on. There was something about the second one, a dessicated rasp that reminded him of insect wings, which made him furrow his brow. It didn't sound right somehow.

That was when he spied the tear in the cloth.

It was a small hole. A mere slit, really. Probably from some random arrow. Strange to find one here; but he'd been told the fighting had swirled everywhere, there at the end. Battle raged clear to the vast supply-wagon fort even farther back down the Chausée Imperial toward the village.

Until Shiraa bit that devil Raguel in two. Neat as you please.

The Grey Angel's end, or ends, had left all of the Crusaders whose souls he'd controlled blinking in befuddlement. Some began to cry; others wandered, hopelessly confused. And others were simply blank, as if in reaching etherically into their heads the Grey Angel had broken something in there.

That was most by far of the Grey Angel horde. A minority, of course, consisted of those who had willingly taken up the Crusade. And partaken eagerly of its dark rewards.

Those had vanished over the horizon as quickly as they could, once Raguel fell. Exhausted as they were surprised, the victors let them go. Over coming weeks and months they would hunt the willing collaborators down. Years, if that was what it took. Rob thought he himself might ask permission to join the hunt. Although he doubted there'd be any shortage of applicants.

Ask Karyl's permission as well as his Emperorship's, he reminded himself. He might be a Barón Imperial now, but Nan Korrigan's boy had his priorities on right-way to. And lucky he was his dear friend and comrade was also his liege lord, all through the magic of Imperial decree.

Again the voices whispered to him. Again his gaze strayed toward that hole. That inviting little hole.

He finished, shook himself, stuffed himself back in place, drew his drawstrings tight. No good walking about the camp with Little Rob peeking out all uninvited; unworthy of his aristocratic dignity, that was.

So was eavesdropping, of course. Not to mention lèse-majesté at the very least.

But then, Rob reasoned, *things happen for a purpose in this fine world the Creators have made. Haven't we all seen the same today?*

And so that hole . . . plus Rob . . . plus those voices . . . well, surely it all added up to the Creators' manifest Will. Had to. There could be no denying.

And Rob, being a pious man—however temporarily and under the direct influence of recent frightening spiritual manifestations as well as truly epic quantities of drink—was never a lad to defy his Creators. Not openly. No indeed.

He took out his dirk and, slipping the tip into the little tear, improved it ever so slightly.

It might be that his hand was not altogether unused to such a task.

He got the hole large enough, he thought, to peep through without holding it open with his fingers and risking getting caught like a lummox. The words swam into focus, like little fishes from the murky bottom of a pond to clearer water near the surface.

"Please, Fray Jerónimo," Rob heard, and it seemed Felipe halfway sobbed the words. "I know what you told me before. But I confess: I still have doubts. The most terrible, terrible doubts. Have I truly done the Creators' Will, by defying Their own appointed emissary?"

Rob peeked inside. At first he could make out little. He was peering into a rear corner of this back room, made into an alcove by a movable screen. The only light came filtered through the paper from a single oil lamp on the screen's far side. Felipe sat on the other side as well.

Ah, Rob thought, trying to sharpen well-blurred vision, *so there you are, my mystery lad. Let's have a look at you, then.*

Every eye in the Empire, it seemed, had striven without success for just such a glimpse at the power who sat invisibly behind the Fangèd Throne. And now to Rob went the golden prize! He called that no less than his due.

Shadow resolved to shape.

By some sheer twist of luck, Rob managed not to shriek. Managed indeed to stumble away into the night without gibbering aloud, though terror threatened to dissolve his bones within him.

Because Fray Jerónimo, sitting in a chair in simple cowled brown monk's robes, was not a man.

He was, quite unmistakably, a Grey Angel.